Drowning World

Drowning

World

A NOVEL OF THE COMMONWEALTH

Alan Dean Foster 1946-

BALLANTINE BOOKS • NEW YORK

Drowning World is a work of fiction. Names, places, and incidents either are a product of the author's imagination or are used fictitiously.

A Del Rey® Book
Published by The Ballantine Publishing Group

www.delreydigital.com

Library of Congress Cataloging-in-Publication Data

Foster, Alan Dean, 1946–
    Drowning world : a novel of the Commonwealth / Alan Dean Foster.—1st ed.
      p. cm.
    "A Del Rey book"—T.p. verso.
    ISBN 0-345-45035-3
    1. Humanx Commonwealth (Imaginary organization)—Fiction.   2. Life on other planets—Fiction.   I. Title.
PS3556.O756 D76 2003
    813'.54—dc21

                                        2002026279

Book design by Joseph Rutt

Jacket illustration by Mark Harrison
Jacket design by David Stevenson

Manufactured in the United States of America

First Edition: February 2003

10 9 8 7 6 5 4 3 2 1

For Gil Serique, because of . . .

Mamiraua, the flooded forest, wherein we saw the three-toed
sloth, the pink dolphin, and the elusive white uakari.
The power of Iguazu.
The *candomble* ceremony in the favelas of Salvador.
The great blue hyacinths of Piaui.
The birds of Itachiaia.
Cozying up to capybaras and caimans.
The sultry feast in the little restaurant in Tefé.
The homemade passionfruit liqueur on Mother's Day in Bahia.
The marketplace in Manaus and the ice cream there and in
Barreras.
And, most memorably, the swim with the giant otters in the
Pantanal.

Drowning World

1

Jemunu-jah didn't want to have to take the time to rescue the human. If it was foolish enough to go off into the Viisiiviisii all by itself, then it deserved whatever happened to it. Kenkeru-jah had argued that it was their *mula* to try to save the visitor, even if it was not spawned of the Sakuntala. As he was ranking chief of the local Nuy clan, his opinion was listened to and respected.

Jemunu-jah suspected that the much-admired High Chief Naneci-tok would also have argued vociferously against the decision to send him, but she was still in transit from an important meeting of fellow Hatas and was not present to countermand the directive. As for the war chief Aniolo-jat, he did not seem to care one way or the other where Jemunu-jah was sent. Not that the cunning Hata-yuiqueru felt anything for the missing human, either. All the war chief wanted, as usual, was to conserve clan energies for killing Deyzara.

Perhaps it was Jemunu-jah's cheerless expression that caused the two Deyzara passing him on the walkway to edge as far away as they could without tumbling right over the flexible railing. The speaking/breathing trunk that protruded from the top of their ovoidal hairless skulls recoiled back against the edges of their flat-brimmed rain hats, and the secondary eating trunks that hung from the underside, or chin region, of their heads twitched nervously. Their large, protuberant, close-set eyes nervously tracked him from behind their visors. Another time, Jemunu-jah might have found their excessive caution amusing. Not today.

He supposed Kenkeru-jah was right. Chiefs usually were. But for the life of him, he could not understand how the death of a missing human, and a self-demonstrably reckless one at that, could affect the clan's *mula*. But the chief had made a decision. As a result, he now found himself directed to present himself to the female in charge of the human community on Fluva. Since Lauren Matthias's status was equivalent to that of a senior Hata, or High Chief of the Sakuntala, Jemunu-jah would be obliged to put his own feelings aside while showing her proper respect. He smoothed his long stride. Actually, he ought to be proud. He had been selected as a representative of his people, the best that Taulau Town had to offer. But if given a choice, he would gladly have declined the honor.

At slightly under two meters tall and a wiry eighty kilos, he was of average height and weight for a mature male Sakuntala. Though smaller than those of a Deyzara, his eyes provided vision that was substantially more acute. From the sides of his head the base of his flexible pointed ears extended out sideways for several centimeters before curving sharply upward to end in tufted points. The outer timpanic membrane that kept rain from entering his right ear was in the process of renewing itself, slowly being replaced by a new one growing in behind it. As a result, the hearing on his right side was at present slightly diminished. It would stay that way for another day or two, he knew, until the old membrane had completely disintegrated and the new one had asserted itself.

His short, soft fur was light gray with splotches of black and umber. The pattern identified an individual Sakuntala as sharply and distinctly as any of the artificial identity devices the humans carried around with them. In that respect he felt sorry for the humans. Despite some slight differences in skin color, it was often very difficult to tell one from another.

His cheek sacs bulged, one with the coiled, whiplike tongue that was almost as long as his body, the other with a gobbet of khopo sap he alternately chewed and sucked. Today's helping was flavored with gesagine and apple, the latter a flavor introduced by the humans that had found much favor among the Sakuntala. He wore old-style strappings around his waist to shield his privates, while the bands of dark blue synthetics that crisscrossed his chest were of off-world manufacture. Attached to both sets of straps were a variety of items both traditional and modern, the latter purchased from the town shops with credit he had earned from providing services to various human and Deyzara enterprises.

Now it seemed that despite his reluctance he was about to provide one more such service. Despite the prospect of acquiring *mula* as well as credit, he would just as soon have seen the task given to another. But Kenkeru-jah had been adamant. He was as stuck with the assignment as a kroun that had been crammed into the crook of a drowning sabelbap tree.

Raindrops slid off his transparent eyelids as he glanced upward. Not much precipitation today: barely a digit's worth. Of course, it had rained very heavily yesterday. Clouds, like individuals, needed time to replenish themselves. The fact that it rained every day on most of Fluva seemed to be a source of some amusement to newly arrived humans. Once they had been stuck on Fluva for about a season, however, Jemunu-jah had observed, the weather rapidly ceased to be a source of humor for the bald visitors.

Well, not entirely bald, he corrected himself. A fair number of humans owned at least a little fur. In that respect they were better than the Deyzara, who were truly and completely hairless.

With an easy jump, he crossed from one suspended walkway to another, saving time as he made his way through town. A few humans could duplicate such acrobatic feats but preferred not to. One spill into the water below, arms and legs flailing wildly, was usually enough to prevent them from trying to imitate the inherent agility of the tall, long-armed Sakuntala. No Deyzara would think of attempting the comparatively undemanding jump. Human children could not be prevented from trying it, though.

This was allowed, since the waters beneath the town limits were netted to keep out p'forana, m'ainiki, and other predators who would delight in making a meal of any child unlucky enough to tumble into unprotected waters. That went for Sakuntala children as well as human and Deyzara, he knew. But when *they* jumped, Sakuntala youngsters only rarely missed.

The rain intensified, falling steadily, if not forcefully. Making his way through the continuous shower, he passed more Deyzara. Like the humans, the two-trunks wore an assortment of specialized outer attire intended to keep the rain from making contact with their skin. To Jemunu-jah this seemed the height of folly. For a Sakuntala, it was as natural to be wet as dry. As visitors who came and went from Fluva the humans could be excused for their reticence to move about naked beneath the rain. But the Deyzara, who had been living and working on the world of the Big Wet for hundreds of years, should have adapted better by now. For all the many generations that had passed, they still displayed a marked aversion to the unrelenting precipitation, though they had otherwise adapted well to the climate. The one month out of the year that it did not rain was their period of celebration and joy. In contrast, it was during such times that the Sakuntala tended to stay inside their houses, showering daily and striving to keep moist.

It all seemed very backward to Jemunu-jah, even though he had viewed numerous vits that showed many worlds where it rained only intermittently and some where water fell from the sky not at all. If forced to live on such a world, he knew he would shrivel up and die like a gulou nut in the cooking fire or in one of those marvelous portable cooking devices that could be bought from the humans or the Deyzara. Rain was life. There would be no flooded forest, or varzea, as the humans called it, without the rain that fell continuously for 90 percent of the year.

With the water from the many merged rivers of the varzea swirling ten meters below the suspended walkway and the surface of the land itself drowned twenty to thirty meters below that, he lifted himself up onto another crossway. This strilk-braced major avenue was strong enough to support multiple paths and was hectic with pedestrians. Humans mixed freely with Sakuntala and Deyzara, everyone intent on the business of the day. Nearby, a spinner team was busy repairing a damaged walkway, extruding the strilk that kept the town's buildings and paths suspended safely above the water. The silvery artificial fiber was attached to huge gray composite pylons that had been driven deep into the bedrock that lay far below the turbid waters and saturated soil. On the outskirts of the sprawling community a carnival of lesser structures whose owners were unable to afford pylons hung from the largest, strongest trees.

The single-story building in front of him was the administrative headquarters of the Commonwealth presence on Fluva. Jemunu-jah had been there a few times before, on official business for the greater A'Jah clan. That particular business being of lesser importance, it had not given him the opportunity to meet Lauren Matthias. He had heard that she was very good at her work, not unlike Naneci-tok, and could speak fluent S'aku. Matthias would not have to strain her larynx in his presence. His command of terranglo, he had been told, was excellent.

A single human stood guard outside the building. He looked bored, tired, and, despite his protective military attire, very, very wet. Visible beneath a flipped-up visor, his face was frozen in that faraway expression many humans acquired after they had spent a year or more on Fluva. He was nearly as tall as a Sakuntala. Drawing himself up to his full height, Jemunu-jah announced himself.

The guard seemed to respond to his presence only with great difficulty. Water ran down the human's face. It was not rainwater, as both of them were standing under the wide lip of the roof overhang that ran completely around the front and sides of the administration building. Jemunu-jah recognized the facial moisture as a phenomenon humans called perspiration. It was a condition unknown to the Sakuntala, although the Deyzara suffered from it as well.

"Limalu di," the guard mumbled apathetically. Jemunu-jah

was not so far removed from the culture of his kind, nor so educated, that he did not gaze covetously at the long gun that dangled loosely from the human's left hand. A single swift snatch and he could have it, he knew. Then, a quick leap over the side of the deck into the water below, and he would be gone before the sluggish human barely knew it was missing.

With a sigh, Jemunu-jah shifted his gaze away from the highly desirable weapon, away from the ancient calling of his ancestors. He was here on clan business. He was civilized now. "I am called Jemunu-jah. I have appointment with Administrator Matthias," he responded in terranglo.

Reaching up to wipe away sweat and grime, the guard blinked uncertainly. "Appointment?"

"Appointment," the lanky gray-furred visitor repeated.

Eyeing the Sakuntala with slightly more interest, the guard tilted his head slightly to his left and spoke toward the pickup suspended there. "There's a Saki here to see Matthias. Says he has an appointment." Jemunu-jah waited patiently while the human listened to the voice that whispered from the tiny pickup clipped to his left ear.

A moment later the guard bobbed his head, a gesture Jemunu-jah knew signified acceptance among humans. Parting his lips and showing sharp teeth, he stepped past and through the momentarily deactivated electronic barrier that was designed to keep out intruders both large and small. Another door, Jemunu-jah reflected as he entered the building. Humans and Deyzara alike were very fond of doors. The Sakuntala had no use for them.

Behind him, the guard had resumed his lethargic pose, leaning back against the wall, his expression having once more gone blank as a part of him dreamed of other worlds and of the long-forgotten state of being dry. Rain fell steadily beyond the brown composite decking and overhang. A few streaks of olive green *walus* were visible on part of the porch railing. It had taken only a hundred years for several of the millions of varieties of fungus and mold that thrived on Fluva to learn how to survive on the supposedly inedible specially treated composite.

Chief Administrator Lauren Matthias had red hair, green eyes, a short and solid (but solidly attractive) build that was growing stouter with every passing year, a temper to match her contentious official position, and a desk full of worries. She had been chief Commonwealth representative and administrator on Fluva for just over a year now, ever since Charlie Sandravoe had gone nuts and been granted a hasty medical discharge. Like everyone else, she remembered the day when the well-liked Sandravoe had finally lost it, tearing off his electrostatically charged rain cape and the clothes underneath before flinging himself out the window and off the deck outside the office she now occupied. He'd fallen nearly twenty meters to the water below. Several members of the cultural staff, whose offices were in the building below Administration, had seen him plunge past the window of their workplace, arms at his sides, legs together. Maria Chen-ha had had the best look. To this day, she insisted that the face of the ex-administrator had been oddly calm.

They'd found him floating below, miraculously alive, having just missed cracking his skull on a number of intervening branches. A couple of Deyzara had fished him out of the water and brought him up. Diagnosis had been swift: mental breakdown brought on by too much time on Fluva. Sandravoe had extended his tour of duty several times, receiving a bonus for each extension. His offers had been reluctantly accepted because it was hard to find qualified personnel willing to remain on Fluva for any length of time. Besides having to adjudicate the never-ending turmoil between the Deyzara and the Sakuntala, there was also the often hostile and unpredictable flora and fauna, the interesting new diseases, the voracious molds and fungi, and of course the small and slightly disturbing fact that it rained 90 percent of the year. And the absence of dry land.

There *was* permanent dry land, Matthias knew. Up in the western mountains that ran the length of Fluva's single substantial landmass. The mountains caught the flow of moisture from the western ocean and turned it into rain. The rain fed thousands upon thousands of rivers that, for most of the year, overflowed their banks and drowned the immense tropical woodland that the moisture supported. The result was varzea, where the land lay thirty meters or so below the surface of the merged rivers. It was a morass, it was a mess, and the combination had a disconcerting tendency to drive visiting humans insane.

Not the Deyzara. Imported from Tharce IV a couple of hundred years ago, the Deyzara were well adapted to working in Fluva's sodden conditions. They thrived in its climate, working the plantations that produced dozens of highly valued botanicals and other products. Preoccupied with fighting among themselves, the native Sakuntala had accepted the Deyzara's presence from the beginning. Unfortunately, the Deyzara bred rather faster than the locals, with the result that there were now nearly as many Deyzara as long-arms. Now, a highly vocal and influential faction among the Sakuntala wanted all Deyzara off the planet.

Yet these Deyzara knew nothing of Tharce IV. Some were fourth- and even fifth-generation Fluva-born. The consequent conundrum constituted a mess and morass of a different kind. One that fell squarely in the lap of the resident administrator. Her lap. As if that weren't enough, she also had to deal with the plants and animals that were constantly evolving in their attempts to penetrate the perimeter of Taulau Town and the other tentative Commonwealth outposts that were scattered around the planet. Not to mention the problems she had with Jack and Andrea. Her husband, a plant physiologist with the Commonwealth's research and taxonomy division, seemed reasonably content lately. On the other hand, Andrea had decided last month, on the occasion of her twelfth birthday and for no discernible reason (at least, none that an adult could discern), that from then on her given name would be Fitzwinkle.

And then there was the unnerving problem of Sethwyn Case. "Sethwyn Case—always on the chase," the other women posted to Administration were fond of murmuring and sometimes of giggling. One of many independent contractors who had come to seek their fortune on Fluva, Bioprospector Sethwyn was tall, handsome, bold, with a grin that induced uncommon tremors in parts of her that she had long thought tectonically stable. He would be gone for weeks at a time, always returning with this or that fascinating new specimen or information or, hopefully, profitable discovery.

Once he had checked in, he would always report dutifully in person to Administration. It was not necessary for him to see her to render his report, but he always did so. At such times he would grin and joke and make light of the dangers he had faced. Once or twice, he had brushed up against her. Accidentally, she chose to believe. But there was nothing accidental about that grin or what she felt she saw in his eyes. As if she didn't have enough to worry about.

And now this fool—what was his name?—she checked the hard copy. Shadrach Hasselemoga. This Hasselemoga person, another freelance bioprospector not six months arrived on Fluva, had gone and gotten himself lost in the depths of the Viisiiviisii. One more irritation to add to a list that was already far too big. It was her job, as administrator, to send someone to try to find him. Apparently, and remarkably, the man's emergency beacon had been completely destroyed or, at the least, damaged beyond repair.

She would have sent Case, but he was out somewhere in the foothills of the Varaku mountains. Jillis Noufoetan was on leave at the orbiting station, and Nicolo Manatinga had been laid up with a fever and an infection that mutated as fast as the doctors tried to isolate it. All of which meant she would have to send out a search team consisting entirely of locals. It had been done before, successfully. Staff had presented her with several possibilities, from whom she had selected a couple on intuition and recommendation of past service.

Outside, the downpour was becoming heavier, sealing off the view across the town and into the dense Viisiiviisii beyond. With a sigh and conflicting thoughts of Jack and a certain free-ranging explorer in her mind, she turned and resumed her seat behind the curving desk. Like everything else in the administration building, it was fashioned of resolutely nonbiodegradable materials.

Everything else, that is, except the people.

"Send him in." The desk's omnipickup identified her voice and relayed the request to Sanuel Pandusky, her administrative assistant. It took several tries before Pandusky responded. Pity it wasn't Case, she thought. I'd have to get on his case.

Stop that, she told herself firmly. Settling herself into the chair and letting it mold itself against her, she rested elbows on the desk and steepled fingers in front of her. They pressed against one another more tightly than was necessary.

The doorway barrier dissolved to admit a Sakuntala of average height. As the portal had been designed to accommodate his kind, he did not have to bend in order to enter. His waist strappings and chest straps, she noted, were particularly stylish and well equipped. This was a prosperous local who stood before her. She knew that Personnel would not have sent her anything else.

A couple of empty chairs reposed nearby. She didn't offer him one. In the absence of the traditional suspended seat, the Sakuntala preferred to squat rather than sit. At a gesture from her, her visitor eased back onto his lean but powerful haunches.

"I don't believe we've met before. I am called Lauren Matthias." She stuck out her tongue and braced herself. Though the traditional Sakuntala method of greeting had become second nature to her by now, that did not make the nature of it any less disconcerting.

"I know your status."

His mouth opened and her visitor's remarkable tongue shot out to curl once completely around her face before the end touched the tip of her own protruding organ. Although the raspy eating surface was turned away from her and only the smooth, wet back side made contact with her skin, she still found herself wincing slightly at the contact. That was a considerable improvement over the first time the gesture had been extended. No one had bothered to warn her, and her screaming, shocked reaction had been a source of considerable amusement to her coworkers. Not informing newcomers to Fluva of the nature of the habitual Sakuntala greeting was always a surefire laugh producer.

As quickly as it had emerged, the tongue recoiled, zipping in reverse around her head to disappear back into the visitor's bulging right cheek pouch. Pitiful as they were, Jemunu-jah reflected, at least the humans had tongues. When among the Deyzara, the Sakuntala had to content themselves with touching tongue tip to the end of the Deyzara's eating trunk. It was a matter of some debate as to whether it would be more proper to touch tongue to speaking trunk or eating trunk. For their part, the Deyzara did not care. They tolerated the Sakuntala gesture only because they had to.

"I am called Jemunu-jah."

"I know your status." Matthias fought against the urge to pick up a dehydrating towelette and wipe her face. Most of the time, the Sakuntala tongue didn't leave behind much moisture. But she squirmed internally all the same. "You come highly recommended."

Both flexible ears dipped briefly toward her. "I thank you for the *mulat*. I say openly to you I would prefer another go in my stead."

Well, it would be too much to expect enthusiasm, she knew. A *lotl* was bumping up against the back window, trying to get in. Looking for a nesting place, she suspected. Someone unaware and lumpish to lay its eggs within. Fortunately, the football-size *lotl* were almost comically slow-moving. If one flew too near, a single swipe with the back of a hand was usually enough to drive it away. If it persisted, a quick jab with any sharp object would puncture its air sac and send the parasite spinning helplessly into the water below. Unless it caught you when you were asleep. On Fluva, nobody slept unprotected, either inside a building or out in the Viisiiviisii. Not if they valued their bodily integrity.

"You were the one recommended," she reiterated. "We need the best for this, and you'll be well paid."

"Why not send one of you own people?" As he crouched

before the human chief, Jemunu-jah chewed idly on the lump of the khopo sap stored in his right cheek pouch. The activity did not unsettle humans, he knew, because some of them engaged in similar food-related behavior. A few had even tried khopo sap and liked it, especially when it came with added flavorings. When not being masticated or sucked, he had been told, it was excellent for making temporary repairs to all kinds of machinery.

"Several reasons." She leaned toward him. With the desk between them, it was not perceived as a hostile gesture. One had to be ever conscious of Sakuntala protocol, because they never traveled outside their homes without at least one weapon. Jemunu-jah's was politely concealed, probably somewhere under his waist straps.

"The human who has gone missing is called Shadrach Hasselemoga." Seeing her visitor struggle with the syllables, she added, "I am informed that he is often called Hasa, for short. He's an independent bioprospector working on a loan-and-consignment basis. I haven't met him myself, but I'm told that he's at least as competent as most of his kind. He arrived here only six months ago from one of our colony worlds. His documents are all in order."

Jemunu-jah bobbed his head. "Apparently, he's not quite as competent as all his kind."

She nodded back, meeting the incredibly sharp, penetrating Sakuntala eyes without flinching. "There's been no word from him since he went south nearly a seven-day ago. No communication, no emergency beacon transmission. Nothing. We know what course he took because he filed a flight plan, but he could have deviated in any direction at any time."

"What about satellite tracking? Does not that keep constant position of all your skimmers?"

A well-educated Sakuntala indeed, she reflected. The report on this native had been correct. "Mr. Hasselemoga's bounceback failed two days into his journey. We don't know why. For a bounceback and an emergency beacon on a properly equipped and maintained skimmer to both fail simultaneously is very unusual. Six months is not a lot of time to learn about Fluva. Some of my staff speculate he may have gotten lazy, or overconfident, and turned off his avoidance system, or gone to sleep at an unpropitious moment."

"Or something hit him." Jemunu-jah exhaled through pursed lips. "Viisiiviisii can do that."

She nodded knowingly, having seen vits of some of the varzea's larger known inhabitants. As to the unknown ones, even the Sakuntala were themselves sometimes surprised by what came wandering out of the flooded forest.

"That is why we need someone like you to go and look for him. You see things we cannot, and not just because your eyesight is so much better. You know the varzea. We are still learning about it. I'm told you've traveled in skimmers before."

"*Heesa*—yes. I very much like experience. But I not trained to pilot one."

"Don't worry. We're sending someone with you who is. Someone who has spent as much time in that part of the Viisiiviisii as anyone we could find."

"Another of your scout-kind-people?"

"I'm afraid not. Those of our community who would qualify for a task like this are all busy with other assignments or for various reasons are presently unable to help with the necessary operation." Looking past him, she spoke toward the doorway. "You might as well come in now, Masurathoo."

Despite his education, despite his comparative sophistication, Jemunu-jah tensed at the calling of the name. It was not a human designation. But he did recognize it.

The Deyzara who entered was shorter than the administrator. Like the majority of his kind, alongside Jemunu-jah the mature male two-trunks would have appeared positively insignificant. The oval opening in the traditional body-swathing lightweight rain cape at the front of the head exposed the upper breathing trunk, the two wide eyes, and the eating trunk that dangled downward below that. The Sakuntala's inherent and traditional preference for low-key dress, a natural consequence of trying to blend in with the teeming and dangerous Viisiiviisii, clashed wildly with the unabashed Deyzara fondness for bright colors and garish patterns. But Deyzara were far less fearful of being eaten by one of the varzea's denizens than they were of being considered unfashionable. Defying the inimical realities of the Fluvan Viisiiviisii and the ongoing disapproval of their Sakuntala neighbors, they continued to adhere stubbornly to the customs of their original home world.

At least this one's facial makeup was less gaudy than the ostentatious splashes of color and lurid phosphorescence favored by some of his kind, Jemunu-jah decided. The Deyzara's skin was a uniform pale pink that contrasted sharply with Jemunu-jah's own strikingly mottled gray fur as well as with the human's light brown epidermis and short mane. He had to remind himself that he was a civilized person and that he and the Deyzara had more in common than they did in difference. As usual, it wasn't easy.

The human gestured in the new arrival's direction. "This one is called Masurathoo."

Advancing, the Deyzara extended one ropy, rubbery two-digited hand. Lacking a tongue, it preferred the human gesture of greeting to that of the Sakuntala. It was trying to avoid the substitute trunk-touch.

Hiding his distaste, Jemunu-jah flicked his own tongue out and around the hairless head, making contact with the dangling eating trunk only briefly before executing an immediate retraction. He had often seen Deyzara shaking hands with humans or Sakuntala, a gesture they seemed able to manage effortlessly despite having only two digits to the human's five or the Sakuntala's six.

"Ah, I am informed that we shall be working together. I hope you will not find it too disagreeable an experience, as I am prepared to do whatever is necessary to locate this unfortunate human who has gone missing."

Jemunu-jah took a care not to clench his pointed teeth, even though those sharp incisors were offset so as not to damage his

own mouth. He could only envy the more galactically sophisticated Deyzara his perfect terranglo that in some ways sounded
more polished than that of the administrator herself. That the
newcomer was as soft-spoken as the rest of his kind did nothing
to diminish his eloquence.

Despite what Matthias had said, Jemunu-jah felt compelled
to offer one more objection. "*This* the one I going into southern regions with?"

Distressingly, the human nodded. "Masurathoo is an excellent skimmer pilot. You'll decide where and how to look, and
he will facilitate your efforts to the best of his ability."

"That I will do." In spite of the Deyzara's accommodating
tone, Jemunu-jah could see that the newcomer was himself
something less than overly enthusiastic about the assignment.
No Deyzara would be keen on the idea of being forced to work
in tight, isolated quarters for an indeterminate period of time
with a surly Sakuntala warrior. On the other hand, when there
was good money to be made, a Deyzara would endure almost
anything.

One last time, Jemunu-jah thought briefly about turning
down the task. Since Kenkeru-jah had already promised his
services, to refuse would be to insult his chief as well as bring
shame on his clan. Accepting meant money and *mula*. When a
difficult situation presents itself, he knew, it is sometimes useful
to have no choice.

"Since this an emergency, I can of course leave immediately."
He felt like a hypocrite, but *mula* was *mula*. If he was going to
have to suffer, he was going to wring every bit of gain from the
arrangement.

"I have already seen to the provisioning of the assigned vehicle," Masurathoo informed them both. "We can be on our way
as soon as you wish."

The mournful eyes that humans seemed to find so—what
was the word he had once heard used?—"winsome" stared up
at him. When the pilot's speaking trunk was not in use, compact muscles kept it coiled flat atop his head. The eating trunk

swung lazily back and forth from the lower portion of the skull, its naked hairlessness a distasteful sight at best. He would have to get used to it, he knew, for as long as it took to locate the stupid missing human and bring him back. Or to admit defeat. Given the extent of the region to be searched, the latter was a very real possibility.

"Leave now," he muttered as politely as he could. A glance out the nearer of the two windows showed that the rain was likely to lessen for a little while. That would mean more local traffic but better visibility. "Better to leave town during clearing."

"Precisely what I would have suggested," concurred the Deyzara knowledgeably. He looked back to the administrator. "We will file regular reports; you can be sure of that."

"I have every confidence in the two of you," she lied. "You were the best team that could be assembled." Given the exploration and rejection of every other possible alternative, she thought silently.

Still, it was part of her job to give these kinds of orders and to look after the human contingent on Fluva. Both of the sentients standing before her seemed quite competent. Given that, there was always the slight chance they actually *would* find the misbegotten bioprospector alive somewhere in the unmeasured depths of the Viisiiviisii.

Turning back to her desk's readout as soon as they had departed, she could only hope they might manage to do so before they killed each other.

2

Shadrach Hasselemoga had come to Fluva hoping to make a killing—of the financial kind. He had sincere hopes of making a fortune—always a possibility where the discovery of useful, previously unknown botanicals was concerned. While others might find the combination of soldier of fortune and botanist (with a special interest in mycology) a peculiar melding of professions, to men and women engaged in Hasa's line of work it was perfectly natural. People had indeed been known to kill one another over the discovery and possession of something small, green, and deceptively insignificant. They were willing to go to such occasional extremes because alien botanicals were frequently the key to the gengineering of everything from new pharmaceuticals to artificial flavorings, and much else besides.

Too bad he hated his new posting.

There wasn't much about it he didn't hate, from the constant rain to the molds and fungi that matured so fast you could watch them reproduce on your supposedly spore-resistant clothing. Or on your face, if you weren't careful. One poor *simick* who had gone hunting for a celebrated lotion-oozing slime mold about a thousand kelegs to the north of Taulau Town had been found only a hundred meters from the safety of his skimmer. Apparently, he'd become disoriented in the varzea and had wandered around unaware that the mold he'd collected had enthusiastically transmuted in the warmth of his collection pack into an ambulatory amoeboid state. Its potential lotion-generating properties notwithstanding, it had invaded his body right through the allegedly impermeable material of both pack and clothes, whereupon it had then proceeded to bed itself down nice and comfy inside his vital organs. Harold Tsukakaza, yeah, that was his name. He'd been lotioned to death.

Perambulating slime molds were the least of a person's worries on lush, fascinating, deadly Fluva. There were fungi that put out toxic mycelia and actively hostile basidiocarps, rusts that gave new meaning to an old word (and class), and all manner of nasties that made their homes in the trees or in the waters of the flooded forest. The Viisiiviisii was no place to be marooned. Hard to walk out of the woods when the base of the tree in which you found yourself stranded was twenty meters or more underwater.

Then there were the natives. The happy, smiling Sakuntala and the hardworking, comparatively diminutive Deyzara. Except that the Sakuntala were as likely to cut your head off as offer you a cup of traditional katola and the Deyzara would bow enthusiastically and wave their trunks in their disarmingly disconcerting fashion while quietly picking your pocket. Not that his own kind were much better. Among the many different species of sentients Hasa had encountered in his travels (and there had been many), humans fell somewhere in the shifting middle of the sentient muddle. That they were not as obvious cheats and liars as the Deyzara or as blatant deceivers and cutthroats as the Sakuntala was only due to the fact that power and experience had rendered them a tad more restrained.

Now, seemingly good and stuck in the middle of nowhere, and an unrelentingly hostile nowhere at that, he was going to have to rely on those same self-serving sons-of-bitches to extricate him from a bad fix not of his own making. Hasa was reasonably willing to take responsibility for his own mistakes. But he'd done nothing wrong this time, certainly nothing that should have led to his current imbroglio.

He'd done everything right prior to setting out: had the skimmer thoroughly overhauled and checked out, paid any overdue bills, settled with that thieving Dararpatui who ran the Kus supply depot, notified the proper authorities of his tentative flight plan, and registered his intentions with Administration. All so he could find himself, a week out from town, locked in a frantic uncontrolled dive down into the yawning depths of the Viisiiviisii. When oral commands failed to effect the necessary adjustments to his craft's plunge, he'd taken manual control, only to find that the relevant instrumentation was also locked and unresponsive. At the last possible moment, he'd thrown himself to the left and activated the craft's emergency self-contained landing sequencer. It, at least, had worked, as evidenced by the fact that he was still alive, mobile, and bitching.

Ripping himself out of the swollen cocoon of sofoam that had saved his life, he'd rushed the control console, only to stumble and fall. Not because he had been injured in the crash, not because he was suddenly overcome with dizziness, but because the floor of the skimmer was pointed down and sideways at respectively sharp angles. Recovering from the slip, he noticed immediately that the protective climate-controlled canopy was cracked in at least a dozen places. He was made aware of this fact because he was sitting in the rain. Also because several blue-striped tree branches now extended inside the skimmer. A head-sized flying creature was presently perched on one. It stared at him out of eyes that were so deep-sunk it seemed they must be set in the back of the animal's skull. In actual fact, they were positioned in the center, where by rotating they could stare as easily out the back of the skull as the front.

"Get out of here, you neeking goscack! I'm nobody's dinner yet!" Reaching down, he picked up a piece of some instrument that he hoped was not essential to the skimmer's functioning and threw it.

Letting out an unexpectedly melodious tootle, the weird arboreal with the internally gimbaled oculars dodged the chunk of airborne apparatus as it spiraled up and out of the wounded skimmer. Multiple wings extended out of the sides of its head and rotated parallel to the ground. In addition to providing lift, the spiral-screw wing system was an excellent design for shedding precipitation. Nature was ever so goddamned inventive, he told himself sullenly. Trying to taxonomize the bizarre creature would twist a bemused biologist's bowels.

Shadrach Hasselemoga was only mildly interested in it. The life-forms that commanded his attention were the ones that put out leaves and sent down roots or popped ballooning basidiocarps out of decaying wood. They didn't have internally pivoting eyeballs. Or, for that matter, eyes of any kind. At least, not usually.

Turning back to the console that was shielded from the ubiquitous rain by a still intact portion of the skimmer's transparent canopy, he spoke in the direction of the omnidirectional voice command pickup. There was no response from the skimmer's internal controller. This was hardly surprising since nothing was lit, indicating a complete loss of power. The emergency backup node was supposed to be sufficiently armored to survive all but a hundred percent destruction of the rest of the craft. The fact that he could now sue the manufacturer of said device for false and misleading claims was at present of little comfort. When he tried it, the craft's manual instrumentation proved equally demised.

Something was not right. Yes, the skimmer's environmental dome was shattered. Yes, the craft had suffered serious damage. But certain components on the sophisticated vehicle should still be functional. The air-circulation system, for example, was independently powered. Even in the event of catastrophic energy failure, it should still be cycling atmosphere. But it was as silent as the communicator.

Alternately cursing the rain and his undeserved ill fortune, he made an attempt to effect temporary repairs, something someone in his position had to be skilled at. No luck. He attempted to coerce the skimmer's computation unit to effect minimal internal resuscitation. No chance. He tried cursing and beating and threatening the variegated deities of half a dozen different religions, not all of them human. The multispecies heavens ignored him.

He was stuck.

As he morosely contemplated his indisputable stuckness, a line of brilliantly iridescent blue-and-crimson kindling came marching in single file through a gap in the broken dome. Wending their way toward where he was seated, their multiple short, jointed legs striding along in unison, they looked for all the world like a monkish procession of deeply religious stick insects. They had bulging black four-lensed eyes, slender quadruple slowly weaving antennae, and disagreeably sharp proboscises. Looking down, he gazed sternly at the first of the twenty-centimeter-long intruders. It halted in front of his leg. Delicate, sensitive antennae tapped gently, tentatively, at the hydrophobic tropical weave of his pants. The hypodermoid proboscis probed, searching for an opening between the raindrops that ran down his leg.

His off-world blood would probably give it indigestion, he knew. Without giving it the opportunity to sample the possible stomachache-inducing effects of imported alien body fluids, he raised his foot and brought it down firmly. There was a muted *crunch*. Green-and-yellow goo splotched across the floor.

Instantly the dance line of intruding ambulatory twigs did a united about-face and, without breaking stride, proceeded to take their leave of the skimmer. There was no violent counterattack, no attempt to gain retribution for the death of their point twig, no multiple keening high-pitched wail of despair. But as they exited the craft back along the branch they had used to enter it, each one deliberately and pointedly defecated on the still gleaming composite rim.

Go ahead, he thought irately. Take your turn. Fate has already done to me what you are only doing now.

He needed to take stock, he knew. Best to do so before
nightfall. If those responsible for such things were doing their
job, he would be located and lifted out of here before the onset
of twilight, let alone darkness. But one never knew. As those in
his position were well aware from long and bitter experience,
the number of complete and utter morons inhabiting government posts was inversely proportional to the distance from recognized centers of civilization. It might happen that he would
be compelled to spend a night, or even two, out in the Viisiiviisii before a rescue-and-recovery team arrived from Taulau or
another Commonwealth outpost. Should that come to pass, it
would be nice to have a few small items readily available. Water
would never be a problem on Fluva. But it would be nice not
to have to search for food. A dry place to sleep would also be
welcome, and a weapon or two was imperative. The Viisiiviisii
was not a benign place for the solo visitor to go camping.

Thoughts of a dry place to sleep caused him to rise and
scramble to the far side of the skimmer. Having briefly blacked
out at the moment of impact, he had no idea of the terrain on
which he had landed. Reaching the outer wall, he stuck his
head out into the full force of the rain, leaned through a wide
gap in the shattered dome, and looked down. A single mono-
syllable emerged from between tightened lips. It was foul.

His incapacitated skimmer was resting amid a tangle of broken branches and trailing vines some twenty meters above the
placid water, held aloft by trees whose bases and buttresses
were submerged in at least another twenty meters of tannin-
infused muck. A plethora of unpleasant possibilities rushed
helter-skelter through his brain.

Then there was a loud *crack*, and the necessity to think was
obviated by the need to grab onto something solid and unmoving. It was a futile gesture, because the entire skimmer was already moving—downward.

The supportive branches beneath it having finally given way
under the weight of the intruder, the skimmer banged and
bounced in an inglorious and quite noisy descent toward

the water below, banging off trunks and smashing through branches at the astonishing rate of one irate invective per second. It landed stern-first with a great splash, its back end sinking halfway under the surface before it finally stabilized atop a pile of exhausted wood.

Breathing hard, teeth clenched, Hasa picked himself up off the slanting deck. An intermittent morbid gurgling continued to rise from the part of his craft that was now underwater. His initial reaction was to kick the console, the walls, the floors, everything around him. He wanted to hurt every corner of the craft that had so rudely betrayed his trust. But he didn't dare, because further violent movement risked destabilizing his already precarious roost. Losing the skimmer didn't worry him. If it sank, it sank. Fine and good riddance. Once safely back in town he would eagerly apply to collect the insurance. But it could not be allowed to sink before he had recovered and stowed somewhere safe and stable those few vital elements of survival he had mentally inventoried only moments earlier.

Moving as carefully and slowly as his temper and the rain-slicked floor of the skimmer would permit, he made his way to the back of the vehicle. The storage lockers he sought were now underwater. Opening them and extracting their contents meant working up to his neck in the placid nutrient-rich liquid. He did not worry if the food paks, for example, were spoiled or not. Everything on Fluva that was subject to invasion and spoilage by mold or fungi was sealed tightly against such intrusion. Anything that wasn't did not last more than a week before it was overwhelmed by the planet's incredibly fecund, moisture-driven flora.

So the food paks he dragged out were still secure in their self-cooking wrappings. He located a repeating pistol and packets of old-fashioned explosive shells. Fancy neuronics and electrics didn't work well on alien worlds where the neutral tolerances of inimical local life-forms had yet to be calibrated. Either of the former might do no more than give a tickle to an onrushing carnivore. Explosives, on the other hand, had the virtue of not being species- or nervous-system-specific. They were marvelously egalitarian in their lethality.

Locating two rain capes, he immediately slipped one over his head. Though his tropical suit was ostensibly fully water-repellent, a person couldn't have too many layers of rain protection on Fluva. The rest of the gear he crammed into a backpack that he hung on a sturdy branch on one of the trees located safely outside the downed craft. If the skimmer's unseen suspect wooden supports suddenly gave way, sinking it to the ground twenty meters below, he would still have his limited store of salvaged supplies. This essential survival task completed, he crawled carefully down the branch he had used to reach the other tree and back into the skimmer.

Why he decided to check on the emergency beacon he didn't know. Even though the rest of the skimmer had lost all power, including backup, whatever had caused the trouble should not, could not, affect a unitary-sealed emergency beacon. That device would be secured firmly in the center of the skimmer's hull, in the region of greatest protection, sending out its powerful locating signal together with details of the accident that had caused its activation. If outside the regional pickup range of Taulau or any other town, the signal would then be picked up by one of the satellites orbiting the planet and relayed to the nearest appropriate outpost. But having secured his emergency supplies, he now had nothing left to do. So for the hell of it, he decided to check the beacon.

What he found made less sense than anything he had encountered since he'd hit the water.

Removing the appropriate panel in the center of the deck, he made sure it was fastened to a sticktight on one wall so it wouldn't go sliding down into the water that filled the lower half of the skimmer. He'd already spent enough time fumbling around under the surface while scavenging his emergency supplies. By now the water inside the immobilized craft had grown still, and there was no telling what sorts of parasites or other indigenous nasties might have infiltrated the partially submerged hull.

Beneath the panel, a transparent vacuum seal shone dully. Though it lay under a still intact portion of the skimmer's canopy, rainwater running down the inclined deck threatened to enter the protected space. Rolling up the second rain cape, he used it to rig a temporary barrier to divert the steady trickle around the opening. Turning back to the cavity, he fingered the necessary visible touch pads in proper sequence. The panel slid aside.

His brows drew together. In the diffuse light that filtered down between the trees from a cloud-filled sky it should have been easy to pick out the glow of multiple indicators on the outside of the beacon box. That it was dark and devoid of light didn't necessarily mean the device wasn't working—but it was not a good sign. Not a good sign at all.

It meant making one more plunge into the water that filled the aft section. Nothing darted from the water to assault him, and he held his breath religiously to avoid ingesting any of the untreated fluid. Emerging with toolbox in hand, he returned to the opening and cracked the beacon's seal.

Passing the tester over the device produced nothing: not so much as a chirp from the auditory indicator or a squiggle on the small screen. It should have lit up with half a dozen different readouts. Instead, it was as flat and dull as a politician in the absence of media. Of course, the crash landing could have damaged the tester as well, but like most tools, it was almost too simple and straightforward to hurt. And it was too much to expect that both the supposedly invulnerable emergency beacon as well as the much smaller tester had suffered similar critical damage during touchdown. A smashup serious enough to cause them both to fail would have done much worse to his far more fragile human frame, sofoam cocoon notwithstanding.

Pondering the unreasonable unlikeliness of it all, he happened to glance at the right side of the beacon. It should have

looked exactly the same as the left side, the top, the front, and
the back. But it did not. Even in the poor light he could make
out the thin but distinct line running the length of the box,
about midway up the side. Frowning, he traded the tester for
another tool and traced the latter along the line. The beacon
popped open: something it should not do outside an authorized inspection-and-repair facility. Wary of the rain, he used his
body to shield the box as best he could as he leaned over and in
for a closer look.

As with any similar device, the beacon's internal components
were solid: drawn, painted, flashed, or strobed in place. None
of which explained the hole in the middle of the lower right
quarter. The fissure had not been made with a drawer, painter,
flasher, or strober. Something large and heavy had been used to
smash a hole in the surface of the unit. Even in this day and age
there were uses for low-tech. The hole might have been made
with something as simple as an old-fashioned hammer. It might
have been made by a rock. The means was unimportant.

Circuitry had been shattered. To fix it would require the resources of a fully equipped shop and a skilled flasher. He had
neither. The dimensions as well as the nature of the destruction
led to an unavoidable conclusion.

Someone had entered, opened, and deliberately damaged the
beacon. Considered thoughtfully, this implied that whoever
had done so had presumed that the beacon might soon be put
to use and that the perpetrator preferred it not be available at
such time to perform its designated functions.

Eyes widening, he removed a portable work light from the
toolbox and stuck it to his forehead. Further examination re-
vealed everything he now suspected and far more than he
wanted to know.

The skimmer's power monitor had been adjusted to show a
full charge when in reality he had departed Taulau on less than
a tenth of that. Guidance systems had also been tampered with.
In fact, once he got deeper into the craft's instrumentation he
had a hard time finding something that had not been tampered

with. It implied more than casual destruction. In as professional and methodical a way possible, someone had gone to considerable trouble to ensure that no matter how skilled its pilot, this particular skimmer would never be able to return its passenger to his point of origin.

Sabotage.

But why him? Sure, he had enemies, both personal and professional. He knew most of them by name and took perverse pride in the extent of the list he had accumulated. But though he went down that list from beginning to end and back again, he could not settle on the identity of a single person willing to go to the extreme of killing him. Priding itself on the maturity of its citizens, the government of the Commonwealth frowned on individuals who used murder to settle personal disputes. That did not mean killings were a thing of the past. After all, many of the Commonwealth's citizens were human. But such killings were not frequent. They were even less common on outpost worlds like Fluva, where residents often had to rely on one another to survive, much less prosper.

Besides, most of his enemies were not unlike himself: straightforward and to the point in their dealings. Though they displayed many qualities, deviousness was not often among them. Anyone wanting him dead would like as not have confronted him face-to-face or at least tried to jump him on a town walkway or in his rented apartment at night. He stared at the several instrument panels whose interiors he had exposed to the light. This was too complex. It hinted at motives beyond a simple desire to see a certain Shadrach Hasselemoga dead.

Whoever they were, they had been very thorough. It wasn't enough to ensure that his craft would crash well beyond any outpost of civilization. They had gone to the trouble of disabling the emergency beacon as well. No emergency beacon meant that even if anyone thought to come looking for him, they were going to have a hell of a time finding him in the tangled mass of vegetation and waterways that comprised the Viisiiviisii.

Looking up, he saw that the sloping angle of his touchdown had smashed a narrow pathway through the trees. That, at least, should be visible from the air—depending on how heavy the overcast and intense the rainfall whenever someone came skimming by. And with each passing day, the fecund varzea would send out more and more shoots and leaping vines and fast-growing spores in an attempt not to close the gap but to make use of the bounty of sunlight it presently provided. Given the astonishing rate of local growth, within a week or so the edges of the gap would be filled with a ragged assortment of fresh, opportunistic vegetation. At least until then, he had no choice but to stay close to the skimmer. Ultimately, it might be all that would remain even slightly visible from above.

Sitting there beneath the cracked and broken canopy, the rain spattering monotonously around him, he listened to the resurgent cries of the Viisiiviisii and pondered a thought that rode roughshod even over the legendary Hasa anger.

I could die here, he realized with sudden clarity.

Though he had never considered himself immortal and knew better than most that the universe would continue on quite comfortably without him, he had always believed himself more durable than his fellow humans. Given the inherent dangers of his chosen profession, he had from the beginning anticipated a possible early demise. Indeed, he had been through a number of difficult scrapes, only to have survived them all with both body and bank account intact. But such incidents had all been natural consequences of his work. Never before had anyone set out to kill him with such detailed malice aforethought.

The more he contemplated his situation, what had happened to him, and how it had happened, the angrier he became. It grew and seethed and boiled within him until it seemed that any alien raindrops that struck his forehead would surely be turned to steam from the mere contact. Anger matured into fury, and fury into a determination to learn who had done this to him and why. And once he had learned that to his satisfaction, once he had established it to a certainty and without a shadow of a doubt, then the residents of Taulau Town would do well to conceal themselves inside their homes and places of business and lockseal their doors and wait out his wrath much as they would one of the occasional monster storms that came thundering down off the steep slopes of the western mountains. Such a storm would be as a gentle breeze compared to the kind of weather a livid Shadrach Hasselemoga was going to bring to unsuspecting Taulau.

Assuming he could get out of his present situation alive, of course.

3

aneci-tok acknowledged the deferential salutations of her fellow villagers as she made her way toward the High House. She walked with the special short stride that signified a person of rank. In the Days of Distant Memory, villagers would have lined up to link their long, strong arms together to form living chains for her to use in crossing open spaces between the trees. Like many traditions, this had been abandoned with the arrival of Commonwealth culture. With spun-strilk pathways linking homes, ceremonial buildings, shops, and stores, the Sakuntala no longer had to leap between trees or weave lianas or make bridges of their living bodies. Roaming might not be as much fun, but it was undeniably safer.

Off to her right, a Sakuntala spinner crew was busy putting the finishing touches on a wide porch surrounding a new food-and-services outlet. It was one of the few in the community that was owned by a Sakuntala family, as opposed to by the Deyzara. Or by Deyzara fronting for a Commonwealth enterprise or for other Sakuntala. Sadly she shifted the coils of her tongue from one cheek pouch to the other. The world was changing so fast, it was impossible to know what new marvel was going to manifest itself next. Or what to do about it.

As a Hata, or High Chief, she was the recipient of reverential salutations and hand signs from the inhabitants of Chanorii Town. A few tongues shot out and lingered respectfully before recoiling. If some seemed more indifferent than was usual, that was to be expected. On this day Chanorii was full of Hatas and Hata-nius, or mid-level chiefs. Not to mention the war chiefs known as Hata-yuiquerus.

They were there to discuss making a new kind of war on the Deyzara. That, she knew, was going to be the most difficult thing to decide next. She did not look forward to the coming debate. There was going to be much passionate disagreement. Voices were going to be raised. Tongues would be rudely extruded. These things always happened when the Sakuntala conferenced. But this conclave promised to be far more raucous than any she could remember having attended.

In addition to the respected Hatas who had been carefully considering the question for some time now, every Yuiqueru, or war chief, within a thousand keleqs had come to Chanorii. What was surprising was how many seemed to lean toward a maintaining of the status quo and the peace it engendered. This was not because the war chiefs possessed any special love for the Deyzara. On balance, they probably disliked the two-trunks even more than did the average Sakuntala. The problem was, and the reason an open expulsion of Deyzara was simply not decreed by the Council of Hatas, that it was not merely a question of Sakuntala versus introduced Deyzara. A third party was involved.

This strange, foreign, difficult-to-comprehend mass organization of alien beings who collectively called themselves the Commonwealth.

Fluva had not yet attained full Class V Commonwealth status—but it was on the verge. Many wonderful things had been promised when that moment arrived. Having seen what Commonwealth technology had already wrought on her home world, Naneci-tok could well believe it. The trouble was that in order for Fluva to be accorded the status of a full Class V world, certain social as well as technical accomplishments had to be realized. One of these was the absence of internecine warfare.

The Sakuntala had always fought among themselves. It was an old and well-established tradition. The Commonwealth authorities had no problem with that. Such intervillage or interclan combat was permitted under the laws that governed internal social compacts. But warring against other sentients for the sake of eliminating a different intelligent species fell under a different set of regulations altogether. It was uncivilized. It was anti-Commonwealth. It was not allowed.

Knowing this should weigh heavily on the Council's final decision. Going after the Deyzara on an organized basis might mean the end of Commonwealth assistance to Fluva. Over the past two hundred cycles, the Sakuntala had grown more than a little fond of the benefits of Commonwealth aid and technology. There were the wonderful tools, the varied and new forms of entertainment, introductions to new cultures, the promise of the opportunity to visit other worlds. New foods, new methods of processing them, new art, new music, all manner of small devices and inventions that made life easier and safer and healthier. Since the coming of the Commonwealth, the Sakuntala for the first time in their history had experienced significant reductions in a previously high rate of infant mortality. Respected elders now lived truly impressive life spans. As a Hata, she could look forward herself to the opportunity to actually enjoy her old age, instead of dying of heart rot or dermal asimatosis or sacral calcification as her ancestors had.

But in return for all these wonderful things, the Sakuntala were forced to put up with the Deyzara.

Not all Deyzara were bad, she knew. On an individual basis, many were actually somewhat agreeable to be around—except when they were eating, of course. Unfortunately, they continued to adhere to the customs not of Fluva but of their ancestral world of Tharce IV.

It would be a simple matter to blame the troubles on the humans of the Commonwealth. If they had not brought the first Deyzara to Fluva, there would be no Deyzaran problem. But it was not nearly so simple, she knew. Busy fighting among themselves, her own ancestors had welcomed both the Commonwealth and the goods and services it brought with it and the Deyzara. If the Sakuntala had stopped fighting among themselves and gone to work enthusiastically for the humans and their friends, it would not have been necessary to bring the Deyzara to work the gathering and plantations in the Viisiiviisii and the small shops and businesses in the towns. But the Sakuntala were more interested in fighting one another as each clan sought supremacy over its historical enemies. So the dilemma that existed today had multiple sponsors, Commonwealth and Sakuntala alike.

She knew that the possibility of solving the problem by repatriating the Deyzara to Tharce IV had been debated in secretive discussions among the humans and their allies. It had been dropped for several reasons. For one thing, it would be very expensive. More critically, the Deyzara in Taulau Town and Chanorii and elsewhere considered themselves Fluvans. Their great-grandparents had been born on Fluva. They knew nothing of Tharce IV. Furthermore, or so she had heard, though the inhabitants of that distant world made the right mouth noises about accepting refugees, they really did not want hundreds of thousands of strange immigrants dumped in their comfortable planetary lap. So it looked like the Deyzara were on Fluva to stay. Unless certain of the Hatas and Yuiquerus had their way.

Her tongue rambled aimlessly between cheek pouches. It was a bad business, this. Though the Sakuntala were accustomed to warfare, war always brought suffering. As for her personal feelings toward the Deyzara, she was ambivalent. She neither liked nor hated them, as so many of her fellows did.

If only the Deyzara had made a greater effort to blend in with the Sakuntala! To gain knowledge of the ways of *mula*, to participate in the various complex but learnable katola ceremonies. To mute their own gaudy tastes and incessant activity. True, it had made them successful in ways only a few Sakuntala were now starting to match. From the beginning, the Deyzara had grasped the intricacies of Commonwealth commerce, passed on to the first immigrants to Fluva by their Tharcian progenitors. These the Sakuntala were forced to learn from scratch. Many of her kind were making great progress in mastering such matters. The estimable Jemunu-jah, for example. But it took time—and the Deyzara had arrived already familiar with many of the intricacies.

It had to be admitted that a few of the Deyzara had made the transition. Without entirely abandoning their own ways, they had learned well those of the Sakuntala and willingly deferred to them as the original inhabitants of Fluva. But all too many Deyzara still remained isolated from their neighbors, keeping strictly to their own customs and dealing with those of the Sakuntala only when necessary. These Deyzara had no *mula,* none. One way or another, she knew, this would have to change.

When consulted about the situation, humans invariably reiterated that such adaptations took time, citing from their own history of mutual convergence with the very different beings called the thranx. Naneci-tok had only seen thranx one time. There had been several of them, leaving the Visitor Greeting Center in Lokoriki Town. They had kept close together and avoided all but the main walkways. This was because, she later learned, while they loved the rain and the humidity, they were terrified of open water. Not only could they not swim, but they also had a distinct tendency to sink like stones. Since, like every other community in the Viisiiviisii, Lokoriki was built above the water, this rendered their visits to Fluva infrequent and unpalatable except in the brief time of the Dry, when the land lay exposed and naked to the air. Strange creatures, the thranx, though the humans seemed very fond of them. But then, though humans were closer in shape and appearance to the Sakuntala than the Deyzara, it had to be admitted that they also had some very peculiar tastes.

Chanorii was an ancient place. Compared to many other towns and villages that had adapted modern ways, designs, and materials, a large proportion of the buildings were still of traditional wood-and-vine construction. Not the High House she was walking toward, however. Of far more recent vintage, it had been built with advanced Commonwealth technology. The spun strilk that supported it (instead of the traditional woven lianas) was linked not only to surrounding trees but also to pylons of tough composites that had been sunk deep into the earth itself, far below the waterline. The best of such material did not rot in the perpetually rainy climate of Fluva and was impervious to the numerous fungi and small crawling things that would have eaten their way through comparable wooden posts in a matter of weeks. But even composites had to be checked from time to time and were subject to regular maintenance. For one thing, the active yananuca vines loved the support these strange new "trees" provided and would pull smaller or incompetently footed pylons down.

The structure itself was similar to those the humans erected for their own use, but entirely in keeping with ancient Sakuntala customs. Constructed of spun and sheet composite in the traditional form of a square, it had no openings on the shielded and armored lower level. In ancient times, this was designed to keep out predatory branch walkers like the nironve and slitherers like the bai-mou. For its part, the Viisiiviisii made no distinction between materials and methods. Maintenance teams were kept perpetually busy cutting away opportunistic lianas and leapers, aerial roots that reached down to the water, and spirocyte fungi that tried to penetrate buildings from below.

Hatas and their advisers and attendants entered through the single circular, easily defended opening in the roof, using ample built-in handholds to swing themselves over to the eskachi, or drying area. In the old days, a series of elaborate shaking gestures would be employed to politely shed the moisture one had accumulated on one's fur. Nowadays, a portable sensing evaporator imported from the thranx world of Evoria did the job faster and more efficiently. *But not,* she reflected as she walked toward her assigned place, occasionally entwining tongues with friends and acquaintances, *half as gracefully.*

The line of chairs suspended from the ceiling formed a circle around the central shaft. These days such seats hung from spun composite, not vines cut from the heart of the Viisiiviisii. The composite strands were stronger and lighter. What they lacked in warmth and weave they made up for by being impervious to decay. It was a trade-off that was hard to argue with.

Rain pouring through the entrance in the roof fell through the open center of the High House to spill out through a slightly larger hole in the floor. When the occasional rare shaft of sunshine pierced the clouds, the raindrops were illuminated from above, giving this central core of falling water the appearance of dripping diamonds. Traditionally at such moments, those not speaking would murmur a soft "Hauea!," an old entreaty to the gods to make sure the rain did not stop. Because if the rain stopped, as it did seasonally for one small part of the year, it meant that, among other things, predators could walk freely along dry ground from tree to tree, seeking prey. That was not so important anymore, in these days of imported advanced weaponry, alarms, and protective barriers, but old fears died slowly, and hard.

She slipped regally into her seat and began the slow, steady rocking back and forth motion that indicated she was ready to participate in the forthcoming discussion. All around her, other Hatas were moving back and forth or side to side to their own personal, unheard rhythms. Skillfully synced, a mobile seat (swings, the humans called them straightforwardly, but without reverence) could convey almost as many meanings as words. Direction was as important as velocity. Her own uncomplicated motion indicated that she was ready to listen but not to speak. Not yet.

Molavil-isi was the last to arrive. An old and wizened Hata, he had come all the way from distant Hiokavaru. Before the advent of the Commonwealth, distance and dangers would have rendered such a journey impossible. Now, with the aid of a skimmer, it could be accomplished in a matter of days. Wonderful things, skimmers, Naneci-tok felt. Her ancestors would have been astonished to see her traveling freely above the treetops, without the aid of branches or walkways. All thanks to the arrival of the humans and thranx and their grand interstellar civilization. Unfortunately, along with skimmers and energy weapons and communicators they had brought the Deyzara. How to deal with the latter without losing the former was the great question this meeting had been organized to try to settle.

The Hata-tanasua served as shaman-advisers to multiple clans. Cherished by all who had enjoyed the good fortune to know him and to experience his wise ministrations, the sage Manarapi-vea formally convened the gathering by intoning the opening to the katola ritual. Holding the first carved bowl of katola at eye level, he kept his tongue twice wrapped around it as he paced deliberately around the central column of falling rain. Conversation quieted immediately. Seats grew still. The katola ceremony was among the most revered of Sakuntala customs. Also among the most anticipated, as good katola was treated by the Sakuntala much as fine wine was by the humans. That in sufficient doses it was also a powerful hallucinogen only served to enhance its appeal.

There would be none of that during the debate, she knew. The ceremony would be carried out in moderation. Everyone would need their wits about them. Indulgences such as agreeable hallucinations could come afterward, during the informal gatherings that were sure to follow.

Halting not far from her, Manarapi-vea inclined both ears and head slightly forward and offered the bowl. Naneci-tok was only mildly surprised. Though there were others present who were senior to her, this was her territory. Manarapi-vea was not only being polite; he was also being politically correct.

Making sure her tongue was tucked well off to one side in an empty cheek, she accepted the bowl in both hands, grasping it firmly with all twelve fingers. As the Hata-tanasua chanted the appropriate phrases, she took a single long swallow. Ceremonial, katola drinking might be—but it was also a fine treat. The tepid liquid slid readily down her throat. Even as she handed the bowl back, she felt her stomach start to grow numb. A distinctive tingling began in her toes and fingers. The woven strappings that covered her midsection and upper torso seemed suddenly looser than usual.

Around the circle Manarapi-vea went, circling the column of rain that continued to pour through the corresponding openings in ceiling and floor, offering katola to Hata, Yuiqueru, and Hata-niu alike. There were no Hata-naus present. The matters to be discussed were too important to allow the lowest-ranking chiefs a say in the outcome. Only when everyone had sipped of the venerable liquid made from the sap of the Oli'wiu did Manarapi-vea raise his voice. Everyone seated around the falling rain that drowned the land and gave life and protection to the Sakuntala from marauding predators joined the Hata-tanasua in reciting the ancient verses of understanding. It was said:

"We come here today to make a Talking. Today and here, we are all of one clan. Today and here, every Hata may say what they will, as they will, without fear of being slain by a neighbor."

There was more. Naneci-tok knew it by heart and recited it from memory, but her thoughts were already on the debate to come. One that without question was going to have a profound impact not only on the future of the Sakuntala but also on their present.

It was expected that Cecolou-tiu, as the eldest in attendance, would speak first. She did not disappoint. With the aid of the pair of Hata-nius flanking her, she eased out of her chair. Once erect, she stood without assistance. Her fur was almost entirely gray, with only the barest hints of the dark black and green pattern that had once identified its owner.

Gazing around the expectant circle, she had to squint hard through the column of rain to make out those chiefs sitting in chairs directly opposite her. But even aged, weak Sakuntala eyes were remarkably acute. When she finally spoke, her words rang out through the meeting room clear and strong.

"You all here know me. You know I not speak without first thinking. Not easy, thinking at my age. But this significant what we talk here today. Very important not make wrong decision. I think hard and harder about what to do about loutish, tawdry, thieving Deyzara. Must for sure do something." A chorus of supportive murmurs arose from many of the assembled. "So believe when I say I think hardest that this talk of trying drive all Deyzara off Fluva is talk-making of idiot people."

More supportive muttering echoed her statement as she slowly resumed her seat, but Naneci-tok noted an equal number of confused mumblings as well as unmistakable indications of outright dissent. As both began to quiet down, a singular presence slipped forward out of his chair. Unusually tall even for one of his kind, Aniolo-jat was a Yuiqueru with a growing reputation among the more radical elements of the Sakuntala. He had drawn considerable attention not only for his military prowess, demonstrated in the usual interclan battles, but also for a wiliness not usually attributed to mid-status chiefs who specialized in combat.

Ears and eyes alert, he gazed silently around the assembly until he was satisfied that he had everyone's attention—or at least that of the nonsenile. He spoke softly and carefully, without any of the ground-scraping gestures or traditional howls that usually accompanied the assertions of a war chief. Naneci-tok was as intent on his words as any of her colleagues. Here was a kin brave and thoughtful. One any female would be glad to mate with and any warrior proud to follow.

Without hearing a word, she had already come to the conclusion that he was very, very dangerous.

His initial comments only reinforced her preliminary opinion: they were completely unexpected.

"I agree with knowledgeable and wise Cecolou-tiu. Is folly to think we can kill some Deyzara and just push rest off our world." Wide eyes and astonished murmurings from his supporters

showed this was not what they had expected to hear from one of
their most admired and aggressive colleagues. But such was the
commanding power of Aniolo-jat's presence that none rose from
their chairs to try to channel him. There was some violent swinging, however.

The Yuiqueru's voice rose just enough to be heard over the
chorus of creaking wood and quivering supports. "I have no
more love for the hairless ones than any of you. But I am real-
ist. I have made some study of politics of our new 'friends' and
benefactors, the Commonwealth. Its history shows it will tolerate some local fighting. But not killing of all one kind of species
by another. They have special word for that. So . . . we may kill
some Deyzara but not slaughter all." His mouth twisted into
the Sakuntalan equivalent of a sardonic smile. "I contain my
unhappiness at this."

"What then we do, Yuiqueru Aniolo-jat?" asked one of the
neutral members of the assembly.

The war chief turned toward the speaker. In replying to her, he
continued to address all of them. "We still fight. Planning been
ongoing for some time now. Very soon all is readied. We pick
careful which Deyzara to kill. Not wealthiest ones. Not technicians. We still need learn from them." He turned slowly, trying
to confront each one of his fellow chiefs individually. "Most
Deyzara think they smarter than any Sakuntala. But we know we
not stupid. Just some bit behind. We smart enough to learn, even
from our enemies. We kill specific Deyzara. Kill some offspring
just to show hint of irrationality, strike greater fear. Idea is to put
Deyzara in position of permanent scaring. Not eliminate. Just
render always inferior. If they always in fear of us, they always be
willing accommodate whatever we ask." Taking a mouthful of
rain from the central column, he sprayed his open hands with it,
held dripping fingers up for all to see. "Water runs. Fear clings.
The Deyzara are naked. We will clothe them in fear."

Behind him, on the other side of the rain, Yeruna-hua
stepped from his chair to speak. Brilliant pupils blazed, and the
other Yuiqueru's yellow-and-black fur stood erect.

"Aniolo-jat speaks thoughtful but speaks too much caution. I say forget Commonwealth. Not mind reaction of off-worlders." He raised an arm high. "Kill every Deyzara! Kill them all!"

The chant rose around the circle. But while spirited, it was far from universal. Aniolo-jat let it run its course before finally interrupting, having to raise his voice only slightly to do so.

"A cubling may not always have what it wish for. In this new, wider world of stars and other beings that live around them, the Sakuntala are still cublings. The wise offspring watches, and learns even from parents it dislikes. It is the foolish one who bravely steps off the branch and into waters of Viisiiviisii, to swim boldly—until is taken by a giimatasa."

It was an image burned into the memory of every Sakuntala. The wild swirl of water, the helpless cries of the trapped, the inability to do anything but watch until the doomed disappeared into the depths: no one, not even a Hata, was immune to such a possible fate—or the memory of it. When it was quiet again, Aniolo-jat resumed speaking.

"We *could* possible kill most Deyzara and see rest flee into sky. But then what happen?" Wrapping his tongue several times around his face, he briefly covered his eyes. "Commonwealth do one of several things. Punish us."

"Not afraid of humans!" Yeruna-hua made a challenging cracking sound with his own fully extended tongue, snapping the tip like a whip. "Humans small and weak. They have cubling tongues, and they slip and fall from trees and walkways like legless shumai. My young ones strong enough to rip off their arms."

"*Heesa,* that is so. But not all strength is in arms and tongues. Humans have better weapons than Sakuntala."

"Not anymore!" shouted someone Naneci-tok could not identify. "We have them now also. Buy and trade for them. For 'protection' from Viisiiviisii and for 'hunting.' "

"We do have them," Aniolo-jat readily agreed. "And from our other sources. But still not so many as humans do. And if

necessary, they have bigger weapons they can bring to Fluva. I
have learned of these things. They have machines that can find
person in middle of night, in depths of Viisiiviisii. They can
hear sound of talking from ship in sky. We learning of these
things and how use them—but we still not have all, or enough.
Someday, *heesa*, but not yet.

"Besides, are other punishments humans can use. We do this
to all Deyzara, maybe humans just go away." Listening closely,
Naneci-tok admired how the Yuiqueru's shrewdness came into
play. "Commonwealth go away, Fluva and Sakuntala revert to
living in stick-and-sap houses in trees." Reaching to his waist,
he tapped his small communicator. "How many here want to
go back to talking with howler drums? How many like watch
vit recordings? How many getting rich trading with and working for humans? No Commonwealth—no wonderful technology toys. No money."

It hit home, she saw clearly. Anyone could rouse a crowd
against the Deyzara. It took a chief with a mastery of both war-
craft *and* wordcraft to make the often fractious Sakuntala *listen*.
Every chief present in the High House knew that being in the
Commonwealth offered advantages too great to abandon.

"What about our culture? What will become of the Sakuntala?" another chief asked, almost plaintively.

"We will keep that which makes us what we are." Aniolo-jat
spoke with conviction. "We will take what we wish from Commonwealth. But to do so we must make sure Deyzara are kept
down. They must agree to set of demands. Foremost important, they must agree to limit their breeding. Fluva must stay
forever in dominion of the Sakuntala." A loud chorus of
"Hauea!" underlined this declamation. This time, Naneci-tok
noted, the response was nearly universal.

"We must do this without bring Commonwealth retribution
down on us. Especially on us personally." His ears flicked out
to the sides in an expression of knowingness. "And as you
know, we now have friends who have agree to help us."

No one would disagree with the Yuiqueru's evaluation, she

knew. There was too much potential individual wealth at stake. Among the Sakuntala themselves, alliances and treaties and declarations were always shifting. To get the people to do anything in concert was historically difficult. In that, she knew, lay perhaps the more formidable weapon possessed by the Deyzara. The trunked ones knew that the Sakuntala were as likely to fight one another as they were to do battle with any outsiders.

Aniolo-jat seemed to have it all figured out. Of course, if even a few of the Deyzara decided to fight back, using those same Commonwealth weapons that had been spoken of so admiringly, then Sakuntala also would die. And if some of the humans chose to aid their embattled Deyzara associates, that would mean more death still. But death in combat was no stranger to the Sakuntala. It was part of their culture—far more so than it was of the Deyzara's.

The human reaction remained the principal unpredictable element. How would the Commonwealth government on Fluva react to an attempt to minimize forever the influence of the local Deyzara? Would they interfere at all? As the wily Aniolo-jat had already pointed out, Commonwealth money and goods were too important to risk losing. The other variable was the reaction of the clans. How closely would traditional rivals and competitors cooperate in an attempt to get rid of the Deyzara? And for how long?

And exactly who were these new "friends" the cunning Yui-queru had spoken of?

Too much was at stake to leave to chance. The more she struggled to reconcile Aniolo-jat's seductive words with what she felt to be right, the harder the veins in her ears throbbed. Could a decision on so weighty a matter be made so soon? Today, even? She wished fervently for wise personal counsel. But her mother was dead. *She* was the counsel, now. A look cast in Cecolou-tiu's direction brought no relief. The aged Hata had fallen asleep.

A sudden thought gave her hope. "Before making any decision here, I would wish us to hear from the learned Jemunu-jah."

The reaction from the assembly showed that even those who most strongly supported Aniolo-jat recognized the name. Though Jemunu-jah was not even a Hata-nua, his reputation was known to even visiting chiefs. Even the bellicose Yeruna-hua grunted considerately.

"Ah, Jemunu-jah," Aniolo-jat murmured in a way Naneci-tok did not like. "The famous, the clever, the hardworking Jemunu-jah. The Jemunu-jah who has been well schooled in Commonwealth ways. I, too, recognize the extent of his knowing. I, too, would desire hear his opinions on this so very important matter." The Hata-yuiqueru's ears dipped forward in a gesture of sadness and regret.

"Distress-saying, there a problem. Jemunu-jah is gone away for a while just now."

"Gone away?" blurted a minor Hata-niu. "Gone away where and how?"

"The human Hata female Matthias ask for Sakuntala help in find one of their own who gone lost in southern Viisiiviisii." He turned a slow circle. "You all know that kind crazy-person human, go out by self or as couple to collect stinking stuff that Commonwealth tanasuas take apart to make medicine and other things." He lowered his voice significantly. "Jemunu-jah not go alone, though. He make traveling with help . . . of Deyzara."

The last was too much for Naneci-tok. The imputation inherent in Aniolo-jat's tone could not be allowed to stand unchallenged. Rising from her chair, she did not still its swinging but let it continue to rock back and forth behind her as an indication of her distress.

"I know well Jemunu-jah. He among smartest of all not-Hata. *Heesa,* he work close and well with Deyzara. Also humans. Jemunu-jah work well with all and any who respect his smartness. He is Sakuntala ear to toe, proud and true." Turning slightly, she focused her attention on the patiently waiting Aniolo-jat. "Who send Jemunu-jah away into Viisiiviisii at this so important time?"

"Why, human Hata Matthias specifically ask for best of local Sakuntala. Specifically ask for one who speak human lingua well. Specifically ask for one who can work with Deyzara. Who else so qualified but Jemunu-jah? Not worry about the skillful one. He return safe and soon."

Heesa-mu, she thought to herself—*but not soon enough to participate in this debate and offer his opinion.* Someone in the High House was being too clever by half, and she did not think it was wise but dozy old Molavil-isi, who had barely stirred during the course of the discussion.

Yeruna-hua's tongue flicked out to slap the wooden floor—a strong sign of disgust. "What could that one have to say that make any matter? He is with humans all time. Work with humans, talk with humans, help humans." Piercing eyes blazed. "This one think that oh-so-clever Jemunu-jah maybe not so Sakuntala proud and true anymore. This one think maybe he now become very tall, very good-hearing, good-seeing, nice-pattern-fur *human*!"

Attempting to counter a serious accusation on behalf of one not present to defend himself, Naneci-tok saw her incipient defense drowned out by the perplexed muttering of her fellow Hatas. At the same time, she found herself wondering if the combative outbursts of Yeruna-hua arose from within his own heart or if he was acting as a spear point for the more "reasonable" Aniolo-jat. The Sakuntala were masters of shifting alliances. But she could not be certain. Either each Hata was honestly propounding his own agenda or else they were displaying the same kind of shrewdness Aniolo-jat attributed to the absent Jemunu-jah.

It might not have mattered even if that praiseworthy individual had still been in Chanorii and available to address the High House. He was not a Hata and unless invited to do so beforehand could not speak at a traditional assembly such as this one even to defend himself.

A young and neutral Hata-niu rose somewhat timidly from her chair. "If we do move against Deyzara as Aniolo-jat proposes,

someone like Jemunu-jah who work close with both humans and
Deyzara could be caught in middle."

"*Heesa-mu*," muttered the relentlessly belligerent Yeruna-
hua, "that would be serious loss indeed."

As expected, Aniolo-jat took a far more rational view of the
possibility. Whether he believed it or not, Naneci-tok reflected,
was another matter entirely.

"Jemunu-jah is skillful enough to take care of self. Time
here-now is for worry about future of all Sakuntala—not individuals." He turned another slow circle. "I say to you, my fellow Hatas, that all future of our people will be decide here
today, and that we must make right decision." He paused for
emphasis. For a long moment, the liquid percussion of rain
spilling through the central opening of the High House was
the only sound in the circular chamber.

"Otherwise, we and our cublings can forward look to long
lives of prosperity and good health as part of this great star-
place Commonwealth—working low jobs for Deyzara. Where is
the *mula* in that?"

As an appeal to reason as well as emotion, Aniolo-jat's speaking clearly moved the Hatas. Others spoke after him—some to
agree, others to dispute. Naneci-tok used her chance to point
out once again that moving against the Deyzara might well
bring the Sakuntala into direct conflict with the Commonwealth and its superior technology. Her words were listened to
by most. But not all. Yeruna-hua and his own small circle of
virulent supporters were as ready to kill humans as they were
Deyzara. The amount of support that showed itself for this extreme position frightened her. By contrast, Aniolo-jat appeared
reasonable and almost restrained.

Which was probably the idea, she knew.

When the vote was finally taken, it was still raining. The sun
did not show itself from behind the clouds, as it sometimes did
in the evening. This was taken as a good sign by Manarapi-vea;
he spread his arms and ears wide to intone the ceremony of
parting. More katola was passed around, followed by bites of

hot pipa fruit that enhanced the katola's narcotic effect. The Hatas weaved and chanted in their chairs, their multiple swinging disturbing the column of rain in pleasing arcs.

Through the relaxing hallucinogenic haze induced by pipa and katola Naneci-tok tried to sort out the import of what had been decided. Her own people would not stand by as events unfolded. They could not, lest they be subjected to more than approbation by the other clans. They would join Aniolo-jat and Yeruna-hua and the others in a coordinated attack against preselected Deyzara targets. The aim would be to "persuade" the Deyzara to agree to the combined Sakuntala demands before the humans could decide to intervene. If this could be done, even an awakened Cecolou-tiu agreed, then everything the cunning Aniolo-jat predicted might well come true, at small sacrifice to the Sakuntala. The alternative proposals put forth by Naneci-tok and others among the Hatas who believed in equal treatment for all, even Deyzara, were politely but firmly voted down.

It was to be war, then. No, not war, Aniolo-jat insisted. A quick, overwhelming bite, like a nougusm striking a bloated laja, then stepping back to watch its prey collapse from the shock. It would all be over before the distant Commonwealth tribes could make up their minds what to do about it. With the aims of the Sakuntala achieved, these tribes would accept the result. Of this Aniolo-jat was certain. While the Sakuntala knew little of other Commonwealth peoples, he had seen enough of humans to know how their system functioned.

As for Yeruna-hua and his ilk, she doubted they even cared about the underlying causes of the forthcoming course of action. They just wanted to kill Deyzara, preferably as many as possible. And perhaps even a few humans, for the *mula* that would accrue to whoever did the killing.

This not a good time, she told herself when she finally rose shakily from her chair to exit the High House. Her own advisers and clan would be waiting anxiously to hear the details of what had transpired within. She tried to convince herself that

Aniolo-jat was right, that the Sakuntala had on this day decided on the correct course of action to ensure their control of their world far into the future. But she was far, far from sure that was the case. Extended to the sides, her ears seemed to catch strange sounds at play. The pipa-katola combination working its magic, she decided.

Not all of her own people would be disappointed in the decision taken by the Hatas. Many were of like mind with Aniolo-jat and even Yeruna-hua. It was her task to lead them, to advise them, but not to control them.

If only Jemunu-jah had been present to offer the benefit of his knowledge. Away helping the humans to find a lost one of their own, Aniolo-jat had told the assembly. For a brief moment the katola fog cleared. Had the human Hata Matthias truly asked for Jemunu-jah specifically? Or had his name been put forth as the most suitable candidate available by another party? If so, who was the other party, and why had they specifically proposed Jemunu-jah to go?

She thought she might ask that question of Aniolo-jat, who was nothing if not responsive to questions. But he was not nearby and she was very tired. She decided she would ask it of him tomorrow.

If she remembered.

4

It was raining more heavily when Jemunu-jah and the Deyzara Masurathoo left the office of the Hata Lauren Matthias. A few humans, huddled against the rain and looking characteristically miserable, passed them on their way to the Administration Center. Jemunu-jah observed them pityingly. Their bodies shed water and they swam well, so why did they always look so unhappy? A human acquaintance had once said something to him about "eternal leaden skies, perpetual damp, and depressing gloom." It made no sense. The rain brought life. It kept the water high, forcing wandering predators to swim instead of run. It refreshed and cleansed.

At least the Deyzara were more stolid in their acceptance of Fluva's climate. Not that they had much choice, being permanent residents. They had long since made their peace with the unremitting rain. Glancing to his left, he watched his unwanted new companion's eating trunk flop loosely against the smooth lower portion of the skull as its owner tugged his wide-brimmed rain hat tighter down on his naked pate. How did this Masurathoo feel about his adoptive home world and its native inhabitants? When they were cooped up together in a small skimmer Jemunu-jah knew he was likely to find out.

Protruding beneath the hat, the speaking trunk uncoiled from the top of the Deyzara's head. "Please excuse me for pointing it out, but I can tell that you are not very personally pleased with this arrangement, though it shall prove financially and professionally advantageous to us both, I think."

"Heesa," Jemunu-jah replied with curt courtesy.

Round, baby-soft eyes turned to goggle up at him. "Do not think you are alone in your emotions. I am similarly less than happy with the present arrangement, and would have much preferred to contract this business with another of my own kind."

At least they had that much in common, Jemunu-jah mused. "I feel same way. Two Deyzara searching by themselves step out of skimmer in Viisiiviisii, that two less Deyzara on my world." He waited for the other to disagree by retorting, "Our world," but the two-trunk was either too preoccupied or too smart to respond overtly to the deliberate challenge. What he did say mildly surprised the Sakuntala.

"As much as it pains me to admit it, you are most probably correct, sir."

Though it was at most a mild honorific, and a human one at that, it was not what Jemunu-jah had expected to hear.

The Deyzara raised a hand and pointed. Following the line formed by the two soft opposing digits, Jemunu-jah found himself looking at what at first glance appeared to be a pair of transparent perambulating storage containers advancing up the walkway. As they drew nearer, he saw that each protective layer sheltered one of the other major partners in the Common-wealth, the hard-shells who called themselves thranx. They were progressing with agonizing slowness, as if (despite their use of four trulegs and two foothands to additionally steady themselves) they feared each step would send them tumbling into the water below.

"Look at them." Though he knew it was not a mature reac-tion, Jemunu-jah could hardly contain his amusement at the sight. "They step like newborns."

"It is well known that they are unable to swim, or even to float." Above his eyes, Masurathoo's speaking trunk bobbed gently from side to side as he spoke. "One should pity these two, as it is most clearly evident they would rather be anywhere else than here."

As they came closer to the two thranx, Jemunu-jah experienced a sudden highly uncivilized urge to bump into the nearest and send it stumbling toward the walkway railing, just to see how it would react. Curious as to what Masurathoo would think, he voiced his desire to his shorter, softer companion.

"Oh, Mr. Jemunu-jah, sir, that is thought most unworthy of a civilized being!" Hesitating, the Deyzara lowered his voice. "But one that, I confess, could prove highly amusing in its consequences."

Something else they unexpectedly had in common, Jemunu-jah realized. A little humor could go a long way toward defusing the tension each felt in the presence of the other. That was going to be increasingly important once they were both restricted to the limited confines of a small scout skimmer. Of course, he wasn't going to *actually* bump into one of the clearly terrified thranx. Still, if he should happen to do so (entirely by accident, of course) and if it did stumble toward the edge of the walkway, he could grab and steady it in an instant. No harm done. The two hard-shells were very close now.

He had not yet decided what to do when the chigyese landed right on top of the alien he was unworthily contemplating nudging. The chigyese had a soft, flexible body that enabled it to squeeze into narrow clefts in the branches of trees. There it could swell itself with water, rendering it impossible for would-be predators to extract. To move about the trees it had a dozen long, glistening tentacles lined with fine hairs. It was not very strong, it had poor eyesight, and its tiny mouthparts were adapted not for biting but for sucking plant juices from new growth.

None of which was known to the two thranx. As the anxious chigyese sought to free itself from the suddenly hysterical surface on which it found itself, the thranx on which it had landed began hopping about on all six legs while flailing frantically at the soggy object clinging to the back of its b-thorax. Instead of helping, the hard-shell's horrified companion was tripping all over its six legs while uttering frantic cries for help. In the panic of the moment, they spoke in Low Thranx instead of terranglo. Acutely conscious of the deadly water below, both visitors lurched away from the railing. This only sent them careening wildly toward the railing opposite.

Jemunu-jah would have helped, had he not been overcome with laughter. Masurathoo tried to call out to the two visitors that the chigyese was quite harmless and that if the one afflicted by its presence would only stand still and let it go free, it would crawl away as fast as its arms would carry it. Unfortunately, his speaking trunk kept emitting small bubbles, this being the Deyzara method of expressing laughter. It was a reaction he was unable to control. Jemunu-jah noted the phenomenon with interest. He'd heard about it, but this was the first time he had ever seen a Deyzara laugh. Usually the two-trunks were so businesslike it made one want to scream. Or cut off their speaking trunks.

Meanwhile, the poor chigyese was doing its best to extricate itself from its hopping, flailing, wildly chittering host. Slipping on the perpetually damp walkway, the thranx thus afflicted fell down, kicking and fighting with all eight limbs. This finally allowed the traumatized chigyese to find purchase on a different surface. It proceeded to scramble clear. In less than a minute its long arms pulled it through the side of the railing and it dropped from sight over the side, hopefully to land this time on a more amenable and less feverish surface.

During the commotion, the protective coverings worn by both thranx had been worked into a tangled shambles. Helping her companion to his feet, the female struggled to untangle her knotted ovipositors before fighting to adjust her own rain shield. It seemed to Jemunu-jah an unnecessary activity, since by now both hard-shells were soaking wet. Moisture sputtered from the breathing spicules that pulsed madly with exertion on either side of their exposed Thoraxes.

"That," he declared as he and Masurathoo continued on

their way, "is funniest thing I see since adolescent relative Moukie-jeu get swallowed by ourulu plant and need to spend three-day having female relations de-sap him hair by hair."

"It was certainly most amusing." Words instead of bubbles issued from the Deyzara's speaking trunk. "They were displeased that we stood by and watched without providing any assistance."

Jemunu-jah looked down sharply. "You can do hard-shell's click-talk?"

"Dear me, no." Using one hand, Masurathoo raised the end of his speaking trunk higher than its internal muscles alone could lift it. "We make sounds and words by sending air over the inflexible ridges that line the insides of our *cotos*. To manage thranx speech requires the ability to snap something flexible against something unyielding. Humans and Sakuntala have internal mouth organs called tongues that are capable of doing this. We do not. But while I cannot speak High or Low Thranx, I can manage some of their meaning-rich gestures, and I can understand some of that speaking."

It was not meant to be a soliloquy on superiority, Jemunu-jah knew. Nevertheless, he reacted defensively. So many Deyzara were not shy about flaunting their intelligence, their mastery of terranglo, or the ways of the Commonwealth. They could not help it, he supposed. But it was a poor way to endear one's kind to such as the Sakuntala.

We just as smart as you are, he told himself with certainty. You just had head-start period on us. Given time and education, he felt, the Sakuntala would catch up.

Unless they took a shortcut by eliminating the Deyzara altogether, as certain rabid Hatas and Yuiquerus like the notorious Aniolo-jat frequently expressed a desire to do.

Having shared mutual amusement at the discomfort of the two thranx, Jemunu-jah found himself in a slightly better mood by the time he and Masurathoo finally reached the transportation depot. Suspended by thick strands of strilk from dozens of pylons and massive trees, the port was designed to serve the close-in needs of several communities. The main port, where the shuttles that shifted people and goods between the surface and orbiting KK-drive ships landed and took off, was located a number of keleqs to the north, atop the only piece of semisolid land in the entire region that rose above the waters of the Vii-siiviisii year-round. For ages it had been an important hunting ground. No sane Sakuntala would live there, of course, since solid surfaces were also favored by carnivores. Its clan owners now relaxed in Commonwealth-supplied leisure, their traditional hunting territory having been leased for the port.

Even though they could be counted among his own clan's old enemies, Jemunu-jah did not begrudge them their good fortune. He was only upset that his people had not been able to share in it. And of course, no one had expected the T'kuo to share with the A'jah or any other clan. That was not the Sakuntala way.

It was one of the ways that was going to have to change, he knew, if his kind were ever to catch up to the Deyzara. The clans would have to stop fighting among themselves and learn to cooperate. Despite the example posed by the races that made up the Commonwealth, such changes were proving difficult to instill. Something else, some other force, was going to have to be found to unify the Sakuntala.

He intended to check in with the depot master himself. Irritatingly, his companion beat him to it. Something about the Deyzara obliged them always to speak first.

"Good morning, my friend." Masurathoo waved his speaking trunk politely at the human attendant, addressing her in perfect, barely accented terranglo. Jemunu-jah knew that, unlike the Sakuntala, humans were not disturbed by such movements. But then, he knew, humans had spent many hundred-years among many different kinds of intelligent beings and were used to strange shapes and gestures.

Peering out at them from her dry, dehumidified office, the stout middle-aged human female pushed back her hydrophobic cap and smiled at her visitors. Her expression showed that she was not used to seeing a Sakuntala and Deyzara walking alone together.

"Mornin'." Her eyes went skyward. "Think it'll rain today?"

Jemunu-jah knew he should have smiled, but he had heard the joke far too often from far too many humans. It had to be allowed in the Deyzara's favor that they did not repeat it.

Standing in the morning downpour, he pushed his way roughly past Masurathoo before the Deyzara could venture any additional expressions of politesse. Though he was eloquent for a Sakuntala, Jemunu-jah knew his own terranglo could not equal that of his companion. But it was more than adequate.

"I Jemunu-jah, this Masurathoo. We are to go search Viisii-viisii for missing-absent human Hasslema. . . . Hasmogi—Hasa. We have authorization from office of Lauren Matthias for use of one scout skimmer."

There! Surely that was as clear as the silently watching Masurathoo could have managed.

It certainly was clear enough for the human attendant. She bobbed her head in the fashion Jemunu-jah had long since come to recognize. "Yep, the office let us know you were coming. You're all set to go, fueled and provisioned." She hesitated as she started to exit the office. "It's just the two of you then, is it?"

"Verily, that is correct," Masurathoo confirmed, getting in a couple of words before Jemunu-jah could respond. Magnanimously, the Sakuntala let it pass unchallenged.

The attendant led them out onto the small staging area and into an open hangar protected from the rain by a hypo curtain. Inside, a number of skimmers were being serviced by human techs and their mechanical subordinates. Emblazed with the hourglass/infinity symbol of the Commonwealth, their 'craft was just large enough to accommodate four humans. It would allow the two of them to carry out their survey in comparative comfort.

"Here you are, guys." The woman eyed Jemunu-jah. "You might have to do some bending over near the back, Saki." She proceeded to supply details about the specific model, addressing herself to Masurathoo on the assumption that he was going to be doing the piloting. The fact that she was correct did little to assuage Jemunu-jah's quiet humiliation.

Have tolerance, he told himself. The female was a bureaucrat, not a diplomat. Still, the longer the conversation went on, alluding to terms and technology he did not understand, the more uncomfortable he felt. He forced himself to listen and, where possible, to learn. To give in to his rising anger and embarrassment would be to react exactly the way someone like Aniolo-jat would wish.

When at last the human female finished, they boarded the compact, powerful craft and made their own check of provisions. That, at least, he could do as well as Masurathoo. The inspection concluded to their mutual satisfaction, they settled into the two seats forward. Though designed to accommodate a human backside, the particular curve of the flight chair allowed Jemunu-jah to sit comfortably without putting pressure on the tail that emerged from the back of his waist straps.

Receiving clearance from port control, Masurathoo smoothly powered up the craft and guided it out of the hangar. A large cargo skimmer lifted in front of them, rising above the clearing in the trees on its way to another town. In the rain gloom, the glare from its traveling lights caused Masurathoo to shield his eyes with one arm.

"Too much shining to see safely, I fear," he commented unnecessarily.

"No brighter than what you wearing," Jemunu-jah couldn't resist observing.

Lowering his arm, the Deyzara glanced down at the swirl of fabric that spiraled up his body to enclose his torso in a tornado of pink, bright blue, and chartreuse fabric splashed with black ovals and squares.

"In deference to the seriousness of our enterprise, my friend, I have come garbed in my most subdued attire."

"Your subdued attire will make you target for first predator that see us the instant we step outside skimmer craft."

A single bubble formed at the tip of Masurathoo's speaking trunk before expiring with a single soft *pop*. "Then I must rely on you, my most esteemed and knowledgeable companion, to exercise your natural talents on my behalf to ensure that I do not become a meal for some indifferent wandering horror."

Not until we have accomplished our goal, Jemunu-jah thought silently, before quickly quashing the thought as dishonorable. Much more of that and he would lose *mula*, he decided. But it wasn't going to be easy to moderate either his words or his thoughts.

In spite of himself, he admired the skill the Deyzara displayed in raising the skimmer above the tops of the trees. Rain continued to fall around them as Masurathoo pivoted the craft in midair, turned south, and accelerated along the course heading that had been filed by the missing human. Finding their objective in the absence of an actively broadcasting emergency beacon was going to be difficult, Jemunu-jah knew. But not necessarily impossible. His people had spent thousands of years evolving to find one another, and other things, in the depths of the rain-swept Viisiiviisii. Smaller things. The skimmer they were hunting was larger than the one they were flying. If it only boasted a working light or two, he might well be able to spot it while soaring over the varzea below.

He settled himself down to searching, disdaining the use of the auxiliary equipment in the skimmer's storage. Monitoring instruments was Masurathoo's job. A Deyzara's job. *He* would rely on the incredibly sharp vision with which Nature had equipped the Sakuntala.

They made steady progress southward along the course that had been plotted for them by the Commonwealth navigation section without seeing a thing. By the afternoon of the fifth day, Jemunu-jah had acquired a grudging admiration for the skills of his companion. Not only did Masurathoo prove to be a superb pilot, but he also showed himself to be equally adept at manipulating the skimmer's food sourcer. While not sufficient to endear the Deyzara to Jemunu-jah, it went some ways

toward tempering his view of his companion. Even the usual
flatulent Deyzara pronouncements on everything from proper
social intercourse to life in general were muted and carefully
timed. There were surprisingly few moments when Jemunu-jah
experienced the familiar Sakuntala desire to wring the Deyzara's
short neck.

For his part Masurathoo had become, if not actually comfortable around the tall, brooding Sakuntala, at least reasonably
confident his companion was not going to slit his throat and
drink his blood while he slept. This Jemunu-jah was an unusual
example of his kind. While his terranglo grammar and pronun-
ciation were still awkward, he showed a much greater command of vocabulary than was usual for his people, together
with an inherent intelligence and curiosity that was almost—almost but not quite—Deyzaran in its perspicacity. So much so
that Masurathoo finally felt comfortable asking about it.

That was another thing about the Deyzara, Jemunu-jah reflected as he worked to compose a reply to his companion's
question. They had no hesitation about prying into one's personal history. In this instance, however, he felt it arose from
Masurathoo's genuine curiosity about him and not from the
usual Deyzaran desire to gain some sort of commercial or personal advantage.

Sitting back from the canopy through which he had been
watching the Viisiiviisii slide past below, he spoke without turning: "Family always thought me strange. On rare nights when
rain would stop and sky clear, others would stay inside houses
to avoid attentions of possible predators. I more inquisitive
than fearful. Especially at night. Would go outside, sit on porch
or branch, and look up at stars. Unreachable lights shimmering
through the mist. Always wanted to touch them."

"Now you very much can," Masurathoo observed approvingly, "thanks to the great Commonwealth."

"No, not yet." Jemunu-jah turned to regard his companion.
"Other things must be settled first." He did not elaborate, and
Masurathoo did not press for details. "Besides, I have not

enough money. Enough . . . credit. That one reason why I finally decide take this task—though not really wanting to."

"Something else we have in common then, sir. I admit openly this was not my first choice of assignment for this and forthcoming weeks. However, as you have so clearly stated, the remuneration is very good indeed. Also, it provides a most excellent opportunity to ingratiate myself to the Commonwealth authorities, whose contacts are of significant assistance in improving one's standing within the local business community."

Jemunu-jah knew of a human term that was both more succinct and more applicable to the condition Masurathoo was describing. It was *sucking up*. The Deyzara were masters at it. No Sakuntala could do it. We have too much pride, he told himself. Too much individual dignity and self-respect. Where the line was to be drawn between pride and arrogance, however, was still a matter of some debate among those Sakuntala who had done successful business dealings with the humans and the thranx—and the Deyzara themselves. Couldn't one have both self-respect *and* credit? The contradiction led many Sakuntala to simultaneously despise and envy the Deyzara. That was not a healthy condition.

"Why do the Deyzara work so hard to please the humans?" he blurted. "Why you abase yourselves before them so blindly?"

Masurathoo looked over at him in surprise, his trunk weaving in mild agitation. "It's not blindness that is at work, dear me, no. We know exactly what we are doing, my friend. It is much easier to do business with a friend than with an enemy. Most intelligent beings are susceptible to flattery. Humans and thranx and many others of the Commonwealth are no different, no. It is simply good business practice."

"Then why," Jemunu-jah asked pointedly, "don't you do the same to us?"

He expected the Deyzara to hesitate and was surprised when Masurathoo did not. "No reason to. We do not do enough important business with the Sakuntala. In such instances, flattery would not only be a waste of time, it would be seen for what it was: a calculated falsehood."

"But it would improve relations."

"I can see that." Masurathoo adjusted a control, and the softly humming skimmer turned a half degree to port. "It works both ways, my friend. Perhaps if the Sakuntala would treat us with more respect and less contempt, we would be inclined to respond more warmly, with an expression other than fear."

As he returned to scanning the Viisiiviisii below, Jemunu-jah reflected on the Deyzara's words. Clearly, if real progress was going to be made in defusing the tension that had been growing between the species, there were going to have to be changes made on both sides. His great and honest fear was that the Deyzara might be more amenable to such modifications than his own kind. Patience was a virtue not even the Sakuntala associated with themselves.

It was while he was contemplating ways of breaking through such an impasse that the glint of something not organic sparked behind his retinas and set off an alarm in his brain.

5

Wiping warm, clinging raindrops from his face, the only part of him that was not directly protected by the rain suit, Hasa labored over the open compartment that held the inert emergency beacon. It was incumbent on him, as a freelance bioprospector, to learn how to repair in the field a good deal more than just the gear he used to study plants and other growing things. If he'd had a partner, it would have been easier. Responsibilities could have been divided, specialties shared. He'd tried a partnership some seven years earlier. Following its dissolution Hasa hoped the man's arm would regenerate fully under treatment and that he would enjoy his enforced retirement.

That was the one and only time Hasa had worked with a partner.

Others had offered, only to be rebuffed. Hasa was smart enough to know his personal limitations. They did not include having to deal with the individual peccadilloes of others less competent than himself. Since he believed firmly that nearly everyone else in his field fell into the latter category, it seemed that he was destined to always work alone.

Others would have listened to music or maybe watched a headsup while they were working in the heat and the rain. In contrast, Hasa's efforts in the field were accompanied by a steady muttering the likes of which were unlikely to ever make the numerous lists that charted the rise and fall of popular culture. He couldn't even keep himself good company, the realization of which fact did nothing to improve his demeanor.

Reaching back for the small laser welder, he touched something sticky. Turning, he saw that a branch or root had fallen through a crack in the canopy and onto the skimmer's slanting deck. The broken wood was oozing sap, into which he had inadvertently pushed a few fingers. The same yellow-tinged goo covered half the welder. His muttering rose in intensity for a moment as his face twisted into an even tighter grimace than usual.

His fingers would not move.

They might as well have been welded to the deck. Cursing aloud, he turned around and grabbed his imprisoned right hand with the other. As he did so, rain slid down the front of his rain cape and the shirt beneath, warm and cloying and alien. A sharp yank failed to dislodge the blond substance. So did a steady pull. His booted feet slid on the smooth deck, unable to gain much of a purchase.

By this time the goo had crept over his hand, up his wrist, and was making steady, silent progress up his arm in the direction of his elbow. It emerged from a seemingly unending supply provided by the root or branch. From the wrist to the tip of his fingers, it had already hardened into a transparent polycarbonate-like casing. Nearby, a second branch was creeping visibly in his direction. Sinister yellowish gunk oozed from its open, hollow tip.

What would happen if he became completely covered in the rock-hard substance was a vision he chose not to entertain. It would not be a pretty way to die.

His mind working furiously, he considered his options. The laser welder would probably melt the material, but the welder had been sealed to the deck by the first oozings. With his right hand now firmly stuck, he strained with his other hand to reach back down into the small tool chest that was secured beside the open compartment. The small hammer he picked up bounced harmlessly off the hardened saplike material. When he missed and accidentally struck the still soft portion of the ooze, it threatened to grasp and hold the hammer fast. There was nothing else like the welding laser in the tool chest.

The crawling goo had ascended past his right elbow and was climbing toward his shoulder. The second invasive root had been joined by a third. He had to twist and shuffle his legs and lower body sideways to keep them from being enveloped by the new invaders.

Nothing in the tool chest worked on either the roots or the fluid they were so copiously disgorging. A couple of bottles of strong solvent proved useless. The directions on one claimed that its contents had the ability to dissolve metal. Maybe so, but the powerful liquid had no effect on the creeping golden goop. Jabbing the ooze with assorted sharp instruments was an exercise in futility.

The stuff was up to his shoulder now and showing no signs of slowing down. His right arm was completely immobile, and he couldn't move his legs any farther without dislocating his hips. A couple of brightly colored legless miwots had settled in one of the trees opposite. Fortunately for him, they were scavengers only of curiosity. He cursed them anyway, adding a few choice words for the root system of the large epiphyte that was threatening to entomb him alive inside his own vessel.

Reaching down into the open compartment one more time, he risked electrocution by grabbing a live conduit and yanking hard. Desperation and adrenaline lent strength to his efforts. The conduit protested at this treatment by parting in a small shower of sparks. Desperately he thrust the raw end against his inhumed right arm and was promptly rewarded with a truly terrible stink.

The yellow material dissolved away like so much solidified piss. Whether the flow of electrons upset its internal pH or shocked the host epiphyte or affected the molecular bonds of the substance he didn't know and didn't care. A couple of moments later he was completely free. Rain washed the dissolving yellow goop away as freely as if it had been lemon soda.

First he fixed the conduit, shoving the torn ends back together until they automatically resealed. Then, picking up the liberated welder, he thumbed it to life as he climbed out of the skimmer and into the full force of the morning rain. Tracing the intruding roots back to their origin, he proceeded to cut the offending epiphyte from which they emerged into quarter sections and then to further slice the quarters into smaller and smaller pieces. A flurry of finger-size winged things, long and blotched but with oversize sucking mouthparts, appeared as if from nowhere to feed on the exposed chunks of goo-giving plant that were now open to the elements. A grim-faced Hasa welcomed their help.

Coming to the realization that expending so much energy in the taking of revenge on a simple plant was neither efficacious nor good for one's mental balance, he left the final annihilation of the glue root (as he named it) to the delirium of small flyers who had swarmed to feed greedily upon it. His anger at his narrow escape did not keep him from taking samples of the plant body, the motile goo-dispensing roots, and the yellow gunk itself. It might well contain the genetic source material for any number of possible useful materials in addition to a tremendously powerful adhesive. These samples he filed as carefully in the small armored specimen case built into his pack as if the organism in question had not tried to subject him to a slow, agonizing death. Escape, retribution, and scientific assaying completed, he returned to the open compartment in the deck and was preparing to resume work on the emergency beacon when he heard the whine.

Looking up through the rain, he saw a dim shape emerging from the low-hanging cloud cover. It floated just above the tops of the tallest emergents. Lights glowed along its sides and bottom.

It took him a moment of anxious fumbling to pull the short-range emergency flasher from his service belt and activate it. Intended to be visible only over a modest distance, its glow was largely suffocated by the falling rain. But if those on board the slow-moving craft had the proper equipment operating, it should automatically detect the signal from his handheld and set off an internal alarm.

Sure enough, the craft began to veer toward him almost as soon as he activated the pen-size device. Though it was unlikely to improve any chances of detection, instinct took over and he began waving the device along with his arms.

"That's right, yes! Over here, I'm down here!"

No question now but that they'd detected him. It was a small skimmer, he saw, squinting up through the rain. Now it was descending rapidly in his direction. He could finally relax and save his curses for whoever had set him up. Soon he would be back in Taulau, sipping something cool and sweet while giving his story to the authorities. For once, he would be glad to cooperate with them.

The skimmer continued to head for him. By now they ought to have spotted his own downed and useless craft, if not the gesticulating, waving figure standing atop part of the broken canopy. They were still heading rapidly in his direction. Rather too rapidly. He frowned. Behind him, unexpectedly and inexplicably, a couple of telltales on his skimmer's own main emergency beacon had sprung to life, after being dark ever since his abortive touchdown.

His rescuers should be slowing down by now. But there was no indication they were reducing velocity preparatory to making a soft landing alongside his vehicle. It was close enough now for him to notice an occasional shudder, as if the skimmer was proceeding under competing forces. Fascinated by the sight, he was as rooted to the spot as the trees that emerged from the slow-moving water around him. Only when it became clear that the oncoming craft was not only not slowing down but also showing no indications of stopping did he make a frantic last-second dive for the safety of those same trees.

"*Hauea,* do something!"

Masurathoo's eyes bulged out even farther than usual as he

struggled with the controls of the bucking, plunging skimmer. Moments earlier the craft's automatic detection equipment had signaled the nearby presence of a suddenly activated emergency beacon. Homing on it, they had quickly made visual contact with a downed skimmer that could only belong to the human they had been sent to rescue. The instant the Deyzara had locked their skimmer's tracker on the signal, control of their own craft had been lost.

Now Masurathoo was desperately trying to regain it, fighting the manual instrumentation as they sank downward in an uncontrollable dive. He was too busy to wonder what had happened. The agitated Sakuntala waving his long arms in the seat next to him was not helping matters.

"I assure you that I am doing the very best that I can!" At the moment Masurathoo was wishing for more than his two arms. "Nothing is responding properly. It is as if, I am remorseful to say, control of our craft has been taken over by an outside source."

"Override it!" Jemunu-jah stared helplessly at the bank of instruments. Though he could not pilot one himself, he knew that flying a skimmer was not as complicated as operating certain other Commonwealth machinery. It was designed to be easy to operate. What was the problem? Why was the stupid Deyzara letting this happen? It served him right for placing his life in the hands of one of the two-trunks! The fact that if they crashed Masurathoo might also die was not allowed to intrude on this line of reasoning.

Crash they did, snapping off branches and smashing through small trees before coming to rest alongside the same craft they had been sent out to find. Water erupted in every direction, scattering all manner of small life-forms. As the skimmer began to settle, Masurathoo leapt from the pilot's seat (which is to say he extricated himself as rapidly as was possible for one of his kind to do so) and began grabbing food paks and other items from an emergency locker. Stunned by the sudden turn in their fortunes, a dazed Jemunu-jah joined him.

As if in a dream, their mortally wounded craft began to

slowly sink into the depths of the Viisiiviisii. Though Fluva was in the first third of the Big Wet, there was still twenty to thirty meters of water under their vehicle, which was not designed to cope with an extended period of submersion. As Masurathoo threw the emergency release and several portions of the canopy slid aside, Jemunu-jah found all his childhood fears of being trapped in the water flooding in on him.

"This way. Hurry, please!" It was not so much that Masurathoo was desperate to save his Sakuntala companion as he was fearful of being caught alone out in the Viisiiviisii.

Jemunu-jah snapped out of his reverie long enough to grab some gear of his own. Shoving the compact food containers into the storage pouches that hung from his waist and chest straps, he sprang clear of the subsiding skimmer, easily passing the less athletic Deyzara in the process. Pausing on a lower half-submerged branch, Jemunu-jah reached back to help his companion to safety. Together they stood there in the rain watching as the skimmer sank beneath the surface. Loud bubbles constituted its only tombstone.

"What happened?" Standing in the rain in now sodden bright wraps of fabric, clutching a couple of food paks in one two-digited hand and a small pistol in the other, a despondent Masurathoo gazed blankly at the spot where the skimmer had been swallowed by the Viisiiviisii. "What could I possibly have done wrong?"

Jemunu-jah paid little attention to the Deyzara's mumblings. As soon as they had emerged from the skimmer, old instincts had taken over. His sharp eyes were scanning their immediate surroundings, looking for any sign of the numerous and resourceful predators that stalked the flooded forest.

"I don't know you do anything wrong, two-trunk. But I do know we stand here very long on this place by the water surface where so much disturbance occur, we quick-soon have nothing to worry about except how fast something else can digest us." He glanced upward. "We have to get higher. Up away from water." Eyeing a suitable branch, he swung himself upward.

With a resigned sigh, Masurathoo moved to follow. Everything Jemunu-jah accomplished with ease was a struggle for the Deyzara. But he persisted. His kind had determination, if not physical ability. Several times, Jemunu-jah waited for his companion to catch up. Occasionally, shaking his head in disbelief at the typical inherent Deyzara clumsiness and lack of athleticism, Jemunu-jah reached down and back to help him.

Eventually they reached a sheltered place beneath a brace of saminio leaves that were growing close enough together to give them some shelter from the steady downpour. Not that Jemunu-jah needed it. His kind were as comfortable out in the rain as they were inside a house. Masurathoo, however, was inordinately grateful.

"I am so very terribly sorry to have let you down like this." Drenched and hunched over in his colorfast wraps, he looked thoroughly miserable. His speaking trunk drooped down over his face, blocking one of his eyes—the physical equivalent of a whisper.

"We don't know it at all your fault." Without quite knowing why, Jemunu-jah found himself inclined to be forgiving. "Maybe something fail seriously within skimmer's controllers."

"Certainly it did." His speaking trunk rising as his eating trunk sucked up a casual drink from a small puddle in a hollow on the branch, Masurathoo eyed his indigenous companion. "But I am puzzled and concerned as to how and why it should have done so just as we made contact with the one we were sent to find."

"Speaking of that contact," Jemunu-jah added as he turned his attention back to the falling rain and the wild, wet Viisiiviisii in which they now found themselves stranded, "I wonder if anyone survive here for us to rescue?"

His answer came in the form of a solid blow to the lower portion of his back, just above the tail. As he fell forward and reached out to grab something to keep himself from plunging through to the water below, he caught a glimpse of the solid, fast-moving shape that had struck from above. Masurathoo's lack of a scream was instructive—as was Jemunu-jah's first sight of the creature that had surprised him.

Landing lithely on both feet, the human kept the majority of his attention focused on the more dangerous Sakuntala while not neglecting to monitor the movements of the startled Deyzara. As Jemunu-jah rolled over, back aching, he found himself gazing down the barrel of a surprisingly large handgun. Occasionally the muzzle would shift to cover the motionless Masurathoo. Most of the time, however, it was aimed in the Sakuntala's direction. The human's stance was tense, Jemunu-jah noted, and beneath the hood of the rain cape he wore his small but efficient eyes were in constant motion. The big, muscular male was clearly very unhappy with something.

Well, Jemunu-jah mused, in that he had company.

"Who are you," the human asked sharply, "and what do you want with me?" For good measure, he repeated the query in both S'aku and Deyzar.

With Masurathoo still overtaken by the rush of events, it was his companion who replied. "I am Jemunu-jah. This my associate in current mission, Masurathoo."

The human's eyes narrowed and his weapon remained leveled. "What would prompt a damn dumb native and a bug-eyed Dez to be traveling together in this godforsaken corner of the Viisiiviisii?"

"We came rescue *you.*" Jemunu-jah bristled at the name-calling. Off to his right, he saw that Masurathoo was similarly offended.

The human made a nonverbal grunting noise, deep and primordial. "Did you, now? Fine job you've made of it." The muzzle of the gun gestured meaningfully toward the place where the newcomers' skimmer had sunk.

Wiping rain from his eyes, Masurathoo was emboldened to speak up. "I am compelled to point out that the instant we detected your location our craft's controls locked up. Despite my most energetic efforts, I was unable to free them. The dire consequences of this you have obviously observed for yourself."

The Deyzara hesitated a moment, his speaking trunk bobbing nervously. "May I say, sir, that while our efforts thus far may admittedly be somewhat lacking in efficiency, I find your attitude more than a little insupportable."

Jemunu-jah tensed in anticipation of a reaction from the human. But humans, he knew, did not always react as expected. They were far more individualistic and less predictable than, say, a Sakuntala.

Hasa peered sharply at the Deyzara. "You say your controls locked when you detected me?" Reaching with his free hand through a slit in the rain cape and into an opening in his pants, he brought out the pocket beacon and began rolling it back and forth between his fingers. "I crashed here because my own controls locked up. Also, my skimmer's main emergency beacon failed. Part of it reactivated only when you appeared."

"Integrated instrumentation such as a vessel's emergency beacon is designed to be inviolable and fail-safe," Masurathoo pointed out.

"Tell me something I don't know, squid-face." Both of the new arrivals wondered what a squid was. To Masurathoo's way of thinking, it did not sound complimentary. But then, it was rapidly becoming clear that this human was as disagreeable a personality as had been rumored.

"First I crash out here on the edge of nowhere. Then you two come prancing along to find me, and as soon as you locate me, *you* crash." As he glanced skyward, blinking up at the rain, he holstered his weapon. Jemunu-jah thought about making a leap for it, decided against it. If necessary, there would be better opportunities later. He had to remind himself that he was here to rescue this contrary person, not fight him.

"It occurs to me," the human continued, "that somebody doesn't want me found and brought back."

"I understand." Finally able to relax now that the imposing handgun had been holstered, Masurathoo settled himself under a protective leaf. "Can you think of anyone who might wish such a misfortune to befall you?"

Hasa laughed without hesitation. It was a bold laugh, ringing out through the rain and the flooded forest. Jemunu-jah winced. The Viisiiviisii was not a good place to call attention to oneself.

"On how many worlds? Here on this dismal dump I could name maybe a hundred." His expression turned serious again. "I just can't think of anyone who'd go to these lengths. Those who come immediately to mind might like to stick a gun in my face or an explosive purgative up my ass—but they wouldn't get this elaborate. No need to." He squinted back out into the damp and the gloom. "There's more behind this, I'm beginning to think, than a desire to see Shadrach Hasselemoga become food for fungus."

"Then we must look for a motive." To emphasize the point, Masurathoo touched the end of his speaking trunk to the tip of his eating trunk. Jemunu-jah shuddered slightly. The sight was repellently suggestive of two samul worms mating. "Besides, um, personal adversaries, who else might have reason to benefit from your demise occurring in so complex a fashion?"

Hasa contemplated his new companions in isolation. Jemunu-jah didn't like the way the human was looking at him. But then, he found that he did not like much of anything about this person. Had he known how thoroughly unlikable the human really was, he would have refused the assignment in spite of the Hata's order.

A bit too late for that now.

"I've been hearing that the natives are restless," the human was muttering. "Or rather, more restless than usual for you Sakis. Couple of sources told me they thought something big was up. They just didn't know what." He stared relentlessly at Jemunu-jah. The gaze was of an intensity sufficient to unsettle most humans. It did not bother a Sakuntala, who could stare down an eagle.

"There always activity among my people," he responded truthfully—and uninformatively. "It possible some might try to take advantage of such a situation as this by blaming it on others." He looked to his companion for confirmation.

Masurathoo was appropriately outraged. "My people would never do such a thing! I am insulted. Insulted!"

"But not absolutely, one hundred percent sure that it couldn't be the case?" Hasa commented thoughtfully.

Both trunks wilted, droplets running down their naked lengths. "No. How could I possibly say that? This whole situation in which we find ourselves is so unthinkable, so bizarre, that I fear nothing can be ruled out." Moon eyes regarded the tall Sakuntala. "Which means that it is also entirely possible, sirs, that elements among the Sakuntala have instigated our present difficulties with an eye toward blaming them upon my people."

"Why would they do that?" Hasa pulled the leading edge of his rain cape lower on his forehead.

"As one more rationale for trying to drive us off this world, which has been a major desire of certain radical elements among the Sakuntala ever since my ancestors were first brought here. Any excuse, however absurd, to wreak violence against the Deyzara is keenly welcomed by such hostile groups."

Jemunu-jah accepted the accusation quietly. He had to, because he knew it to be true.

The tension between the two of them seemed to amuse the human. "You folks really don't like each other much, do you? Well, if it means anything, I don't like you, either. I don't like ignorant, big-eared, thieving primitives. I don't like mincing, snake-faced, money-grubbing immigrants. And I don't like this stinking, soaking, moldering muddle of a planet."

"My goodness gracious. Is there anything that you do like, Mr. Hasselemoga?" Masurathoo gave voice to the same response Jemunu-jah had been considering, only in far more polite terms than the Sakuntala would have managed.

The human smiled at the Deyzara. "Yes, there is. I like money. I like the compliments I get when I discover and bring back something useful. I like my privacy. I like certain other things you farcical resident freaks wouldn't understand. Understand *that* about me, respect *that* about me, and maybe we'll get out of this together."

Understand I do, Jemunu-jah thought darkly. *Respect,* however, was not a term that he found he could apply to the human.

"Just to be fair," Hasa added, "there are certain brainless bundles of morons within the Commonwealth who think humans and thranx should stay off any world not already classified Class Two or above. While I'm not personally acquainted with representatives of any such organizations on this dirt ball, that doesn't mean they aren't here. They could've been the ones responsible for putting me down, and for working to prevent any rescue." He smiled broadly. It was an easily recognizable expression Jemunu-jah had come to associate with human amusement. In the case of this particular individual, however, it clearly had other associations and meanings.

"Being around my own kind most of the time, I've no illusions about what they're capable of. So there's enough potential blame to go around. Don't worry. When we get back I'll find out who's responsible, and deal with them in my own way." Implicitly suggesting that the Deyzara would be useless in such an undertaking, Hasa focused his attention on Jemunu-jah. "You can help if you like."

"You seem very sure we will get back, sir." Masurathoo found that more and more of his attention was being drawn away from the ongoing conversation and toward their saturated, inhospitable surroundings.

"I'm always sure I'm going to get back. I've been in bad situations before, and I'm still here."

"You not spent time on foot in Viisiiviisii," Jemunu-jah countered. The human just glared at him but said nothing.

"Well, I daresay that our present obligation is to make ourselves as safe and comfortable as possible while we await our own rescue." Masurathoo began searching for a drier place among the leaves and branches.

"What rescue?" Hasa snorted. "Want to bet that whatever took over your skimmer also disabled its emergency equipment, just as it did mine?" Pulling it from his service belt, he waved the compact short-range beacon he had used in his futile attempt to signal the incoming skimmer. "Right now this is all we've got that we know works. I wouldn't want to bet that Commonwealth Administration would be in any hurry to send out a second craft to look for you. Not for a while. They'll assume you're taking your own good time looking for me." Rising and turning, he peered off into the flooded forest. "Sitting around waiting to be picked up didn't do me much good, did it? I'm not going to hang around here waiting for another skimmer that may or may not be on its way."

"I agree." Jemunu-jah moved to stand closer to the human. "So much noisemaking will have attract many meat eaters. They all around this place, waiting to sample taste of food that talks."

Masurathoo rose so fast that he bumped his head on an overhanging branch. "What meat eaters, where?" He gazed worriedly out into the rain. "I do not see anything."

"They there. They always there. Strange noises draw them close, make them curious. Better to leave this place and let them explore Mr. Hasselemoga's skimmer." Raising a long fur-covered arm, Jemunu-jah pointed eastward. "Are many villages scattered throughout deep Viisiiviisii. If we can find one, we have food and safety. Better than wait here for rescue craft that may not come."

"And a village will have contact with another village, which might have contact with another, that in turn has contact with an outpost of civilization." Hasa was in full agreement with the Sakuntala. Jemunu-jah refrained from pointing out that *every* Sakuntala village was an outpost of civilization. This was neither the time nor the place to launch into an extended argument with the human. That, and possibly more forceful objection, could come later. Right now he needed the human, if only to have something edible to shove between himself and a marauding casokul.

An agitated Masurathoo eyed both his companions askance. "You will please excuse me if I take leave to disagree with the both of you. Our best chance for surviving this regrettable situation is to remain here, near our downed craft that others are sure to come looking for."

"Looking and finding are two different things." The human was already focusing his efforts northward, in the general direction of distant Taulau. How many Sakuntala villages might lie between that teeming outpost of Commonwealth civilization and their present location no one knew. Nor did Jemunu-jah's presence guarantee them a cordial reception even if they managed to reach one. But anything was better than sitting still doing nothing. Also, Hasa agreed with the native: all the commotion was bound to have drawn the attention of local predators. If either skimmer had remained intact and above water, he might have decided differently. On the other hand, without such protection from the roving hazards of the flooded forest, he felt that the sooner they vacated the area, the better.

Besides, if you stayed in one place in the Viisiiviisii for any length of time, things would start to take root on you.

"Something else," he added. "Whoever did this, for whatever reason, might not be completely confident that just marooning me out here is enough to do the job. After a while, they might decide to come and check on the results of their handiwork personally." He patted his side arm. "Since this is about all I've got in the way of defensive ordnance, I'd rather not be around in case they show up." His attention turned back to Jemunu-jah.

"All right, big-ears—this is your country. Pick a direction. I usually lead, but when someone else knows the territory better than me, I'm not ashamed to follow."

"It is not that simple. We cannot just go straight northward." Turning, Jemunu-jah indicated a complex of interlocked trees and lianas. "Except for places where is no other choice, we must keep above the water." His eyes focused on the human. "Rain is life; flooded forest is death."

"Pithily put." Hasa gestured broadly. "Lead on, Junko-juke."

"Jemunu-jah," the Sakuntala corrected him, biting back the words he really wanted to use. Selecting a branch just above and in front of him, he reached up and pulled himself to a higher level. They *had* to get farther away from the surface of the water.

"You are both, you should please excuse my expression, making a big mistake." Masurathoo showed no sign of moving from beneath his leaf. "We *must* remain with our downed craft if we are to have any hope of being found." Using both hands and both trunks, he made a four-limbed gesture into the depths of the rain-washed Viisiiviisii. "Go in there and we will be lost forever. All too many times this place has swallowed the most confident and experienced of individuals."

"I'm already feeling swallowed." Displaying both strength and agility, Hasa had followed Jemunu-jah up onto the higher branch. "No one's forcing you to come, mashed potato. Stay or follow; it makes no difference to me." Lowering his voice meaningfully, he glanced over at Jemunu-jah. "If he stays behind, maybe he'll draw the carnivores."

The Sakuntala did not respond. It would have been unseemly and would have cost him *mula*. Like him or not, Masurathoo was his associate in this joint venture. Still, the human's words contained a certain merit . . .

Jemunu-jah started walking, bracing himself with his long arms and balancing gracefully on the branch. Following behind, the human matched him stride for stride. Masurathoo remained where he was, stubborn and utterly convinced.

Or rather, he did so until his companions had advanced out of sight. Only later did the Deyzara catch up to them, panting hard, his breathing trunk swollen and reddened with the effort, his splendid body wrappings already shredded and torn.

They were forced to stop early for the night so that he could recuperate. Left to his own devices, Hasa would have pressed on. But he was smart enough to realize that he stood a much better chance of getting somewhere if he stayed with the Sakuntala, and Jemunu-jah would not leave Masurathoo behind. It was, he explained, a question of *mula* and of doing what was right.

Besides, it was abundantly clear to Jemunu-jah by now that the Deyzara would be much easier to shove in front of an oncoming predator than would the human . . .

6

No one spared more than a casual glance at Aniolo-jat and Yeruna-hua as they made their way toward the nakobo tree. It stood off by itself, surrounded by water and connected to the rest of Hasawa Village by a single narrow footbridge. The walkway wasn't even made of strilk but was woven in the old way, from braided vines. Pale red fungi and lavender-hued mold covered large sections of it, showing that it was little used. Using his tongue, Aniolo-jat snapped off a piece of huim and chewed it as he and his companion made their way across the swinging viaduct. Below, a surface-feeding takuwolu kept spitting acid in their direction. But the walkway was too high. After several tries, the finned, snakelike predator gave up and swam off in search of more accessible prey.

Reaching the isolated tree, Yeruna-hua scanned their immediate surroundings. Only a light drizzle was falling, making it possible for them to be seen from the village. No one was looking in their direction. Hasawa was a small community, out-of-the-way and unimportant. It was also, significantly, a "pure" village. Not even the usual Deyzara food shop marred its Sakuntala nature.

As Yeruna-hua kept watch and used his own body to shield his companion from the sight of others, Aniolo-jat reached out and pushed on several light brown shelf fungi. Unusually, they did not break off under the weight of his fingers. Even more unusually, they stayed down instead of springing back up when he pushed on them. In response, a rust-stained section of the tree slid aside, admitting the pair not to a woody interior but to one lined with pale composite paneling. Entering, they shut the barrier behind them.

No one in a place like Hasawa would expect someone to step inside a tree. Had anyone been able to follow the two Yuiquerus who did so, he would have been even more surprised to see them descend a series of spiral steps and finally pause before another doorway. This one was flanked by a pair of warriors armed not with spears and hunting bows but with neuronic rifles. One versed in such matters would have noted immediately that they were of familiar Commonwealth manufacture.

Beyond the door, a large meeting chamber awaited their arrival. The chamber had been constructed outside the tree, beneath the water. During the short dry time, when the water receded and the land was once more briefly exposed to the air, it would look from the outside like a cluster of dead logs. It would not fool anyone on close inspection. But by that time, Aniolo-jat was sure, its exposure would not matter.

A dozen other Yuiquerus had assembled in the room, swinging solemnly back and forth in their hanging chairs. In place of the traditional central gap open to the rain, an artificial column of falling water had been installed. At the far end, Sakuntala who had received and passed various forms of advanced training were busy operating modern communications equipment. They were in touch, Aniolo-jat knew, with other branches of their organization in towns and villages throughout the Viisiiviisii. His own portable communicator rode comfortably in the holding pouch secured to one of his chest straps. Everyone else in the room was similarly equipped. And armed.

He and Yeruna-hua were the last to arrive. There was no need for introductions. Everyone knew everyone else by name. They had been working together, across clan lines, for some time.

In a way, Aniolo-jat knew, that was the greatest accomplishment of all. Not the arming of those present and their followers. Not the maintenance of secret links unknown to the Council and other Hatas or to the Fluvan representatives of the Commonwealth. Not even the development of their plans. No, it was the fact that the alliance had been able to sustain and develop its purpose across clan lines. Identifying the individuals who were present, he was able to count with pride the number of ancient rivalries that had been set aside on behalf of the greater good.

Sesesthi-toa, for example. Her extended clan had been arguing and fighting with his own off and on for hundreds of years. If some of the other Hatas among her clan knew she was working closely with a Yuiqueru of the Jat, they would remove her from their inner consultations and demote her in status, or worse. That they had both been able to overcome their mutual animosity was a source of great pride to him—though she still refused to touch tongues with him.

Yeruna-hua slipped into the vacant swing seat next to him as Aniolo-jat settled himself into position. By the speed and direction of his swinging he indicated that he was present, aware, and ready for the meeting to begin. Iwoko-jei declared for silence. As he was a Yuiqueru and not a Hata-tanasua, there was no opening invocation, no katola-drinking ceremony. Though some were secretly sympathetic to their aims, Aniolo-jat knew, no Hata-tanasua would openly bless such a gathering—or its intentions. It didn't matter, he knew. That could, and would, come later.

"The time has come at last," Iwoko-jei was saying. He was so excited, he could hardly keep his tongue coiled in a cheek pouch. "All our planning, all our hard work, is about to blossom like hyreath flower. Brothers and sisters, the day for us take back our world is at hand!"

A united chorus of "Hauea!" followed the senior Yuiqueru's impassioned declaration. Next to him, Waruna-hia stilled her chair.

"The western and eastern trees are ready. When appointed time arrives, our fighters will attack every Deyzara institution and business concern within our region. As instructed, we will try concentrate on property. There will be some deathing. Is unavoidable." She smiled humorlessly. "Many of those who are with us are young, and hungry for killing."

Aniolo-jat spoke up. "Must be no massacres. Mass deathing may possible compel Commonwealth authority to act. Is vital that they be kept out of this. Property destruction alone will not be enough allow them act on Deyzara behalf."

"That iss sso," declared a new voice. It was oddly inflected, and its mastery of S'aku, while commendable, tended to slide past certain syllables rather than fasten firmly on the necessary diphthongs. "Lissten well to the one called Aniolo-jat. Like the resst of you, he thinkss much as we do." A clawed hand moved in a gesture of third-degree approval.

Iwoko-jei turned his seat in the direction of the voice. "If our good friends have something to add, we are all us here, as always, eager hear their words."

The speaker and a single companion stepped forward from where they had been monitoring the Sakuntala who were operating the advanced communications equipment. They did not speak from the traditional hanging chairs. Even if they had been inclined to try them, they would have found the swinging seats uncomfortable. For one thing, their tails were much thicker than the slim tufted appendages possessed by the Sakuntala. For another, the special suits they were forced to wear in order to survive on Fluva might have caught and torn on a rough part of the chairs, and this the two strangers would not risk.

Favoring as they did a desert climate with no more than 10 percent humidity, their lungs could only tolerate the intense dampness of the Viisiiviisii for about an hour before saturation threatened to clog the moisture-phobic alveoli in their lungs. Furthermore, they were particularly susceptible to many of the airborne spores and eggs that exploded into the atmosphere whenever the interminable rain let up long enough to allow local flora to propagate. Their special suits were lightweight, both to shed the rain and to protect them from the fecund Nature in which they found themselves submerged. Most important of all, the small but extremely efficient dehumidifiers they wore over their snouts both dried and warmed the air they took into their lungs.

"As you all know, the final promised weaponss sshipment arrived lasst night and wass dissperssed locally."

Both Aniolo-jat and Yeruna-hua acknowledged this with approving flicks of their extraordinary tongues.

Thessu RDDTYTW replied with a fourth-degree sign of concurrence. Next to him, Jallrii BQQHHJR gestured satisfaction. The two AAnn officers were pleased that everything was going so smoothly. Pleased because it meant that all their hard work over the previous several years was finally reaching fruition. Pleased because its success would mean promotion for them both. Pleased because they were advancing the aims of the Empire. But pleased especially because it meant the two reptilian operatives might soon be able to make their final bows and gesticulations to this sodden hell of a world and return to civilization and a decent climate, where they would once again be able to breathe air that did not congest the lungs and stink of everlasting moisture. This whole world of Fluva stank of rot and decay.

Thessu continued, addressing himself to Aniolo-jat. Even though the Yuiqueru in question was not senior among those assembled in the secret meeting chamber, Thessu and Jallrii had long since decided he was the most clever and forward-looking among them. Which was another way of saying that of all the smelly, waterlogged, rain-loving natives they were forced to deal with, he was the one who thought most like an AAnn.

"Once fighting hass begun, we will continue to ssupply you as before. As alwayss, we musst be circumsspect in our work lesst we alert the local Commonwealth authoritiess to our activitiess." He accompanied his words with a second-degree gesture signifying importance. "It iss vital that the nature of the assistance we have been providing to you remainss unknown, at leasst until all of our mutual goalss have been accomplisshed. If you can achieve what you have promissed as quickly as you indicate, there sshould be no problem. By the time the local humanss and thranx come to gripss with the sscale of your movement and can requesst and receive insstructionss on how to deal with it, much less formal assisstance, it will be too late for them."

"Too late for the Deyzara," Waruna-hia declaimed aloud. Cries of determination and agreement supported her observation.

Thessu and Jallrii exchanged comments of their own by means of gestures whose meaning was unknown to the assembled Sakuntala. Like many other species, the indigenous natives of Fluva communicated only by speech and expression. They lacked the added sophistication of exchanging meaning by means of limb movement that was common among the higher races like the AAnn. Or, it had reluctantly to be admitted, the thranx and, to a lesser extent, humankind.

Aniolo-jat waited for emotions to settle before speaking again. "How can we expect our good friends the AAnn to help us directly in fight to remove the Deyzara?"

His tail switching back and forth, Jallrii took over for his colleague. "As we have previoussly explained, we cannot be directly involved in the fighting. If we were to do sso, and ssuch participation by uss was disscovered, it would change radically the nature of the Commonwealth ressponsse to your uprissing. It would become a matter of the Commonwealth verssuss the beloved Empire. But if all hosstilitiess remain local, then Commonwealth government reaction sshould alsso sstay confined to local action, at leasst long enough for you to accomplissh our joint intended aimss."

Thessu spoke up. "As long as your actionss perssisst, we will continue to ssupply you with weaponss when, where, and as feassible. You will of coursse alsso have access to our advanced communicationss facilitiess, and to our sstrategic advice."

"The Sakuntala not need advice from anybody on how to

fight!" a belligerent Yuiqueru put in, rocking violently in his chair. Several self-confident exclamations echoed this sentiment.

"We did not mean to imply that you did," Thessu responded deferentially, with a slight clacking of his sharp teeth. "We meant only to offer."

"Your offer gratefully acknowledged." Aniolo-jat met the AAnn's catlike gaze evenly.

Yess, a clever one, that Aniolo-jat, the AAnn officer reflected. When events on Fluva began to settle down, he and Jallrii had already decided who would be chosen to occupy the position of prime contact with the Empire. It was good of the natives to have made the choice for them. The others could be dealt with as necessary: rewarded for their efforts or shunted into positions of largely ceremonial importance or, if they proved particularly recalcitrant to acknowledge the new order of things, disposed of. He had no doubt that the Yuiqueru Aniolo-jat would be cooperative in all aspects of realigning the social order on Fluva. It was always helpful when the usual one or two semi-intelligent natives announced themselves. It saved having to sift through the populace to find them.

"There are to be no massacress," Jallrii was saying. "That iss the only thing that could sspark rapid and direct involvement by Commonwealth peaceforcerss."

"Of course not," another war chief agreed. "Maybe just a little massacre, here and there. Out of sight of witnesses and Commonwealth people." His look of feral anticipation was sufficient to freeze a Deyzara in its tracks. "Easy to hide much in Viisiiviisii."

"You will have to rein in ssuch dessiress," Thessu warned him. "Your aim iss to rid your world of as many Deyzara as possible. Remember—forcing them into the major townss will keep the local Commonwealth authoritiess bussy trying to assisst and care for thoussandss of refugeess. The more they can be kept occupied, the less likely they are to learn of our ssurreptitiouss proactive activitiess among you.

"Once it can be demonsstrated that the only way to protect

the Deyzara iss to remove them from thiss world and repatriate them to Tharce IV, you will have achieved that which you wanted." He signed first-degree significance, even though none among the Sakuntala recognized the gesture. "As ssoon as that has been carried out, the new governing council, repressenting all your clanss, will announce that Fluva iss ssevering any affiliation with the Commonwealth. Upon itss withdrawal, you will declare your dessire to be repressented in future matterss of interstellar import by the gloriouss Empire, may the beloved Emperor Navvur W besstow his most lucid and luminouss blessings upon you."

Iwoko-jei slid out of his chair. "We look forward to day when our AAnn friends move more freely among us, and to reclaiming of our world. Deyzara have Tharce Four and Commonwealth worlds to welcome them." His burning eyes roamed the circle. "Sakuntala have only Fluva. Soon we take back our home!"

"One matter of ssome concern remainss." Thessu was not quite ready to acknowledge that the meeting was at an end. "For thiss to work, it iss vital that our effortss be ssupported by a ssufficient majority of Ssakuntala. Are you, at thiss late date, confident that thiss will be sso?"

Aniolo-jat spoke up before Iwoko-jei could reply. The senior Yuiqueru glared at the younger war chief but chose not to make the breach of etiquette an issue. Now was not the time. Aniolo-jat could be reprimanded later.

"It is true there are some who may oppose what we intend. But they are Sakuntala all. Once fighting begins, all reluctant ones will eventual join. They will have little choice. If after we have begun are still important ones who choose not participate, they will be dealt with appropriately. At the time, or afterward."

He smiled at the two AAnn, marveling once again at the effort it required on their part for them simply to be able to walk about and breathe properly in Fluva's atmosphere. Because of this, they could never constitute more than a small presence on his world. Unlike the humans, for example, who were better able to tolerate Fluva's constant rain and damp even though they were not fond of it.

He felt that he understood the aims of these toothy-snouted beings better than most of his fellow Yuiquerus. The tough-skinned, thick-tailed visitors did not want to possess and exploit Fluva so much as they wished to deny it and its resources to the humans and the thranx. An alliance would give them an out-post of influence within Commonwealth space, much as one clan historically sought to destabilize an enemy by forging a union with dissident families belonging to the same clan. Sur-veying the circle, he eyed his fellow Sakuntala conspirators with fond contempt. Bold, robust fighters, every one of them. But they lacked vision. They could not see beyond killing Deyzara or driving them off Fluva. As a consequence, few of them would ever rise to become anything greater than Yuiquerus. Whereas he had been exposed, from listening to these AAnn, to greater possibilities.

Properly supported and backed, a Sakuntala could aspire to rule more than a single clan. Aniolo-jat did not want Iwoko-jei's standing, for example, or even that of Cecolou-tiu. The position he wanted belonged to the female Lauren Matthias—only it would be given to him by the AAnn, not by humans.

Let the Hatas and the Yuiquerus glory in their newfound sta-tus, in their complete dominance over their individual territo-ries. Once the Deyzara had been dispossessed and removed from Fluva, many Sakuntala would revert to old ways. Tradi-tional rivalries would reassert themselves even as the culture as a whole continued to make progress through further contact with the AAnn and their advanced technology. The Hatas would need someone to come to for advice. Someone to rule on internal disputes. Someone to distribute the aid and assis-tance the AAnn had promised to provide and to communicate requests on their behalf.

Him.

The position was already his. He knew it from the way the two AAnn officers acted when they spoke to him. They were happy to have found someone to handle the task, and he was more than happy to accept it. He would be paramount among his kind, a Hata among Hatas. All that was necessary was for everything to proceed as planned with the expulsion of the Deyzara. He was ready to accept the mantle that would then be handed to him.

Let it begin.

Jaruntamee was just opening his small shop when the four Sakuntala appeared. At first he thought they were customers and hurried to get his new display in order. The Sakuntala had proven fond of specialty sweets imported from Dargala, and he was doing a good business selling them to those who had hard credit to spend.

Then, as the rain turned from downpour to drizzle, he saw that they were holding not the traditional carry baskets but weapons. Though he was but a simple shopkeeper, he had no trouble identifying the slender, wicked-looking devices. Even in the dim light, they were unmistakable. One gleamed as if new, while the others looked old and worn. That did not render them any less ominous.

Startled by the sight, he rationalized that the Sakuntala were hunters who had acquired more sophisticated tools of their trade than springbows and spears. Only when they stopped in front of his shop and he could make out their expressions as clearly as their weapons did the shock of realization hit home. Dazed, he searched the street of suspended strilk for support, found none. His was the first place of business to open for the day. He was about to pay for his industriousness.

Though none of them pointed a gun directly at him, the respite was brief. Two of the tall forms brushed past him as if he didn't exist, nearly knocking him off his feet. When he saw what they were pulling from the carry pouches attached to their waist straps, he started forward.

"Gentle Sakuntala," he began anxiously, "if I have given offense to you, please to let me know what it was and I will endeavor most strongly to make amends. I have no idea what has prompted this anger of yours, but I assure you that—here now, you can't do that!" He started forward. "You must stop! I am telling you most strongly, you cannot—"

Something struck him hard from behind, knocking him down. As the Deyzara had no knees but only a system of entwined ligaments and tendons in their arms and legs to support them, he folded rather than crumpled. At first he thought he had been shot. But the angry ache in his back was not accompanied by spreading blood.

His vision was blurred, but not his hearing. Though not as acute as that of Sakuntala or humans, it was good enough to overhear the Sakuntala laughing and chattering among themselves. All around him, he heard the rising cries of his neighbors as they were rousted from their homes and businesses by other armed indigenous. As he lay stunned in the rain on the now slightly swaying walkway, he wondered what had brought this on. Ever since the Deyzara had come to Fluva there had been rampages against them by the native populace. But these had all been sporadic, unorganized, and of brief duration. What was happening around him now smacked of careful preplanning. Furthermore, in the old days his attackers would simply have shot him. These seemed almost at pains not to do so.

He tried to rise, but a furry foot in his back kept him down. As he struggled to keep his trunks from being crushed beneath his face, he held back the words he wanted to shout. The fact that he had not been shot did not mean he could not provoke them to do so.

So he lay quietly and sobbed within himself as he watched his business burn.

In Udredruta, the Salamthi family was just concluding their morning mutual ablutions when two armed Sakuntala burst into the house.

"Here now!" Both trunks waving angrily, the senior of the two females present immediately placed herself between the junior wife and their pair of mutual offspring. "What is the meaning of this intrusion?" She waved both hands and all four digits at the much taller intruders. "Get out, get out, both of you! You are not invited; you are not welcome here. Bursting in like this armed, and in front of the broodlings! You should be most ashamed of yourselves, oh yes."

Raising the battered but still serviceable pistol he was holding, the nearer of the two Sakuntala shot her cleanly between eyes and speaking trunk. Hoots of shock and alarm rose from the surviving female. So terrified were the two broodlings that they expelled air through their eating as well as their speaking trunks.

The other Sakuntala growled at his companion. "We not supposed to kill them. Only frighten and chase from house. Yuiqueru Getouka-via will be unpleased."

"May Getouka-via suffer a kensuk in his bowels." The raptorish eyes of the other native were wild. "Ever since I a prewarrior I have watched Deyzara make most credit, take best home places. For years I see them looking at me like I a therruna just drop from top of whirltree. I hate them. I hate their clothes that hurt the eyes; I hate their smell; I hate their food. I hate everything about them." As he looked down at the body of the senior female, lying smoking on the floor of the house, his expression did not change. "Let Getouka-via be unpleased. I, Nevairu-kei, am very pleased." Raising the wonderful pistol that had been assigned to him, he leveled it at the two broodlings. Eyes rolling back fully into her head, both trunks quivering in fear, the junior female nonetheless placed herself between the weapon and the offspring.

Taking his companion's forearm in a strong six-fingered grip, the other Sakuntala forced the muzzle of the weapon down. "This not about Getouka-via. It not about you or me. I like Deyzara no more than you. But is greater end at stake here." Both highly mobile ears inclined in the direction of the terrified remnants of the typical Deyzara family. "You remember talkings. Killing offspring the sort of thing that might bring humanx intervention. Better for us that Deyzara offspring walk away and humanx peoples have to feed and house them. Keep humanx authorities busy." He smiled. "Feeding and housing take more time than dumping in Viisiiviisii. You want vengeance, my friend—or results?"

The other Sakuntala's initial, archetypal reaction at being grabbed was anger. Then it cooled, and common sense took over. It was a measure of how much the Sakuntala had advanced in the hundreds of years since their initial contact with the Commonwealth.

"My blood says kill them, but my mind says you speak wiseness." Lowering the pistol, he fumbled in another pouch until he found one of the compact conflag packages. Taking it in his free hand, he broke the seal as he had been instructed and threw the activated handful against the back wall of the gathering room. The incendiary material contained in the package immediately set the wall aflame. It would burn, he knew, even in the rain, drawing the components necessary to sustain combustion from the very material it was consuming. The broodlings began to hoot even louder. The Sakuntala's ears twitched. It was a revolting sound.

"Let's go to next house." The thrower's eagerness could not be denied. "Maybe they will have weapons and try resist. Getouka-via say we can shoot any who resist with weapons."

"We must first decide what is weapon sufficient to justify shooting back."

The pair continued their conversation as they strolled nonchalantly from the now flaming structure, leaving the junior female and the broodlings to make their way to safety as best they could.

Outside, a collective trill of massed panicked Deyzara hooting could be heard even above the falling rain.

In Nesawiti, a pitched battle was under way between their Sakuntala assailants and a handful of Deyzara determined to defend their community center. After two hours of exchanging fire with their indigenous attackers, they were forced to surrender when the main cables supporting the structure were severed

by Sakuntala wielding cutters. With the building listing dangerously to one side and threatening at any moment to fall into
the swirling waters below, they marched out and sullenly
turned their weapons over to their tormentors. Expecting to be
slaughtered, they pleaded only for the lives of their families.
Though it could not be said they were delighted with the consequences, they were certainly surprised to find themselves only
beaten, instead of killed.

More unexpectedly still, after razing and looting the interior
of the dangling building the attacking Sakuntala left them to
deal with their wounds and their misery. Someone found an
undamaged cargo skimmer. Piling themselves and their families
into the well-used but sturdy vehicle, tending to those who
were most seriously injured, the survivors of the outpost rose
above the trees and limped toward the nearest community with
a Commonwealth station.

Nilsson was finishing his midday ration, while Erla had just
cracked a container of pink grape juice. Mist rose from the
cylinder as the contents automatically chilled to her preset preferred temperature. Next to her, Nilsson reached up to bat a
wandering tseth off his shoulder. It had its augur unsheathed
and was making a strenuous effort to bore through his shoulder armor. It buzzed angrily as it fell, broken-winged, toward
the water seven meters below. Something long, slim, spotted,
and yellow-black that Nilsson did not recognize thrust a pair of
stem-mounted jaws skyward. One snapped shut around the
body of the tseth with an audible popping sound before sliding
back beneath the surface.

Chewing idly, Nilsson studied the spot where both creatures
had vanished before returning to the last of his meal. Sometimes he wished he were a xenobiologist. Most of the time he
did not. What he did wish was that his term of service on this
world was six months further along. Then he would be packing
to leave.

He knew his partner felt exactly the same. Commonwealth
insistence notwithstanding, Fluva was no place for sensible

human beings. But a presence was required, and like it or not, they were part of it. Erla had just put the freshly chilled drink to her lips when a dozen Deyzara came running along the walkway toward them.

Adults all, they were moving as fast as they were able. Deyzara were not naturally gifted runners, and their sandaled twin-digited feet tended to slip even on the dimpled, perforated artificial surface. They accelerated noticeably as they neared the end of the walkway, which began to sway beneath their weight. The reason for the terror Erla felt she saw in their goggling eyes soon manifested itself. Coming up hard behind them were half a dozen Sakuntala, wild-eyed, sharp teeth flashing, ears pointed forward like knives. Most of them carried intricately carved spears or traditional war clubs fashioned from jokobo or segleth wood. But two—Nilsson put aside the last of his food and Erla set down her drink—two of them carried shock rifles. Held them correctly, too, at the appropriate end, with two thin fingers resting on each trigger.

Stationed on the periphery of Taulau Town, the two humans had spent months shedding water without engaging in anything more strenuous than popping a few predators that had tried to climb from the water below up into the trees. Suddenly faced with a small but unprecedented crisis, they reacted with admirable speed. Erla unlimbered her own gun while Nilsson activated his before speaking into the communicator pickup of his duty suit.

"Central, this is Twenty-three. Corporal Nilsson speaking." He squinted through the rain at the thoroughly terrified Deyzara and the pursuing Sakuntala. "We have some kind of an incident in progress here. There appear to be—"

Central dispatch interrupted him. The voice at the other end (probably Fasoli, he mused) sounded unusually harried. "Wait your turn, Twenty-three! I'll put you in line with the others."

The others? That didn't sound right. What was coming down here, besides rain? Leaving the line open, he picked up his own rifle and moved to stand alongside Erla.

"Business dispute, you reckon?" he murmured.

She shook her head, having pulled the helmet's protective visor down over her eyes. "Too many locals involved. You see the rifles?" He nodded. "Where did the Sakis get shock rifles?"

"Don't know," her partner responded tersely. "Right now I'm more interested in finding out if they know how to use 'em."

Upon reaching the sentry's position, the Deyzara did not race past. Instead, they alternately stumbled and fell to a halt, clustering as tightly as they could behind the two humans. Their always pungent body odor was powerful with perspiration, and their blaze of usually immaculate colorful attire was uncharacteristically torn and dirty. One elderly individual, his breathing trunk pulsing sharply as he strained to suck air, stood as close as possible to Nilsson. It was plain that he and his companions were in the last stages of fear and exhaustion.

"Please, respected sir! You must protect us! The Sakuntala—they have all gone mad, quite mad! Houses have been burnt, businesses looted, families forced to flee for their very lives. Help us!"

Erla blinked in the Deyzara's direction. "Say what? We haven't heard anything like that." Her gaze shifted to her partner. "Have we?"

His attention remained focused on the onrushing Sakuntala. "Not yet." Reaching up, he tapped his communications pickup with one index finger. "Something's not right. Not just here, either."

At the sight of the two armed humans, the six Sakuntala slowed. Those holding the rifles fingered them in a fashion sufficiently familiar to suggest to Nilsson that the natives did indeed know how to use the advanced Commonwealth weapons.

"What's all this about, now?" Erla demanded to know, holding her ground.

The Sakuntala exchanged glances. They were barely breathing hard. It was clear they had been toying with the Deyzara they had been chasing and, had they wished to do so, could have overtaken them at any time. That in itself was suggestive—though of what, precisely, neither Commonwealth soldier could be sure.

One of the Sakuntala armed with a club stepped forward, holding the weapon out parallel in front of his torso to show that he meant, for the moment, no harm. "We have begun this thing to take back our world. Not involve humans. Not want hurt you."

"The feeling's mutual." Nilsson spoke softly but did not lower his weapon. "So if you'll just turn around, or go around, we'll all be content and nobody'll get hurt."

Looking past the sentry, the speaker glowered at the pitiful Deyzara. "Step to left or step to right. Both steps make safe for you and me."

Erla glanced back down at the huddled refugees. She did not think much of the Deyzara. Neither did she have any particular affection for the Sakuntala. But she was quite fond of her rank.

"How about you step back and they step forward? That'll have the same result: nobody'll get hurt, and whatever this is all about can be sorted out later."

The Sakuntala hesitated. Nilsson's eyes shifted slightly to the right and he raised the muzzle of his gun. "If you're thinking of using that old shock rifle, big-ears, you'd better make sure you don't miss with your first shot. Mine's a stable repeater, and I could kill you and all five of your buddies before you have time to figure out what you did wrong."

"Not to mention," Erla added, tapping her chest plate, "that we're wearing armor and you're wearing fur. Take it from me: in a firefight, armor is better."

Several of the Sakuntala fell to murmuring sharply among themselves. Disagreement was palpable. Finally they turned and, with a couple of murderous backward glances, loped back the way they had come, disappearing among the rain and the trees.

As bawling, appreciative Deyzara crowded close around him, pawing him with grateful two-digited hands, Nilsson barked into his pickup, "Fasoli, what the hell's going on?" He tapped the tip of the lightweight pickup again, making it bounce slightly. "Fasoli, dammit!" The dispatcher didn't answer.

He was very, very busy.

Such actions were being repeated, on scales both larger and smaller, throughout a large portion of the inhabited Viisiiviisii. It rapidly became apparent that unlike in the past, the attacks were not random outbreaks of anti-Deyzara violence but were being well coordinated. In the face of the ferocious (but by no means universal) assault, those frightened Deyzara who were able to do so fled their small settlements. Seeking protection and aid, they began to converge on the larger, more developed towns and municipalities. At first they were taken in by relatives and friends. But as the full dimension of the attacks and the scope of the tragedy became clear, more and more sought shelter in public facilities. These were rapidly overwhelmed by the number and desperation of the refugees with which they were being asked to cope.

Calls began to go out. Information traveled through the troubled Viisiiviisii. Eventually it reached Taulau.

Where it all ended up, metaphorically if not literally, on one desk.

1

Brushing idly at the softly humming brim of her fully charged rain cape, Lauren Matthias gazed glumly at the chaos before her. Hundreds of Deyzara were packed into the port's staging area, a sea of mooning eyes, bobbing trunks, and pale rain-slicked heads. There was hardly enough room for those already there while more were arriving every hour on foot and via transport. Flocks of gauzy-winged, serrated-beaked voukopu soared overhead, skimming from one tree or building to another in search of the dead meat they seemed certain was to be forthcoming.

Gosling was a good man, but the strain was already showing on his face. He was nominally in charge of a refugee agency that had not even existed forty-eight hours earlier. Though doing his best, he was clearly overwhelmed by the scope of the task before him.

"They keep filtering in," he told her in his sorrowful, laconic manner. "Some of the other towns are worse."

"So I've been told." Walking past the families was hard. Broodlings gaped up at her out of impossibly wide, confused eyes: they had been forced to surrender the familiar, sometimes at spear or gunpoint, often in the middle of the night. Most families had brought some food with them. That would soon begin to run out, she knew. Then it would be the responsibility of the Commonwealth, as the administering authority, to feed them. She had already made arrangements for individual teams to set aside their regular duties in favor of hunting-and-gathering expeditions. That would help. Whether or not it, in combination with the usual warehoused supplies available in each community, would be enough remained to be seen.

The Sakuntala could help—except that the Sakuntala were the cause of the crisis. The trouble was that many of those who did not agree with the methods being employed by the radicals, and there were many, had been intimidated into refusing assistance. Others gave tacit approval to the end the radicals were striving toward even if they did not agree with the means that were being used. A dangerous majority were indifferent. The result was a carefully crafted conundrum knotty enough to test the skills of a senior diplomat.

Which she was not. She was only an administrator.

Jack was being as supportive as possible. He could hold her and tell her that everything was going to be all right, but he couldn't make decisions for her. At least Andrea had settled down. The scale of the emergency and the extent of the overt violence had pushed adolescent concerns onto the back burner. In other words, Matthias knew, the events of the past couple of days had forced her daughter to grow up a little.

"We can handle another thousand max, maybe." Gosling was studying the crowd. His staff was methodically settling groups in empty hangars and available storage buildings, trying to provide every family and individual with at least a modicum of shelter. There was no pushing or shoving among the Deyzara. It was not that they were an especially docile people, just that they were used to, and respected, the benefits of organization.

"Any more than that and port operations will begin to be compromised."

Matthias's mouth tightened. "We can't have that, Eric. Local transport is going to be more important than ever, and we're going to need space for some big boys to land and unload here."

"How soon until the first relief ship arrives?"

"Couple of weeks. The government on Praxiteles has been as helpful as you could ask for, but it still takes time to get relief material together, shuttled to orbit, loaded, and delivered. Tharce Four is putting together an enormous shipment, as you might expect, but there's no telling when that will get here. That's what happens when the world you're on lies on the fringes of settled space." She checked her chronometer. "I've got to get back to the office. I'm meeting with representatives of both species."

Gosling sighed. "These things blow up among the Sakuntala all the time. Maybe this one will disappear as quickly as it surfaced."

"Let's hope so." Privately, she was seriously concerned. This uprising was different from the periodic outbursts of violence that were so much a part of Sakuntala culture. An uncharacteristic amount of planning was involved. The radicals were acting in concert all across the Viisiiviisii. Then there were the reports that some of the insurgents possessed advanced weaponry, and not the kind used for shooting game. A hasty check of stores showed nothing missing from the armory. Where had shock rifles and neuronic pistols come from? The radicals would need outside help to acquire such weapons. Who among her staff or the limited number of successful Sakuntala traders or even rogue elements among the Deyzara could have smuggled in such weaponry?

Her thoughts had no rest as she took the slider back to Administration, dodging pedestrians as she navigated the web of suspended spun-strilk walkways. Deeper inside Taulau Town life went on as usual, with none of the turmoil attendant on the activities at the port. The surrounding signs of normality served to settle her nerves somewhat. By the time she reached Administration and parked the slider in its charging slot, she was feeling a little better. Unseen lightning illuminated the clouds, and distant thunder boomed. Not a good sign. The rain on Fluva usually fell without such dramatic accompaniment.

She barely had time to slip out of her rain suit and cape and enter her office before she found herself besieged by a pair of Deyzara. Her assistant looked in helplessly. Matthias waved him off.

"I'll handle it, Sanuel. That's what I'm here for."

The assistant eyed the three visitors uneasily. "Let me know if you need anything, Administrator. Anything at all." Somewhat reluctantly, he stepped back out into the outer office, closing the door behind him.

The single Sakuntala present, Matthias noted as she sat down behind her desk, looked troubled but not angry. For that much she was grateful. The two Deyzara were making enough noise to drown out the sound of rain on the trees outside her window.

Raising both hands, she managed to get the pair to sit down. Next to them yet distant, the female Hata Sakuntala crouched silently on her haunches, her tail moving back and forth behind her in slow, measured arcs.

"You absolutely for certain must do something!" The male Deyzara's trunks were wandering all over the place.

"Yes." His female companion glared over at the serene Sakuntala. "Our people are being driven from their homes; they are having their property looted and destroyed. There have been injuries and killings. All of this is decidedly unprovoked. We demand Commonwealth protection, and that the perpetrators of these miserable, cowardly acts be brought to justice and appropriately punished!"

Matthias nodded as she folded her hands on the desk. "I'm still gathering information."

"Information? I will give you information!" Quivering with anger, the male's speaking trunk threatened to snap off his head and go careening around the room on its own. "I will give you so much information it will make your hirsute head hurt! Why, Administrator Matthias, down in Kawili District alone there have been—"

Raising a hand once more, she interrupted what threatened to become a lengthy diatribe. Hooting softly, the Deyzara subsided.

Turning to her left, the human administrator found herself gazing at the waiting Sakuntala. The female appeared neither smug nor upset. That did not mean, Matthias told herself, the indigenous representative would be receptive to queries.

"Hata Naneci-tok, can you give me some idea, any idea, what has prompted this unexpected violent outbreak? Before I can decide what to do next, I have to know what's going on." Both Deyzara joined her in facing the Sakuntala. Their expressions, though nowhere near as versatile as those of human or native, were severe enough to be recognized.

As the Hata shifted her long, slender legs, the strappings around her waist and thighs made small clacking sounds. "There always been element among my people that not accept presence of Deyzara people on Fluva. Has inspired unpleasant incidents for long time. But always carried out by small, isolated groups of unhappy individuals. This something much different."

Matthias wished she could read the Sakuntala better. It was impossible to tell whether this Hata was being honest or devious. She hoped for the former.

"I've received reports that some of the Sakuntala involved in this disturbance have come into the possession of advanced weaponry. One of the first things I did was order a complete check of my government's limited local inventory of such items. Nothing is missing, not even a field knife. Therefore, the armaments I am hearing about must have come from somewhere else. Do you have any idea who is supplying the radicals with such dangerous ordnance?"

"I have no more idea than you," Naneci-tok replied truthfully. Several times her tongue flicked out to tap the floor, a sure sign of personal discomfort. Looking to her left, she regarded the Deyzara out of eyes that were sorrowful as well as penetrating. "You not the only ones who have been deceived."

The Deyzara were not mollified. Snapping the two digits of her left hand together sharply, the female once more assailed the human administrator. "If the Sakuntala Hatas can no longer control their own people, then we must assuredly have protection from Commonwealth forces. If we accept, albeit reluctantly, that the local authorities are no longer able to enforce restraint among all elements of the indigenous population, that clearly leaves us at the mercy of its most fanatic components. We have begun to resist, to fight back, but we would prefer that the Commonwealth intervene on behalf of what is right."

Wonderful, Matthias thought moodily. Just what she needed: an all-out civil war between the two local sentient species.

"I can't authorize armed intervention on behalf of the Commonwealth in the absence of proof of extensive casualties. There have been some confirmed deaths, but nothing on a scale that would allow me to justify Commonwealth intervention."

"Why not?" the male inquired bitterly. "Because it might mean some humans would die, instead of just lowly Deyzara and Sakuntala?"

"We will go and speak to the local representatives of the Church," his companion declared.

Matthias eyed her regretfully. "I can tell you right now that the United Church will not intercede with force in favor of one side or the other. The local padres are authorized to defend themselves and their missions, but not to intervene in such matters. Nor will they, since they minister to Sakuntala as well as Deyzara."

"Then what, I ask, are we to do?" The male's frustration threatened to overwhelm the heart-hammering efforts of his overworked circulatory system.

It was an honest, and a good, question, Matthias knew. The radicals were being very clever. Instead of perpetrating a massacre that could bring Commonwealth intervention, they were apparently making a conscious effort to avoid casualties. Deyzara were being beaten, their properties looted and destroyed, but except in a few isolated instances, killing was being avoided. The two-trunks were not being slaughtered—they were being herded. Into towns, where pressure was growing on her own people as well as on private enterprises to house and feed them. One way to alleviate such pressure would be to move refugees off-world, where adequate facilities existed to care for them.

Which, she reflected, was precisely what the extremist groups among the Sakuntala wanted. Once the Deyzara were off-world, she doubted that even the moderate elements among the Sakuntala would allow any to return.

Who had advised them on such a plan of action? Knowing the Sakuntala as she did, she found it hard to credit the fanatics among them with such cunning. The radicals were known for their audacity, not their restraint. Someone was helping them with advice as well as with advanced arms. But who? A few elements among the Deyzara themselves might benefit from seeing a large number of their colleagues ejected from Fluva. That was a hard possibility to countenance. What of her own kind? Could she trust every human on Fluva? Take the inventorying of weapons, for example. Without seeing for herself, how did she know if the report that had been hastily compiled and sent to her was wholly accurate?

She wished Jack were there, seated beside her. His steadying presence would have been welcomed. But it would have undercut her authority and prompted whispering. People sat near her to have *her* support, not the other way around. She felt very alone.

The trio of locals was staring at her and she became aware she hadn't said anything in too long. They were waiting for an answer to the Deyzara's question. Taking a deep breath, she folded her hands in front of her and sat up as straight as her tired back would allow.

"This is what I am going to do for now. Any Deyzara that enters a chartered community will be given the protection of the local Commonwealth authorities. Food and shelter will be provided insofar as resources permit. The radicals will not be allowed to harass refugees."

The female Deyzara indicated satisfaction. "What about those of us who are trapped outside such municipal boundaries and who are unable to reach such designated areas of safety? And what about the destruction of property?"

"First things first. The situation continues to evolve rapidly and unpredictably. I have already relayed a space-minus communication to my superiors and am awaiting a response. I can't do anything more until that's received." This did not satisfy the apprehensive pair, but they could think of no hard objection to raise. The Deyzara understood procedure.

Relieved by the ensuing silence, Matthias turned to the Hata. "Meanwhile, I expect the Sakuntala hierarchy to do everything in its power to curb ongoing hostilities and to try to rein in the more extreme elements among the clans."

"This we already doing," Naneci-tok replied, "and not because of human directive. Is presently much confusion among my people." Raptor eyes flashed. "Real danger is that young ones are swept up in fervor and excitement of upheaval. Fighting is to Sakuntala what breathing is to others. Spirit moves body; body forgets brain." She looked genuinely uncomfortable. "At such times is hard to speak reason to young ones. When mouth is wide open and screaming, makes hearing difficult."

"I know that the Hatas will do their best." Matthias found herself sympathizing with the visibly distressed female. No such sympathy flowed from the furious Deyzara as they rose to depart and communicate the results of the meeting to their people.

Alone again in the office, Matthias turned to watch the rain falling outside the window. For the moment, she had done all she could. Despite what she had told the Deyzara, she doubted authorization would be forthcoming from Earth or Hivehom for the use of weapons in support of the Deyzara and against the Sakuntala. If hundreds were being slaughtered it might be different. But in the absence of mass killings, cautious bureaucrats would want to avoid at all costs being seen as taking sides in what was inarguably a local dispute. She knew how the system worked. They would agree to provide only humanxitarian aid.

Which meant that if the Council of Hatas proved unable to control the radicals, the extremists might well succeed in their aim of getting a large number of Deyzara permanently expelled from Fluva. Could she allow that to happen? What did it matter to her? First and foremost, her job was to oversee the Commonwealth presence on the Big Wet, not to get involved in local fighting.

But it bothered her that she was being out-thought and out-maneuvered. Especially since she had no idea by whom.

At least she had succeeded in somewhat reassuring the Deyzara's representatives without riling the Sakuntala's chosen Hata. That was something. Now, if things would just calm down for a day or so and give her some time to delve a little deeper into the source of the disturbance, maybe learn what groups and individuals were behind it all, she might be able to find ways to stabilize the situation. To induce, for example, some of the less unruly Sakuntala to give up fighting and return to their homes.

Most important of all, she needed to find out how and where they had managed to obtain sophisticated weaponry. It had to be admitted that the latter troubled her more than anything else, especially since armed radicals and human patrols had nearly come to blows at several outposts. If a couple of her people got killed, as opposed to just threatened, it would alter the existing dynamic dangerously. Then she would have to worry about restraining her own staff as well as the Sakuntala.

She found herself pleading with unseen forces: I'm not asking for much. Just a day or two, a brief but real cooling-off period when nothing of significance happens . . .

Pandusky stuck his head in, smiled apologetically, and entered. "Sorry, Administrator, but I thought you should see this right away."

Thoughts of a possible break evaporated. "What is it now,

Sanuel? If it's another batch of reports about fleeing Deyzara being chased by rabid Sakuntala, I've had about all I can handle for one morning."

The smile returned. "Good. Then maybe you'll look on this as a change of pace instead of another crisis." Pulling a hand projector, he flipped it to life.

A three-dimensional map appeared, floating in the space between them. Within it, a tiny skimmer-shaped dot of light was visible traveling south from Taulau Town.

"That's the rescue team we sent out to find that missing bioscout, Hasselemoga." As he paused, the light disappeared. "That's the location of the last contact, aural or automatic, that we had with the rescue team. Thirty hours ago."

She frowned at her assistant as the map vanished and he slipped the projector back into a pocket. "If contact was lost thirty hours ago, why am I just finding out about it now?"

"Because permanent contact wasn't terminated until just this morning. Prior to that, the skimmer's instrumentation was doing its job, staying in touch with Port Base. The trouble is, the last thirty hours of communications turned out to be blank. Nobody thought to check the transmissions for actual content until they stopped altogether." He looked apologetic. "So they likely were traveling for thirty hours or so on unknown vectors. We have no way of knowing if they changed course during that time. If they did, it's going to be hell to find them."

"As good a description of the Viisiiviisii as any." Resting her head in her hands, she stared down at the desk.

Pandusky waited silently for several moments before finally breaking the silence. "Administrator Matthias? Lauren? What do you want me to do?"

"Tender my resignation, effective last week." She looked up. Pandusky was not concerned. He'd heard it before. "I'm sorry, Sanuel. It hasn't been a very good couple of days."

"No," he agreed somberly, "it has not."

"And now this." Spinning her seat, she waved at the window and the rain-swept varzea beyond. "First this reprobate but supposedly competent Hasa person goes missing. Now you're telling me that the skimmer we sent out to find him has done likewise?"

Pandusky pursed his lips, following her gaze to the window. "Do you suppose the Sakuntala insurgents could be responsible?"

Her gaze narrowed as she swiveled back to face him again. "You think they could have shot down both skimmers?"

Pandusky shrugged. "From what I'm hearing, they certainly have the firepower to do it."

She made a face. "Doesn't make sense. If they did so, it would gain them very little. If they tried and failed, they know it would allow us to justify sending patrols against them."

"Something else, then," the assistant surmised. "But what?"

"Maybe the Viisiiviisii itself." Matthias turned thoughtful. "These wouldn't be the first two skimmer crews to disappear out there. But to lose one sent to find another, that suggests something more than a feral coincidence."

"So what do we do? Do you want me to try to put together another, better-armed team to go look for the both of them?"

She shook her head. "First of all, I'd like to have a better idea of what might have happened before I send a third skimmer after two. Second, we can't spare anybody right now anyway, in case the extremist Sakuntala decide to try to test the patience of Commonwealth authority even further. We can't do anything until things settle down here."

Pandusky nodded. He was staring out the window again, at the raw, wet forest beyond. "That means if this Hasselemoga and the two we sent to look for him are still alive, they're going to have to find a way to survive on their own for a few days out in the open Viisiiviisii."

"Maybe a few weeks," she added. "Maybe longer. It can't be helped. I need all personnel to attend to their assigned stations until further notice."

Pandusky nodded again and excused himself from the room. Once, by dint of a mistake, he had been forced to spend a few hours alone in the Viisiiviisii. Once was enough, and he knew he had been fortunate to survive the experience. He did not care to think about what it would be like to try to survive in the flooded forest for a few weeks.

Later that afternoon he returned to the office to deliver a personal entreaty from the supervisor of the skimmer port at Kaxanti Town. Administrator Matthias was nowhere to be seen. He finally located her—standing outside on the porch, beyond the rim of the protective overhang. She was capeless and soaked, dripping wet from head to toe, her red hair plastered to her face and neck like stranded seaweed as she stared out into the Viisiiviisii.

"Administrator Matthias?" he asked hesitantly.

At first he thought she hadn't heard him. Or that if she had, she was not going to respond. Finally, she turned, looked hesitant, then smiled and brushed wet hair back from her forehead. Across the way, a sokot was eyeing her speculatively. A tentative, timid predator, it disappeared back into the rain and the branches as soon as she moved.

"It's okay, Sanuel. I was trying to clear my mind." She glanced down at herself. "If only the state of affairs in which we presently find ourselves was as easy to tidy as my clothes."

He nodded understandingly. "Just shove everything out in the rain and let the Big Wet wash it away. I'm afraid it's not going to be that easy, Administrator." He stepped aside as she moved back under the overhang, heading for the open doorway. "Can I make you something to drink?"

"You could," she told him wryly, "but much as I'd rather be otherwise, I'm afraid I'm going to have to stay sober if we're going to resolve any of this with a minimal amount of bloodshed and mayhem."

"Is that resolution going by Commonwealth or Sakuntala standards?" Pandusky asked her as they reentered her office. She elected not to respond.

Maybe because she had no answer.

8

The maccaluca gazed down at the potential prey out of the shape sensor that ran horizontally across the upper half of its face. It was not so much an eye as an instrument for analyzing interruptions in the patterns of light. The unique organ of perception had evolved to automatically filter out rain, thus enabling the maccaluca to see as clearly as if no rain was falling. In the brief dry season, when this evolutionary advantage was denied to it, it had great difficulty catching food and chose instead to hibernate in the high hollows of the great trees.

Now it "saw" the three figures moving below it as sharply as if they were not currently making their way through a torrential downpour. Other inhabitants of the flooded forest gave it a wide berth. For while the upper portion of the maccaluca's face was given over to its distinctive cream-colored organ of discernment, the rest of it was mostly mouth.

Half a dozen many-jointed arms allowed it to move rapidly and with great flexibility through the branches and vines. Once, it paused to pin a plate-sized fungi-browsing falek between the opposing pincers on one arm. Mewping futilely, the unlucky falek disappeared down a dark gullet. The snack only increased the maccaluca's interest in the more substantial food that was moving below it. Silently it began a gradual descent, its dappled brown-and-green fur together with the red and yellow lichens that grew upon it allowing it to blend in perfectly with its sodden surroundings.

Hasa broke trail while Jemunu-jah brought up the rear. Between them, the disgruntled and markedly unhappy Masurathoo kept up a steady stream of complaint. At least, the Sakuntala thought, the Deyzara had stopped griping about the damage to his clothing.

"I am compelled to point out once again that I think we should have remained at the crash site."

And I am compelled to remove my side arm from its place of resting and blow your speaking trunk clean off your head, Jemunu-jah mused silently. *But I won't. At least, not yet.*

"Save you energy for walking," he replied tersely.

"Walking where?" The Deyzara fluttered a flexible arm at the surrounding Viisiiviisii. "Deeper into damp deadliness? Nearer to death?"

"Didn't you hear the human and I consulting? Coming this way, he flew over small village a number of days' trek northeast from here. We reach it, maybe they have communications facility. Few communities on Fluva completely isolated anymore. We rest and eat there until pickup can be sent out for us."

Masurathoo snorted through his eating trunk. "*If* we can reach it, and *if* they have any means of communication with civilization. Those few isolated communities to which you refer are most unlikely to be found, sir, in this unvisited and unmapped portion of the Viisiiviisii. They might just as well decide you are a hereditary enemy, that we are your friends, and choose to have us for dinner—as courses and not guests."

Jemunu-jah bridled at the insult but said nothing. He could not, because he knew the two-trunk's words to be true. There were still large areas of Fluva the Commonwealth presence had not yet touched. Were still cousins who lived according to the old ways.

"I prefer take chance with Sakuntala meat eaters than with those that dwell in forest. At least can talk to former."

Hooting derisively, Masurathoo struggled to descend to the

larger branch below. They were traveling very close to the water now. The stagnant rain-spattered surface was only a few meters below the branch they were presently traversing. All manner of ferocious organisms dwelled in that water, he knew, hatching out of the dry ground and maturing rapidly as soon as the rains began to fall and the forest to flood. Many lurked just beneath the surface, waiting hungrily for food to fall from the trees. A considerable number were vegetarians. Those that were not—he shuddered—those that were not were best encountered in harmless education vits or in museums. They were a varied and impressive lot, inspiring in the many different ways of killing they had evolved.

He wanted to ask his companions to climb higher, away from the water, challenging as the effort would be to his already weary muscles. At best, they would ignore him. At worst, his suggestion would inspire more jokes at his expense. He had poor grounds for argument, he knew. Both the Sakuntala and this Hasa person were far more at home than he in the depths of the Viisiiviisii. He was going to have to rely on their expertise to get out of this alive. He knew it, they knew it, and he knew they knew it.

So he kept his mouth shut and plodded on in comparative silence, nervously trying to divide his attention between the slippery, uncertain route ahead and the ominous shadowy sheen of water below. All the while, he wiped constantly at his eyes. Rain battered them despite the protection provided by his electrostatically charged wide-brimmed hat and rain cape.

He was concentrating on some small movement in the water when he stumbled and fell. The aqueous disturbance seemed to intensify as he slipped toward it on the rain-slickened wood. Kicking frantically, his sandaled feet smashed through a clump of punky purple fungi, shattering the alien basidiocarps and sending thousands of spores shooting prematurely into the damp air. An instant later, his feet and legs were in the water. He didn't fear the water. Unlike the thranx, the Deyzara were excellent swimmers. But like anyone living on Fluva, he very much feared what lurked within the water.

Powerful arms grasped his own as he scrambled desperately to gain a footing on the semisubmerged branch. One set of arms was covered in light gray-and-black fur, while the other was nearly as bare as his own. Working together, human and Sakuntala easily dragged their clumsy companion clear of the water.

Lying on his back, Masurathoo first checked to make sure he hadn't lost any of the survival gear attached to his waist belt. To his considerable relief, everything was still where he had secured it. He had to rely on his own resources, he knew. The likelihood of either of his companions sharing their own supplies with him was small.

But . . . they had pulled him out of the water.

"What happen?" Jemunu-jah's tone reflected little in the way of actual concern.

"I saw," wide, bulging eyes turned to the right, "I certainly saw something moving most noticeably in the water."

Sakuntala and human exchanged a glance. "What you see?" Jemunu-jah inquired further.

"Movement. I assure you that it was quite noticeable, if not especially distinctive."

Straightening, Hasa turned his head sideways and spit, an action both the Deyzara and Sakuntala found interesting. "You saw movement in moving water. No wonder you panicked." He shook his head in disgust. "The Sakis are afraid of their own shadows and the two-trunks are still gooking around in the trees. What a world."

Having once again managed to insult two species in one sentence without the slightest regard as to how the two local representatives of those species might react, he turned to resume the trek eastward. There was a small gap between the half-submerged branch they were standing on and a dry branch opposite. He paused there, not waiting for his cohorts but judging the distance. Though it was modest, the slickness of both surfaces made even a short jump tricky.

Being Deyzara, Masurathoo had no elbows. Instead, he stiffened the longitudinal binding tendons in his arms to raise himself to a half-sitting position. As he did so, he saw a rustling of leaves directly overhead. Though he could see nothing behind them, he was immediately certain of one thing: the activity was not being caused by falling rain.

"Up . . ." He swallowed. "Something is moving above us."

Hasa turned his head slightly but didn't look back. "Sure. Probably whatever came leaping out of the water." He continued to gauge the short jump in front of him.

"No, it is verily true, sir!" The Deyzara started to get to his feet; in the absence of bones, it was a graceful, flowing, noiseless movement. "Please, look!"

With a sigh, Jemunu-jah started to tilt his head back. At the same time, both ears inclined sharply forward. Behind the sound of droplets landing on leaves and wood, there was something else: a faint scratching. Frowning inwardly, he trained preternaturally sharp eyes on the cluster of leaves and epiphytes the Deyzara had singled out. Cat pupils expanding sharply, he reached for his pistol and threw himself to one side.

Extending his speaking trunk to its full length, Masurathoo let out a piercing hoot and rolled, landing in the water with a clumsy splash. Mouth parted so wide it made it appear as if its head were split in half, the maccaluca landed on the branch where the Deyzara had been barely a second before. The branch bent noticeably under its weight. One clawed leg slashed at Masurathoo's back but caught only brightly dyed material. Spinning ferociously, the predator extended three other limbs in the direction of the rapidly retreating Sakuntala.

Jemunu-jah raised his pistol and squeezed the trigger. Another instance, he knew, where Commonwealth technology was a welcome improvement over traditional implements. Facing down a maddened, determined maccaluca was no time to lament the passing of culture.

He tripped just as he fired. The shot went over the mac-caluca's flattened egg-shaped skull to split leaves and bring down a large cluster of aerial roots. Behind the monster, Shadrach Hasselemoga could be heard cursing in a multiplicity of languages.

Lying on his back, Jemunu-jah struggled to bring the gun up and around for a second shot. His right arm had become entangled in some chest straps that had come flying up toward his face when he'd tripped. The maccaluca was very close now. The fully agape mouth was lined with a thousand needlelike finger-length teeth designed to clamp down and not let go. Rain, usually a familiar friend to the Sakuntala, was in his eyes.

Something half as big around as their now submerged skim-mer erupted from the water on his left to clamp triple jaws around the body of the maccaluca. Jointed clawed legs waved wildly and the predator screamed, a high-pitched howl that was almost a hiss. Its limbless attacker slid straight back into the water from which it had exploded, dragging the luckless mac-caluca down with it. In their wake, water boiled and bubbled for a moment or two. Then all was silent once more.

The querulous peeps and edgy screeches of the Viisiiviisii re-sumed, in vivo counterpart to the continuous rain.

Still holding one of his two pistols, Hasa had moved to stand close to Jemunu-jah. He did not offer the taller Sakuntala a hand up. Reaching over his head, Jemunu-jah grasped a small branch with both hands and pulled himself erect. Together they stared at the place where the maccaluca had been sucked down.

"That's a new one on me." The human spoke as if he had just been presented with a holiday greeting vit. "The maccaluca I recognize. What was the thing that got it?"

"Vuniwai. Only third one I ever seen myself. They not common."

The prospector spit anew, this time into the water. "Glad to hear it." He turned. "If I had a hundred credits for every nar-row call I've had in my life, I'd be retired now."

Jemunu-jah took a step in the human's wake, then halted.

His sharp eyes searched the surrounding varzea. "Wait. Where is the Deyzara?"

Hasa halted, his brow creasing. "You're right. Two-trunks has up and gone missing. Did the macca get him?"

"I don't think so. If it did, I not see it." Bending, he began to scan the water. When he finally straightened, it was to pick a spherical bowai fruit from its supportive basket of glasslike fronds and toss it into the shadowed surface.

It landed next to what appeared to be a particularly robust pink stick. The stick promptly surfaced, followed by the thoroughly waterlogged Deyzara. Having rolled into the water to escape the maccaluca's attack, Masurathoo had remained there completely submerged, breathing through his trunk.

The Deyzara was trying to look in every direction at once as he swam back to the semisubmerged branch where his two companions waited. "Is it gone?"

"Yeah, it's gone." Hasa's eyes suddenly widened. Crouching, he reached for his side arm. "There's another—right behind you!"

Letting out a hysterical hoot, Masurathoo spun wildly, kicking up water in every direction. When he finally calmed down some, he saw there was nothing behind him but a small taleki making its brightly patterned ponderous way across a supportive line of dink molds. Chortling loudly, the human turned away and strode back to the gap he had been contemplating crossing moments earlier. Suffering from a momentary surge of compassion, Jemunu-jah reached down to help the saturated two-trunks back up onto the branch. Every one of the six fingers on his left hand was needed to keep his grasp from slipping.

"Why did Hasa he say there was maccaluca there?" he wondered aloud.

Masurathoo started to run part of his wrappings through two strong digits to strain water from the fabric. Abruptly aware of the futility of trying to do so while standing in the midst of rain that hardly ever ceased, he gave up and let the limp material fall from his hand. It slapped wet and heavy against his leg.

"Some humans, if the wretched truth must be told, find the most extraordinary things a source of great personal amusement. Not excluding inducing terror in others."

Both turned to regard their muscular, insular companion as he easily jumped the watery gap. Despite Masurathoo's silent wish, the vuniwai did not erupt from the water a second time to swallow the Deyzara's tormentor. Sputtering water from both trunks, he resignedly started to follow.

Later, once they had climbed to a comparatively safe height above the water, Jemunu-jah murmured softly to the miserable Masurathoo, "If it of any kind solace, know that I not find human's action funny, either."

The Deyzara turned goggle eyes on his much taller, leaner companion. "It is most considerate of you to say this thing." Water spilled in tiny cascades from the wide brim of his rain hat. "I most assuredly *did* see movement in the water. Perhaps the next time neither of you will be in quite such a rush to enjoy laughter at my expense."

Jemunu-jah dipped his head and ears slightly in the Deyzara's direction. "Perhaps," he admitted.

But that won't keep us from laughing at the sorry sight of you, he mused as he followed the soggy lump of pink flesh deeper into the trees.

Their first night away from the shelter of the skimmers was terrifying to Masurathoo. A highly educated administrator and executive, he had spent all his life in the developed towns of Fluva. In his mind and those of his fellow managers, *camping out* and *going to hell* had interchangeable meanings.

At least, he reflected as he sat in the supportive crook of several large branches some five meters above the water, he was traveling in the company of two tough individuals. They were used to surviving such conditions (even, he reminded himself with a certain degree of satisfaction, if they were incapable of

recognizing the potential danger to be found in a pool of unnaturally disturbed water). All he had to do was remain in one
piece, keep up with the pace they set, stay between them, and
he would get out of this with both trunks intact.

Anyway, that was what he kept telling himself, over and over.

A truly deafening cacophony of mewlings, howls, roars,
peeps, twitters, hisses, and scratching sounds filled the air when
the exhausted clouds finally cleared for a while. Able at last to
slip out of his rain gear for a few hours, Hasa carefully laid his
attire over smaller branches in the hope it would dry out a little. The human, however, did not stop there but continued dis-
robing until he was completely naked. Squatting down, he set
out a small emergency light and began eating his evening rations. In a wishful dream, the light would be seen by any skimmers or aircraft that happened to pass overhead.

Unaccustomed to the sight of an unclothed human, Sakuntala and Deyzara contemplated their naked companion. Hasa
was completely oblivious to their stares. He would have reacted
exactly the same had he been traveling with a dozen of his own
kind. In the Viisiiviisii, any inhibitions vanished as rapidly as did
clean clothing.

After a moment's hesitation, Masurathoo removed what remained of his own brilliantly colored but badly tattered attire
and laid it out as neatly as he could manage over the same welcoming branch, alongside the human's garments. Jemunu-jah
observed this procedure in silence. His own strappings were as
comfortable wet as dry and were designed to reflect his status
and wealth rather than enclose his body. Of course, he had his
fur to keep him comfortable in the constant rain and damp.
Deyzara and, with spotty exceptions, humans had no such natural protection and were forced to make do with bulky, binding
coverings of artificial fabric. He felt sorry for both of them.

"You would like your garments to be dry," he stated
thoughtfully.

The naked, muscular human glanced up at him. "Damn
right I would. Kind of an impossibility, though, out in the Vii-

siiviisii. Even if your rain gear stays fully charged and keeps the rain off you, your clothes get soaked with sweat while you're working or walking. Either way, a man ends up sopping wet by the end of the day."

"Would you like have them dry for little while, anyway?"

Pale blue eyes narrowed. "What is this—Sakuntala humor?" Holding a half-full cup in one hand, Hasa gestured with the other. "You can't make a fire out here. Nothing'll burn. And I'll be damned if I'll use up the charge in my cutter to dry my underwear."

"True so. But can find heat."

He disappeared into the tangle of branches and vines. An apprehensive Masurathoo watched him depart. "Whatever he is thinking of, is it wise to go looking for it? The darkness conceals many dangers."

"Shut up, two-trunks." Hasa's expression was as sour as his tone. "Something I've always wondered. If a Deyzara presses the end of his breathing trunk against his eating trunk, can he snort food out of his own stomach?"

Masurathoo's own eating trunk recoiled at the image that was raised by the human's words. This Hasa was by an order of magnitude the most unpleasant example of his species Masurathoo had ever encountered. Brutish, uncouth, racist, devoted only to his own well-being, he was not the sort one would want to encounter at a party or official function. How well such characteristics were suited to survival remained to be seen.

To Masurathoo's very great surprise, he gave vent to what he was feeling. It was most atypical of him, and he was startled by his own audacity.

"I—I don't like you, sir. Not even a little bit."

Hasa looked up over his cup. Though promulgated by such small eyes, Masurathoo noted, an unbroken human stare could be exceedingly unnerving.

Tossing aside the remnants of his coffee, Hasa laughed loudly, indifferent to whatever menacing creatures lurked nearby that his voice might alert.

"Well, I'll be damned! Somebody once told me a few of you baby-butt skinned shopkeepers had guts. I didn't believe 'em. Glad to be corrected." He indicated the side arm that lay among the Deyzara's clothes. "Maybe you'll get a chance to use that. I'd like to think that the next time some purple-pussed fiend drops out of the trees on top of us, you'd be able to save my ass for a change."

It took Masurathoo a moment to classify the colloquialism. "I would think, sir, you would have a greater care for your brain."

For some unknown reason, this set the human to laughing again, much harder this time.

Hasa had settled down by the time Jemunu-jah returned. In his long, thin arms the Sakuntala carried more than a dozen sausage-sized lumps of dark blue flesh. Tiny cilialike feet allowed them to creep slowly over and around one another, forcing the Sakuntala to continuously turn back one creature after another lest it crawl out of his arms. Dozens of what appeared to be glass tubes protruded from their backs.

Carefully he set them down underneath the branch that held the two sets of clothing, human and Deyzara.

Pivoting carefully on his naked backside, an uncertain Hasa eyed the result of the Sakuntala's hunting. "Look like oversize millipedes. Are they good to eat?"

"Nawenaa might be tasty, but too dangerous to try to eat one." Jemunu-jah settled down on his knees next to his slow-moving menagerie, his body straps flapping around him.

"What are they?" Masurathoo had never seen anything quite like the lumpy, seemingly helpless creatures. "Poisonous? Or do those silicaceous growths on their dorsal sides break off and shatter inside a predator's mouth?"

"No, not poisonous. And not break off. Watch."

As Hasa and Masurathoo looked on, Jemunu-jah took a clawed finger and poked one of the slow-moving organisms in its side hard enough to draw blood. Letting out a barely audible keening, it immediately curled up into a ball, exposing to the watching world only the glassy spines on its back. Hearing their companion's cry, the others did likewise. While human and Deyzara watched, the spines began to glow. Yellow at first, then a deep red-orange.

"Nawenaa can produce chemical reactions in their bodies that generate heat. This rises up into and warms the spines on their backs." He smiled at his companions. "Hungry predator that bites nawenaa ends up with burned mouth." Reaching down, he carefully prodded another of the creatures. The glow on its back intensified.

Even from where he was sitting, Hasa could feel the concentrated blast of heat. He nodded in the direction of the unexpected exhibition of biothermics. "That's why I'm here," he observed. "This place is full of interesting, and potentially profitable, life-forms. Growing things are more my line, though. Especially macromycetes." Rubbing his chin, he eyed the Sakuntala sagely. "Long as we're traveling together, maybe you could point out to me one or two rare growths that have unique properties? I'd share any ensuing profit with you, of course."

"Of course you would." Jemunu-jah's tone was impossible to interpret. "I might be able to find you interesting fungus, or flower. But I only do such a thing for someone who helps me."

Rising, Hasa moved to check his clothes. Bathed in the warming heat from the agitated nawenaa, they were indeed drying out. "Hey, we're all in this together. Got to help one another or we're not likely to make it out alive, right? You can count on my help, Jemunu-jah." His smile widened. "As sure as my name's Shadrach Hasselemoga."

"I have no way of verifying that," the Sakuntala replied dryly enough to earn a commendation from a Deyzara solicitor. "Will settle for now for you being a little nicer. No more insults." Seeing the appallingly naked Deyzara staring at him, he added, "To either of us."

The human glanced from one alien to the other. "All right, it's a deal. The help I can promise. No insults—hey, we are who we are. But I'll work on it. How's that?"

"Enough for now." The Sakuntala poked a nawenaa that was trying to crawl away back into the pile. "Another hour, you have dry clothes, I think."

Jemunu-jah was as good as his word. Compliments spilled from both human and Deyzara the following morning as, for the first time since they had been forced down in the Viisiiviisii, they were able to don their respective rain gear over dry clothing. The gear kept the rain that began to fall with first light away from their attire.

By evening, as Hasa had observed the night before, both human and Deyzara were once again soaked with perspiration. This time, Jemunu-jah could only comment on their sodden clothing with a hum of compassion. Not for the first time, he was intensely puzzled by the fact that among all the advanced intelligent species he had encountered personally—human, Deyzara, and thranx—only the Sakuntala possessed a proper covering of fur. No doubt, he told himself, it had something to do with the rains of Fluva. An evolutionary adaptation, he had read. Quite possibly there was a direct link between inherent native intelligence and hairlessness.

He chose not to ponder any further ramifications.

9

The following day offered a rare mid-morning break in the rain. A good time to pause, rest, and eat, since sunlight was the time of the hunters. Freed from the need to see through mist and rainfall, predators scrambled to gorge themselves on prey exposed to the light. In the brief period of open air and bright illumination, an orgy of consumption ensued. Carnivores large and small seized the opportunity to seek out and hunt down those who relied for cover on the otherwise omnipresent rain.

It was also a time of riotous propagation. Swelling visibly beneath the stimulus of the rarely seen sun, millions of basidiocarps burst, sending forth trillions of spores. Settling on branches and leaves, these formed hyphae that reproduced in situ to create new growths, new mycelium.

Other plants exploded in billows of fertilized seeds, while some growths reproduced in ways new to Commonwealth science. Jemunu-jah could give names to these without entirely understanding the processes involved. It was as if the life of the Viisiiviisii, quiescent and huddled in dark places during the persistent rain, momentarily set aside all its caution in a frenzy of reproductive enthusiasm. The same activity took place during the brief dry season, but in a more measured and stately manner. All around them, Hasa reflected, Nature was shooting up on sunshine. He marveled at the outburst of life force, searching it for profit.

They hunkered down in half a split branch and waited for the pandemonium of life to subside. As they sat quietly, it was possible to watch all manner of carnivores, plant and animal alike, busy at the business of catching and consuming prey. It was also important to keep fruiting bodies and certain wind-blown seedlings from taking root on one's clothing and skin. Certain prolific rusts and opportunistic fungi were capable of establishing themselves within minutes of making contact. Hasa had always had trouble with wax accumulating in his ears. That was problem enough. He did not want to dig in one morning and find something blossoming there.

They looked out for one another. Not because they wanted to, not because friendship had suddenly bloomed among them, but because if they weren't careful and alert, other things might. So Hasa brushed red dust that was actually emukawa hyphae from Masurathoo's sloping shoulders, Jemunu-jah picked needle-rooted bohlaka seedlings from Hasa's bald pate before they could take root, and Masurathoo delicately and somewhat tentatively groomed the fur on the Sakuntala's back in search of arthropoidal flyers who sought to lay their eggs therein. For once, Jemunu-jah saw an advantage in not sporting fur. It was impossible for a bug to hide itself and its parasitic intentions on the Deyzara's or the human's bare skin. The natural oils in Jemunu-jah's fur gave him some protection from the vermin that during the dry season and these isolated episodes of sunshine would otherwise try to set up housekeeping for their offspring inside his body.

It was tempting, particularly for Hasa and Masurathoo, to keep moving while the sun was shining. Every time they considered doing so, something within range of their sight or hearing died or screamed. It was as if the Viisiiviisii had gone momentarily mad, as if the clock of life had suddenly decided to run forward at triple speed. Step out of their place of shelter and concealment and there was no telling how many or what kind of lurking killers might leap upon them.

Not all were leapers or flyers. As the morning wore on and the clouds finally began to gather themselves once more, the sharp-eyed Jemunu-jah pointed to a branch in the tree opposite theirs. The branch hung low over the water, but not so low that they wouldn't have passed close to it while resuming their way northeastward.

"Tawalakuikin," he murmured.

When Masurathoo couldn't get his speaking trunk around the word, Hasa supplied the simpler terranglo equivalent. "That one's been classified. Called a darter."

"Why?" Masurathoo was as unfamiliar with the creature as he was with its name.

Hasa's expression was as flat as ever. Sunlight was dimming as dark cumulus continued to coagulate above the treetops. If the predator in question was going to make a last move before the rain resumed, it would have to strike soon.

"Watch."

In appearance, the darter was neither attractive nor intimidating. Its long, low, flat body lay draped over the branch on which it reposed. Carpeted in stubby brown bristles, its neckless torso and short, thick legs looked barely capable of moving it forward. Each of the half-dozen legs terminated in a single curved hoof or claw that was designed to grip wood rather than prey. No fangs hung from the upper lip of the pointed snout; no stinger protruded from the stunted, useless tail. But the four jet-black eyes arrayed across the front of the head were alert and glistening, and the narrow, forward-pointing ears reminded Masurathoo of Jemunu-jah's. More than anything else, the darter looked like a sharp-eyed rug.

A pod of pekawa put in an appearance on the water. Pale, fat, and lightly feathered, they were more buoyant than they looked. A flotilla of tiny pink eyes encircled the head that jutted straight up from the plump central body, giving each individual a full and

constant 360-degree range of vision. Its four finned feet could
send a pekawa shooting rapidly away in any direction. Where a
duck would have glided across the surface of the water, the
pekawa advanced in short sprints, scooting from cover to cover,
never lingering too long in any one spot. With their eating apparatus located on the undersides of their bodies, they never had to
dip their heads below the surface to feed. This allowed them to
dine while keeping continuous watch for potential predators.

Masurathoo tensed. Positioned above the active, always moving pod, an ordinary predator might have flexed its muscles or
claws. Not the darter. Instead, it slowly and quietly began to
swell.

It was several times its original size and no longer flat when
something shot silently from its pointed proboscis. Hasa was put
in mind of the tongue of a frog or chameleon. But what fired from
the darter's muzzle was tipped not with glue but with spikes.

They struck one of the mature pekawa right where the neck
met its bulbous body. Trying to escape, the pekawa jerked violently several times while the rest of the pod scattered. The
spikes held fast. Within less than a minute, the unfortunate
creature lay quivering on the surface of the water. Attracted by
the commotion, other disturbances appeared, moving toward
it. Before the curious submerged carnivores could investigate
the dead pekawa, the darter was reeling in its catch. Masurathoo and his companions watched as the arboreal predator
began to suck up its prey through its versatile expanded snout.

Hasa enlightened the Deyzara where he was resting: "Those
spikes contain a powerful poison that dissolves as well as kills.
They're propelled by air the darter sucks in and uses strong
bands of abdominal muscle to expel. It doesn't have any teeth
because it doesn't need them. It doesn't move fast because it
doesn't have to. It'll make a leisurely meal of the pekawa's insides as they liquefy." He rose. "You could walk right up to it
now and give it a pat and it would ignore you. It'll certainly ignore us as we pass."

Though the human was true to his word and both he and

Jemunu-jah passed less than an arm's length from the quietly feeding predator, Masurathoo still gave it as wide a berth as the surrounding vegetation would allow. The darter was an unlovely sight, but not as gruesome as the slowly liquefying remains of the pekawa. Masurathoo's mind conjured up an unwanted image of himself similarly darted and dissolving, his muscles and organs sickeningly subsiding into an easily ingestible lump of red ooze while he was still alive, his—

He forced himself to concentrate on the path ahead, aware more than ever how much he was compelled to rely on his companions to warn him of or protect him from such barely detectable dangers. Every rustle of leaves, every whisper of tiny legs tiptoeing across protruding shelf fungi, every still of mold, portended in his mind something horrific, indescribable, and lethal. How he longed for his clean, antiseptic office back in Taulau! If his friends and family could see him now, they would simultaneously hoot at his bedraggled appearance and bemoan his unhygienic surroundings.

Self-pity, he knew, would not get him out of the Viisiiviisii. It slew the sympathetic as callously as the exploiter. Momentarily absorbed in such thoughts and temporarily distracted as rain began to fall again, he nearly tripped over the slow-moving creature that had emerged in front of him.

His startled whoop turned Hasa right around and brought Jemunu-jah up fast from behind. When they saw what had sent Masurathoo fearfully toppling backward into the brush, they exchanged a laugh. Or at least, Jemunu-jah laughed, in the manner of his people. The human's corresponding loud verbalization suggested contempt as much as amusement.

"A sevasalu," Jemunu-jah explained. He did not offer the fallen Deyzara a hand up.

As he struggled back to his feet, Masurathoo saw that if he had landed only a little more to the left, he would have missed the cushioning cluster of parasitic plants that had broken his fall, and plunged right through to the water below. Remembering the triple-jawed vuniwai, he shuddered.

Ears rotating back and forth in a sign of exasperation, Jemunu-jah sighed softly. "Sevasalu not dangerous. Interesting, yes, but not dangerous."

Taking a couple of tentative steps toward the beast that was making its careful, languid way into the denser foliage, Masurathoo made an effort to see what was so interesting about the animal. When he finally screwed up sufficient courage to move near enough, he needed no further explanation from Jemunu-jah or Hasa.

Advancing slowly on four short legs equipped with inward-facing gripping toes, the sevasalu carried its head low, swinging it deliberately back and forth as it grazed on the fungi that sprouted profusely from many branches. Prehensile lips enabled it to pluck the choicest pieces from holes and cracks in the wood. Heavy-lidded eyes with doubled pupils added to the appearance of a creature that existed in a perpetual state of near-somnambulence. Instead of fur, it was covered with small green scutes. This armor provided a certain amount of protection from roving predators. What really kept it safe, Jemunu-jah pointed out, was the taste of its flesh. Impregnated with alkaloids, it was exceedingly bitter.

From the base of its neck the sevasalu's spine split in two, one backbone running down each side of its body. Between the two was a deep swaybacked depression filled with rainwater. Within this mobile pool dwelled small plants, whirling arthropods, tiny vertebrates, and the occasional larger amphibious predator. There were even a few fruiting fungi whose free-floating mycelium drew nutrients from the decaying bodies of dead creatures and other detritus that sank to the bottom of the sevasalu's deeply swayed back. As a by-product of feeding, the mycelium excreted certain strong alkaloids. Absorbed into the sevasalu's body, these were what gave its flesh the unpalatable taste that caused wandering predators to avoid it.

The sevasalu carried on its back a miniature self-contained ecosystem.

Setting aside for the moment all fear of his surroundings, a thoroughly entranced Masurathoo followed the sevasalu as it made its deliberate, lazy way down a branch running parallel to theirs. So absorbed was he in investigating this new, motile zoological wonder that he threatened to fall behind his guide. Seeing that the human was steadily expanding the distance between them, Jemunu-jah did his best to chivy the Deyzara forward.

"We will see more," he told Masurathoo. "Hurry up."

Reluctant to take his leave of the most fascinating creature he had yet encountered in the Viisiiviisii, Masurathoo nevertheless forced his attention away from the indifferent sevasalu and back to the trail-breaking Hasa.

"Most marvelous, I think!" Carrying a world on its back, the sevasalu was quickly swallowed up by the dense vegetation and the intensifying rain. "What happens if it falls, or trips and turns over?"

"The sevasalu is very surefooted," the Sakuntala assured him.

Hasa commented without turning as he pushed relentlessly forward, "Same thing that happens if a planet turns over. Everything living on it dies."

Bending one flexible ear across his head, Jemunu-jah used the pointed tip to scratch the back of the other one. "A sevasalu that loses its world will go down into water to fill it back up again. Not with water. Rain does that. But with population of small things. Then it must find right kind of fungi in trees. Rub against bulbs, get spores to grow in water on back. Start new little world."

"Speaking of going down into the water . . ." Hasa's voice trailed off.

One hand firmly gripping a liana for support, the human had stopped and was staring at something. Droplets coursed off the top of his rain cape and ran down its transparent back. Catching up to him, Jemunu-jah and Masurathoo soon saw what had brought the seemingly indefatigable Hasa to a halt.

The Viisiiviisii was a labyrinth of merging rivers. They had finally come to one too wide for branches and vines to span.

"What now, sirs?" Masurathoo eyed the turgid, slow-moving waterway uneasily. "It is time for everyone to put their engineering skills to the test and construct a temporary craft to use in crossing, yes?"

"No." Hasa eyed the Deyzara querulously. "You people are good swimmers. So are the Sakis." He indicated the river. "Current here is practically nonexistent. With a village maybe another couple of days' trek from here, I'll be damned if I'm gonna sit around and try to bang out a boat."

Masurathoo touched the pistol slung at his hip. "I must say, with the three of us working together I do not think it would be too very difficult to burn out the interior of a log and fashion a crude but serviceable dugout."

"Why don't you try digging out some sense?"

While the human slipped out of his rain cape and began to fold and pack it for carrying, Jemunu-jah commenced an examination of his own gear to ensure that all was secure. He did not bother to check whether any of it was capable of withstanding the proposed crossing. He didn't need to. The first prerequisite of anything imported for use outside a building on Fluva was that it had to be waterproof.

Masurathoo watched these preparations with increasing apprehension. "Surely, my friends, you are not suggesting that we swim across this potentially deadly watercourse?"

"Nope." Hasa efficiently stowed his folded rain cape in a storage pouch at his belt. "We're not suggesting. We're doing." He looked back at the reluctant Deyzara. "Same rules apply as always. Come with us or stay here." The by now familiar humorless smile returned. "I'm sure you can make yourself a dugout or a raft or something in a few days." He glanced up into the trees. "Plenty of building material to work with. So long as you don't become something's lunch in the meantime." Having expended himself of that less than useful advice, he started down, using branches and vines to descend toward the waterway. Disdaining the vines, Jemunu-jah simply used his long arms to lower himself from one branch to the next.

Once again, Masurathoo was faced with the decision to follow or stay behind. And as before, he had no choice. He tried to steel himself. What was he so afraid of? So long as he kept the human in front of him and the Sakuntala behind, he was screened from any attack. Unless, he reminded himself, it came at him from either side. Or from below.

Stop this, he told himself. You are as competent as either of these two vulgarians and more intelligent than either. Use that intelligence, and a little common sense, and you will soon find yourself safely on the other side. Besides, the human was right. The Deyzara *were* good swimmers. And thanks to the design of his respiratory apparatus, he could submerge completely and still breathe, while a human or Sakuntala would soon drown. *He* was the one with the natural advantages.

Starting downward, he began to hyperventilate. Not out of nervousness but to charge his lungs with extra oxygen. In the water, his boneless legs and arms would allow him to move more agilely than his muscular but stiff-jointed companions. In his mind's eye he saw himself swimming circles around both. But only in his mind's eye. Once in the water, he intended to travel only one way, and that was in a straight line toward the opposite shore.

No, not shore, he corrected himself. The shore in the Vii-siiviisii was far beneath his feet, where the trees of the forest took root in the submerged soil of sodden Fluva. No one would see any "shore" hereabouts for another half year yet.

Hasa was already in the river, his arms moving from front to side as he treaded water. Jemunu-jah was slipping in alongside him. Masurathoo soon joined them.

"Ready?" Hasa eyed the Deyzara dubiously. "Once we start out, we stay together and move fast. Falling behind's not a good idea."

From the depths of new assurance Masurathoo stared back at the human out of damp, protruding eyes. "If you are of a mind, sir, I will race you."

Hasa hesitated, then responded with a tight smirk, "Maybe you *will* make it out of here without becoming flacc food." He turned serious. "No racing. No wasted motion. No flailing around, no splashing. Slow, steady kicks only. I was right about the current: there isn't any." He turned to Jemunu-jah. "Ready?"

The Sakuntala's ears were aimed out to the sides, listening intently for any untoward noise or the sound of something large entering the water. "Floating wastes time. Talking wastes time."

Responding with a terse, somber nod, Hasa turned and struck out across the open water.

This wasn't so bad, Masurathoo found himself musing when they were halfway across. The rain was not coming down hard enough to obstruct their vision, nothing armed with tooth or fang appeared to challenge their transit, and the enveloping water was warm against his hairless body. Supported by anywhere from three to a dozen thin-skinned floats apiece, platforms of dark blue, pale red, and yellow fungi drifted past like so many electrified flowers. So brilliant were their colors and patterns that they seemed to mimic iridescence electric even in the rain.

Something small and bright sprang from one miniature mushroom barge to another. Its action was soon being imitated by more and more of the finger-sized creatures. Each had a single powerful leg protruding from the middle of its underside and a single eye on top. In between was a cylindrical body lined with bioluminescent spots that flashed every color of the rainbow. Springing between gaudy floating fungi, the brilliantly adorned creatures looked like dancing jewels.

Marveling at the glittering miniature ballet, Masurathoo found that he was approaching the far side of the river faster than ever and seemingly with greater ease. With each contraction, his muscles were growing used to the effort. Only when he tried to linger to examine a particularly radiant cluster of fungi and its shimmering, energetically hopping passengers did he realize he was moving toward the looming forest wall *without* making any effort.

"Giimatasa!" Jemunu-jah was yelling. Masurathoo did not know what a giimatasa was. He did know that Jemunu-jah did not shout unless the Sakuntala had good reason for doing so. In the Viisiiviisii, that reason was not likely to be benign.

Flexing hard, Masurathoo tried to change course, found himself unable to do so. Something was dragging him and his companions south of their course, in the direction of a dark coiled mass of tree that loomed out over the river. Searching as he swam, he sought evidence of something inimical hiding in the tree, saw only a few small pius—tiny brown-and-blue winged creatures that were little more than balls of fluff composed of wiry, rain-shedding feathers. Further examination showed that the tree itself was nothing more than what it appeared to be and not some monstrous lurking predator in woody disguise.

Nothing had latched onto his body. No tentacles or ropy limbs swathed his legs or torso. No claws or jaws had snapped shut on his arms or neck. In the absence of visible or tactile interference it was impossible to tell what was pulling him toward the tree. Then it occurred to him that it was the water itself that was dragging him southward downriver.

Fighting hard, Hasa soon curved around to face him. Then the human seemed to be behind him, with Jemunu-jah to the north. Masurathoo felt himself moving faster and faster. In addition to the physical discomfort and bewilderment he was feeling, he found himself growing dizzy. Then he looked down and saw the giimatasa.

Or rather, part of it. Only the open maw was visible, inky dark and menacing. That and the large swiftly stirring fins that were generating the artificial whirlpool that was sucking them down toward the riverbed. It was shallow here, close to the shore beneath the shadowing tree. Shallow and a bit of a back-water. This made it easy for the giimatasa to spawn its prey-snatching vortex. Having detected the three bodies swimming in its general direction, the creature had set in motion a singular feeding behavior that threatened to draw all three of the travelers into the waiting mouth below. Even as he was being sucked downward toward a horrifying death, Masurathoo found himself wondering by what astounding physiological mechanism the giimatasa managed to take in and simultaneously expel such vast quantities of water.

Recognizing the danger, the human had finally ceased trying to swim clear of the inexorable eddy and had drawn his side arm. Jemunu-jah did likewise, but his shot went astray. It was hard to keep one's head out of the water, battle the drag, and aim at the same time. Fumbling with his own weapon, Masurathoo had to struggle just to hang on to it. When his head was pulled underwater, it was hard to know which way to thrust his breathing trunk.

With his feet scraping whirling fins and the outer edges of the gaping oral cavity, Hasa fired repeatedly downward. Though the water absorbed much of the energy from the explosive shells, enough penetrated to discourage, if not kill, the giimatasa. The finning slowed, the mouth closed, and the whirlpool buckled. They were free again, but underwater.

Moments later, one head after another broke the surface of the river. Without waiting to see if his companions were all right, Jemunu-jah struck out for the near shore. The great tree that had seemed so ominous now extended welcoming branches down into the water, providing convenient handholds for him to pull himself up and out. Relieved but worn out, the Sakuntala helped the exhausted Masurathoo drag himself up onto the branch on which his taller companion was sitting. Together, they contemplated the section of river from which they had narrowly escaped.

Jemunu-jah's sharp eyes scanned the surface, shifted quickly to the surrounding undergrowth. "Where is the human?"

Rolling onto his side, Masurathoo studied the river with bulging eyes. "I most greatly fear that I do not see any sign of him."

As Jemunu-jah was considering whether to slip back into the water to search for their companion, Hasa's head broke the surface. Sputtering and cursing, he spotted them sitting on the low-lying branch. A few kicks and he had rejoined them.

"What happened?" Jemunu-jah studied the human, shorter but so much broader of torso and thicker of limb than himself. "Did giimatasa try a second time to drag you down?"

"Hell no." Sitting in the light but steady rain, Hasa removed his rain cape from its pouch, unfolded it, and slipped it over his head and body. A flick of the activation control showed that it still retained more than half its original charge. The cape's electrostatic field repelled water, keeping the falling drops a fraction of a centimeter away from the actual material. When the field was on, the transparent fabric was always dry to the touch.

"After the whirlpool collapsed, I went back down to try to kill the sumbitch. You can see it pretty clearly when it's not generating a killing vortex. Looks like a big, fat olive green lump half buried in the bottom muck. Nothing much shows but the mouth and all those fins it uses to create a whirlpool. I didn't see any eyes." He wiped river water from his face. "Probably detects potential prey by sensing pressure changes in the water." Squinting into the rain, he glanced upward. "Locating in a calm place under something like this big overhanging tree makes sense. The water's easier to eddy and the tree's shade helps conceal it from unsuspecting victims." His gaze returned to the river. "And other predators."

Jemunu-jah indicated agreement. "One of first things Sakuntala parent teaches cublings is where is safe to swim and where is not." A long, slender arm reached out toward the water. "I not know this place, so not able to predict what might lie in wait here."

"That's the Viisiiviisii for you." Hasa seemed none the worse for their near-death encounter. "Chock-full of lies. The big clawed meat eater that crosses your path isn't hungry, but the water is." He rose from where he was seated. "Squatting here philosophizing ain't bringing us any closer to that village."

"Please." Having risen to a sitting position, Masurathoo discovered that was as far as his weary body was willing to take him. "I am afraid I must impose upon you both for a brief respite. I have to rest." When neither of his companions responded, he waved a double-digited hand. "If you must go on, then do so. At the moment, the Grand Nasuth himself could not stir me from this spot."

Hasa deliberated. "Maybe the Grand Nasuth couldn't, but I bet if I pushed you back into the river you'd get moving quick enough."

Masurathoo fluttered both trunks. Emerging from his speaking trunk, his voice sounded like it was still underwater. "I would only commence a slow floating downstream. My strength is fled. I *must* rest."

Espying a comfortable cluster of soft-stemmed seglet basidiocarps, Jemunu-jah sat down in the middle of the chubby, bulging fungi. A number of the taut fruiting bodies burst beneath the weight of his angular backside. Instantly knocked down and washed away by the rain, the prematurely released spores were condemned not to reproduce but only to serve as food for hungry scavengers.

"It do no harm to camp ahead of schedule for a change. Fight against giimatasa has made me hungry early."

" 'Hungry early,' eh?" Hasa did not move to join them. "Sounds like an itinerant musician." He indicated the water that was flowing slowly past in front of them. "Camping by a river's not a real good idea. While it's full of good things to eat, it's also full of things that want to eat you."

"Ordinarily I agree with you." Jemunu-jah was setting out his gear. "But this place of water is safe because giimatasa is here. Its presence keeps other meat eaters away."

Masurathoo eyed the turgid flow uncertainly. "Then I am

correct in assuming it will not bother us up here, on these branches?"

Utterly at home in the varzea, Jemunu-jah leaned back against the convenient stalk of an emerald-striped mushroom that was nearly as tall as he was. "Giimatasa kills with whirlpool. Has no arms, nothing else with which to fight. Not like darter or casoko. Or nougusm," he finished with a wary look.

Confronted with one fellow traveler who was completely exhausted and another evidently preparing to spend the night, a dissatisfied but resigned Hasa found himself a suitable resting place slightly higher, where several intertwining branches formed a constricted but adequate sleeping platform. He chose to remain with his companions not because he felt uncomfortable about forging ahead or traveling by himself, but because he was prudent enough to know that in a place like the Viisii-viisii it was useful to have someone always watching your back.

Even if that someone was a skinny sumbitch like an overeducated, know-it-all Sakuntala or a goggle-eyed, malodorous wimp of a Deyzara.

10

Expecting chaos, Lauren Matthias was not disappointed. Having been almost completely taken over by the several departments responsible for local affairs, the skimmer port had been transformed into the largest refugee camp on Fluva. Thousands of displaced Deyzara crowded onto the main liftoff platforms, spilled over onto walkways and service chutes.

Supported by deep-driven pylons, the central portion of the port was as sturdy as anything ground-based could be on Fluva. But the ancillary facilities, like most of the structures added later by the Commonwealth, were underpinned or hanging from cables of strilk. The strands wouldn't break, she knew, but the same could not be said for the trees or smaller pylons to which the glistening lines were attached. As she was escorted toward the port's administrative offices, she saw at least two seriously stressed spinner crews working nonstop to reinforce dangerously overloaded lines.

"I'll come with you, if you want," Jack had told her that morning. Smiling, he'd added, "If only so that you'll have someone around you can talk to without having to worry about their individual or cultural political agenda. No one's getting much work done at the lab these last few days anyway."

She'd seriously considered taking him up on the offer, before finally turning him down. "Thanks, sweetie, but it wouldn't look good. People on staff as well as independents and natives would start wondering if maybe you had some influence over Commonwealth policy."

"Don't I?" He'd punctuated the comment with a playful kiss.

She had to smile back. "Of course you do." She put a finger to his lips. "But don't tell anybody—it's a Church secret between me and the Last Resort."

"You're the Last Resort here," he'd reminded her.

That was the thought she carried with her now. Even by Commonwealth standards, Fluva was a long way from the government and Church nerve centers on Earth and Hivehom. While bureaucrats on both worlds dithered, she was the one on-site. The one faced with issuing life-or-death edicts. The one responsible not only for her own people but, to a lesser extent, for the Deyzara and the Sakuntala as well.

She didn't want it. What she liked was the routine, the sane, and the predictable. Signing off on directives that came from her superiors, implementing modest improvements, and facilitating the humdrum. Instead, she was faced with a refugee crisis not of her own making and an escalating interspecies war. She would have been within her rights to ignore it. Within her rights but not her conscience. Had the situation been reversed and it had been the Sakuntala who were being driven from their homes by the Deyzara, she would have reacted in exactly the same way.

True, the Commonwealth was responsible insofar as it was its shortsighted decision that had allowed the emigration hundreds of years ago from Tharce IV to Fluva. But that had nothing to do with her. She wasn't hundreds of years old. Neither, she reflected, were the Sakuntala who were presently on the rampage, but she knew that argument was useless. It had been tried decades ago and had had no moderating effect on the determined predecessors of the extremists who were behind the current uprising.

The steady caterwauling of Deyzara broodlings overrode the usual forest sounds. The massed squealing did nothing to

discourage the active predators who had gathered in large numbers in the water beneath the port. Occasionally, she had been
told, they would pick off the isolated Deyzara who lost his
footing and fell from a walkway or port structure. Few lingered
to mourn such losses. The collective communal anguish was
too great, too extensive, to allow for much in the way of individual sorrowing.

Deyzara body odor was strong enough to be detected even
through the rain. With so many crowded together so closely,
the stench bordered on the overpowering. Still, she wore no filtering mask over her face. While the need for it would have
been understood by the Deyzara, who were quite aware of their
own fragrance, it would not have been tactful. Striding through
the temporary shelters that had been erected and the thousands
of ropy limbs, writhing trunks, and bulging eyes, she tried to
breathe through her mouth as much as possible.

Falu Bedara was a small man with thick artificial implants in
his eyes that made him look more than a little like a Deyzara
himself. His arms moved continually, as if he were conducting
unseen music, when in reality he was only accompanying his
own agitated oratory. As a result, his rain cape was constantly
hurling repelled water in all directions. Matthias tried to keep
as far from those flailing limbs as courtesy allowed. One thing
she didn't need, one thing no human on Fluva needed, was
more water to be thrown in her face.

Bedara was one of those people who lived inside proscribed
procedures. At this he was expert, and without his hard work
administering such procedures she knew that the bedlam at the
port would have been ten times worse than it was. Consequently, she respected his efforts without feeling any particular
fondness for their supervisor.

". . . another thousand bubbles by the end of the week, at
least," he finished, referring to the lightweight and simple-to-
erect aerogel shelters that had been pressed into service on behalf of the refugees. She had not paid much attention to his
long recitation of needs. The refugee effort was short of every-

thing, and there was no overflowing government warehouse ensconced on any of this system's empty worlds or dead moons capable of providing the desperately needed supplies.

"I'll authorize whatever you deem necessary for the short term," she replied absently.

"That's all very well and good, Administrator Matthias," Bedara huffed, "but given the predicted shortfall between what we have been able to scrounge already and what is likely to remain in the—"

She turned on him sharply. She was shorter than most of her subordinates, and in this instance she was able to take full advantage of the man's modest stature. "I can't give you what we don't have, Falu. You know better than I what's in the storehouses. And despite the desperateness of the situation here, I have to keep in mind the needs of other communities besides Taulau."

He flinched, but only for a moment. "I understand, Administrator. I only want to do my best."

"Nobody else on staff could handle this any better than you are, Falu." There, she thought. That ought to satisfy him, even if she was obviously grading him on a curve that began and ended with him.

It did. "Thank you, Administrator. I assure you I will do my utmost to justify your continuing faith in . . ."

But the administrator had lengthened her stride, and his words were lost in the cacophony of mewling, hooting Deyzara.

Port Administration's offices were a refuge from both the sound and smell of the refugee flood. She embraced it readily, if not gracefully, as she pushed back the hood of her rain cape, striding straight over to Harriman's desk. Looking more than a little disheveled, the younger woman was in no mood for formalities. That was fine with Matthias, who felt similarly. Though engrossed in a tridee projection, Harriman, Matthias noted right away, was carrying a side arm. Stopping in front of the desk, she gestured in its direction and spoke without ceremony.

"Expecting trouble, Nichole?"

"Prepare for every eventuality. That's what the handbooks tell you." The tired blonde smiled wanly. "They just don't prepare you for an eventuality like this."

"I just finally managed to lose Bedara."

"Lucky you." Harriman made a face. "I have to deal with him every day."

"Try to be understanding. He's good at what he does." Matthias indicated the hovering projection. "How are we doing—really?"

"About as well as could be expected. Maybe even a little better." Harriman leaned back in her chair. "Thanks to the bubbles, most of them now have a place to sleep out of the rain. A large number brought food with them, and we've been able to supplement that enough to prevent any hunger, let alone starvation. It helps that the Deyzara eat only soft foods and that those are easier to store and transport, not to mention rehydrate." She summoned up a reluctant smile. "The Commonwealth can be proud of its representatives on Fluva."

"Hang the Commonwealth. We need to settle this soon, before our facilities are overwhelmed. And overwhelmed they will be, if this keeps up."

Murmuring to her desk, Harriman snuffed out the projection and turned to her superior. "How is it in the other towns?"

"Pretty bad. A few better, where moderate, reasonable Sakuntala have been able to intervene." Her expression darkened. "Several worse. There have been some killings."

Harriman nodded somberly. "I've heard. Word gets around. Much more of that and the Deyzara won't wait for us to adjudicate. They'll start finding weapons of their own and fighting back. Then we *will* have a tragedy on our hands." She hesitated. "Well, a bigger tragedy." She gestured toward a window. "A few of these Deyzara can trace their lineage on Fluva back five generations. Some of them have lost everything. They'll be petitioning for redress."

"Let the government on Earth and Hivehom worry about

that," Matthias responded impatiently. "Our job is to try to take care of these people until they can safely return home." She shifted in the chair, the transparent material of the deactivated rain cape crackling beneath her. "Let me see your latest."

Harriman obediently called forth a series of descriptive projections. Viewing them while occasionally asking pointed questions, Matthias was not pleased with either the visuals or the figures. They were as remorseless and unforgiving as Bedara's statistics. The conflict had to be brought to an end, and soon, or the ability of her people to manage the situation was going to fall apart. In the mayhem that would follow a collapse of local Commonwealth authority, deaths on both sides were sure to be numbered in the thousands. Then there was the still small but slowly escalating threat to her own people.

Her attention was briefly diverted by movement she glimpsed out of the corner of her eye. A pair of Sakuntala had entered the administration building. They were young but well dressed, with finely decorated and embossed strappings that served to emphasize their height. One was a Hata-nau, or Low Chief, while his attendant companion was a commoner. It must have taken more than the usual quotient of Sakuntala nerve to make their way here through the teeming mass of Deyzara refugees, she reflected. One of Harriman's subordinates took them in hand.

Assuming they were on some kind of port-related business, she did not give them another thought until she saw them coming closer, picking their way carefully between workstations. Absorbed in their own assignments, staff engaged in manipulating data and projections ignored the two lanky green-and-brown-furred natives. They must have a question for Harriman, she was thinking even as she saw the Hata-nau reaching into one of the larger pouches hanging from his torso strappings. That was not what tipped her off: it was the ears. A strolling Sakuntala's ears were always pointed outward, in opposite directions, to pick up as much ambient sound as possible. They pointed directly toward something only when their owner was engaged in person-to-person conversation, confronted with a threat—or about to pounce on prey.

The two Sakuntala were not talking with anyone, including each other, there was nothing in the room to threaten them, and as for prey . . .

There being nowhere to run and no place to hide, she did the only thing she could. It was also the last thing the Sakuntala expected. Rising abruptly from her chair, she extended her arms, lowered her head, and charged straight at the oncoming native. She hit the startled visitor low while he was still trying to take aim with the pistol he had pulled from his pouch. It was brand-new, still gleaming with the pride of its thranx manufacturers.

Though eager to make use of it, the Hata-nau was not entirely familiar with the lethal device. By the time he had succeeded in slipping one of his six fingers around the trigger, he was down on the floor with his would-be victim on top of him, flailing madly at his face. While the Sakuntala were possessed of considerable lean strength, the willowy build that made them so agile in the forest also left them vulnerable to a straight-ahead attack by a stockier opponent. Though she would have been loath to admit it, Matthias weighed more than her prospective assassin.

Before he could throw her off or bring his weapon to bear, half a dozen alerted workers were on top of him. A sizzling sound terminated the shouts of the Hata-nau's companion. Breathing hard and brushing back hair as she rose, she saw one of the other office workers looming over the body of the other Sakuntala. The pistol she held tightly in her right fist was pointed down at the prostrate native. He lay unmoving, except for the smoke that coiled upward from the hole in his forehead.

Concern writ large in her expression, Harriman was at Matthias's side in an instant. "Are you all right, Lauren?" Her gaze shifted to the two prone bodies; one dead, the other defiant. "O'Morion, what the hell just happened here?"

"Death to Commonwealth!" the pinioned Hata-nau rasped. "Death to thieves of Fluva! Those who stay, we kill!"

Swallowing hard, her throat dry, Matthias strove to project an air of calm above the pandemonium that had enveloped the office. "I'd say that explains it pretty plainly." Under the direction of a trio of armed officers who had arrived in response to an emergency call from a member of the staff, the surviving assassin was secured and hauled away, facedown, long arms bound behind him.

Matthias restrained one officer briefly. "If you can, find out if they are acting alone or, if not, who sent them. They could be acting on behalf of a clan, a family, a single fanatical Yuiqueru, or someone else. Or they might have decided to do this on their own." Her expression contorted as she watched the bound assassin being removed from the room. "The extremists' extremist."

"Don't worry, Administrator." The officer's face was flushed with anger. "We'll get the answer out of him. If we have to, we'll just turn him over to some of the local Deyzara who've lost loved ones in the uprising."

"No," she replied firmly. "This doesn't involve the Deyzara. Do what you can, but do it properly, following prescribed procedure."

The officer was visibly disappointed. "As you wish, ma'am." Turning, he hurried off in pursuit of his colleagues.

Walking back to Harriman's desk, she resumed her seat. "We were going over arrival projections for the next week, I believe."

Lips parted, Harriman slowly sat down in her own chair. "Are you sure you want to continue with this, Lauren? We can pick it up anytime. Don't you want to go home, or at least back to your own office, and get some rest?"

"No, I'm fine," she insisted, straightening the upper half of her jumpsuit beneath the rain cape. "I played a lot of competition contact sports when I was younger."

"You took that Sakuntala right down." Harriman did not try to disguise the admiration she felt for her superior.

"Once I saw the gun starting to come out, I didn't have any choice except to get right in the middle of him. He was ready for me to run or try to dodge, not attack." Smiling, she patted her right hip. "Nice to know a low center of gravity is good for something." With a hand, she gestured at the projection that still hovered, undisturbed, above the center of the desk. "Let's get on with it." Harriman did not see the administrator's other hand. Lying out of sight in her lap, it was shaking badly.

It didn't occur to Matthias, more rattled than she would have admitted, to try to suppress the news of the attempted assassination. As a result, it was all over the port and then the rest of Taulau within a couple of hours. The Hata High Chief Naneci-tok came as soon as she heard the news. She arrived alone, Matthias noted, without an escort, braving the derogatory and abusive hooting of the Deyzara refugees massed outside the Port Administration center.

"I heard what happened." As Naneci-tok spoke, Matthias was ashamed of herself for reflexively noting the position of the Sakuntala's ears. Both faced outward, to the sides. "This a terrible thing, terrible!"

"It was that," Matthias agreed as she took leave of Harriman and Port Administration. "But it's over, and no one was hurt. Except the one attacker who was shot, of course."

Together they exited the double door that was designed to keep out rain as well as excessive heat and humidity, not potential killers. In light of the attempt on her life, the procedure for native access, Matthias knew, was one of the things that was going to have to be changed, perhaps permanently. That was not how interspecies relations were advanced, she knew, but under the circumstances she saw no alternative.

Outside, with her hood up and the rain coming down steadily around them, they headed for the small personal skimmer that would convey them back to her office. "If the radicals now feel confident enough to target humans as well as Deyzara, it shows that this uprising has moved into a new and far more dangerous stage."

"May only be a few crazies." Naneci-tok spoke thoughtfully as droplets coursed down her slender form, hanging momentarily from the tips of her body strappings and fur before falling to the tarmac. "May have decided to do this dreadful thing without Hata or clan approval." Piercing eyes met her own. "I ask, as Hata for Taulau territory, that you only warn your people about what has happened. Ordering payback will only make situation worse."

Matthias could not conceal her surprise. "I had no intention of ordering a reprisal." Even as she replied, it struck her that Naneci-tok was speaking, albeit in terranglo, as if to a fellow Sakuntala. Among her people, given what had just taken place inside the port building, instant reprisal would have been the order of the day.

"That's not how the Commonwealth works," she explained. "We have advanced beyond such things." At least, government policy had, she knew. The actions of individuals were something else again.

"That good to know. I will see to it that all Hatas are so enlightened. It will help."

Matthias's skimmer was parked on the other side of a single covered walkway beneath the open overhang that fronted the nearest maintenance-and-storage hangar. As they approached, a quartet of thick-beaked kolari spread perforated leathery wings and glided down toward the water. The holes in their wings allowed them to sieve away rain that would otherwise have weighed them down and rendered flight a more arduous proposition.

Every creature on Fluva, Matthias reflected, had evolved its own method of dealing with the constant rain, some of them unique and found nowhere else. She was particularly taken with the blind jilp, to whom Jack had introduced her soon after their arrival. Standing motionless out in the heaviest downpours, the jilp thrived in and relied on steady rain for its survival. Clusters of the harmless, attractive, knee-high russet- and pink-colored browsers could be seen standing with the flowerlike orifices that crowned their bodies spread open to the rain. They fed by straining a constant flow of rainwater through their bodies, in the top, out the bottom, filtering out and living upon whatever tiny creatures were washed down out of the trees and macromycetes by the rain. A boring life, that of a jilp. But it seemed to suit them.

Pondering the static jilp, Matthias did not notice the heated shouts of recognition and resentment that had begun to rise above the general din. It was impressed upon her that something out of the ordinary was happening only when they suddenly found their way blocked, not by knots of imploring refugees but by Deyzara faces distinguished by red-rimmed bulbous eyes and angrily darting trunks.

"Look, brethren—a high Sakuntala walks alone among us!"

"The She-Hata shows nothing but contempt, I have to say."

"She thinks that because she can see easily over us, we do not exist in her eyes."

"Bring those eyes down to ours, so that she may see the pain in them that her people have caused."

"Bring her down; bring her down; bring her down!"

Initiated by the most militant among the crowd, the cry was taken up with an enthusiasm and a speed that startled Matthias. Confronted by a single Sakuntala Hata, those who had been forced out of their homes, had their livelihoods destroyed, or seen friends and relatives ill-treated found in the isolated Naneci-tok a target for their accumulated hatred. No rocks were thrown (there were no rocks in the Viisiiviisii), but someone found a branch and hurled it. It struck the now wary Naneci-tok on one shoulder and bounced off. Other objects started to come flying through the air: pieces of wood, empty containers, battered sandals. There wasn't a lot the irate Deyzara could throw. Every emergency food container was soft and either edible or biodegradable. Only the satiated would hurl uneaten food, and there were not many of those in the crowd.

Feeling something hard strike at the back of her knees, where she was most vulnerable to being brought down,

Naneci-tok started to reach for her side arm. Matthias was quick to restrain her.

"No shooting! We'll get out of this." She nodded forward. They were almost to the walkway. Once on the strilk-suspended accessway, the crowd would be able to follow only two abreast and would find itself slowed accordingly.

That was all she needed now, she reflected worriedly: a shooting incident. Self-defense or not, if the Hata accompanying her shot down one or two Deyzara, the huge mob might well get completely out of control.

Then something struck her in the face, and she was forced to place survival above procedure.

Staggered by the blow, she reached up. Several fingers came down covered in blood that the rain of Fluva rapidly washed away. Something opaque and sticky had begun to obscure the vision in her left eye. The Deyzara were all around them now, pressing close, hooting and chanting wrathfully. For the first time, she felt the weight and presence of the mob, and was frightened. Would Harriman or anyone else step out of their dry, comfortable dens long enough to see what was happening? And even if they did, could they arrive in time to do anything about it? She and Naneci-tok were trapped. Because of the press of bodies, they couldn't move forward, back, or to the side.

There was, however, still one avenue of escape open to them. Being Sakuntala, Naneci-tok didn't hesitate. It took all her strength to take the stocky human with her, but she was not about to leave her friend the administrator to the mercy of a mob that was rapidly spinning out of control.

Followed by a flurry of thrown objects, the two females went up into the trees. Matthias felt the Hata's lean but powerful arm around her waist as the cries of the infuriated Deyzara receded beneath them.

"You must to help self now," Naneci-tok told her as they settled on a branch that was much too thin. "I can't carry you anymore."

Are you implying that I'm overweight? Matthias found herself thinking reflexively. But of course she was. Practically any human would be. Grown Sakuntala could fling themselves through the trees with apparent ease, but they could not carry much of a load while doing so. To them, humans and Deyzara were solid as well as short. Naneci-tok might be nearly two meters tall, but Matthias doubted the Hata who had saved them both from the mob weighed more than fifty or sixty kilos.

Looking down through the rain, Matthias saw the frustrated Deyzara still gesticulating furiously below. She and Naneci-tok couldn't go back the way they had come. Nor could they make use of the walkway. It had been taken over by other Deyzara who expected the human, at least, to descend and try to cross on it. For the moment, their rage and resentment had overcome the fact that she was not their traditional enemy. It was enough to make her a target of their ire that she was accompanying one of the hated Sakuntala.

"This way." Naneci-tok gestured encouragingly. "We go around."

Around? Wiping blood from her face, an uncertain Matthias eyed the route the Hata was proposing. It consisted of a winding path through vines and loopers, utilizing branches and broad-shouldered shelf fungi made slippery with rain. The other alternative was to sit and wait, hoping the mob would grow bored and trickle back to their shelters and emergency rations before she stumbled and fell.

If I'm going to slip and fall, she told herself firmly, I might as well do it while trying to get out of here.

"Okay," she muttered uneasily, clinging tightly to a chartreuse looper with one hand, "but take it slow. I've never done anything like this before."

As at home in the trees as on a solid surface, Naneci-tok eyed the administrator in surprise. "You on Fluva for years and never make road through the forest?"

Matthias offered up a wan smile. "Canopied skimmers are more my speed."

Naneci-tok grinned. "You smart incubator. I bet you learn quick."

I will damn well have to, Matthias told herself as she eyed the water some thirty meters below. If she fell and survived the splash-down, there was no one around to fish her out before several of the Viisiiviisii's water-loving predators found her first.

"There is one other thing," she told her long-limbed companion. "I'm in pretty good shape, but . . . I'm afraid of heights."

"Watch me and stay close. I will go slow and grab you if you fall. Follow my back end."

Matthias did as she was told. It worked even better when in her mind's eye she substituted Sethwyn Case's backside for that of the slender, furry Hata. She discovered she could follow it easily as it appeared from behind the moving strappings, the muscles twitching as . . . Though she was able to justify the imported mental picture as a matter of survival, she felt guilty nonetheless.

Moving safely but guiltily through the trees, human and Sakuntala followed a roundabout course toward the skimmer maintenance block. They arrived safely fifteen minutes after Naneci-tok had first snatched the administrator up into the branches. Matthias was soaked to the skin despite her rain cape, having been forced to twist into extreme positions in order to complete the journey. Despite her saturated self she was unnaturally ebullient. Other than a slightly sprained right ankle, her grazing head injury, and a flurry of scratches, all of them minor, she was unhurt.

Wait till I tell Jack about *my* morning, she mused excitedly. A glance backward showed that a few of the enraged Deyzara had advanced almost all the way across the linking walkway. Now seeing that their quarry had already reached and was about to enter a vehicle, they gave up, turning back in disappointment, their fury unrequited.

"I didn't think I could do that." As she spoke, she was unsealing the skimmer portal. The same remote that she used to open it simultaneously activated the interior instrumentation.

"It not hard to travel through the forest in place like this."
Naneci-tok gestured at the surrounding foliage as she followed
the human into the skimmer. She had to bend nearly double in
order to enter.

In less than a minute they were airborne, racing through the
rain back toward the administrative and operational center of
Taulau Town. The port, with its skilled but overworked staff
and surging throngs of despondent, fuming Deyzara refugees,
was left behind. Only physically, Matthias knew. She could not
blot the sight of hundreds of despairing moon-eyed faces from
her mind.

This has got to be stopped, she told herself. The Deyzara
must be allowed to return to their homes and businesses in
safety, and the senior Sakuntala are going to have to cooperate
in putting an end to this uprising. What was happening to the
always fragile but long-running concord that existed between
the two species was illogical and irrational.

Just like the Sakuntala often were themselves, she reminded
herself dourly. No matter. She would see the situation resolved.
She would *not* tender her resignation in the face of a crisis, no
matter how insolvable it appeared to be or how intractable its
components!

If only, she thought as she guided the skimmer over the
town and toward the ever-nearing refuge of her office, the en-
mity between Sakuntala and Deyzara did not seem as abiding
and permanent as the perpetual drenching, remorseless rain.

11

I will try my best obtain a *pahaura,* a decree, from the Council—or at least from as many of High Hatas as I can—declaring this rising and the actions taken against the Deyzara an illicit thing." Vertical pupils locked with Matthias's round ones. "But I only one Hata. Can only do so much."

The administrator rubbed at the scratches on her right forearm. "I have a feeling you can do a lot, Naneci-tok." She grinned. "I just went tripping through the trees of the Viisiiviisii, something I never imagined myself ever doing, or imagined I ever *could* do." The smile vanished. "Now is the time for each of us to do things we never imagined we could do."

The Hata agreed somberly. Her tongue flicked out to wrap briefly around the administrator's face, then withdrew into a cheek pouch. With that, Naneci-tok turned and departed.

Matthias watched the Sakuntala Hata fade into the rain-dimmed distance. Wincing as she pivoted on her sprained ankle, she pulled her rain cape a little tighter around her upper body and limped from the covered parking area toward the main entrance to Administration.

There were four guards there now. Posted at the portal ever since the scale of the troubles became apparent, they were now armed with rifles as well as side arms. None of them looked sleepy or bored. Her approach was noted immediately.

"Pause and identify yourse—" The guard finished with an

expletive. All four of them crowded around the administrator. They were taller than she was, and for a bad moment she was mentally back at the port, surrounded on all sides by a surging mob homicidal in intent.

The feeling passed quickly. "I'm fine, thank you. Well, maybe not fine. But I'm okay."

"The infirmary . . . ," a tall blond woman began.

Matthias pushed past them, leaving a pool of slightly stunned expressions in her wake. "No time for that. I'll get patched up here. Too much to do."

She was more right than she supposed. When she had finally managed to reassure her staff, each of whom wanted to treat her assortment of bruises and scratches personally, she found a Deyzara delegation waiting for her in her own office. Oddly, their presence affected her less than had the knot of four guards outside. Perhaps, she decided as she removed her filthy and torn rain cape and dropped it to the floor before she slumped behind her desk, because for the first time in hours she was in a place that was wonderfully, delightfully, blissfully dry. But not quiet.

Nearly a dozen Deyzara had crowded in to see her. According to Sanuel, they had been waiting hours for her to return. It was a measure of their distress that not one remarked on her visible, if minor, injuries, a most un-Deyzaran oversight. Ordinarily, death would have to be approaching for a Deyzara to be reduced to rudeness. But then, these were not ordinary times, she reminded herself. Just that morning, a very large number of Deyzara had been somewhat more than rude to her. Reaching up, she felt gingerly of the slowly healing wound on her forehead. Forget diplomacy, she decided. For the moment, anyway.

"Be quiet up, all of you!" Just to make sure she was not misunderstood, she repeated the admonition in Deyzar.

The combination of words, tone, and volume had the intended effect. Silence descended upon the delegation, accompanied by not a few shocked looks. Several of those present had engaged in prior dealings with the Commonwealth administrator. At none of those had she ever raised her voice, much less delivered what sounded suspiciously like a command.

It was the very most respected entrepreneur, Tasumandra, who finally took notice of the scratches on hands and arms and the raw red scrape on the human's forehead. "I do not mean to remark on something that may be unpleasant to take notice of, but you appear to have suffered some recent injury."

"Yes." Inner calm and a habitual sense of professionalism had returned along with the comparative quiet. "I have suffered a recent injury. At the hands of the Deyzara, I must add."

Hootings of disbelief mixed with concern greeted this disclosure. "Where did this regrettable episode take place?"

She was calling up a projection from her desk. "At the skimmer port. I was walking with a Sakuntala Hata when we were attacked."

"Ah, refugees." An older female's trunk bobbed back and forth as she spoke. "While I personally regret the incident, it most certainly falls within the range of the recently possible." Her eyes were unusually wide, even for a Deyzara. "People are very angry."

"They have a right to be." Matthias spoke while studying the latest news. "I don't dispute that. But it doesn't give them the right to go and attack any Sakuntala they encounter."

"You protect the Sakuntala," another delegate countered accusingly.

"The Commonwealth extends its protection to any and all who seek it," she responded tiredly. "As chief administrator here I favor no side above the other. For your information, two young Sakuntala tried to kill me while I was on business at the port. My coworkers and I stopped them just before the Hata I referred to arrived to see how she could help with the current situation."

A pair of Deyzara exchanged knowing glances. Given their bulging eyes, the exchange was hard to miss. So were their chromatically clashing clothes. In fact, with so many characteristically overdressed Deyzara in the room, any need for artificial lighting seemed all but superfluous.

"A most interesting coincidence," the first murmured. "Two of them attempt to assassinate the administrator, and then a Hata shows up immediately after the attempt fails. Almost as if to see what has happened. What excellent timing."

"So very much so," responded a colleague. "Just in time to offer their 'help'—or view the executed, depending on the exigencies of the moment. One would not think to associate such punctuality with the Sakuntala."

Matthias leaned forward so sharply, she pushed herself partway into the projection. "It *was* a coincidence. I happen to know the Sakuntala Hata in question."

"Oh, surely no one can dispute that," observed another sardonically. "Of course, to say such a thing presumes that one actually can 'know' a Sakuntala. Just as one can 'know' the animals of the forest, or the decaying fungi of the Viisiiviisii." Calculating whoops rose from the assembled.

Matthias chose not to argue the matter further. A hastily convened meeting in her office wasn't going to settle several hundred years of differences between Deyzara and Sakuntala. Anyway, her concerns were more immediate.

"I understand your anxiety. Believe me, I do. I'm just reviewing the latest news right now." She indicated the information-rich projection that continued to hover above her desk. "I assure you that the Commonwealth government is aware of the situation developing here on Fluva and is preparing an appropriate response. Meanwhile, I will continue to use every resource at my command to deal with the immediate needs of your people, and to seek a solution to these unexpected and objectionable actions that are being perpetrated by a minority of disaffected Sakuntala."

There, she thought. That was straightforward, reassuring, and diplomatic at the same time. Diplomatic in that if word of it leaked out to the Sakuntala, she had said nothing that could be construed as favoring the Deyzara.

Her visitors' reaction showed that they wanted more action and stronger language but didn't quite know how to press for it. Finally, one of the youngest delegates spoke up.

"At the risk of embarrassing myself with my forwardness, Administrator Matthias, I have to very much say that something needs to be done *now*. This is no longer merely a matter of displaced persons and stolen goods." Both trunks stretched toward her imploringly. "Our people are being *killed* out there. Their homes are being destroyed, their occupations ruined, their lives cast aside like old namurand shells. I fear most strongly that we cannot wait for distant decisions to be made on faraway worlds as to whether a committee should be appointed to look into the matter of the minor troubles on far-flung Fluva. If the Commonwealth cannot or will not do something about this, then we us ourselves will have to respond as best we can. We are not green frashera, to be nudged unresistingly into the cooking pot."

Hootings of support rose from other delegates. Matthias saw quickly that she would have to nip this new line of thought in the bud.

"Are you talking about armed resistance?"

The young Deyzara was not intimidated. "If we do not defend our property and ourselves, then who will?"

"The Commonwealth Authority on Fluva will," she told him quietly. "I will."

Trunks and arms gestured. There was a moment of silence; then another delegate spoke up. "When?"

"Right now. Today. This afternoon. I'm scheduled to conference with my military people in a little while." She wasn't, but it was a meeting she had been intending to set up, and she might as well call for it in an hour or two.

"And Commonwealth soldiers will be deployed to defend the Deyzara?" a senior delegate inquired. "Or are you going to attempt to halt this continuing outrage with strong words?"

"You're asking me to make a decision before the decision makers have met. Everything takes time."

Several of the delegates conferred. She could see their trunks swaying hypnotically, hear the soft chirp of their alternating hoots. After a few minutes, the improvised caucus broke. Tasumandra adjusted his burgundy, gold, and hot pink wrappings.

"We do not wish to appear obdurate. We understand most clearly what you say when you declare that you need time to evaluate and render decisions on such weighty matters." With great dignity, he flipped a loose fold of sparkling gold material over his sharply sloping right shoulder. "We will give the Commonwealth Authority until tomorrow to respond, and not with trunk-twisting messages bemoaning its anguish over the continuing catastrophe. The Deyzara will expect action of a kind sufficient to keep people from being driven from their homes, or being murdered in their beds.

"If not," he added as he turned to head for the doorway, "I fear most assuredly that the Deyzara will be left with no choice but to defend themselves."

"Fight the Sakuntala and they will make what's happened so far seem like a holiday recreation."

The delegation paused, clearly uncomfortable at her words. But Tasumandra was not to be deterred. "Without question a great many of us will die horrible deaths. The Sakuntala will butcher us in the trees, or force us into the water. If fortune favors us, we may hold our own in the towns, where our skills at organization may go some ways toward offsetting the natural combative talents of our enemy." He looked back at her from near the doorway.

"If we move to defend ourselves most vigorously, Administrator Matthias, either we will kill enough of the Sakuntala to make them stop this, or they will slaughter us. Should either scenario eventuate, there is one thing that I can say for a surety. Speaking as a bureaucrat myself, I would not wish to be in your sandals when the time comes for an evaluation of your performance here."

With Tasumandra's final words serving as both parting and warning, the delegation filed slowly out of her office. Left with only her thoughts and a swirling mass of information that offered up not a single line of encouragement, she knew that the Deyzara was right. If the Sakuntala succeeded, her efforts to mediate would be accounted a complete failure. If the Deyzara managed by violent means to somehow put a stop to the uprising, she would be upbraided for failing to find a peaceful solution to the problem. If neither side prevailed and the discord continued, she would be faulted for not doing enough. If she gave the order for Commonwealth soldiers to intervene, she would be assailed for using force against a technologically inferior species of sentient.

She was damned if she did, damned if she didn't, and twice damned if she did nothing at all.

Her hesitant assistant appeared in the open doorway. "Uh, how did it go, Administrator?"

"Wonderfully well," she replied without a trace of sarcasm. She noted the hard copy he held in one hand. "What have you got for me now, Sanuel?"

He approached and passed it over. "Didn't know when you might get to your messages. This one I thought you ought to see right away. Copied it out to make sure I didn't forget about it." He made a soft clucking sound. "Bad news, I'm afraid."

At least that's settled, she decided. She *was* damned. It took only a moment to peruse the missive. Sitting back in her chair, she rolled her eyes at the ceiling. Outside, a heavy shower was pounding the overhang and the porch. It did not distract her. After about a month on Fluva, one hardly noticed the perpetual drumming sound anymore.

"There's no time stamp on this. When did it come in?"

Pandusky looked apologetic. "Right after you left to go to the port. I heard about what happened there."

She scanned the note a second time, hoping that by subjecting it to her vision the content might somehow transmogrify into something less aggravating. It did not. Her gaze shifted to the window. It was raining hard enough now to obscure the view of the nearest trees.

"This Hasa person has become a real headache. I'm afraid I may lose my temper when I finally meet him."

"If you get to meet him." Like his boss, Pandusky's attention was focused on the deluge outside. "He's been gone a long time without contact."

"Only a few days," she murmured. She was seriously in need of a bath. Her scrapes and scratches demanded it.

"You and I both know that's a long time to be stranded in the Viisiiviisii. He could be dead."

She swiveled back to face Pandusky again. "Too bad he didn't have the grace to notify us of that in advance." She tapped the hard copy. "We could have avoided this." As Pandusky stood silently before her, she leaned forward slightly, resting her head in both hands. "I'm sorry." Taking a deep breath, she looked up. "That was a loutish thing to say. This Hasselemoga may not be beloved of his colleagues, but he's a Commonwealth citizen operating on a difficult world and as such it's our job—my job—to extend full assistance to anyone who runs into trouble. Now I'm informed that the team sent out to look for him has itself disappeared without a trace."

Pandusky nodded slowly. "For two up-to-date skimmers to go down in the same general area and for the emergency beacons on both to fail is an extraordinary coincidence."

"If it is a coincidence," she muttered by way of reply.

His features scrunched into a frown. "I don't understand, Administrator."

She met his gaze. "We're in the midst of a Sakuntala uprising against the Deyzara that's as widespread as it is unexpected. Somehow, from somewhere, these radical Sakuntala have acquired an unknown number of advanced weapons. That is inexplicable. So is the 'coincidence' to which you've just referred. I'm just wondering if there could be some connection between this current surge of inexplicables."

Pandusky pondered his superior's comments for a long moment, finally shook his head in bewilderment. "Even if both were attacked by extremist elements, their emergency beacons should continue working. What possible connection could there be between the Sakuntala uprising and two of our own skimmers going missing and completely silent in the southern Viisiiviisii?"

"If I knew that," she replied flatly, "it would be explicable. The Sakuntala and the Deyzara I chose for the follow-up mission were the best, and the brightest, I could find to crew the rescue skimmer. Still, given the animosity between their respective species, it's not inconceivable that a fight might have broken out between them. But even if one killed the other, or they both died as a result of an accident, that still doesn't explain the nonresponsiveness of their own skimmer's emergency beacon. Same goes for the beacon on this Hasa's vehicle. The latter failure is exceptional. To experience two such failures within as many weeks of a tried-and-true fail-safe technology is more than that: it's suspicious."

He nodded. "What do you want me to do?"

She steepled her fingers, thinking hard. "Call someone at the inner port you personally trust and have complete confidence in. Ask them to do some circumspect checking. See if anyone who isn't directly authorized to do skimmer maintenance and repair has been spending an unusual amount of time in the area, even if only to talk with friends. Warn your contact to be as discreet as possible. If someone *is* responsible for the disappearance of the two vehicles and the corresponding failure of their emergency gear, they're not likely to think twice about eliminating any perceived inquiry into their activities."

"Sabotage," Pandusky murmured. "But why?"

Sighing heavily, she slumped back in her chair. The material immediately flexed to mold itself to her new posture. "It's inexplicable, remember? Tell your contact to ask especially about any Sakuntala who might have been seen lingering in the vicinity. I've never met one myself who was capable of incapacitating a skimmer once it was airborne, much less deactivate a sealed internal emergency beacon in a way that would not trigger a blowback alarm. But then, until a little while ago I'd never imagined one pulling a punch pistol on me, either. New revelations raise new expectations—not all of them good."

Turning, he started toward the door. "I'll find somebody trustworthy; don't worry. I have a couple of people in mind."

She waved him away. "Let me know the minute they find anything even remotely suspicious."

As the door closed behind him, she swiveled back to face the window. The cloudburst had let up, giving way to the moderate rain that passed for normal daytime weather on Fluva. It was a good thing, she reflected, that the sun did come out occasionally or she feared she might forget what it looked like. Hard as the perpetual gloom was on adults, it was no wonder Andrea was having such a difficult time coping. Lauren mused that her daughter's deciding to call herself Fitzwinkle was less destructive than any number of other things the girl could do.

And what could *she* do? Her mandate to interfere in the affairs of Commonwealth sentients was severely proscribed. If the Sakuntala and the Deyzara had been evenly matched, she could have sat on the sidelines and watched them beat each other senseless until they ran out of arms, energy, and willing combatants. But they were not evenly matched. They never had been. Ever since they had come to Fluva, the Deyzara had relied on at least the threat of Commonwealth intervention to protect them from the repressed ferocity of the Sakuntala. Now a large group of the indigenous had chosen to challenge that nebulous threat. Because, she suspected, someone had provided them with advanced armaments. No need to fear Commonwealth intervention, they had apparently been convinced, if you have Commonwealth guns yourself. Running down the source of those highly illegal imports was yet another problem she had to deal with.

It was a good thing the Sakuntala didn't know she was all but powerless to intervene in the conflict. If she ordered her small but well-armed and well-trained garrison to intercede on behalf of the Deyzara, it would look to her superiors as if she was favoring one resident sentient species over another. That would not sit well in certain departments on Earth and Hive-hom. If she could show that she was doing so to prevent geno-cide, that would provide an after-the-fact justification for her actions. But the extremist Sakuntala were being too clever by half. In most uncharacteristic fashion, they seemed to be delib-erately trying to avoid causing fatalities. They were herding the Deyzara, not (with a few exceptions) murdering them.

Was that sufficient grounds to validate an order to intervene? And if she did, there was another consideration. One that lin-gered on the fringes of every argument she could make in favor of helping the Deyzara. One that refused to go away, no matter how much she wanted it to.

The prospect that the much more numerous moderate Sakun-tala, who like all their kind enjoyed a traditional passion for war-fare, would join their radical brethren in the fighting if they felt that the self-proclaimed neutral Commonwealth Authority had chosen to side with the Deyzara. That and the even more dis-turbing possibility that, equipped with modern weapons, the Sakuntala might succeed in defeating the limited number of sol-diers under her authority.

While she did not want to be chastised and demoted for tak-ing the wrong action, even less did she want to preside over a massacre.

"Too bad about those two skimmers, hey?" The tall, muscular figure expressed unashamed concern for the missing. "Man, I wouldn't want to be stuck out there in the damn varzea. I don't care how much experience you've got. The Viisiiviisii *eats* people."

The mechanic who had been painting new circuitry in an open compartment in the side of the cargo skimmer switched off his firing lenses, pushed them back up on his head, and wiped sweat from his brow.

"Me, I'd sooner shoot myself now than get stuck out there."
He nodded in the direction of the hangar portal and the mist-
shrouded rain-swept forest beyond. "They say if you lie in one
place for more than thirty minutes, some fungus or mold will
find a way to enter your body even through the toughest envi-
rosuit." He bent to check his equipment. "Natty's Pub is about
as close to the real Viisiiviisii as I want to get."

The other man laughed. "Good place, Natty's. Best baked
spud suds on Fluva. Somebody told me he brews his beer using
local hops—or the native variant thereof."

"Just as soon you hadn't told me that." The painter was
making adjustments to his sprayer, fine-tuning the application
settings. "Now I've got to wonder if maybe some night the
beer won't start to drink *me*." He was waiting for his most recent application to dry, so the synaptic connections would set
properly. "How about you? Spent much time out there?" For
the second time he waved in the forest's direction.

His visitor shrugged. "I get out now and again. All part of
the job." Turning, the taller man gazed toward the rain-soaked
varzea. "Wouldn't be any hassling going on now if that idiot
prospector Hasselemoga hadn't managed to go and lose himself. And then the rescue team they send out goes and vanishes
while looking for him. That's what happens when you send a
couple of locals to do a human's job. It's still weird, though."

"Real weird," the mechanic agreed readily. "Two emergency
beacons failing like that."

"Wonder who did the last service checkouts on both skimmers?" The visitor eyed the mechanic thoughtfully.

The painter put up both hands. "Whoa there, brother. Wasn't
me. I'd have remembered. Authority's already been through
here, questioning everybody, and that was one of the first questions." He returned to his paraphernalia. "By rights, somebody
ought to be in line to catch hell. But there aren't that many of us
who do that kind of preflight checkout work, and everybody's
work pad checked out clean. I know *mine* did."

The other man nodded. "Anybody else have access to vehicles besides pilots and mechanics?"

"Just the usual service teams and automatons." The mechanic looked penetratingly at his visitor. "Are you implying something, bro, or are you just fisq hunting?"

"I'm just curious. Me, when I go out I make sure to run my own preflight systems check. I'm just wondering, that's all."

The mechanic was now thoroughly involved in his visitor's speculations. "Wondering what, bro?"

The taller man looked away. "Just farting in a vacuum. Wondering if maybe somebody might want a prospector, or just a human, to disappear in the Viisiiviisii, for reasons of their own. Seems to me anybody who would do something like that to an unsuspecting prospector wouldn't hesitate to interfere with a rescue team."

Moving closer, the intensely interested mechanic lowered his voice. "You got anybody in mind?"

The visitor glanced around to make sure they weren't being monitored. Everyone else in the hangar was busy with their own work. "I've got a couple of ideas, sure. Hasn't everybody?"

Eyes narrowing, the mechanic scanned his coworkers. "Not one of the people in here, surely. I know all these folks pretty good. There isn't one I wouldn't trust with my life."

"Who said anything about people?" The visitor's eyebrows rose slightly.

Realization dawned on the mechanic. "Oh. I see. Who, then?"

"Like I said, I got a couple of ideas." The visitor turned to depart. "Just keep one thing in mind. All these poor, put-upon Deyzara who keep flooding into town? Isn't it true that their kind will do anything for money? *Anything.*"

Angling toward a pair of techs working on the engine of a transport skimmer, the visitor headed across the hangar floor. Behind him he left one preoccupied mechanic alone with his thoughts, including a few unsettling new ones.

12

They were being watched.

They had all overslept. Not that anyone had an appointment to keep. The marvelous moss bed Jemunu-jah had found nestled in the crook of four intersecting blue-green branches of a strong kapolu tree was more than a meter deep and probably hundreds of years old. That didn't keep Hasa from eagerly bedding down in the middle of the softest part, blissfully indifferent to the deaths of the thousands of growths that were crushed beneath his weight. The result was the best night's sleep he'd enjoyed since the crash of his skimmer.

Sitting up and adjusting his rain cape, he saw that he was the only one awake. That was unexpected. His own experience-toughened reflexes notwithstanding, the Sakuntala Jemunu-jah would normally be the first one to awaken to the presence of an unseen intruder. Both he and Masurathoo relied on the Sakuntala's forest skills to warn them of the presence of any especially furtive visitor. But the native slept on, indifferent to any imagined visitation. As he lay on his back with both ears relaxed, his tufted tail stretched out to one side, it was possible to envision his completely relaxed form not responding to every single presence.

Hasa wasn't taking any chances. You didn't get many in the Viisiiviisii. Rising, he surveyed the scenery that surrounded their unexpectedly luxurious place of rest. Though his vision was not as acute as Jemunu-jah's, it was unusually sharp for a human. Years of experience had contributed to a heightening of his senses. It was one of the main reasons he was still alive.

There was definitely something out there, and it definitely had its eyes on them. If they *were* eyes in the normal sense, he reflected. Several difficult-to-classify inhabitants of the Viisii-viisii exhibited some remarkable adaptations to light. A number of them were able to perceive shadowing and movement with the aid of sophisticated organic instrumentalities that could not properly be called eyes.

The air was filled with the calls and cries of unseen creatures that rose above the patter of falling rain and the *drip-drip* of individual droplets wending their way downward from the tips of leaves and fungi. The sounds made by the concealed were sharp and clear, designed to be discernible above, or rather through, even a substantial downpour. Through the trees flashed something with the sheen of polished ivory, trailing feathers or filaments that were tipped with luminescent gold. They might constitute the tail of some fantastic flying organism, the bright metallic appendages designed to attract potential mates. Or they might be a mimic protruding from the mouth of something large and hungry, designed to attract the potential mates of another creature with a false tail similar in color and shape. Eat, mate, live, die. That was life in the Viisiiviisii.

Come to think of it, wasn't that life everywhere?

Standing there in the rain, he waxed momentarily philosophical. Here something waves gold-tipped tails or tentacles. On less wild worlds we wave credit balances and guns. The means are different but the ends the same. Eat, mate, live, die. Personally, he was more comfortable in a place like the Fluvan Viisii-viisii than in an urbane metropolis on Earth or New Riviera. Here, at least, the maneuverings of the local predators were straightforward. He would far rather confront a nironve or a bai-mou than a lawyer.

Water ran in rivulets away from the repulsion field that kept the outer layer of his rain cape dry. Reaching down, he removed one of the two collectors that were built into the waist and gulped down the filtered, cooled contents. The water was clean and refreshing. You could also sip it straight from any branch or leaf, but in doing so you ran the risk of imbibing possibly harmful organic detritus along with the life-giving liquid. Not to mention bacteria or internal parasites. And water so sipped would be tepid. Cooled and filtered was better. After his pistol, his versatile rain cape was the most important item he had salvaged from his downed skimmer.

Such thoughts served to churn memories of the debacle. They were wasting time here. He had things to do, places to go, people to beat the crap out of. Turning away from contemplation of the saturated yet beautiful forest, he moved to wake Jemunu-jah. As he turned, his boots sank into the soft, spongy moss.

There it was again. Straightening, eyes narrowing, he whirled and scanned their immediate surroundings. A small knot of perouku were making their way up a sloping branch hung with diademite floss. On the rare occasions when the sun showed itself, the floss would sparkle like diamonds, the light triggering active spore dispersal throughout its surroundings. Showing no interest in the floss, the perouku ambled on short black legs up the branch. Miniature rain shields protected their upper bodies and the young that rode there, clinging tightly to the short fur that sprouted from the adults' backs, from falling drops. Though they had four eyes apiece, they were focused on their ascent and ignored the outsiders in their midst.

When he completed his circle, still without having espied anything that might be staring back in his direction, Hasa found Jemunu-jah standing awake and alert behind him. The human's sharp turn had been enough to awaken the sleeping Sakuntala.

"What is?"

Beneath the rain cape, Hasa let his right hand fall away from his gun. "I've been up for a few minutes. Can't escape the feeling there's something out there that's watching us."

Large vertical pupils scanned the rain-washed Viisiiviisii. "Feelings are not scientific. Maybe forest spirits."

Hasa eyed the taller native quizzically. " 'Forest spirits'? And you say *I'm* not being scientific?"

Having completed his cursory scrutiny of their surroundings, Jemunu-jah looked back down at him. "A forest spirit can be many things, and can announce its presence in many ways. Not always by scream or shout."

"Or a stinger delivered to the buttocks. Your words fail to reassure me." Turning away from the Sakuntala, he peered once more into the dank forest depths. "Don't be coy with me, big-ears. Is there something out there or not?"

"Just like forest spirits, there are many creatures who hunt by not moving. Who sit and wait for food to come to them. Like giimatasa in water." He leveled a stare past the human. "I don't see anything like that."

"Well, I suppose that's something, anyway."

They stood together for a couple of moments, surveying the forest, listening to the ceaseless litany of soft chattering sounds that emerged from the rain-swathed interior. Finally, Hasa shrugged and moved to gather up his gear.

"Maybe I've spent too much time looking at the Viisiiviisii. Now I've got it in my head that it's starting to look back."

"Forest spirits can be very deceptive." Jemunu-jah wished to be understanding.

"So can creeping dementia." Hasa fiddled with his pack, making sure it was sealed against moisture. When he saw the Sakuntala eyeing him quizzically, he added by way of explanation, "Think of it as a kind of parasite." That was easier, he decided, than trying to explain the inner workings of the human mind: a discussion for which he was not in the mood.

But though he dropped the matter, his skin continued to crawl, and not from any new infestation of microscopic life-forms. At which point Masurathoo let out a half hoot, half shriek of such intensity that it rose well above the sound of falling rain, the cacklings of unseen forest denizens, and the bioprospector's own restless thoughts.

"It has me!" the Deyzara was screaming. "Something has got hold of me!" He was thrashing around on the moss bed, flailing behind and beneath him with his flexible arms.

Weapons drawn, Hasa and Jemunu-jah were at his side in an instant, flanking their panic-stricken companion. "Where?" Jemunu-jah queried the spasming, contorting Deyzara. "Where do they have you?"

"Everywhere! They are all over me!" Rain-cape-clad arms continued to flail away beneath the convulsing form.

Holstering his gun but not securing it, Hasa bent carefully toward the Deyzara, whose naturally protuberant eyes now threatened to pop out of his head. "Whatever it is, it's got him from below. Let's try to turn him over."

Jemunu-jah managed to get hold of the Deyzara's ropy, wildly kicking legs. Together, he and the human simultaneously lifted and twisted. Masurathoo was not heavy. In an instant, he was lying on his ventral side, still lashing out and hollering.

That was when Hasa finally identified the preponderance of hooting that was emerging from the Deyzara's speaking trunk. They were not yells of pain. Stepping back, he frowned down at the bouncing pilot.

"Son of a bitch. He's not squealing in agony. He's *laughing*."

"Laughter?" Jemunu-jah stared uncertainly at their pink-faced colleague. "Amusement? I don't understand."

"Look at him. At the way he's moving. See any wounds? Any blood?"

Careful to avoid being struck by the Deyzara's flailing whip-like limbs, Jemunu-jah bent over the shuddering body. "No. But I do see kaema." Extending his right hand, he gestured with his three middle fingers.

Peering at where Jemunu-jah was pointing, Hasa saw an ear-size bulge attached to Masurathoo's back. Dark green splotched with black streaks and spots, it was clearly visible through the transparent rain cape and between shredded folds of shockingly bright attire.

While Hasa did his best to hold the twitching, gurgling Deyzara down, Jemunu-jah unsealed and removed their companion's rain cape. Unwinding their companion's body wrappings proved more difficult, as there were as many different ways for a Deyzara to arrange his attire as there were clashing colors to choose from. Eventually, the Sakuntala managed to expose the Deyzara's ventral side from neck to lower torso.

At least two dozen kaema had attached themselves to the smooth bright pink skin. They either had been living in or had come up through the moss mass. Hasa studied them in fascination. They looked like so many green limpets fastened to pink granite. He spoke the first thought that came to mind.

"Parasites?"

"Actually, no." Sitting back on his haunches, the Sakuntala no longer appeared concerned. "The kaema are benign travelers. Left alone, they do no harm to those they choose to ride. Attach themselves to any creature traveling through forest." Making a six-fingered cup shape with one hand, he held it out over the convulsing Deyzara's bare back. "Underside of kaema looks like this. Secure to travel host with suction. Drop off when reach a place they like." His lips parted, showing sharp teeth. "Sakuntala usually not bothered. Hard to get a grip on fur with suction."

Hasa silently digested this explanation. "Then why is this fool laughing hard enough to tie his trunks in knots?" He eyed the pale exposed flesh with undisguised distaste. He'd seen newborn babies with darker skin. Newborn human babies, he corrected himself. The transient image of a newborn Deyzara broodling was sufficient to raise the bile in his gut.

"I think I know." Jemunu-jah regarded the occupied Masurathoo with some sympathy. "Outside of kaema cup is lined with tiny legs. What you call, I believe, cilia. To make travel host move, and keep moving, kaema move these legs against its skin, causing irritation."

Hasa let go of the Deyzara's arms and stepped back. Left alone on the moss bed between his companions, Masurathoo continued his violent twisting and hooting, his half-naked body now exposed to the falling rain. The prospector shook his head slowly.

"Obviously the damn things don't rub off. What do we do?" Intending to try to pluck it free, he started to reach for one of the toothless but persistent vermin.

Jemunu-jah forestalled him. "Suction is too powerful. Any grip strong enough to pull away kaema will also pull away skin and flesh."

Hasa's fingers continued to hover over one of the green-black protuberances. "It ain't my skin and flesh." A bit reluctantly, he drew his hand back. "Okay then. They can't be pulled off. What then?"

Jemunu-jah was reaching into one of the pouches attached to his waist strappings. "Fire. Is fire in Viisiiviisii only in time of fleeting dryness. No creatures have resistance to it."

The prospector examined their sodden surroundings. "Makes sense." Glancing back down at poor Masurathoo's body, he considered how best to proceed. Weakened by non-stop laughter, the Deyzara's movements were beginning to slow.

Having withdrawn a small cylinder the size and shape of a pencil, Jemunu-jah knelt beside the quivering body. At the Sakuntala's touch, a small blue light emerged from the tip of the device. Working carefully and deliberately, he touched the beam to each kaema. One by one, they dropped off the Deyzara's back. Smoke curling upward from the center of their shells, a few scuttled out of sight, burying themselves back in the moss. Those that clung longest to their intended transport suffered deeper burns. When they finally fell off, they lay atop the moss bed and did not move.

Only when the last of the persistent outriders had been expunged did Masurathoo roll over onto his back. As he sucked in air through his breathing trunk, it expanded and contracted with the effort. After a few minutes, he was able to sit up, then stand. With as much dignity as he could muster, he began rewrapping himself with his frayed folds of garishly hued apparel. Warm rain coursed down his face and exposed pink torso.

Grudgingly, Hasa felt compelled to ask, "How you feelin'?"

"Exhausted. Embarrassed. Most highly mortified." A strip of gold and blue wound itself around his upper body, over one shoulder, and down his back. Though intricate in execution, the mannered procedure of Deyzara dressing was only interesting the first time it was observed. "My entire back feels as if it has been flayed by flies."

"The itching will pass," Jemunu-jah assured him. "Better to laugh at such things than scream in pain."

"One reaches a point where it becomes exceedingly difficult to tell the difference." Right arm quivering, he used the two wide, strong digits to fasten a length of wrapping beneath his other arm as he turned his gaze on Hasa. "I appreciate your not shooting at me in a misguided attempt to rid me of the damnable affliction."

"Don't mention it," Hasa replied without breaking a smile. "You sure you're okay?"

"There will be some small marks," Jemunu-jah commented. "In a few days, they all faded away. Next time, be more careful-ing where you put down your backside."

Masurathoo's reply was, for an instant, the coldest thing in that part of the Viisiiviisii. "Thank you for that most small admonition. And now, if you don't mind, I find myself entirely too open to the elements." Bending, he moved to recover the rain cape that the ministering Jemunu-jah had set aside. In so doing, his foot crashed through a narrow place in the moss bed, promptly sending him headfirst into the shallow depths of the soft green pad.

As they worked together to pull him out, Jemunu-jah and Hasa found that even without the presence of any hitchhiking, tickling kaema on their bodies, it was their turn to laugh.

● ● ●

Another river. Wider than the one they had been forced to swim previously. Wider and this time boasting a significant current.

Recovered from his humiliating encounter with the kaema, Masurathoo contemplated the broad waterway that stretched out before them with understandable trepidation. Though there was nothing to suggest the presence of another giimatasa, or something even worse, he had no doubt that the river's unseen depths were home to other kinds of predators as resourceful as they were voracious.

"Raft," he declared curtly.

"No time." Though his tone was unchanged, even Hasa was a bit discouraged by the width of the watercourse. "If we wanted to spend a lot of time in one place, we would've stayed with the skimmers."

"I tell you right here and now, sir, that I am not swimming that. Our last aqueous excursion provided more than enough excitement for me. I have no desire to repeat the experience."

Nearby, Jemunu-jah was scrutinizing the trees that grew right to the edge of the open water. "Not much here good for making raft anyway." He looked back at the Deyzara. "Since we also cannot make a skimmer out of leaves and vines, we have to swim. Deyzara are good swimmers. You show that before."

"Not as good as the local flesh eaters."

Hasa was willing to concede the Deyzara's point. "Maybe we don't have time to build a boat, but we might look around for some kind of natural protection. Thorns, poisons we could dump in the water around us. That sort of thing." He focused on Jemunu-jah. "I don't recognize anything useful here. You got any ideas?"

The Sakuntala paused, then gestured approvingly with his tongue. "Maybe something we passed a little while ago. I think it will do what is needed. But it will be difficult make work."

Hasa frowned. "Difficult how?"

Turning, Jemunu-jah beckoned for them to follow. "Easier to show than explain."

Back within the trees five minutes later, they stood on branches looking down at a cluster of blossoms floating on the water. They were undoubtedly the most beautiful flowers Shadrach Hasselemoga had ever seen in his life, on any world. Without question, collectors of rare and exotic flora would pay a fortune for their seeds, seedlings, cuttings, or samples. While he had no idea what Jemunu-jah had in mind, he did know that the Sakuntala had unintentionally led him to a new source of income.

"Where are the thorns, or are the leaves toxic?" He found himself enthralled by the beauty floating on the water at his feet.

"Vatulalilu has no thorns, no poisons." After making a quick scan of the surrounding waters for lurking predators and finding none, Jemunu-jah started down. His companions followed.

Up close, the individual blooms were even more spectacular. From a cream white center individual metallic blue petals as long as Hasa's arm thrust outward in all directions. They shaded from a pale turquoise, to a deep royal blue, to, in a few isolated instances, dark purple. Gold flecks danced within the anthers. Each time a raindrop landed on one of the leaves, the spot where it struck seemed to explode with golden fire. From the center, crimson stamens curved up and out in graceful arcs, to terminate in pistils tipped with black the color of obsidian. The breathtakingly beautiful blooms were, without question, the most stunning single life-form Hasa had yet encountered in his exploratory forays through the Viisiiviisii.

Yet . . . he had spent too much time on too many treacherous worlds to accept the alluring display of floral beauty unquestioningly. True to Jemunu-jah's words, no thorns or other protective adaptations were visible. That did not mean they did not exist. Needing sunlight, the vatulalilu had put down its long roots where its spectacular blossoms were not blocked by spreading branches or overhanging fungi. It stood open to the rain and the intermittent sun. This also exposed the staggering display of color to any wandering herbivores who might hop, swim, or fly past. Yet insofar as he could tell, the closely packed water plants had not suffered a single tear or bite mark. Despite advertising its presence with an unsurpassed burst of color, the vatulalilu pushed its blossoms toward the sky unscathed.

"I know." He spoke aloud in reply to his own unasked question. "The flowers have a bad taste. Probably concentrates ammonia or something in the leaves."

"Not bitter." Standing in the rain to one side of the eruption of efflorescence, Jemunu-jah once more wielded the small flare tool he had employed earlier to remove the tickling kaema from Masurathoo's back. Stretching out his arm, he drew the blue light of the versatile cutting tool across one huge bloom, leaving several cuts in half a dozen petals.

Human and Deyzara both tensed, but nothing happened. After a respectful pause, a mystified Hasa stepped forward to inspect the damage. A pale liquid the color and consistency of honey oozed from the multiple cuts. It was thick enough to maintain its texture in the rain.

He leaned closer. Jemunu-jah had assured them nothing about the vatulalilu was toxic. Could it be corrosive? Extending one tentative finger toward the thick goo, he half expected the Sakuntala to warn him off. Instead, Jemunu-jah continued to stand off to one side, watching silently. A suspicious Hasa drew his hand back anyway. At that point, he caught his first full whiff of the golden ooze.

He retched so violently that he fell backward. Only reflexes honed from years of exploring the most inhospitable reaches of alien worlds allowed him to grab onto a couple of branches and keep from falling into the water below. Eyes wide, he continued to vomit with such vehemence that he felt like his stomach was going to rise right up through his throat and burst out his mouth.

Observing this, the always alert Masurathoo took a couple of prudent steps backward along the branch on which he was standing. "What ails our unhappy colleague?"

Ignoring the heaving human, Jemunu-jah walked back to the

plant and began making measured slices on every blossom.
Honey-hued fluid promptly began to flow from each successive
cut. When he was satisfied with his destructive but measured
handiwork, the Sakuntala put away the flare tool. Using his
long fingers, he began to scoop up the thick, sticky liquid and
smear it strategically on his body. Every now and then, with a
look of resigned expectation, he would pause to throw up.
Each time one of these startling episodes of strenuous but
measured upchucking concluded, he would resume the work.

Eventually, Hasa's digestive system had nothing more to
give. Too weak to be really angry, the prospector rose to his
feet to confront the Sakuntala.

"You scrawny, underhanded excuse for an alien monkey-rat!
You could have *told* me the plant was protected by an olfactory
defense!"

Methodically applying daubs of golden goo to his fur, the
Sakuntala regarded him out of double-lidded eyes. "If I had de-
scribed in detail what going to happen, would you still have
been willing undergo the experience?"

Hasa started to respond, hesitated, then replied in a low
murmur of grudging acceptance, "Not likely."

"You see?" Having exhausted the supply of glistening golden
stink from one flower, Jemunu-jah moved on to the next. "You
need not put it on you bodies. The vatulalilu sap will stick
plenty enough to your clothing."

Masurathoo's speaking trunk hardly moved. "Plenty enough
for what purpose, my dear Jemunu-jah?"

"The scent of vatulalilu flower holds its strength even in
water. Well covered in it, we can safe swim the river that blocks
our way. Water dwellers may come close to us, but nothing will
bite."

"I can believe it. With that stench smeared all over, I wouldn't
want to come too close to me, either." Swallowing hard while
fighting to steady what remained of his stomach, Hasa clenched
his lips and advanced on the nearest spray of blindingly beautiful
blossoms. Turning off his rain cape, he removed it, folded it

neatly for a second time, and stuffed it into its vacant pouch. Reaching down, he scooped up a fingerload of the shimmering liquid and began to spread it across his chest. He promptly gagged, fought down the automatic reaction, and continued to battle the retching reflex as he treated first his torso, then his limbs.

Masurathoo watched until his companions were almost finished. Then he sighed softly through his breathing trunk, moved forward to join them, and began to emulate their actions. Hasa paused in his work, his expression one of grim expectancy. Jemunu-jah did likewise.

Manifesting supreme indifference to the vatulalilu flowers' ferocious fragrance, the Deyzara blithely smeared large fingerfuls of the potent syrupy extrusion all over his body. After several minutes, he finally noticed the dumbfounded stares of his companions.

"What? Oh, I understand. You're wondering why I am not regurgitating the remnants of my last several meals all over the forest."

"You could say that." As familiarity with the golden fluid did not breed acceptance, Hasa was still having to fight down a constant and all but overwhelming urge to puke.

Masurathoo returned to the work at hand. "That is easily explained. We Deyzara have a well-known tolerance for strong odors." He held a double-digited handful of the goo up to the end of his breathing trunk, a gesture sufficiently profound in its implications that it very nearly did make the queasy Hasa throw up all over again. "To me, this substance smells only slightly sweetish."

"And yet," Jemunu-jah observed, "there is an internal scientific logic to this. Deyzara smell so bad naturally it not surprising they would not be bothered by essence of vatulalilu. Petal perfume would be hard to detect over own body odor."

Masurathoo was suitably indifferent to the implied insult. "Spoken as by one with no experience or knowledge of the subtleties of fine fragrances." Having sufficiently smeared his rapidly shredding body wrappings with the pungent plant extract, he strode serenely between them, exuding confidence (and much more) as he headed for the suddenly no longer terrifying river.

Both wobbly from the effects of repeated upchucking, his companions followed rather more shakily. They did not exchange a word but, upon reaching the river's edge, conspired simultaneously to pick up, swing, and throw the wildly protesting Deyzara headfirst into the waiting water.

13

Matthias did not want to go back to the skimmer port. Swamped with requests for authorizations, statistics that had to be evaluated, decisions that had to be approved, subordinates who had to be coddled, and delegations of Deyzara desperately in need of reassurance, she barely had time to leave her office long enough to say hello to her family before collapsing into the cooled, dehumidified airbed alongside her husband. But the call had been both cryptic and urgent.

This time she took no chances. It was all very well and good to put on a brave front, to pretend that the official Commonwealth contingent on Fluva was neutral and favored neither side in the ongoing fight. Unfortunately, reality conflicted. She had no desire to be surrounded again by an angry mob of hungry, dispossessed Deyzara.

This time when she arrived at the port, she was accompanied by a pair of armed peaceforcers. Instead of landing some distance from her intended destination, her skimmer touched down directly opposite the main service facilities. Flanked by her guards, she moved quickly through the rain and into the building, hardly glancing at the milling crowd outside. Actually, she noted, things appeared to have settled down somewhat since her last visit. Bedara and his team seemed to be getting things under control. She chose to believe that was the case as she moved deeper into the arched structure.

Tarik Bergovoy was waiting for her. Unusual for a Commonwealth resident of Fluva, he sported a neatly trimmed white beard. The longer they stayed on Fluva, the more inclined resident humans were to engage in general depilation, since body hair offered an inviting mobile nesting site for all manner of tiny opportunistic creatures. Not Bergovoy. In addition to his beard, he flourished a full head of curly gray-black hair in hirsute defiance of potential infestation.

"Administrator." They shook hands. His fingers were thick and rough, though the ambient humidity that softened everything made them feel more creased than calloused.

They spoke while strolling toward the rear of the main hangar. At present, several large skimmers were undergoing servicing. Flashes of actinic light like miniature thunderbolts sparked from the undersides and flanks of various craft. Half-hidden by the open panels behind which they were working, painters were laying down new circuitry. Mechanicals scurried to and fro across the bare, dry floor, ferrying equipment and supplies to preoccupied workers. More sophisticated mechs carried out automated, less sensitive repairs on their own, without human supervision. At the far end of the hangar, a solitary thranx was tuning some particularly delicate and expensive piece of apparatus recently arrived from Amropolous.

"Things going okay here, Tarik?"

He shrugged diffidently. "Every now and then we have to bring in a couple of peaceforcers to evict some shelter-seeking refugees from one corner of the facility or another. That's supposed to be Sanderson's job, not ours. Interrupts our work here."

Wim Sanderson was head of port authority. "I'll have a word with him," she assured the chief mechanic. "That's not why you got me out of bed to come down here. Why didn't you just message what you had to tell me?"

Bergovoy glanced around. His manner was casual, but his eyes were not. "Didn't trust the system. I know it's supposed to be secure, but you never know." He returned his attention to his guest. "In response to your requests, I had the service records on the two missing vehicles compiled. They were more interesting for what wasn't there than for what was."

She eyed him intently. "You want to elaborate on that?"

Bergovoy absently stroked his beard. He did not look at all, she reflected, like Saint Nick. More like one of the red-suited fat man's assistants: the one who did the dirty work in some dim, windowless basement of the toy workshop.

"It was cleverly done, but not so perfectly that someone who knows how to read maintenance records couldn't spot the anomalies. Of course, you'd have to be looking for something like that or you'd just gloss over them. That's what happened until I went digging for specifics. Certain details had been altered. Others—not many, but of significance—were missing altogether. It was a good job, but not perfect. Suggests that whoever was involved was knowledgeable, but no expert."

She took a moment to scan their surroundings herself. Satisfied that they were not being watched, she looked back up at the chief mechanic. "It follows that whoever went to the trouble of manipulating official records might also have gone to the greater trouble of manipulating the related skimmer instrumentation."

Bergovoy nodded solemnly. "Instrumentation, onboard equipment, explicit vehicular functions—that I wasn't able to determine." His expression darkened. "I pride myself on running a good shop here, even under Fluvan conditions. We service all Authority vehicles here as well as a goodly number of private craft. People depend on us, on the quality and reliability of our work." Turning slightly, he gestured toward the rain-swept forest.

"No way would I let one of my people send a suspect vehicle into town, much less out into the Viisiiviisii. Nothing leaves here unless it's had all its systems, even the noncritical ones, double–checked out. Whoever altered those service records knew they were sending people in harm's way. I don't know exactly what was done to those two missing skimmers, but the consequences speak for themselves." Holding up a fist, he slowly clenched and released his powerful fingers. "When we find out who it was, I'd like to request the pleasure of a face-to-face conversation with them."

She ignored the appeal. "Any idea who might be responsible?"

He shook his head sharply. "I'd hate to think it was any of my people. But only qualified users and technicians have access to hangared craft."

"*Authorized* access," she corrected him.

He nodded. "I always thought we had adequate security here. But this isn't Brisbane, or Chitteranx. Of course, port security's been stepped up since this crisis with the Deyzara and the Sakuntala, but both of the skimmers in question set out and went down before all this got really cranked up."

He went silent then. In lieu of further questions, she waited for additional comments. When he looked up at her again, he appeared uncertain.

"Come on, Tarik," she encouraged him. "Whatever it is you're thinking, even if it's no more than pure speculation, I need to know. I'm working in the dark here."

"It's nothing conclusive," he muttered. "Just a possibility. There's no proof of anything."

She smiled up at him. "I'm a professional bureaucrat, Tarik. I'm used to separating suspicion from fact. I don't jump to conclusions."

Pursing his lips, he nodded understandingly. "All right, then: here it is. Personnel records show that among those who worked on not one, but both, of the stray skimmers were a service specialist name of Charukande and a parts tech named Dalindidretha."

The names were sufficient identification. "I didn't know you had Deyzara technicians working here."

"Sure. They're good, too. Although I don't work directly with any of them, I made sure to check the performance stats on both of these. Nothing but good reports, high-grade evaluations. I haven't spoken to them about this, or about anything else related to the disappearances. I figured that was your department." His voice dropped slightly. "Or Security's."

As powerfully as the chief mechanic's words resonated, she knew she had to move slowly on his observations. If word got out among the refugees that two of their own kind were being investigated for sabotage, it would only add one more layer of disruption to an already unruly state of affairs.

"Do you have any definite reason to suspect them?"

Bergovoy didn't hesitate. "None whatsoever. Like I said, their records are clean." His expression changed. "Changing the subject a little, I want you to know that I can understand why someone might want to get rid of this Hasselemoga person."

Her brow furrowed. "You do? Why?"

"Never met him myself, but from what I've been told, he's a pretty disagreeable character. There's also apparently quite a bit of professional jealousy where he's involved. Apparently, he's as good at bioprospecting as he is at pissing people off." The chief mechanic's eyes bored into her own. "Two reasons someone, or several someones, might have for seeing to it that he has to try to walk out of the Viisiiviisii."

"Nobody walks out of the Viisiiviisii," she commented absently.

"If you follow that line of reasoning," Bergovoy was continuing, "it makes sense that whoever wanted to see the last of this guy would do their best to make sure nobody finds him."

She pondered the speculations. Somehow, it didn't quite jell. Something was missing, something that lay somewhere between motive and manipulation.

"I can see the envious wanting to get rid of the competition or somebody they dislike. That's one thing. But eliminating a rescue team means taking on the Commonwealth Authority. The first is personal; the second implies much greater concerns."

Bergovoy was clearly interested. "What greater concerns?"

She sighed heavily. "If I knew that, we'd have a pretty good idea who's responsible. Thank you for your help, Tarik." She started past him.

"One more thing, Administrator." The mechanic was smiling humorlessly. "If you do find out who's responsible, you will at least let me know, won't you?"

Her expression was grim. "If I find out, Tarik, everyone will know."

Though she spent much of the rest of the day dealing with those administrative matters that absolutely, positively required her personal attention and could not possibly be put off, she was no nearer clearing her work backlog than when she had started. New data arrived faster than it could be processed. It kept her hard at work after dark. No one wanted to travel home in the dark. Under cover of the rain-swept night the stealthy inhabitants of the Viisiiviisii crept inside the town limits, only to melt away again at the first sign of cloud-masked daylight. In the dark and rain, even modern safeguard technology sometimes failed to offer sufficient protection to those who had the nerve to venture outside their cosseted homes and places of work.

Nocturnal travel was safer for her than for others. Her skimmer's programming transported her to the residency compound without any need for human input or guidance. Like those of the other Commonwealth residents, her home was suspended from strong strilk cables attached to an intricate support network of composite pylons. In addition to windows in the roof and walls, there were two in the floor: one in the living room and another in Andrea's. Standing on one of the transparencies, one could look straight down at other residences or to the water far below. A terrestrial spider would have felt right at home with the layout.

Jack was waiting for her. She reflected on how things had changed. When they had first settled in on Fluva, she had often arrived home before him, since he'd needed to spend a lot of overtime familiarizing himself with the lab. Now she was the one trundling home after dark.

Though perfunctory, their kiss was enough to lift her spirits, if not her energy level.

"I've made you some supper. You haven't eaten?"

She shook her head, mustered a weary smile. "Are you kidding?" In the small combination kitchen/dining room, she settled in behind the table and dug into the meal he had prepared. She was almost too tired to eat. Skimmers and supervisors, she reminded herself: all need fuel.

Sitting down across the table, he watched her for a while, leaving her alone until she'd downed some of the food. "Another bad day?"

"Here, lately, they're all bad." While it might be an odd shade of indigo, faux pasta made from a local fungus slid easily down her welcoming throat. "Today was *special*, though."

"Uh-oh." He crossed his arms over his chest and looked sympathetic. He was very good at that, she realized gratefully. "What now?"

"Those two skimmers that went down in the south? The bioprospector nobody seems to like and the rescue team that was sent after him? Bergovoy, the chief mechanic out at the port, says their maintenance records were tampered with. More than a hint of funny business there."

Her husband's expression turned solemn. "That's not good."

"There's more." She gestured with a utensil. "Two of the last techs to work on both craft are Deyzara."

He let out a soft whistle. "Bergovoy implicated them?"

"Only by inference." She took a long swallow of cold fruit juice. She could never pronounce the Sakuntala name for the fruit from which it came, but the juice was delectable. "I can envision why somebody might want this bioprospector out of the way and, to a certain extent, anyone who might try to rescue him. What I can't imagine is why this might involve the Deyzara."

Slumping in his chair, one foot fiddling idly with her right leg under the table, he contemplated the ceiling. "Maybe it's not so different from trying to ascribe cause and effect to predator and prey in the lab. A xerexl wants a puorot dead so it can have it for lunch. Okay. Why would the Deyzara want a bioprospector dead? Furthermore, why would they not want him found and brought back alive?" He lowered his gaze. "To the xerexl, food is the most important thing. What's the most important thing to the Deyzara?"

She didn't hesitate. "Money. Commercial success."

Picking up the pitcher, he refilled her empty glass. "When you get back to the office tomorrow, try to connect predator with prey."

She frowned. "You think money's behind this?"

"Money, or some kind of business advantage. *If* the Deyzara are involved. Don't you think it's worth checking out?"

She nodded slowly. "Yes. Yes, I do. You know, Jack, sometimes I think you're a little bit of a genius."

His face creased in mock outrage. Outside, something on the fringe of the deep forest howled plaintively. "What do you mean, 'little bit'?"

It was two hours before she could find time for Pandusky to even begin to run a search of relevant records. It was midafternoon when he finally transferred what he had been able to unearth to her office. Sitting straight in her chair, she deactivated all communications, including the emergency line, as she contemplated the information floating in the air above her desk.

There was no attempt to conceal the data that jumped out at her. Why would there be? By itself, it was the perfect image of innocuousness. There was no need to mask straightforward business dealings. The fact that several firms were involved in exploring a certain section of the great southern Viisiiviisii was to be expected. Companies as well as individuals were busily engaged in seeking out useful, exploitable resources throughout both varzea-covered continents.

However, the search she'd had Pandusky run focused on one small portion of the southern part of the northern continent: the general region where Shadrach Hasselemoga and the rescue team sent to find him had both gone missing. It turned out that only three companies were working in that same general vicinity. Two had their own teams in the area, while the third was an umbrella support group for individual prospectors. Besides their mutual interests, the three companies had one other thing in common.

All were owned and run by Deyzara.

Sitting back in her seat, she contemplated the hovering words. Circumstantial evidence to be sure, but right now it was all she had to go on. At best it was mere coincidence. But at the other end of the speculative spectrum, it was more than a little suggestive.

Three Deyzara outfits all prospecting in the same region. A disagreeable but highly competent outsider starts sniffing around the same area. Inexplicably, he vanishes. So does the team sent out to find him. Deyzara technicians are reported to have worked on both downed craft.

The Deyzara were known to all but worship commercial achievement and to strive for financial gain. That was a truism and not a generalization. The Deyzara themselves made no apology for it. But they had limits. Although she was not intimately familiar with its often arcane details, Matthias did not think the modern Deyzara code of business ethics extended to sanctioning the murder of rivals, much less that of individuals incidentally involved on the periphery of competition, like the missing rescue team. Besides, the lost crew included one of their own. Suffused with curiosity as well as information, she now began to run a few database searches of her own.

Insofar as she was able to tell, the individual known as Masurathoo was not and had never been in the employ of any of the three Deyzara businesses under suspicion. Did that make him a more likely target or less of one? What better way to throw an investigation into murderous sabotage off the track than by disposing of one of your own people? She decided Masurathoo's participation could not be used to either confirm or deny Deyzaran involvement.

Research and speculation indicated that Deyzara might be directly involved. The question was, were they guilty of anything? Or *was* it simple coincidence that Hasselemoga had vanished in a region being worked by three Deyzara firms? No question but that his demise would give all three companies a freer hand in the region in question. A carefully crafted and complex assassination-by-disappearance would give deeper meaning to the phrase *killing the competition.*

Since her arrival on Fluva she and Jack had made a number of good friends among the Deyzara. In its way, their time-honored avariciousness was almost quaint. Certainly she had never felt physically threatened by it, nor had she ever met anyone who was. Deyzara ruthlessness was confined to computation and the manipulation of figures. Otherwise they were generally considered to be mild in disposition and, if anything, excessively polite in their dealings with others. The notion that one or more of them had resorted to multiple homicide to gain a possible business advantage was hard to countenance. Besides, she had no proof of anything. Only tenuous possibilities and imagined links.

Unfortunately, that was all she had.

Was it enough to order action against any of the Deyzara companies concerned? The Deyzara could be exceptionally closemouthed where business dealings were involved. Accusing them directly might shake loose one or more individuals willing to expose a plot in order to save themselves. If there *was* anything to shake loose. If there was a plot.

But sending peaceforcers to bring in the principals of a Deyzara company could further exacerbate the current political situation. At the very least, there would be an outcry that the Commonwealth Authority was singling them out without any hard evidence to back up whatever accusations it might be thinking of making. Giving the local Deyzara the impression that the Authority even suspected some of their own of such a crime carried with it the automatic, and dangerous, corollary that the Authority favored the Sakuntala. That was not the kind of sentiment she wanted to spread right now. As always, it was vital that her office be perceived by both sides as being impartial. If that perception was lost, she risked sacrificing any ability to influence the Deyzara. They would respond by sending appeals to higher Commonwealth authority that bypassed her—if they hadn't begun to do so already. The volume of anxious space-minus communications between the local Deyzaran community and their ancestral home of Tharce IV had risen noticeably since the beginning of the Sakuntala uprising. She had no way of knowing whether any of those coded private communications included attempts, either direct or veiled, to undermine her authority on Fluva.

She would have drummed her fingers on the desktop if she hadn't been so tired. Instead, she banished the square of floating facts. Addressing the desk's pickup, she asked to be connected to the skimmer port, maintenance division, chief mechanic's office.

Bergovoy was out on the floor, supervising work inside a cargo skimmer. His portable conveyed a tridee of its owner from the shoulders up, detailed down to the sweat on his forehead, as her call was automatically forwarded to its intended destination.

"What can I do for you, Administrator?" asked the hovering projection.

"I was just wondering, Tarik. The Deyzara technicians you said worked on those two missing skimmers. I can see how someone with a modicum of practical mechanical knowledge could cause them to crash. What's hard to accept is that both skimmers' internals were manipulated subtly enough to force

them down at a specific place and time. Not to mention simultaneously disabling every bit of backup instrumentation."

The projection nodded. "If that's indeed what happened,
then it was certainly a sophisticated piece of sabotage."

She studied the projection closely, wishing he were there in
person. "Too sophisticated for your Deyzarans to manage without help?"

Bergovoy considered the question. "Hard to say. The two-
trunks we're talking about are good workers. Whether they're
good enough to bring off something like this is something else
again. I don't see any way to know for sure without testing
them on similar procedures. If they are responsible, then I suspect they'd be sharp enough to figure out the purpose of the
testing. They'd fail intentionally, and we wouldn't know any
more than we do now. Except that if they are responsible,
they'll have been warned that they're under suspicion." He hesitated.

"If you want, I can set something up with them, try to ascer-
tain their competency level."

"No, no." She sighed wearily. "I really just wanted your
opinion, Tarik. If the techs in question *are* responsible for
what's happened, the last thing we want to do is let them know
that we suspect their involvement. Just keep an eye on them."

"Like I told you before, Administrator. Anything out of the
ordinary crops up, you'll be the first to know." As he turned,
she had a brief glimpse of the tech crew he was working with
before he clicked off. They were all human.

Something small and beige was smacking against her window, trying to get inside. A pensive glance showed a creature
the size of her open palm. It had multiple translucent wings, a
stout sausage-shaped body, and a single large compound eye
stretched across its front. Yellow splotches decorated the
smooth abdomen. It had no thorax or neck and no visible legs.

The third smack was hard enough to prompt the window to
respond with a small defensive electric charge. Stunned, the
would-be intruder drifted backward, hovered a moment in the

damp air, and then whirled around to whir back into the
trees and the rain. She continued to stare at the place where
it had vanished. Mulling over its disappearance unexpectedly
prompted a new line of contemplation.

Sentients, like the native fauna of the Viisiiviisii, were always
moving in and out of the forest, their paths and purposes often
concealed by the vegetation and the constant rain. The Fluvan
varzea was an excellent place in which to hide methods and
motives. Suppose the Deyzara weren't behind the sabotage of
the two missing skimmers? Suppose another party, knowing
that Deyzara technicians had worked on both craft and also
aware of the involvement of Deyzaran-run companies in exploring a certain section of the southern Viisiiviisii, decided to
exploit that knowledge to make it *look* like the Deyzara were responsible? Who would benefit from such a deception?

Naturally, the Sakuntala came first to mind. In the context of
the current uprising, it would be much to their benefit to have
the irritation of the Commonwealth Authority turned away
from them and focused instead on the Deyzara. Motive was
certainly there. The only trouble with that scenario, she reflected, was that while the Sakuntala were famed for many qualities, subtlety was not among them. That was not to say the
cleverest among them, individuals like the missing Jemunu-jah,
could not have devised such a plan. But conceiving and carrying out were two different things. Were there Sakuntala techs
accomplished enough to have made the necessary alterations to
the missing skimmers' instrumentation? That was one possibility Bergovoy had not discussed. And if they were not sufficiently accomplished to have carried out such sabotage on their
own, who might have advised them? For that matter, who
could have advised the Deyzara techs on matters of sabotage?
Was there anyone else besides Deyzara or Sakuntala who potentially stood to benefit from the disappearance of Shadrach Hasselemoga and the team sent to find and rescue him?

She probably should have made the connection sooner between such possibilities and the possession by the Sakuntala radicals of advanced weaponry. But she'd been so overwhelmed with work, so swamped with the refugee crisis, that she'd had little time left for speculating further afield. She addressed the desk sharply.

"Call to Major Bredel."

The head of Fluva's peaceforcer contingent appeared above the desk less than a minute later. He looked as harried as she felt, she decided.

"Morning, Charles."

The holo nodded once. "Administrator Matthias. If there's a problem, I hope it's minor. We're stretched pretty thin here right now."

"I know," she told him understandingly. "I'm sorry, but there's something that needs to be done."

He looked resigned. "I can't spare any people to run an observation. Those who aren't trying to keep Sakuntala fanatics from burning every Deyzara building they come across are busy dealing with security at the refugee encampments."

"This is nothing like that. Do you know those two AAnn the government accredited as observers? Thessu and Jaill or Jaal or something?"

Some of the officer's fatigue seemed to slough away. "Why?" he inquired sharply. "You've found something out about them?"

"No. At least, not yet. I just need to talk to them. Ask them a few questions."

"About what? No, no, don't tell me. I'm already dealing with far too many outlandish suppositions. Talk to me again when you have facts you want me to act on." His expression turned thoughtful. "So you need to talk to our AAnn guests, hmm? Might take a while to track them down. From what I hear, they spend a lot of time out in the forest, traveling from community to community. On the lookout for commercial possibilities, or so I'm told."

"Just find them and bring them in."

"It'll be done. Suppose they don't want to come?"

"Have your people explain that there's been some trouble with their accreditation."

Bredel matched her thoughts. "They'll wonder why a simple bureaucratic procedure can't be performed remotely."

"All right then," she replied impatiently, thinking fast, "say that I've received a report they might be particularly vulnerable to a new virus that's just been isolated by our biomed division, and that I'm concerned for their welfare."

The major chuckled. "That should confuse them. From what I hear, this isn't an especially healthy climate for AAnn." His tone changed to one of warning. "If you think they're up to something, Administrator, and they are, they might still resist."

"Have whoever picks them up say that I insist."

He nodded tersely. "I'll let you know when they've arrived."

14

I t did not take nearly as long as she had feared for the AAnn to be brought in. Like every other vehicle on Fluva that was designed to travel through the Viisiiviisii, that of the duly accredited Imperial observers was equipped with a specific iden- tification and locator beacon. They showed up the following morning, short-tempered and out of sorts. With the AAnn, one expected nothing less.

She waited for them to be brought into her office. Thought- fully, she had ordered in a couple of chairs with larger gaps in their seatbacks, to accommodate AAnn tails, which were thicker and more muscular than those of the Sakuntala. With plenty of other things to worry about even before the advent of the ex- tremist Sakuntala uprising, she hadn't wanted the belligerent reptiloids on Fluva. But the accreditation of AAnn observers pre- ceded her appointment as administrator. Since then, several pairs of them had come and gone. She checked a hard copy. These two, Thessu and Jallrii, were the latest. Floral pharmaceuticals were the specific interest of these two, or so their official dossiers claimed. Try as she might, it was hard to envision a couple of can- tankerous AAnn spending their time picking flowers.

Their mutual outrage preceded them. As soon as the door opened and the sound-absorbent bubble that enclosed her of- fice was violated, she was able to hear their sputtering and hiss- ing. It sounded like someone had dumped a vit player in the middle of a barrel of snakes and was rolling the result in her direction.

Then they were inside, their special suits hanging rumpled around them, the dehumidifying masks that covered their snouts making them look as if they had just stepped off an asteroid instead of the front porch. Slitted pupils glared at her from behind wraparound protective lenses designed to keep ambient moisture out of eyes that were used to excessive dryness. She glanced briefly at the custom varzea garb and the heavily laden service belts they wore beneath the protective outer suits. The heat from the multiple layers of attire wouldn't bother them. AAnn thrived in the heat. It was the humidity they couldn't handle. Despite their specialized outfits they must be moderately uncomfortable, she decided.

Good.

One of the peaceforcers escorting the visibly aggravated pair eyed her questioningly. She waved him off. Her visitors would already have been scanned for weapons. Though shorter than the average human, they were powerfully built, and the claws on their hands and sandaled feet constituted weaponry that could not be checked at the door, as did their muscular tails. She was not overly concerned. If they went berserk and attacked her, she was not entirely defenseless herself. Furthermore, they must know that any hostile action would be observed and recorded and that they would suffer any attendant consequences.

They hesitated when she offered them the chairs but finally accepted in a huff. Perhaps it was the realization that she had gone to the trouble of providing seats suitable for their dimensions. Or maybe they were simply tired of standing.

Introductions were terse and formal. No physical greetings were exchanged, for which she was grateful. The AAnn equivalent of a handshake consisted of gripping the other person's throat with one hand—claws retracted, of course. The one called Thessu clearly had no time for such pleasantries.

"Why have we been brought here, under armed esscort, in

violation of all extant agreementss?" His words were supplemented with a first-degree gesture of displeasure that was notable for its brusqueness.

"Truly!" snapped Jallrii. "What iss thiss nonssensse about a 'new viruss'? We are consstantly monitoring our own immediate environment and have detected nonessuch. We are both of uss in excellent health."

"If you had heard of it, then it wouldn't be new, would it?" She smiled pleasantly, knowing that the AAnn were receptive to a display of teeth. "As chief administrator I'm responsible for the health and well-being of every nonindigene on Fluva. Including guests of the Commonwealth."

"Thiss iss not a way to treat guessts," Jallrii hissed, adding a second-degree gesticulation of annoyance.

"I could not forgive myself if anyone on my tour of duty was to suffer because of an oversight on my part," she replied smoothly. "In matters of medicine, I find it's always better to err on the side of caution."

As much as her words, her demeanor appeared to have some effect. AAnn rage gave way to plain irritation. "Vya-nar," muttered Thessu. "By the-sand-that-shelters-life, if your concern iss only for the health of otherss, then it iss to be commended."

She ran her right index finger over an apparently bare portion of her desk. If she pressed down in a certain place, a hidden alarm would sound and various protective barriers would spring into being between her and her guests.

"Much as I would like to accept your compliment, I'm afraid that I can't. While I am truly interested in your health, as long as you are here I was also hoping you could provide me with some information on other matters."

Jallrii's pupils narrowed even farther, the protective inner transparent eyelids flashing shut over both eyes. It was purely a reflex action, since there was no blowing sand in the room. Indeed, both AAnn would have welcomed an intrusion of intimate airborne grit.

"What other matterss?" he hissed warily.

"From time to time certain minority extremist elements among the Sakuntala lose control of themselves and vent their cultural frustrations against the Deyzara. As you know, we are in the midst of one such regrettable period. Only this one is different. A great number of Sakuntala are involved and there has been considerable damage to property as well as some loss of life."

"Deplorable, truly," Thessu declared, adding a gesture Matthias could not decipher along with an elegant double flick of his pointed tongue. It snapped against the inside of his mask.

"The quarrelss of localss do not concern uss." Though the AAnn visage was not nearly as flexible as that of humans or Sakuntala, Jallrii managed to look smug. "We are only interessted in the pharmaceutical potential of native flora."

"Of course you are." Her smile remained conscientiously fixed in place. "That's why you wouldn't happen to know how the Sakuntala radicals have managed to coordinate their current efforts to a degree unprecedented in recorded history. Not to mention how they've managed to come into possession of advanced energy and explosive weapons."

The pair exchanged a glance. "We would not," Thessu finally responded. "Why would we rissk our possition here, as guessts, to involve oursselves in the sstupid ssquabbling of primitive localss?"

Leaning forward, she rested both elbows on the desk, tapping her lips with her steepled fingers. "That's a question I've just recently been forced to ask myself." As they both began to swell with indignation, she added quickly, "From a purely hypothetical standpoint, of course. Understand, I'm not accusing you of anything. But as administrator, it is my duty to consider even the most extreme scenarios."

That calmed them—somewhat. "What possible advantage could we gain from a fight between nativess?" Jallrii demanded to know. "Ssuch disscord only inhibitss our fieldwork."

"Yes, your fieldwork." She eyed them solicitously. "I'm told you spend most of your time out in the field. It must be very uncomfortable for you."

"Very truly." Thessu let out a hissing sigh. "How we long to conclude our tour of duty in·thiss misserable place! I pine for the hot, dry sands of home."

"As do I," added Jallrii, not to be outdone in expressions of vapid nostalgia.

"You've been here awhile. You must have amassed a considerable body of knowledge, not to mention a first-rate collection of specimens."

Thessu gestured fourth-degree assent. "All carefully ordered and classified according to potential ussagess and commercial value."

She was nodding slowly. "I'm sure it's very impressive. Could I see it? And my husband? He works for Bio, you know."

Thessu gestured apologetically. "I am regretful, but that iss not possible." He ventured the AAnn equivalent of a smile. "We have not worked sso hard for sso long to give away potential trade ssecretess to curiouss humanss."

She didn't think they would, but she was curious to see how they would react to her request. "Then, to be blunt about it, and from a purely hypothetical standpoint, as I said, you've had nothing to do with helping the rioting Sakuntala organize and you haven't in any way helped them to obtain modern weapons?"

"You know what the Ssakuntala are like." Jallrii summoned up a credible shudder. "Violent, unpredictable ssavagess. Truly, to place advanced armamentss in the handss of ssuch primitivess would be to invite chaos! It would be totally irressponssible."

She placed her hands flat on the desk and sat up as straight as her aching back would allow. "My thoughts exactly. Consequently, I can't help but wonder who might benefit from the eruption of chaos on Fluva. Surely not the AAnn—truly."

This time they appeared to hesitate before Thessu finally

responded, "Fluva liess within the Commonwealth'ss ssphere of influence. It would be dissingenuouss of uss to deny that we would prefer to ssee it sshift to an unaligned sstance or, yess, even to requesst some kind of formal association with the Empire."

"That's a very political statement to make for someone who professes that his sole interest lies in flowers."

"The Empire alwayss favorss the sstrong," Thessu observed.

"We are all people of the ssand," an unperturbed Jallrii added with becoming calm. "Wherever we go, the Empire travelss with uss." Behind his mask and goggles, yellow-flecked eyes twinkled. "But to ssuggesst that we may have provided armamentss to thesse uneducated primitivess iss outrageouss!" Both clawed hands moved rapidly, executing a gesture of second-degree indignation mixed with an equal amount of resentment.

"I did not mean to imply any such thing," she replied, when of course that was exactly what she had meant to imply. "And since you haven't been advising the Sakuntala extremists on how to conduct their uprising and you haven't been supplying them with advanced weaponry—Commonwealth weaponry, acquired on the sly so as not to implicate anyone from, say, Blassussar or Pregglin—then it stands to reason that you also aren't in any way responsible for or involved with the disappearance of the human bioprospector Shadrach Hasselemoga or the Sakuntala-Deyzara team that was sent to try to rescue him."

It was a long sentence and it resulted in a long and, as far as she could tell, genuinely perplexed pause on the part of her guests.

It was Thessu who finally replied, choreographing his response with a third-degree gesture of puzzlement supported by second-degree confusion. The elaborateness of his hand movements belied the brevity of his response.

"Who?"

She spoke briefly to her desk. Along with their missing craft, rotating, fully formed images of the unaccounted-for trio appeared above the projection surface.

"You know nothing about any of these individuals, or their vehicles?"

Turning to face each other, the AAnn conversed briskly in their own language. Their hisses and clicks were accompanied by a vigorous semaphoring of hands. Once again, it was Thessu who spoke. For the first time since the conversation had commenced, Matthias had the feeling that her visitors were honestly mystified.

"We know nothing of the oness of whom you sspeak. Why would you think we might have knowledge of them or their whereaboutss?"

"The human bioprospector's disappearance was accompanied by the complete failure of his emergency instrumentation. The same is true of those who were sent into the southern Viisiiviisii to bring him back. One such failure verges on the unprecedented. Two such failures, occurring as they did one right after another, constitute an implausible coincidence. My people have been forced to consider the possibility that both craft were tampered with deliberately. The question is: To what end?"

Jallrii switched his scaled tail back and forth, smacking it several times against the floor. "Not thiss end, Adminisstrator." The AAnn were known to have a sense of humor, albeit one that was singular in nature and rarely experienced by outsiders.

"You are implying, I think," declared Thessu, "that not only may the dissappearancess of which you sspeak be in ssome way connected to uss, but that we perssonally may ssomehow be connected with them." Eyes that verged on the hypnotic bored into her own, compelling her to blink. "How in the namess of the Four Wellss of Perdition could the dissappearance of ssome thickheaded human and ssimpleminded nativess in the unexplored Viisiiviisii be of the sslightesst benefit to my colleague and mysself, far less to the Empire?"

When the AAnn spoke the name of the Viisiiviisii, she reflected, the word emerged as a single long hiss. "You just said yourself that the AAnn favor the strong, who in this conflict you perceive to be the Sakuntala. There are several indications—

nothing definite or verifiable, mind—that the Deyzara might be behind these disappearances. That could indeed be the case, though much remains to be substantiated before any formal accusations can be levied. However," and this time it was Thessu, mesmerizing stare or not, who blinked, "if certain parties who support the uprising of the radical Sakuntala were responsible, it would go a long way toward explaining one aspect of the disappearances that continues to puzzle my advisers and myself."

Jallrii was the perfect picture of reptilian nonchalance. "Truly, the longer such puzzlementss remain unssolved, the more elaborate consspiracy theoriess have a way of becoming. Purely for the ssake of disscussion, how could we in any way be ressponssible for the dissappearance of thosse of whom you sspeak? Ssurely you are not ssuggessting that Thessu and I ssomehow managed to evade your local ssecurity, ssneak into your sskimmer facilitiess, ssabotage the missing craft, and esscape again? All, of course, without being sso much as ssniffed by anyone elsse?"

"I am not suggesting anything of the sort." An eerie serenity had come over her. Outside, the rain continued to fall, indifferent to the confrontation taking place inside the main administration building. "My technicians inform me that a very high degree of technical skill would be required to carry out such sabotage, particularly to manipulate a skimmer's sealed emergency instrumentation. It is a matter of some dispute as to whether any of the Deyzara technicians on local staff possess those attributes. It is also generally conceded that no Sakuntala technician does. That forces one to contemplate other possibilities.

"Now, if a Sakuntala technician or two were to receive from another, more technologically sophisticated source detailed instructions on how to carry out such deadly modifications, it's easy enough to see how the consequences could be blamed on the Deyzara. If they were to be held responsible, especially in the current political climate, this could be greatly to the advantage of the Sakuntala. For example, gullible humans, and I won't deny that there are some, who might otherwise be neutral in the current conflict, might find themselves more partial to the Sakuntala point of view. If the Sakuntala were to be favored, that would naturally also be to the benefit of those who favor the Sakuntala." She smiled pleasantly. "The AAnn, let's say."

She waited for a response. It was not long in coming.

"If what you ssay hass happened, and you are being truthful about the circumsstances ssurrounding it, then we will not deny ssuch a sscenario could be to the benefit of the Empire." Thessu raised his left hand, claws extended. "But I and my colleague will sswear on the ssandss in which we were brooded that neither of uss had anything to do with the incident you sso elaborately detail. Until you sspoke of it jusst now we had no knowledge of the dissappearancess of which you sspeak. We are in no way or wisse involved in the vanisshment of the two craft to which you refer. Wonderful if it iss blamed on the Deyzara, to the benefit of our friendss among the Ssakuntala. We welcome such a development. But . . . much as we would like to take credit for ssuch a clever sscheme, we had nothing to do with it. If indeed the dissappearancess *are* truly due to the kind of convoluted and problematical plot you desscribe."

Jallrii gestured first-degree concurrence. "We are not foolss. While we may approve of the active machinationss of certain Ssakuntala, we would not go sso far as to engage in an action that would take the life of a human, a Commonwealth citizen, ssimply to casst possible assperions on the Deyzara."

"Am I supposed to take your word on that?" she asked candidly. It was a tactless question but one that she felt had to be asked. Each of her previous inquiries had vanished, sunk in a suave sea of AAnn denial.

Thessu signaled no animosity. Among the AAnn, such candor was greatly respected. "It doess not matter if you do or you do not. Given the current ssituation, killing a human or caussing one to meet hiss death, enjoyable as ssome individuals might find ssuch a happensstance, would not be worth the rissk were we to be held ressponssible. Certainly it would not be worth it ssimply to casst the Deyzara in a bad light."

Her visitors reposed in silence, tails switching metronomically back and forth, waiting for the next question. She was out of questions and had received no answers. Or at least, no indictable responses. She was no more cognizant of their possible involvement now than she had been when they had first come through her office door, hissing and complaining. If they were telling the truth, then the session had been a complete waste of time. No, she told herself. Worse than a waste of time. It would leave her looking paranoid and foolish.

"Thank you for your time, sanderlings. I appreciate your answering my questions."

Thessu gestured third-degree magnanimity. "We are ever conssciouss of our privileged possition as mere obsserverss on thiss Commonwealth-adminisstered world, and would do nothing to jeopardize it. I ssympathize with the awkward possition that pressently confrontss you." He showed both rows of sharp, strong teeth. "You musst be under a great deal of perssonal sstress."

"I appreciate your concern," she replied without acknowledging the accuracy of his surmise. "It is truly a difficult time. For myself as well as for others." She smiled back. Her teeth were not as sharp, or as numerous, but they were just as white. "That's why I'd never be able to forgive myself if either of you, as guests here, came down with an infection that could easily have been prevented. I promise you that our best medical people will make certain that doesn't happen."

The AAnn exchanged a glance. "We are in perfect health," Thessu assured her.

"Yes, you may be—for now. But I've been told that this new virus, to which your kind may be particularly susceptible, is truly virulent. I couldn't live with myself knowing that you could be properly vaccinated against it and had missed the opportunity. The medical team that discovered it has gengineered just such a vaccine." Pushing back her chair, she stood behind her desk. "It shouldn't take up much of your time. A three-stage inoculation followed by a suitable period of observation to ensure there are no side effects."

"Sside effectss? Vaccination?" Jallrii's gaze narrowed and the end of the dehumidifying mask over his snout began to show signs of fogging. "What iss thiss talk?"

Reaching down, Matthias touched a blank part of her desk. Immediately the door opened behind the AAnn to admit a brace of armed peaceforcers. She maintained her smile.

"You'll be escorted to Medical. A team is waiting for you there. I look forward to seeing you again once you have been properly treated." She glanced down at her desk. "There will be no charge for this service, of course. It should be regarded as a complimentary benefit of being guests of the Commonwealth."

Surrounding the irate pair, who had risen from their chairs, the peaceforcers began to shepherd them from the room.

"This iss truly unnecessary!" Thessu was hissing loudly. "We are in perfect health! We have no need of inferior Commonwealth mediciness or medical attention. I musst protesst in the sstrongesst termss!"

"Bye!" she called out to them as they were hustled out the door. "I'll see you in a few days, after you come out of quarantine. Be nice to your attending physicians: they have your best interests at heart. Truly."

The door shut behind the stunned, sputtering pair. Jallrii's tail banged into the jamb, and then they were gone. Her office was quiet again, except for the ever-present drumming of rain falling outside.

She slumped back down in her chair, which immediately began to massage her back, backside, and upper legs. By having the two AAnn detained she knew she was running the risk of precipitating an interstellar incident, albeit a minor one. She felt the gamble was worth it. There were only two of them, Fluva was an out-of-the-way world, and it would be difficult for Imperial authorities to build a case against her for holding them for what purported to be medical treatment that was in the claimed best interests of the detained. She felt the worst they could charge her with was being overly hospitable.

Meanwhile, the two would be incommunicado from any off-world contacts. They would also be unable to advise or assist any allies they had acquired among the Sakuntala and would be prevented from causing any mischief while they were being treated for the "newly discovered virus."

She rubbed at her eyes with the tips of her fingers. The inter-view and the mental strain it had exacted had drained her, and she was still no nearer any answers than she had been before it had begun. Questioning, challenging the AAnn, hadn't pro-duced the hoped-for breakthrough. Reluctantly she called up and scanned the latest batch of communications demanding her attention. It was more of the same. Deyzara insisting she do something to put down the Sakuntala uprising. Sakuntala de-manding the Commonwealth acknowledge their ancestral rights and claims. One department after another pleading for more manpower, more material assistance, further instructions. Jack reminding her that he was spending the night at the lab. Andrea wondering when and if her mother was ever going to be able to help her with her studies again. Everyone wanting, wanting, wanting something from her.

It was a dangerous time for Sethwyn Case to come barging in.

He entered as he always did; ignoring Pandusky's protesta-tions and advancing with that confident rolling gait that sug-gested he owned every scrap of territory his big feet came in contact with. Her office was no exception.

Tiredly she waved the anxious, angry Pandusky off. "I'll han-dle it, Sanuel. Just go back to your own work."

Tight-lipped, her ever-protective assistant favored the much bigger Case with a single corneal caveat before backing out and closing the door behind him.

Case promptly parked himself on one corner of the desk and grinned down at her. Despite her exhaustion, she was uncom-fortably aware of his proximity. Not for the first time she won-dered if it was pheromones or simply sweat.

"Greetings and good things a'coming at you, good-looking." He extended a hand toward her.

She flinched back. "Stow it, Seth. I just finished some verbal sparring with our resident AAnn and I'm really bushed."

Nodding, he pulled out a small stim stick and casually sucked it to life. "Yeah, I saw the hiss brothers being led away. They didn't look any too happy."

A hint of a smile played across her features. "I'm having them held for a while, so we can keep an eye on them until this mess with the Sakuntala and the Deyzara is settled. They're being treated for a theoretical infection."

He laughed. It was a wonderful laugh, deep and rich and booming, and it filled the room. "That's one way to keep 'em out of circulation. They'd better be glad my friends and I don't work in Medical. We'd leave no scaly orifice unprobed." He leaned toward her but kept his hands back. "I *have* been known to play doctor on occasion, however."

Shaking her head, she turned away from him so he wouldn't see how her smile had widened. "Sethwyn Case, you are incorrigible."

He inhaled aromatic smoke. "Actually, I'm very corrigible, when the right person comes along."

She waved at the stim smoke, even though it didn't affect her. "How can you stand those things?"

Holding the stick between two fingers, he eyed it with mock seriousness. "Doesn't hurt the lungs. Tastes good, smells good. Out in the Viisiiviisii, every little touch of home is important."

"How's your luck been?" she asked, honestly interested.

He turned away and his grin faded slightly. "Not so good. Last couple of trips didn't yield anything really worthwhile. It'll get better. I've got a couple of leads on some spots down south that are thick with a new species of emergent that's supposedly festooned with half a dozen promising rusts and molds." He took a long drag on the stick. "Next trip'll be the best. You'll see." Turning back to face her, he leaned right over the desk. "How about a kiss for luck?"

She hesitated, internally conflicted. Eternally conflicted. What harm could a friendly kiss do? For luck. Wasn't part of her job to encourage those who worked under her? Worked under her—she kissed him hurriedly, as much to kill the thoughts (and other things) that were bubbling inside her as to comply with the request.

It lingered far too long. He was very polite about it, but when they finally separated, her lips were much wetter than they should have been. She raised a hand to wipe them dry, thought the gesture might be considered insulting, tried to rub them against each other, and ended up feeling ridiculous. Case just grinned down at her. She felt herself flushing, as if he was reading her mind. The climate conditioning that kept the room cool and dry seemed to have failed.

"How's that?" she finally managed to croak.

"It'll do for now." Reaching out and down, he patted her on the shoulder. "We'll see how my luck goes on the next trip. I might have to come back and lean on you again for a recharge." He slid lithely off the desk and headed for the door. "Take care of yourself, Lauren. You'll get control of this native business. I know you can handle it. You can handle anything."

Trying desperately to think of something clever to say by way of parting, she failed miserably. "Be careful out there, Seth. Some of the more radical Sakuntala have crossed the line and attacked our people."

He was at the door. "Thanks for the thought, good-looking, but don't worry. I'm not concerned about the Sakuntala. They won't bother me."

Then he was gone, the sharp perfume of the stim stick and of his body lingering teasingly in the room.

She found that she was breathing hard, for no discernible reason. Speaking softly, she opened a drawer and drew herself a carbonate drink. The feel of the cold liquid sliding down her throat helped to shock her back to reality.

Damn the man! He was far too attractive. Indecently so. The

way he looked through her eyes instead of into them, the play
of muscles beneath his clothing, that damnable cocksure grin of
his, as if he knew everything you were thinking—it was unfair!
She knew she ought to ban him from her office. Every time he
showed up, she told herself it would be the last time. There had
been a lot of last times.

Pandusky needed something. Forcing away thoughts of
Sethwyn Case, she admitted her assistant. She listened intently
to everything he had to say, commenting where appropriate,
authorizing where necessary. Anyone observing the discussion
would have believed that her attention was focused entirely on
her assistant and the matter at hand.

Even if she did glance more than seemed reasonable at one
particular corner of her desk.

15

The lingering stink of vatulalilu sap stayed with them as they made camp in a jam of floating fallen logs on the other side of the river. It would not wash off even with the aid of the constant rain. The enduring smell didn't seem to faze the by now acclimated Hasa or trouble Jemunu-jah, but Masurathoo felt as if he would never be clean again.

The jackstraw jumble of rotting wood made for uncertain footing. One log would provide a solid base, while the one jammed up alongside it could be composed entirely of disintegrating punk shot through with millions of mycelium. Hasa found this out the hard way when one foot went completely through what appeared to be an unyielding bouloutu trunk and plunged him into the soupy water up to his waist. It was while they were pulling him out, cursing and complaining, that Jemunu-jah first heard the humming. Leaving Masurathoo to help the fuming human the rest of the way, the tall Sakuntala turned to the south, both ears alert and aimed in the direction of the rising noise.

"What is it?" Upset with himself for having taken the misstep, Hasa was wiping fragments of decomposing wood from his rain-slicked lower extremities. After first trying to help, Masurathoo backed off and left the human to his own devices. Those flat, many-fingered hands were swinging a little too wildly for him to get close enough to assist without risking a swipe across his own face.

Jemunu-jah flicked his tongue backward and fluttered the tip. The human knew enough of Sakuntala tongue language to recognize the request for silence. Neither he nor Masurathoo had to repeat the query, because the humming soon grew loud enough so that they could hear it for themselves.

To Hasa, it sounded like a chorus of male tenors warming up for a Magnificat. Masurathoo found it alien but not surprising. The depths of the Viisiiviisii were as full of new sounds as they were of new sights.

By the time the drifting shapes finally came into view, emerging out of the rain, their deep-throated purring was louder than anything else in the forest. Jemunu-jah's eyes grew almost as wide as a Deyzara's.

"Mokusinga!" he yelped. Turning, he leapt into a gap between several trees and began frantically ripping at what appeared to be some black-striped reeds that were growing out of the water. "Hurry, quickly!"

Masurathoo joined the Sakuntala without thinking. When in the deep varzea, it was always best to do so. But Hasa hesitated, standing his ground on an unwavering log. He had just struggled up out of the organic gumbo underlying the logjam and was in no hurry to submerge himself all over again.

Studying the approaching mokusinga, a species new to him, he failed to see anything sufficiently intimidating to spook someone like Jemunu-jah. Certainly they were not as ferocious-looking as a nougusm or casoko. In fact, he decided as he unholstered his pistol, they looked downright benign. He felt something striking at his backside through the material of the rain cape. Turning, he saw that the Sakuntala was repeatedly tapping him with the tip of his tongue in order to get his attention.

"Hurry, Hasa! Come into the water and do as I am." Demonstrating, he placed one end of a hollow reed to his lips and began to breathe through it. Floating alongside him, Masurathoo did not need to make use of a reed. The breathing trunk on the top of his head would allow him to respirate freely while completely submerged.

Frowning, Hasa took another look at the oncoming mokusinga. The closest was a hovering head-sized ball of glistening winged cilia. Near the front he could make out a semblance of a face buried within: several eyes, a dark round spot that might be a mouth, nothing resembling nostrils. Half a dozen wings kept each of the unlikely and somewhat preposterous-looking quintet aloft. They flew slowly, picking a careful path through the trees, weighed down by the constant rain.

"Don't look like much to me." Drawing his pistol, he raised the muzzle and took aim at the nearest flyer. At the same time, something wrapped several times around his ankles and brought him crashing to the surface of the log. Rolling fast, he aimed his weapon at the source of the upset.

Jemunu-jah gazed unflinchingly down the barrel as he withdrew his tongue from the human's legs. "Stay there and die, then." With that, Jemunu-jah ducked down under the surface. All that was visible was the single reed through which he was respirating and, nearby, a motionless Deyzaran breathing trunk.

Idiot aborigine, Hasa thought as he sat up. He was used to defending himself, not hiding in the muck. As he started to rise, he caught sight of the tree directly behind him. In addition to its own lower branches it now sported perhaps fifty finger-length shimmering spines. Embedded firmly in the wood, they sparkled like spines shaved from a crystalline cactus. Whirling, half crouching on the log, he confronted the approaching mokusinga. They continued to advance slowly. They didn't have to move fast, he saw, because they weren't covered with cilia. They were covered with needles.

As the pair nearest him began to swell anew, filling their bodies with the air they utilized to propel the thousands of spines that covered their bodies, he spun and dived for the watery gap that concealed his friends. Landing with an awkward splash, he tore a pair of reeds off at the waterline, took a deep breath, and ducked under the surface. Behind him, an irregular black splotch appeared on the log on which he had been standing. It had been comprehensively needled. The black hole spread rapidly, eating its way into the thick bole. When it reached the heartwood, it spread explosively. By the time the mokusinga had arrived at the spot where the three travelers were submerged, the tree behind them was dead from crown to roots, eaten away from the inside out by the caustic liquid contained within the forcefully flung spines.

Peering up through the dim water while continuously wiping swirling organic debris from his eyes, Hasa could just make out the ominous hovering shapes of the mokusinga. Exhibiting a menacing awareness, the threatening spheres showed no inclination to move from where they had paused. Next to him, Jemunu-jah was gesturing with one hand while securing his breathing reed with the other. Hasa could only shake his head in response. He had no idea what the Sakuntala was trying to tell him. And it was hard work trying to suck enough air down through the thin reed to keep his lungs going.

How long would the mokusinga linger overhead? he found himself wondering. How hungry were they? Were they clever enough to make the connection between their submerged prey and the couple of reeds and one trunk that poked above the surface? If so, what could they do about it? Could their air-propelled spines be driven with enough thrust to skewer quarry hiding in the water?

A sudden thought made Hasa wonder if, after all, it was not possible to perspire while underwater. All the lurking mokusinga had to do, he realized, was drop down far enough to rest their bulk on top of the reed through which he was breathing in order to force him to the surface. He began searching his immediate surroundings, looking desperately for a better hiding place beneath a semisubmerged log or clump of weeds. In water rich with decaying vegetation it was difficult to see more than a meter in any direction.

Abruptly he felt something inside his mouth. Small and with multiple legs, it either had been living inside the reed when he had ripped it from its stalk or else had crawled down from outside after the stem had been plucked. Now whatever it was, was crawling around inside *him*.

Would it bite? Was it poisonous? The itching from the moving legs was quickly becoming unbearable. If the tiny visitor started down his throat, he would choke and have to shoot to the surface. Where the mokusinga would be waiting for him. The tickling and scratching of tiny feet inside his mouth was driving him crazy. He twisted, he wriggled his lower jaw back and forth, he tried to think of something, anything, he could do to rid himself of the unbearable itching, tickling sensation inside his mouth, but it was no use. He was going to have to—

Something struck the water directly in front of him. Startled, he drew back, found himself tangled up with the hysterical Masurathoo. But the mokusinga that had landed in front of him did not attack. It just bobbed gently in the water for a moment as its lightweight body settled in place.

A glance upward showed that the other patrolling mokusinga were no longer hovering threateningly overhead. Hesitantly Hasa rose upward. As soon as he broke the surface he spit out something small, green, and confused. While it raced speedily away, relieved to be free of the prison of his mouth, he sucked in a long, delicious draught of warm rain and fresh air. The mokusinga were still there, but they were no longer airborne. Except for the one that had landed in the water in front of him, they were all lying on the punky logs of the jam, deflating slowly, their ominous humming stilled.

Jemunu-jah was climbing out of the water. Cautiously he drew near a pair of the stranded needle throwers. They showed no reaction to his approach. Hasa noted that the Sakuntala was careful not to make physical contact with the quiescent creatures.

"I think they dead," Jemunu-jah announced in amazement. "It safe to come out."

Hasa joined him in studying the unmoving predators. Coughing and snapping water away from his trunks, Masurathoo was slow to emerge from the turgid water's protective embrace.

The bioprospector leaned as close to one of the motionless organisms as he dared. There were no visible wounds on any of the bodies, no signs of injury. Yet they were not sleeping, had not suddenly opted for instant estivation as opposed to trying to kill the three people they had chased into the water. They were manifestly deceased.

"I don't get it," he muttered. "I can see maybe one of them just dropping dead. But six? Simultaneously?"

It was Masurathoo, fumbling with his badly torn rain gear, who pointed out the powder. "Look there, my friends. No, not by the spines, please. At the area around the mouth."

His companions did as they were instructed. A dark maroon residue clung to the outer edges of the round suckerlike oral cavity. Inspecting the others, they found the same substance lining every mouth.

Jemunu-jah looked around uneasily, his ears in constant motion, his tongue ball shifting nervously from one cheek to the other. "Something kill them while they are waiting to kill us. But whatever it was, it not eat them."

"Yet." An equally uneasy Hasa found himself looking from left to right, turning a slow circle to closely search their immediate surroundings. Forest noises filtered through the rain. Small brightly colored shapes flitted here and there among the branches and the raindrops. After assuring himself that nothing massive and threatening was moving through the varzea nearby, he turned his attention back to the inert forms of the mysteriously deceased mokusinga.

They were surrounded by the usual phantasmagoria of plants, molds, rusts, and fungi. At the base of a twisted trunk, a carnivorous blue plate fungi snapped shut over a crawling tinworm. That was the only evidence of nonmotile predation occurring in their immediate vicinity. Nothing was emerging, either rapidly or slowly, to consume the bodies of the dead mokusinga except for a few dirty whitish-yellow filaments of some opportunistic subsurface fungi.

There it was again, he thought. That feeling that something was watching them. Was it what had exterminated the mokusinga? If so, he had decidedly mixed feelings about making its acquaintance.

But whatever it was, it had chosen to kill the mokusinga and then ignore them. That suggested either extraordinary good luck on the part of the greatly relieved travelers or something even more improbable and fantastic.

Choice.

Why would anything in the Viisiiviisii choose to slay mokusinga and ignore them? Perhaps, he mused, because he and his companions were not the natural prey of whatever had done the killing? Or maybe they had nothing to do with it. Maybe whatever had slain the spine-armed flyers had only been reacting defensively, protecting itself from a perceived threat. That conjecture made a lot more sense. He voiced his opinion to his companions.

"Forest spirits," muttered Jemunu-jah as he took a drink from his rainwater collector, using his strong tongue to draw the pouch up to his mouth.

"I say that it does not matter." Masurathoo's trunks both bobbed nervously. The Deyzara was still recovering from the narrowness of their escape. "What is important is that we are still alive and unharmed." He glanced apprehensively at the enfolding forest. "Whatever killed the mokusinga may still be here, either rooted in place or lurking about. All the more reason for us to be on our way."

"Nice to hear you say that for a change." Hasa looked briefly to the east before choosing a likely course and starting off. His companions followed, Masurathoo taking middle position as always.

Behind them, the white tendrils of decomposing forest fungi continued with their work, entering the bodies of the dead.

• • •

Two days later the travelers were far more tired. Since they had
left the place where they had encountered the mokusinga it had
rained especially hard. In addition to obstructing their vision,
the severe downpour rendered the already sodden surfaces un-
derfoot even more treacherous than usual. The slippery footing
did not inconvenience Jemunu-jah, who progressed as much by
the use of his long arms and six-digited hands as by his feet, but
it slowed human and Deyzara considerably.

The slower they advanced, the more discouraged they became. Furthermore, despite repeated checks of the global positioning gear that was included with the survival packs they
carried, neither Hasa nor Jemunu-jah was even sure they were
still traveling in the right direction.

"We should have reached the village by now." Hasa sat beneath the shade of an enormous spray of striped gray shelf
fungi. Every time he shifted his backside, a small puff of spores
rose prematurely into the air, only to be washed away as they
were knocked down by the rain. A distant burst of uncommon
thunder rolled through the varzea, and Jemunu-jah flinched in-
voluntarily.

"I understand." Masurathoo had folded himself into the
darkest, driest corner of their temporary mycorrhizal refuge.
"Forest spirits. There is most assuredly no need to be afraid."

"I not afraid." Jemunu-jah glared at the Deyzara. "Childhood stories are always with one." He looked over at the
human. "What about you, Hasa? You have no cubling fears of
darkness and sky shouting?"

Hasa shrugged, staring moodily out at the downpour. "Natural phenomena never scared me. I've always found my own
kind much more frightening. Especially when you're a kid."

Though he found this line of inquiry insightful and interesting, something in the human's voice told Jemunu-jah it would
be best not to pursue it, even under more climactically favorable circumstances. They sat in silence beneath their fungoid
shelter, watching the rain.

By the morning of the next day the deluge had finally slack-
ened, giving way to the more customary steady drizzle. As they
were packing up their gear, wordless with fatigue, Hasa noticed
a small fist-sized herbivore attacking a clump of mushroomlike
basidiocarps growing on a fallen log just outside their resting
place. The fruiting bodies were very distinctive, with handsome
three-sided purple caps that shaded to dark red basidia underneath. Using two sets of blunt projecting teeth, the herbivore
rose up on stumpy hind legs and began to chew into the thick
body of the cap.

Protruding from the decaying wood close to the stem of the
fruiting body were several jet-black tendrils. As the small herbivore gnawed deeper into the basidiocarp, one of these tendrils,
shivering slightly, rose upward. Its tip quivering, it sprayed
something in the direction of the plant eater. The intruder
promptly shuddered, gave several violent spasms, leapt into the
air, and landed on its side. In a moment, all ten legs had ceased
kicking.

Interesting defense mechanism, Hasa mused as he fastened
his service belt around his waist and prepared to don his rain
cape. Interesting, but not surprising. The plant life of the Viisiiviisii had evolved hundreds of ways of defending itself, from
protective mimicry, to concentrating toxins in leaves and fruiting bodies, to throwing caustic spines and other more active
means of repulsing would-be browsers. There was nothing remarkable about the little drama he had just witnessed. The
black tendrils would likely be defensive rhizomorphs, specialized bodies that in this instance were designed to defend the
spore-holding basidiocarps. Both were part of the same largely
hidden underground life-form.

Jemunu-jah was already dressed and ready to be on their
way. Though visibly discouraged with their lack of progress,
Masurathoo was not about to give up and lie down in the moss
and muck. They were both waiting for him.

Well, he was ready, too. Picking up his rain cape, he gathered
the folds around him preparatory to slipping it over his head

and shoulders. At least the rain had let up, he reflected. Glancing down one last time, he happened to notice the protruding jaws of the dead herbivore. White mycelium were already probing the small, motionless body preparatory to entering the dead flesh and beginning their task of starting to decompose the small corpse. Frowning, he moved close and leaned low. There was something around the edges of the diminutive stilled jaws. Some kind of red stain. No, not red. Maroon. He had seen it before.

Lining the open mouths of the exterminated mokusinga.

"It is a good morning and the rain is light, sir." Masurathoo's bulging eyes blinked in his direction. "We should travel while the conditions are favorable."

"Just a minute." Waving one hand in the direction of his impatient companions, Hasa bent lower still, bringing his face close to the unmoving little corpse. There was no mistaking the color or consistency of the residue that lined the dead herbivore's mouth like some kind of bizarre granular lipstick. Was it toxic on contact, he wondered, or did it have to be inhaled or swallowed? One thing he knew for sure: it had been ejected by the upright rhizomorph. That black tendril now lay flat on the ground alongside the stem of the one damaged purple-and-red fruiting body. Seepage was already beginning to cover and heal the gaping wound where the herbivore had been chewing. Curious, Hasa reached for it.

He felt something on his right leg, just above where the jungle boot met the fabric of his pants. Looking back and down, he saw half a dozen of the black tendrils touching his upper calf. Several were unmistakably pointed in his direction. Their tips, he could see clearly now, were hollow. Tubes designed and equipped for spraying lethal sticky maroon powder at any potential predator.

Slowly, very slowly, he withdrew his fingers from the vicinity of the damaged basidiocarp. As he did so, the black rhizomorphs straightened, the threatening tips pointing skyward instead of toward him. They did not, however, withdraw back into the rotting log from which they had emerged. Instead, they continued to feel his leg just below the knee.

"Come along, Hasa," urged Masurathoo. "You are delaying our departure."

Jemunu-jah was eyeing the human more intently. "What is going on, Hasa? What you looking at?"

"I've found something. Or it's found me. I'm not sure yet."

"Found something?" The Sakuntala took a long nimble step toward where the human was starting to sit back down. "Found what?"

"I don't know." He glanced quickly in the Sakuntala's direction before returning his attention to the busy rhizomorphs. "Maybe some of your forest spirits." Keeping his movements slow and predictable, he sat down on the large log that had served as the center of their encampment. Rising hypnotically from the wood, more and more of the rhizomorphs emerged to inspect his body. Some of them were unusually thick, even by the standards of Fluvan fungal growths. A few were giants of their kind, as big around as his little finger.

Seeing what was happening, Jemunu-jah's pupils expanded and he started to reach for his gun. Hasa was quick to wave him off.

"Leave them alone! They're not hurting me. They're just—" It was hard to voice the words that seemed simultaneously appropriate and impossible. "—checking me out." He indicated the dead herbivore. "They killed that small browser. Look at its mouth. It's the same stuff that killed the mokusinga."

Keeping wary eyes on the swaying, probing rhizomorphs, Jemunu-jah knelt and Masurathoo folded himself to inspect the deceased herbivore.

"Never know pannula to do such a thing before," Jemunu-jah finally commented.

"Different species, maybe," was Hasa's response. "I've certainly never seen a macromycete quite like it."

When Masurathoo looked up, both of his trunks were half-retracted. "Coincidence," the Deyzara insisted. "You not saying, human, that we were deliberately saved from mokusinga by a fungus?"

"I *am* saying that we were saved by one. By this particular species." Hasa sat quietly as tendrils now swayed back and forth in front of him like waltzing eels while dozens of others that had emerged from the rotting log continued to poke and prod his seated form. Their touch was incredibly gentle. "Whether it was deliberate or coincidental is what I don't know." He chuckled. It was, Masurathoo noted, a sound most uncharacteristic of the human.

"Saved by a mushroom." Hasa glanced back and up at Jemunu-jah. "Do the Sakuntala have a name for this type of growth?"

His lanky companion moved nearer. "Pannula. We do not eat them. They have bitter taste. They hardly ever encountered near towns."

"Fond of their privacy, maybe."

Masurathoo was following the human's line of reasoning, and he did not like it. "Permit me to inquire, Hasa, if you are claiming some sort of consciousness for this . . . this . . . *fungus.*"

As he did always, Hasa was clearly enjoying the Deyzara's discomfort. "I'm not claiming anything of the sort—yet. But consider: Something saved us from the mokusinga. These tendrils are inspecting me instead of trying to enter my body. Admittedly, that kind of work is usually done by mycelium and not rhizomorphs, but it's still evidence of some kind of restraint, be it directed by intelligence or instinct. And what about that feeling I've been having for days and days of us being watched?"

Pushing back the hood of his rain cape, Masurathoo stepped forward. "In this I fear most strongly that I must be at variance with you, sir. A fungus possesses neither intelligence nor instinct. Nor does it have anything to 'watch' us, or anything else, with."

"The Viisiiviisii is full of surprises, bug-eyes. Say it 'perceives' rather than 'sees.' " As he spoke, several of the inky rhizomorphs had risen high enough to begin investigating his lips.

"Be careful." Jemunu-jah's fingers itched to draw his weapon. "Remember the poisonous residue that killed mokusinga!"

"If this plant wanted me dead, it could already have slain me a dozen times over. Or it could have let the mokusinga do the job." Inquisitive black tendrils touched his lips, felt of the soft flesh. They tickled. And the feeling of being observed, even in the absence of anything recognizable as eyes, was more compelling than ever.

Masurathoo's breathing trunk twitched. "Those may have been examples of similar but different species." He gestured with a flexible arm. "They lie two days' trek behind us. This is a different gathering of growths, in an entirely new location." He indicated the attractive purple-reddish fruiting bodies that sprouted from dead wood nearby. "These are other pannula. Surely you are not claiming an ability for different individual growths to communicate over distance in *addition* to some kind of fungal consciousness?"

"I wonder if different growths *are* involved."

As Hasa spoke, two of the questing tendrils took the opportunity to slip inside his open mouth. Jemunu-jah tensed. The rhizomorphs investigated for a few seconds, tickling Hasa's palate, tongue, and the insides of his cheeks before withdrawing. Finished their exploration, he wondered, or found the human oral environment not to their liking?

"Please not to take offense, sir, but you are not making any sense."

Fascinated, Hasa raised his right hand and spread his fingers wide. Questing rhizomorphs immediately rose to match the gesture, one or two tendrils making contact with each of his elevated fingertips.

"To rise this far above the wood it's emerging from," he said as he moved his hand slowly from side to side, "this easily and effectively, these rhizomorphs must be supported by a much larger mass buried deep within the host tree or, more likely, in the ground itself."

Jemunu-jah gestured downward. "There no ground here, Hasa. Ground here is many kel below top of the water. Pannula lives in trees and deadwood, not ground. Leastways, all pannula I know."

The human replied while continuing to play touchy-feely with the inquiring rhizomorphs. Nearby, ghostly white mycelium had begun to infiltrate the body of the dead herbivore.

"How can you be so sure about that, Jemunu-jah? Have your people ever dug one up? Not part of one, but a whole one, to see how far the spawn and the hyphae actually extend?"

The Sakuntala's snout twitched. "Why would anyone want to do such a thing? All pannula taste bad. Probably this kind also. Stringy stuff in trees and wood probably tastes worse. Be a big waste of time and energy."

Hasa nodded. Opposite him, black tendrils bobbed in mime. "Probably just as well no one ever tried it with one of these. The pannula in question might have taken offense." He was studying the weaving tendrils intently. "We've already seen what it can do when it takes offense."

Masurathoo badly wanted to sit down and rest but could not quite bring himself to do so. The image of sharp, piercing white filaments painlessly penetrating his backside and then rapidly expanding to infest and rot his entire body from the inside out was one he could not shake.

"I daresay that you are trying to make a point, Hasa, but I fear to confess that it continues to escape me."

"Locating, identifying, and finding uses for these kinds of growths are my business, finger-face. I'm thinking that maybe these pannula are analogous to similar fungal organisms on Earth. Very large organisms. In fact, they're the biggest living things on the home world of my species."

Jemunu-jah eyed the nodding strands with new respect. "How big?"

"Big enough so that these rhizomorphs and mycelium could all be part of a single organism." He glanced at the dubious

Deyzara. "This here wouldn't have to 'communicate' with those that killed the mokusinga if they were all part of the same organism. Big enough so that these basidiocarps," and he indicated the tripartite fruiting bodies nearby, "and the ones we saw at the place where we were attacked by the mokusinga could all be reproductive bodies sprouting from the same individual source."

The Sakuntala mentally retraced the ground they had covered during the past couple of days. It was not great, but it was substantial. "That very difficult to believe, Hasa."

"I've studied organisms like this. With all due respect to the accumulated practical knowledge of the Sakuntala, your kind haven't." He turned thoughtful. "One variety is called *Armillaria ostoyae*. It lives a more restricted life than your pannula, living mostly on tree roots. For a long time, my kind didn't recognize it for what it was because by far the bulk of it existed below ground. It took a long time for people to understand that the fruiting bodies and mycelium they were seeing were all part of a single gigantic life-form. One *Armillaria* was found that covered five square kilometers."

Masurathoo performed the quick calculation, translating human units of measurement into those of the Deyzara. "That is not possible!" he finally declared, rolling his eyes.

"It is not only possible; it is," Hasa assured him. Thrusting his hand sharply to his right, he brought it quickly back to his left as the tips of the ebony tendrils sought to match the movement. They continued to follow the lead of his darting fingers wherever he thrust them. "It's sure as hell no less possible than the fact that I'm sitting here in the middle of the southern Vii-siiviisii playing tag with a fungus. Of course, to be certain, DNA samples would have to be drawn from multiple outcrops.

"Think about it. Something like an *Armillaria* is perfectly adapted to life on Fluva. It can live on live trees, deadwood, and in the ground, safe beneath and protected from predatory browsers by the varzean flooding. Its hyphae can reproduce above the water during the Big Wet and on the ground in the short season when the water recedes and dry land lies exposed. Its size means that predation by browsers that can survive its defenses only damages a small portion of the main body. Even if every fruiting body and all the mycelium aboveground were to die or be eaten, the main body of the individual would remain safe beneath the water." Drawing back his right hand, he watched as the black tendrils followed. When he pushed it forward, they retreated.

"If the pannula *is* anything like *Armillaria,* it probably spreads slowly and lives a long time. A very long time. Possibly thousands of years. That might even be long enough to develop some kind of rudimentary awareness."

Masurathoo let out a disdainful snort through his speaking trunk. "A Eurmetian shumai has awareness. That does not mean it is intelligent."

"A shumai wouldn't go out of its way to save us from attacking mokusinga, either."

"We don't know that what happened." Jemunu-jah's observation reflected reasonable caution. "Could have been coincidence."

"Could have been," Hasa conceded. "It also could be coincidence that the pannula simply decided the mokusinga were a threat to it, and we just happened to be in the area. Just like that little browser was a threat to it and we're not. But it sure as hell doesn't explain why these rhizomorphs are following my hand movements and checking out my body without trying to make a meal out of me, or out of any of us."

"Awareness," Masurathoo repeated, "is not intelligence." But despite what he felt strongly to be true, the Deyzara was beginning to waver.

"Why these," Hasa asked aloud, indicating the weaving tendrils, "and not those?" With his other hand he pointed down at the dynamic white mycelium. "I'll tell you why. Because fungal rhizomorphs are specialized. Some are dedicated to breaking up soil to make it easier for the mycelium to spread. Some are committed to entering wood to begin the process of rot. That's

on the worlds I've visited. The rhizomorphs here—they could
be specialized for other functions as well. Defense, for one
thing. For another—perhaps consciousness. A detailed examination of the entire organism's cellular structure would be very
edifying."

"If what you contend contains even a modicum of validity,
sir, then why," Masurathoo observed somberly, "have these
pannula in all these thousands of years not tried to make contact with the Sakuntala?"

The human favored him with that infuriatingly mordant
smile of his. "How do we know they haven't?" He turned the
same expression on Jemunu-jah, who was no less pleased to be
on the receiving end of it. "Awareness and intelligence are a
two-way proposition."

Both ears flicked forward. "Are you implying that Sakuntala
not smart enough to realize when they are being talked to?"

"Hey, the Viisiiviisii is your ancestral home. You big-ears
evolved having to watch out for much more overtly threatening
nasties. Maybe this one particularly highly evolved strain of pannula *did* try to make contact with your kind once or twice over
the millennia. You knock on somebody's door for that long and
they continue to ignore you, eventually you're going to get tired
of trying. Or maybe the pannula, if they are real slow maturing,
are just reaching the point where they feel able to try to make
contact." He shrugged. "Or maybe they just weren't interested
in making contact with people who regarded their manifestations
of consciousness as belonging to unnamed 'forest spirits,' and
chose to wait for some real intelligence to come along. Like me."
Ignoring their simmering indignation, he continued to play finger tag with the agreeable rhizomorphs.

Swallowing his resentment, Jemunu-jah moved to peer over
the human's shoulder. "If by some chance you right and pannula is somehow some kind of sentient, how we make contact?
Pannula is fungus. Has no eyes, no ears, no mouth. Only filaments."

"That might be enough. In ancient times, there used to be

humans who couldn't see, hear, or speak. That didn't mean they were any less intelligent. They learned to communicate solely via touch. Maybe all this species can do is respond to my hand and finger movements, but it's a start."

Masurathoo felt that his credulity was on trial. "I beg to point out, Hasa, that such mimicry can be accomplished by many different species from a number of worlds that are not classified as intelligent."

"I'm sure it can be, but how many brainless mimics would rise to the defense of visitors in peril?" he argued.

"I still think coincidence." Jemunu-jah was not swayed.

"Still could be," Hasa admitted. Rising, he brushed debris from his rain cape. "So let's put it to the test. If the pannula did intentionally save us from the mokusinga, then it has our best interests at heart—even though it doesn't have one itself. If it is intelligent, then our little sojourn here may represent the first formal contact between it and my species. Whether it wants anything to do with either of your kind remains to be seen."

"You flatter yourself unreasonably." Masurathoo found himself unable to take the continuing veiled insults any longer without articulating a response.

"We'll see." Hefting his pack and swinging it up onto his back, Hasa started back the way they had come.

"That is the wrong direction," Jemunu-jah reminded him.

"I know." Having paused and turned around, Hasa was grinning more broadly than ever. "So I've been told."

Jemunu-jah blinked eagle eyes. "*Heesa;* I just told it to you."

"Not just you." Raising an arm, the human gestured. "Look."

Sakuntala and Deyzara turned. Every one of the black tendrils that had previously been standing erect and weaving slightly from side to side was now lying flat with its tip pointing due north.

"They have fallen down," Jemunu-jah commented. "It means nothing."

"No? Let's see." Retracing his steps, Hasa halted beside the

cluster of prostrate rhizomorphs. In response to his renewed
proximity, they immediately straightened. After playing with
the bobbing, ducking tips for a couple of minutes, he stepped
back again. As they began to lie down once more, he moved
forward and deliberately pushed them flat so they faced in a
southward direction. Retreating, he turned once again to re-
trace his previous course.

Behind him, the rhizomorphs slowly lifted themselves and
adjusted their positions until all were once more facing north.

"What do you think now?" he asked triumphantly.

"The alignment could be due to other factors," Jemunu-jah
insisted. "Direction rain is coming from, position of hidden
sun, current temperature. Could be many factors involved."

Hasa nodded. "Or, having our welfare—excuse me, *my* welfare—in whatever a pannula uses for a mind, it could be pointing the way toward the village we've been trying to reach,
assuming that would be the nearest place of safety for us from
marauders like the mokusinga."

Where a human could only cross its arms, Masurathoo was
able to entwine his. "I am not going to proceed through this
horror of a landscape on the basis of directions provided by a
fungus."

Hasa glanced at the third member of the party. "How about
you, fuzz-face?"

The Sakuntala wanted to grab the human by the throat and
shake him. That, he reflected, would have been the reaction of
an uneducated Hata-nau or perhaps one of Aniolo-jat's rabid
followers. He, on the other hand, was civilized. Though every
time he patiently absorbed one of the human's obnoxious jibes
he found himself wishing it were otherwise.

Standing capeless in the rain, he finally thrust both ears forward. "We have been going that direction anyway."

"No, we haven't," Masurathoo objected immediately. "We
have been moving more to the east." A twin-digited hand indicated the prone tendrils. "Those . . . *things* . . . are pointing

markedly to the north. If we follow their 'direction' we could end up entirely missing the village we seek."

"If we haven't missed it already," the Sakuntala murmured.

"We haven't." Hasa spoke confidently. "If it was somewhere behind us, the rhizomorphs would be pointing back the way we came."

He started forward. Jemunu-jah hesitated only briefly before following. That left Masurathoo, for a change, to bring up the rear. Despite the rain, his companions did not have to look back to ensure that the Deyzara was keeping up with the pace. His steady litany of complaint and accusation marked his location and their progress as surely as any of the global positioning devices contained in their emergency kits.

16

As they marched on and on through the rain, Jemunu-jah began to wonder if he had finally lost all his *mula*. Surely if they were on the proper course they should have made contact with the village by now. His reservations were dismissed by the human. It seemed like every time the Sakuntala voiced his uncertainties, they would stumble across another outcrop of pannula. All the same vast organism, Hasa would insist. Another clump of mindless mushrooms, Masur-athoo would counter.

Jemunu-jah was left caught in the middle between his two companions. One insisted that they were being guided, or at least helped, to safety, while the other swore to anyone and anything that would listen that they were only wandering aimlessly through the endless Viisiiviisii until exhaustion and death finally claimed them. For the scion of a warrior clan, the Sakuntala ruminated, he was spending an awful lot of time trying to keep the peace.

Two more days had passed since Hasa had announced his "discovery" of the existence of consciousness among the pannula. Two more days of traipsing through constant rain, avoiding potential pitfalls and predators, while striving to extend their dwindling supplies by foraging in the forest. Two more days of having to listen to the human extol the virtues of a still hypothetical enormous underground organism that might or might not possess, at best, a rudimentary form of sentience.

The rain beat down on the outside of the hollow log in which they had taken shelter. It was a fallen sokulaa, one of the forest giants. But even a sokulaa's specialized roots eventually gave way to rot and the effects of having its lower trunk submerged in water for most of the year. When this one had finally toppled, it had landed atop a dense network of decomposing brethren. That was what had kept its hollowed-out interior above water and provided them with one of the drier havens they had found since leaving their skimmers.

Still, it had proven difficult to go to sleep inside the cylindrical chamber because of the lights. Thousands of them, each one an individual phosphorescent fungus of the kind known to Jemunu-jah as ovatu. Flashing their light in sequence, they formed multiple lines of rainbow luminance all along the interior of the fallen sokulaa. The spectacular streams of color strobed like a giant internal pointer to the far end of the trunk, down where the roots began. There dwelled a single tavawau: a legless, eyeless, antennae-laced carnivore that relied on the ovatu to attract food. Masurathoo was nervous about going to sleep in the same hollow tree as a resident carnivore, but Jemunu-jah had assured him that the tavawau was no threat to them. Even if it could detect their presence, its lumpy body was permanently fixed in place. It was less mobile than a sponge.

So when they awoke, they had ample light with which to view their surroundings, though it took a while for their eyes to adapt to the sequencing flashes of the ovatu. Visible through the rotting break in the side of the trunk that had admitted them the previous evening, morning rain was falling lazily outside their latest sanctuary.

As he was eating an inadequate morning meal from their dwindling store of supplies, Jemunu-jah noticed Masurathoo gesturing oddly to him. Both trunks were gesticulating tersely and the Deyzara's right arm coiled repeatedly in the direction of the rear of the trunk. Finishing the last of his food, the Sakuntala moved to see what the two-trunk wanted. While the diameter of the hollow space inside the fallen tree was generous, he still had to bend to keep from bumping his head against the curving ceiling and its ranks of harmless perfectly aligned pulsating ovatu.

Settling down next to the Deyzara, he spared a sympathetic glance for his companion's badly shredded rain cape and was glad he didn't need one. His fur kept him drier and more comfortable than any garment. The only advantage he saw to the rain capes was that their owners could remove them and clean them separately.

"I am compelled to point out, my tall friend, that if we do not do something to change the present situation, we are going to die here and be food for the first fungus that decides to invade our bodies."

Jemunu-jah started to rise. "If you going to do nothing but complain, I would rather get ready for walking."

"No, no, wait and hear me out, please." Though he was in a position to do so, Masurathoo did not reach out to grab his fellow traveler by the arm. No Deyzara would dare to think of physically trying to restrain a Sakuntala. Instead, Masurathoo used a hand to gesture in Hasa's direction.

The human was seated with his back against the interior wall of the fallen sokulaa. There would be a dark spot there when he moved away, his weight having crushed dozens of the tiny luminescent ovatu. They would quickly be replaced by the dense network of ovatu hyphae that permeated the decaying wood.

In front of him, several dozen black rhizomorphs danced and swayed in reaction to the slow weaving of his hand. For the moment, their burly, resilient, unlikable human looked like a child playing with a new toy. Which, in a way, he was. The delight he took in getting the rhizomorphs to respond to his increasingly elaborate gestures was palpable. It was not shared by his companions.

"Look at him." Masurathoo could not keep the distaste from

his voice. "One might think this was a game. Our lives are at stake and he insists that we should place our hopes for survival in the cryptic actions of a fungus. One whose dimensions are a matter of pure speculation and who he would have us believe is not only intelligent but empathetic. A compassionate fungus!"

"It may not be matter of compassion." Jemunu-jah was reluctant to take sides. In point of fact he could not, because he had yet to decide who was right.

The Deyzara pressed his argument. "Even if this pannula growth—and it is nothing but a growth, no matter how great its actual physical size—is sentient, that hardly means it is capable of, or interested in, helping us. It could be no more than minimally aware of us. The response of its rhizomorphs to the human's hand movements may be nothing more sophisticated than a basal response to movement or shadow. Many plants respond to the proximity of more motile life-forms by closing flowers or curling leaves."

Jemunu-jah regarded the bobbing and weaving of the silent rhizomorphs. "Such plant movements are defensive in nature, or a response to the absence or addition of light. This is different. And what about the lying down of every rhizomorph we have encountered in same direction?"

"I am willing to admit that action does continue to puzzle me. It does not mean, however, that it represents an awareness of our presence coupled with a conscious desire to provide assistance."

"We will learn truth if they point us to village," Jemunu-jah observed sensibly.

"How much longer can we afford to continue that enticing experiment?" Reaching down, the Deyzara picked up his food pouch and shoved it open and unsealed in the Sakuntala's direction. "You see how little real food remains to me. I believe your supplies and those of the human are in a similarly deficient state. Perhaps you can survive on what edible substances the forest can provide. Possibly the human can as well; I am not intimately familiar with the nutritional requirements of his kind. I only know that I cannot.

"Furthermore, every muscle and tendon in my body aches, I am stiff and sore all over, and I feel as if my entire corpus could collapse in a paralyzed heap at any moment. Even my integument is sore."

Jemunu-jah considered. "I have bruises and scrapes myself. Enough for several families."

Masurathoo immediately seized on the Sakuntala's admission. "Our bodies are in sympathy then, if not yet our thoughts." Leaning close and reaching up with his speaking trunk, he placed the end as close as he could to one of the Sakuntala's ears. "We must do something to change our situation, or we risk throwing away our lives because we relied on a fungus for survival. And there is still another possibility to consider."

Jemunu-jah drew back slightly, uncomfortable at the nearness of that whispering trunk to his face. "What, another possibility?"

The Deyzara was not to be dissuaded, not even by Sakuntala sarcasm. "Supposing for a moment that the human is right. Suppose the Viisiiviisii *is* home to gigantic sentient fungi like this pannula. Could it not be sending us around aimlessly, deeper and deeper into the varzea? Could it not be deliberately leading us astray?"

Jemunu-jah frowned down at the two-trunks. "To what purpose?"

"So that we will fall over from exhaustion and hunger, whereupon it can infest and devour us at its leisure."

The Sakuntala was unimpressed by the Deyzara's reasoning. "If that was its intention, why wait for us to die? Why not just invade our bodies while we sleep?"

Masurathoo persisted. "We might sense the attempt and awaken. And if it is intelligent, it might recognize that we have in our possession weapons that could harm it."

Jemunu-jah rose. "Now you giving to it more sense than even Hasa. I don't accept your argument. If pannula want to help us, it helping us now. If it want to kill us, it can kill us anytime."

"And if it's not sentient?" Masurathoo continued. "Or what

if it is, and it's just curious about us? Or generally indifferent? What then, big-ears?"

Jemunu-jah hesitated. "You worry me like young females." He turned to walk back up the hollow trunk to the place they had chosen for resting.

Astonishingly, Masurathoo actually reached out and grabbed the Sakuntala's tail. The Deyzara was desperate.

"Please, my tall friend, you must see what is happening here! The human is so enamored of his supposed discovery that it has bemused his brain. There is more fog in his thoughts than in the forest. Having made what he thinks to be a great discovery, he has become blinded by it. He believes because he wants to believe. This, I do happen to know, is not an unusual occurrence among his kind. I have read of it."

That made more sense to Jemunu-jah than anything else the Deyzara had said. He crouched back down on his haunches. As if to help confirm Masurathoo's words, farther up the hollow sokulaa the human continued to play with the dancing rhizomorphs, oblivious to the conversation and conference that was taking place among his companions.

"Very well. I open to discussion of your beloved possibilities," he muttered. "What suggestions you have?"

"Just this." Masurathoo spared a goggle-eyed glance past the Sakuntala to make absolutely certain the human was not listening. "Today we will follow his lead and that of his beloved fungus. But if we encounter nothing save more of the same, then tonight we will arise well before morning and set off on our own, resuming our original course due east instead of this new track to the north."

"What if we have already miss the village?"

The Deyzara rolled both eyes back into his head, a disconcerting sight at the best of times. "Then we are already dead, and I will never see my family again."

Jemunu-jah gestured understandingly, with ears as well as hands. His tail flicked methodically from side to side. "The human is attuned to the forest. He sleeps lightly."

Masurathoo had anticipated the observation. "I have watched him every time he makes use of his supplies. His emergency kit includes a general human soporific. I will endeavor to obtain some and slip it into his food. Alternatively, when he is sound asleep I will apply it to his lower torso via injection."

Jemunu-jah was impressed. "Bold action for a Deyzara, to contemplate forcibly incapacitating a human."

Reddened, protuberant eyes met Jemunu-jah's own. "Desperation can drive even the civilized to take previously unimagined risks. Are we in agreement?"

Backed into making a commitment, Jemunu-jah still demurred. "Another difficult day lies ahead of us. As we walk there will be plenty time for contemplation of alternatives. I will tell you tonight what choice I make."

"Excellent! I'm confident it will be the right one." Turning away, the Deyzara began to assemble his gear. "It may be the last chance we have to make one."

The light was beginning to fade when they reached the river. One more river, Jemunu-jah thought tiredly. Yet one more. And this one wider and swifter of current than any of those they had previously crossed. They might yet have to pause and expend more of what little remained of their reserves of strength on building a raft with which to attempt the crossing. This unnamed watercourse was sufficiently broad that it might not be possible to swim it. Furthermore, during the approach he had not seen or smelled any vatulalilu. If they were to try swimming so deep and wide a waterway without some form of protection or camouflage they might as well do so with some of the human's clever advertising signs hanging around their necks, proclaiming to every water-dwelling carnivore that dinner had arrived.

He was tired; he was frustrated; he missed his family and clan and home. Now this, a physical barrier greater than any they had yet encountered. Looking up and down the channel, he could see no sign of shallows that might be waded. Swim or make a craft: those were their only two choices, and the first of them was not viable. Not for any creature with a shred of intelligence remaining.

"Might as well camp here for the night. It's early, but we're not going anywhere until morning." Advancing through the rain, Hasa began the search for a suitable site.

Nothing fazes the human, Jemunu-jah thought. No obstacle, no danger. Yet there was no denying that the furless biped possessed common sense as well as intelligence. So much effort, not for clan or *mula,* but in the pursuit of Commonwealth credit. Was Hasa civilized or just smart? Jemunu-jah was beginning to think that the two did not necessarily go together.

As he turned to one side, Masurathoo caught his eye. The Deyzara's plan was typically devious. The Sakuntala were more direct. Yet Jemunu-jah could not see himself killing the human merely because they disagreed on what course to take. He was more inclined to kill the Deyzara simply to shut him up. Briefly, he considered killing both of them. That would leave him alone in the depths of the southern Viisiiviisii. It was better to have companions, even if one talked so much it made his ears hurt and the other dripped contempt the way a horulia shrub shed water.

"Remember what we discussed," Masurathoo was whispering to him out of his fully extended speaking trunk. "Have you come to a decision?"

Jemunu-jah did not look down at the Deyzara. He was contemplating the river, using his exceptional vision to penetrate the rain and study the far side. "Yes, I have. We going to cross this river, on raft."

Masurathoo sagged visibly. "You can't be serious, Jemunu-jah. Even with our tools, it will take at least two days to construct something suitable. And then where will we be?"

"On other side of river," the Sakuntala replied sensibly.

"And what does that gain us? The opportunity to continue this interminable march through hostile varzea?"

"Not interminable, I think." Raising a long, slender arm, he pointed with his two middle fingers. "Look."

Masurathoo could not squint: his eyes were either open, shut, or shielded by double lids. But he could hear the human's shout at the same time he detected movement on the far line of submerged trees.

Whatever it was, it was coming toward them across the river. It took a momentary lessening of the rain for him to resolve the slowly advancing shapes.

There were two rafts. Each supported a pair of minimally clad Sakuntala. A large, dead ti-tokuliu lay in the middle of the nearest. Using long paddles, the Sakuntala were propelling the two unlovely but sturdy craft across the river, their strong arms battling the current. Off to his right, Hasa was gesticulating in the rain, voicing an alternating stream of excited whoops and joyful obscenities.

"Hunting party from a village." Jemunu-jah's eyes glistened as he tracked the rafts' approach. "*Hauea!* Maybe not the village we seek, but right now I will glad to accept the hospitality of the lowliest of clans."

"So will I." Turning at a sudden thought, Masurathoo found himself searching the surrounding trees and deadwood for waltzing black rhizomorphs. None were to be seen. That did not mean, he realized, that the pannula was not present. Its mycelium could be running through the body of the decaying tree just off to his left or through the fallen log under his feet. If it was as vast an organism as Hasa had suggested, it could be everywhere around them.

"Coincidence. We have just been traveling in the right direction all along."

"Right direction, yes," Jemunu-jah agreed. "Original direction we chose, not. How do one give thanks to a fungus?"

"It's coincidence." The Deyzara was insistent—but not as insistent as before.

Peering across the river, the villagers had been astonished to see three strangers staggering out of what they had believed to be uninhabited forest. While their dialect was distinctive, Jemunu-jah had no trouble communicating with them. Hasa and Masurathoo managed less well. It did not matter. What *was* important was that the villagers were friendly, distant relatives of the minor but well-known Kioumatii clan. The hunting party of S'Kio was happy to bring the strangers back to their village.

It was a rudimentary community, Jemunu-jah saw immediately. The dwellings in the trees were suspended above the water by cables of woven vines, loopers, and lianas, not imported strilk. Few signs of modernity and Commonwealth culture had penetrated this far south. There were a handful of advanced tools and utensils, sheets of lightweight rain-shedding fabric, a couple of vermin-proof food storage lockers, and one thing more.

A battered old model but operational communicator.

Their hearts leapt when the village elder informed them of its existence. Its range was extremely limited, they were informed, and it could not talk to one of the Commonwealth speakers in the high sky. But it *would* reach to Tavumacia, the next nearest village. Tavumacia had a more powerful communicator and could talk to not one but a dozen additional villages. Eventually, contact could be made with Taulau Town. *If* the village's own cranky apparatus was in the mood to function.

The visitors spent several anxious moments hovering over the device until it was clear that it would. The message was sent. The village's friends in Tavumacia readily agreed to pass it along. In return, they were told of the Sakuntala uprising.

Then there was nothing to do but wait.

"How long do you think it will take, good sir?"

"What, for us to be extracted from this Sakuntala landfill?" Following a (by Sakuntala village standards) decent meal, Hasa's habitual ire had returned full force. But then, Masurathoo reflected, it had never really left. "Lemme think. Message has to get to Taulau. Once there, it has to be passed to the proper department. Someone has to decide it's legitimate and validate a report. Then the lazy bastards have to organize a rescue. At least they've got the coordinates of the communicator here."

Swinging slowly back and forth in the suspension chair of their host's home, he pondered the motionless debris-stained water of the Viisiiviisii shimmering a few meters below the carefully constructed porch. Here no advanced charged fields protected them from anything inimical that might be waiting just beneath the surface. No automatic weaponry rested ready and armed to blast whatever might emerge. They didn't care. For the first time in many days, the three of them reposed with full bellies, if not satisfied palates. Masurathoo in particular had had a difficult time keeping down the simple village food.

"Couple of days at most," Hasa continued. "Even if they wanted to, educated and enterprising village Sakuntala couldn't fake the kind of electronic identification I'm carrying on me. Administration will send someone." He favored his companions with a knowing smirk. "They don't have any choice. I'm a Commonwealth citizen."

A fact that does not speak well for the Commonwealth, Jemunu-jah thought to himself. Fortunately, the existence of appalling individuals like Shadrach Hasselemoga was offset by the genuineness of persons such as the administrator Lauren Matthias. Jemunu-jah found that he was looking forward to filing an official report of their misfortune and subsequent survival, if only so that she might read it.

Gazing out through the rain from the porch of their host's home, Hasa regarded the unassuming ramshackle houses of the villagers with disdain. "Could've hoped for rescue from a village with something more going for it than this dump."

The fact that Jemunu-jah agreed with Hasa's assessment did not lessen the force of the associated insult. He would have objected, but the human was still talking.

"Okay; we're alive and likely to stay that way for the foreseeable future. As soon as the twits up in Taulau can manage to extricate their brains from their pants, they'll send a rescue skimmer down here to pick us up."

A perfectly horrible thought sprang unbidden into Masur-athoo's ever-wary Deyzara mind. "What if it is sabotaged by the same individual or individuals who incapacitated our craft?"

Hasa was curt but reassuring. "We've explained what happened to us. Unless whoever's responsible for sending out the rescue crew is utterly barren of intelligence, they'll triple check everything before taking off. I think it'll be okay." Leaning back in the suspension chair, he sucked on something brown, round, and full of sweet syrup. "I wouldn't want to be rescued by anyone stupid enough to let what happened to us happen to them."

The human's confidence bolstered Masurathoo's depleted spirits. The Deyzara had decided that Hasa was worth saving after all—just barely.

"Couple of days," Hasa repeated. The rain had intensified. If it started to come down any harder, he mused, they would have to move inside. He didn't want to do that. Like any traditional Sakuntala dwelling, that of their kindly host stank to high heaven. "That gives us time to sort a few things out."

Nearby, Jemunu-jah lolled in comparative contentment in his own chair, idly watching the rain. Amazing how soothing it was; in its sound, its smell, its constancy. He never would understand why it made humans so irritable.

"What things? We have already agreed on a common report."

Having drained the boku of the last of its sugary contents, Hasa let it slip from his fingers. It landed on the otherwise clean deck. Jemunu-jah eyed the human disapprovingly. The least the disagreeable one could have done was throw it over the side, into the water. It would not have taken much of an effort. But then, a lack of concern for others was one of their human companion's most notable characteristics.

Hasa half closed his eyes, blissfully indifferent to the affront he had just delivered to their absent host. "On a report about what happened to us, yeah. We also have to decide what to say, or what not to say, about what we've discovered. Specifically, the pannula." His gaze shifted from Sakuntala to Deyzara and back again. "Are you going to agree with me that it's an intelligent organism? Or are you going to continue to reference it as a purely reactive 'forest spirit,' or just a dumb hunk of fungus?" Rising from the suspension seat, whose swinging he did not still, as would have been proper, he headed for the doorway into the main house.

"I'm gonna take a walk. The rain's not bad, and I'd like to see the rest of the village before we're lifted out of here."

Masurathoo fixed him with both bulging eyes. "Hoping to chance upon some useful undescribed plant or animal the knowledge of which you can steal from the locals?"

As Hasa looked back from the portal, it was clear that he had entirely missed the point of the Deyzara's sarcasm. "Well, of course. That's what I'm doing here. I'm not proud. I've got no problem with letting some dumb native do the dirty work for me."

As he watched their companion depart, Jemunu-jah bristled at the human's offhandedly offensive manner. "We save each other's lives, but I do not like Hasa. He is poor representative of his species."

Masurathoo was slightly more understanding. "If nothing else, I have to say that I find his xenophobia remarkably consistent. You should not feel singled out, my tall friend. Bear in mind that he hates his own kind as well."

"Heesa, that is so." Jemunu-jah regarded the shorter Deyzara. "What he said has merit, however. How are we to describe pannula in our official statement?"

Masurathoo gazed out into the forest. Below, something long and green made a half-hidden leap, leaving behind rain-dappled ripples on the surface of the water. It came nowhere near reaching the floor of the porch. "Do *you* think it is sentient?"

Jemunu-jah pondered the question. "The human is convinced. I am not. My people have always been aware of certain presences in the forest. There no stories of any pannula consciously trying to help them."

"Maybe they did not need help," the Deyzara pointed out. "Or maybe the timing wasn't right, or the moment of contact. Or perhaps, being so familiar with your kind, the pannula was not interested. It might have taken the arrival of an entirely new species, like Hasa's, combined with just the right circumstances, like our helplessness and isolation, to induce it to make itself known."

Jemunu-jah was still not convinced. "The Sakuntala eat fungi. We do not talk to them."

"That may have to change." Rising from his seat, whose motion he carefully stilled so as not to offend any watching Sakuntala, Masurathoo walked to the open edge of the porch. Alive with haunting sounds, masked by rain and mist, the southern Viisiiviisii emerged from the waters of ten thousand conjoined rivers.

"Do you not realize what it means if the human is right about the pannula? It would completely change the sociopolitical dynamic on Fluva."

Jemunu-jah struggled hard to comprehend. "I not sure I understand."

Carefully stepping away from the edge, the Deyzara turned to regard his fur-covered fellow traveler. "Allow me to point out that Commonwealth classification of this world is based on the presence of one indigenous intelligent species and one imported one. The way the Commonwealth government treats Fluva is based on that classification. The situation here is already atypical in that the resident sentient population is almost evenly divided between two different species. If a third is added into the mix, the situation becomes unique."

Jemunu-jah frowned. "I do not see how it changes anything."

"Some of it will be good. The Commonwealth will pay more attention to Fluva. That means more aid credits and a greater voice within the galactic government. But consider this: Where sentience is concerned, Commonwealth and Church policies are designed to safeguard the most primitive."

"Are you saying that the Commonwealth will work to help the pannula before it will the Sakuntala?"

Masurathoo was gesturing with both trunks. "Or the Deyzara. That is the way of things. The government will be especially interested in the pannula because it represents the first evidence of intelligence in a life-form of its kind, although I understand that there are rumors of something similar on another world. They are only rumors, though. The pannula is real." Sorrowfully he eyed the remnant shards of his once striking garments.

"At least one good thing will come of it. If the Commonwealth Authority accepts the human's interpretation of the pannula's actions, it will gain leave to intervene in the uprising promulgated by the extremists among your people. The Authority will be able to use the excuse that it is interceding to protect the interests of the least advanced of Fluva's three resident sentient species."

Jemunu-jah gaped at the Deyzara. "The Authority would shoot Sakuntala to protect a fungus?"

"If they believe it to be intelligent, comparatively helpless, and in danger, yes. Policy would allow them to do that even if the pannula are not directly affected by the ongoing clash."

The Sakuntala's ears bent forward and his tail lay limp on the deck behind his chair. "This changes everything."

"That is what I am saying. Because of its uniqueness, the pannula will become the focus of Commonwealth interests on Fluva."

"It is so absurd."

Masurathoo rolled his eyes. "The policies of governments often are. But both the Deyzara and the Sakuntala have to learn to deal with them." He went silent, turning to gaze again at the rain-swept forest.

Deal with them, Jemunu-jah thought furiously. Unless— what if the Commonwealth Authority continued to remain ignorant of the pannula's hypothesized intelligence? Where would be the harm in that? Even if the bad-tempered human's

assessment was correct, it could be many, many years before
anyone else happened to stumble upon the knowledge.

Could he persuade Hasa to keep silent on the matter?
Jemunu-jah doubted it. It was likely that such a momentous
discovery would mean that honors would be bestowed on the
human by his own kind. Even if the Deyzara did not entirely
believe it, it was reasonable to assume that Masurathoo would
eventually support the human's contentions, if only for the effect it would have on any Sakuntala uprising. Jemunu-jah had
no quarrel with that. He also wanted to see an end to the conflict. But did he want to see it enforced, on some of his own admittedly misguided people, by Commonwealth weapons?

Ancient emotions stirred within him, his mind and heart
boiling with conflict. He could save injudicious Sakuntala
youth from assault by intervening Commonwealth forces and
protect the paramouncy of his kind in the eyes of the Commonwealth government. All he had to do was kill his two companions. Masurathoo would be easy. Jemunu-jah knew he
could take the Deyzara apart with his bare hands. Seeing to the
demise of the feral human would be more difficult but should
still be achievable. Only one thing held him back.

He was supposed to be civilized now.

Murdering his companions would not be the civilized thing
to do. So what if the humans interceded to stop the misguided
uprising of the radicals among his own kind? Did he not seek
the same end? Few, if any, of those involved were likely to be of
his own clan. That realization, at least, placed his simmering
thoughts well within tradition. Let the humans shoot a few
wild-eyed members of opposing clans. From the standpoint of
custom, that would be all to the good.

As to his people suffering a lessening of importance in the
eyes of the Commonwealth while it strove to understand and
assist the pannula, where was the harm in that? Would it not be
offset by the increased aid and attention the Commonwealth
would bring to Fluva?

He was torn. His heart told him to kill, his mind to participate.

Maybe the destiny of the Sakuntala did not rest in his hands, but their immediate prospects did. It was a responsibility he had not asked for and did not want.

"You are become awfully quiet," Masurathoo murmured through his speaking trunk.

A single strike to the back of that naked fleshy skull, Jemunu-jah thought. Then a quick push and the oblivious Deyzara would topple over the edge of the porch to land in the water. Waiting scavengers would make quick work of the body.

Jemunu-jah found himself wrestling harder with his own inner demons than ever he had with a clan opponent.

As he trundled through the village along the crude network of walkways suspended above the water, Hasa groused silently at the time it was taking for deliverance to arrive. He'd have a word or two for the crew of the rescuing craft, and they wouldn't be pretty. A pair of villagers going the other way greeted him with the respect due an honored guest. He snapped out a terse Sakuntala greeting, indifferent to whether they understood him or not. Damn stinking aborigines—he'd be more than glad to get back to Taulau and what passed for civilization on this miserable soggy pustulant tumor of a world.

Even his rivals, of whom there were many, would have to fete him when he announced his findings. Identifying potentially useful botanicals was one thing. Discovering a new intelligent species was several orders of magnitude more significant. While the immediate financial returns might not be as quick in coming, the recognition should lead to a flurry of opportunities. At the very least, he would be generally anointed the leading bioprospector on Fluva. Large companies and trading houses would seek out his advice, for which he could charge, and would be eager to employ him at extravagant rates. Furthermore, the discovery of the pannula would bring more such enterprises to Fluva. He intended to milk his finding shamelessly and methodically for all it was worth. Of course, even though they continued to express skepticism of his conclusions, he would be legally obligated to share the forthcoming plenty with Masurathoo and Jemunu-jah.

Unless . . .

It would be terrible if they failed to return. A real tragedy. No doubt there would be much high-throated keening among Jemunu-jah's clan and corresponding nauseating trunk blowing by Masurathoo's relations if both of them vanished in the Vii-siiviisii. That would be too, too bad. He would be forced to deal with the glory and prospects raised by the discovery of the pannula all by himself. Could one person handle so much fame and wealth?

Though it might take some effort, he was convinced that he could.

There was a problem, however. Though simple, unsophisticated folk who had little contact with civilization, the local villagers had seen him arrive in the company of two ostensibly healthy, alert companions. He doubted they would care one way or another if the Deyzara in their midst happened to vanish one day, but Jemunu-jah presented a much bigger problem. While he was not of their village or a related clan, they knew him now as a respected and highly educated member of an important and influential northern group. His sudden disappearance, coupled with that of Masurathoo, would arouse more than suspicion. They might not take any action themselves, but there was the danger that they might pass their qualms on to the rescue team. Such accusations could place him in a position sufficiently awkward that even he might not be able to find a way to wriggle free.

He cursed himself for lack of forethought. The time to have carried out such intentions would have been days earlier, when the three of them were still alone in the depths of the Viisiivii-sii. But then, the members of the hunting party that had found them might not have been as inclined to assist him as they had been eager to help a fellow Sakuntala like Jemunu-jah.

Like it or not, it looked as if he was going to have to share the success that was coming his way. That left him feeling grouchy and even more out of sorts than usual. Masurathoo remarked upon it when he finally rejoined them later that afternoon. Jemunu-jah did not.

Sakuntala regarded human with unusual intensity while human gazed back with uncommon thoughtfulness. Between them, Masurathoo blithely assumed he was still among not only friends but civilized ones.

It was just as well he did not know otherwise. Already seriously stressed, his highly strung nervous system might not have been able to cope with the disclosure of his good friends' conflicted thoughts.

17

M atthias liked the Other Place. Most eating establishments in Taulau catered to the majority Deyzara and Sakuntala. Few had the inclination and the skills to prepare food that was not only suitable for humans serving with the Commonwealth Authority but tasty as well. The Other Place (a loose transliteration of its Deyzaran name) was one of them.

The proprietor, an obsequious but highly skilled Deyzara named Agruarasa, waited on her personally. It was a point of some pride that the head of the Commonwealth Authority, the human High Hata, chose to dine in his place of business. She listened politely to the familiar stream of sycophancy that spilled from his speaking trunk along with occasional mentions of actual food and then ordered.

It would have been nice if Jack could have joined her for lunch, she mused, but the laboratory complex where he worked was located on the other side of the main port and was too far for an easy commute in the rain. Besides, he would typically be as buried in his work as she was in hers. They understood that about each other. It was one of the reasons their marriage, unlike so many on Fluva, survived.

She was not the only human in the restaurant. Unlike the rest of them, however, she chose to sit by the edge of the dining area, at a small table that overlooked the bustling, rain-washed town, instead of farther inside.

Gazing at the panorama of busy strilk-suspended businesses and homes, offices and meeting places, it was difficult to envision the brutal clash that was taking place elsewhere between harried Deyzara and persecuting Sakuntala. Precipitation ran steadily and peacefully off roofs and walkways, while pedestrians of several races wended their way to and from work and home. Skimmers dropped off travelers and made deliveries. Harmless winged gerulenk and gaseous totolu soared or floated peacefully among walkways, buildings, fungi-infested trees, and pylons. It was all very civilized and serene. A Commonwealth-sponsored facade, she knew, that masked the deeper troubles that bubbled and boiled just outside the town limits.

Hanging from the sloping ceiling (there were no flat ceilings in downpour-drenched Taulau or anywhere else on Fluva), cages full of domesticated varisanu steeped the restaurant in song. In addition to their own inborn harmonic repertoire, the fist-size, sparkle-throated varisanu could mimic any music they heard following a single listening. All four hirsute wings unfurled, red eyes bobbing at the tips of short stalks, one nearby blue-and-gold individual was presently declaiming a superb, if muted, rendition of the princess's final aria from Act Two of *Turandot*. In the same cage, an equally attractive yellow-and-lavender specimen was tootling its way through an entire cycle of atonal Deyzaran folk songs. The consequent counterpoint, she reflected, would have seriously strained the descriptive abilities of the most egalitarian music pundit.

Her server was a senior Deyzara. Less susceptible to mold and rust than a mechanical, the live waiter was also cheaper to operate in Fluva's remorselessly damp climate. Matthias accepted the food appreciatively and was about to begin eating when a visitor intruded on her vision.

Looking up, she found a short, slim man with a mournful expression gazing down at her. She decided he could not have weighed much more than fifty kilos. His hair was thin, blond, and receding. He looked to be about thirty. Worn down early, she concluded. One of those sad individuals who found themselves peeled prematurely off the roll of Life.

"Sorry to break in on your lunch, Administrator Matthias." He spared a furtive glance for the other occupants of the dining area. "I really need to talk to you."

"Here?" She forked food, chewed calmly. Whatever else the man was, he did not appear threatening. "Why not make an appointment with my office?"

"Kind of in a hurry. Don't like formalities." He cast a meaningful glance in the direction of the other chair. "May I? I think it's important."

She sighed inwardly. One of the main drawbacks to being in charge of everything was never having any privacy. People were always confronting you with complaints, suggestions, requests, demands, angry objections to something you'd just done or were going to do or hadn't even contemplated. It went with the job. Hopefully, it wouldn't take long for her uninvited guest to have his say.

"Clifford Kamis," he was saying as he slipped into the chair. "You can call me Clif."

She mustered a smile. "Nice to meet you, Clif. I'm afraid I can't talk to you for very long. I don't get much time to myself, you see, and—"

"I'll be real brief," he assured her, interrupting. "It's about those two skimmers that went missing."

She hesitated with a full fork halfway to her lips, carefully set it back down on the rectangular Deyzaran serving tray. "What about them?"

He stole another glance at the busy dining room. "Everybody's talking about them, but nobody seems to know much of anything."

"And you do—Clif?" She was watching him intently now, her rapidly cooling lunch temporarily forgotten.

He looked away and shrugged uncomfortably. "Maybe. Maybe not. It's just something I seen. I work graveyard cleanup at the port, Administrator."

She nodded understandingly. He had her full attention. "Go on, Clif. Don't worry. Anything you say to me here stays with me, and is between you and me alone."

He was appropriately encouraged. "People are whispering that they didn't come back 'cause they were sabotaged. Talk is that the Deyzara is responsible. Me, I don't see how the two-trunks could bring off something like that. Seems to me you got to really know your way around the insides of a skimmer's instrumentation to bring off something like that, you know?"

Folding her arms, she leaned forward and rested them on the table. "You don't think the Deyzara did it?"

"What for?" He looked out over the town, into the steadily increasing downpour that had replaced much of the original view with a palisade of drumming gray. "I mean, what would the two-trunks get out of it? Especially if they were found out and held to blame. A few folks, they're saying that the Sakuntala did it and are making it to look like the Deyzara are responsible. Now, that makes more sense to me, 'cause right now the Sakuntala need to make the Deyzara look as bad as possible, so's to help justify what their trigger-happy warriors are doing to the two-trunks." He shook his head, lips tightening. "But I've never seen any Sakuntala messing around with skimmers they weren't using. Certainly not late at night, when I'm doing my job. And none of the regular engineering types I've talked with know of a Sakuntala tech skilled enough to carry out that kind of advanced high-level instrumental manipulation."

She took a sip of her drink. "There are a couple of AAnn observers here on Fluva. They might have the necessary skills."

This time when he shook his head, it was with greater certainty. "Still need an expert authority on-site when you're doing that kind of real understated work, or so I've been told by the folks who'd know about such things. And I've sure as hell never seen no lizards sneakin' around the facility."

She forced herself to remain patient. "If not the Deyzara, or the Sakuntala with or without AAnn assistance, then who?"

Now that the time had come to get specific, he wavered. Fighting down a paroxysm of impatience, she reminded him again that whatever he said would be held in strictest confidence. As he leaned over the table toward her, his already soft voice was tempered even further by palpable concern.

"It's just that, working late at night, there ain't a lot to see. So when there *is* something to see, you kind of take notice of it, you know? I didn't think nothing of it when I saw it. Seemed perfectly natural to me at the time. But later, afterward, after that bioprospector fella's skimmer went missing and then the rescue team's also, it kind of got me to thinking.

"See, there was this one time I saw someone working on the prospector's skimmer, real late—and it wasn't him. Next night, I hear that there had been some minor glitches in the port surveillance system. A few days later the system goes down again, for just a little while. That same time it goes down, I seen the same guy working on the skimmer that goes out with the rescue team. Both times, the guy doing the work didn't notice me." He smiled wanly. "I'm not a real noticeable type, you know? I don't stand out. And I don't move around too much or make much noise when I'm doing my work. Took me a while to put everything together." He shrugged again.

"Course, it might not mean a damn thing. Just struck me as a couple of funny coincidences, that's all. The same guy working on both skimmers on the same nights port surveillance goes on the fritz." He eyed her earnestly. "What do you think, Administrator? Am I wasting your time?"

She sucked in her breath. "No, Clif, I don't think you're wasting my time. I don't think you're wasting my time at all. One thing I don't understand is, why bring this to me? Why not report it to Port Security?"

He looked away, clearly ill at ease. "Well, it's like, I don't know the guys who work security all that well. And I'm thinking, what if one of them is working with this guy I seen, to help cover what he's doing? Maybe the security guy is taking down the surveillance system while his buddy is doing whatever it is he was doing to those two missing skimmers? What if they're working something together?"

That could certainly explain, she realized, why the Port Security crew had not been able to come up with any useful information to pass along to her office. "Would," she asked her guest with studied deliberation, "you be able to recognize the individual you saw working on both of the missing skimmers if you saw him again?"

"Oh, hell, I don't need to look at a holo of him. I know the guy. He's in and out of the port all the time, checking out and working on his own skimmer, always making sure it's operational and ready to go. Seen him working late lots of other times. I'm told he's a bioprospector also."

That would make sense, she knew. Someone with a skimmer based at the port wouldn't arouse suspicion when he entered and left the facility, even at odd hours. It shouldn't be too hard for a patrol to pick him up. There weren't that many independent bioprospectors working out of Taulau.

"Give me his name. Don't worry. Whatever happens, your involvement won't be brought up."

Kamis grinned softly. The more she talked with him, the more she liked the soft-spoken little man. "Don't care about him. Don't care if he knows or not. It's the guy I don't know, the security guy who might be helping him out, who worries me."

"I'll see to it that you're given protection. Discreet, of course. Just give me a name. I've met a couple, but by no means all, of the bioprospectors who work out of Taulau."

He met her gaze unflinchingly. "You know one named Sethwyn Case?"

At his intolerable, excruciatingly painful words, more than her appetite summarily drained away. Nausea rose in her gut. She felt suddenly queasy. Hardly touched, the meal laid out before her had abruptly taken on the look and smell of warmed-over offal. Exerting a tremendous effort of will, she took a long swallow of her chilled drink without her hand shaking. In contrast, every bit of her insides seemed to be trembling.

"Are you sure you're not, not mistaken in your identification, Clif? I'm certain you realize how important this is, what you're telling me. You need to be very, very sure."

"Oh, I'm sure," he told her without the slightest hesitation. "It was Seth Case, all right. Both times. Unlike me, the guy's pretty distinctive-looking." He peered a little closer at her. "Is he one of the prospectors you know?"

"Yes." She was having a difficult time breathing. "Yes, he's one of the ones I know."

"You okay, Administrator?" Kamis looked suddenly alarmed. "You don't look so good."

"Swallowed some juice the wrong way. I'm all right, Clif. I'm just wondering. As long as we're talking about this. What reason could Mr. Case have for sabotaging those two skimmers? What possible motive could he have?"

Kamis sat back in his chair. "Hey, that's not something for someone like me to speculate on, Administrator."

"Go ahead, Clif." She spoke more sharply than she intended. "Go ahead and speculate."

"Well . . ." He scratched at the fine blond hair that barely veiled the pale flesh of his skull. "You listen, you hear a lot of things around the port. There's a lot of competition among prospectors."

"I know," she snapped. Seeing him flinch at her tone, she hastened to reassure him. "Sorry. This is—it makes one angry, you understand?" How angry, her guest could not imagine.

"Sure, I understand. If it's true and I were in your position, I'm sure I'd feel the same way."

You have no idea, she thought bleakly. "You were speculating?"

"Yeah. Like I said, lots of competition, to find valuable growths and stuff. I don't pretend to understand everything that's being talked about, but I understand about the competition clear enough. Everyone understands about competition.

"Case, he was pretty jealous of this Hasselemoga's successes.

And this Hasa guy, I never met him, but I get the feeling he wasn't real well liked by his opposite numbers."

"It is my impression that all the other bioprospectors felt similarly about Mr. Hasselemoga."

"Uh-huh. But I didn't see none of them hanging around those two skimmers that've gone missing on the two nights when port surveillance just happened to go out."

From the last time they had talked, some of Seth's words suddenly came back to her in an explosive, damning rush.

"How's your luck been?" she had asked him.

"Not so good. . . . I've got a couple of leads on some spots down south . . ."

Down south. That was where the reviled Shadrach Hasselemoga had gone missing. Had Sethwyn been working the same general area? Was he afraid that his detested but resourceful competitor would beat him to discoveries that Case believed were rightfully his to make? Had he seen to it that Hasselemoga's skimmer would crash and not be able to send out a call for help?

When a rescue skimmer had been sent out to look for the missing prospector, had Case been forced to make sure that it, too, would vanish without a trace, in hopes that no third party would be sent to look for those who had preceded it? Wasn't that exactly what had happened so far? Meanwhile, rumors flew that the Deyzara were behind the twin disappearances. Divert attention. A classic maneuver of the clever criminal. Was Case responsible for them, too?

Kamis was rising to go. "I just want you to know, Administrator, I'm not telling you about this because I've got anything against this guy Case. Or because I happen to like this Hasa fella. I don't even know him. I ain't doing it because I'm any more fond of Fluva than any other human bean unlucky to be stationed here. I'm telling you because I'm a regular church-goer and it's against United Church orison for one sentient to belittle another with intent to cause harm. What happened to those two skimmers may or may not be the fault of this guy Case. Any stuff like that has yet to be proved. But the rumors ain't fair to the Deyzara. That's why I'm speaking up. I'd bet my pension they're not responsible for what happened." He pushed his chair back into the table. "Maybe if you have a chat with Case, you'll find out for sure who is."

She did not follow him with her eyes as he made his way back out through the crowded restaurant. Her vision, like her thoughts, was directed elsewhere. She sat at the table, hardly moving, staring at nothing, until the diffident Deyzara server approached. The two-trunks' speaking organ was bobbing fretfully.

"Your pardon, Administrator Matthias, but is there perhaps something wrong with the food?"

"What?" Absently she glanced down at the intricately inlaid and still heavily laden tray. "No. Nothing at all. I'm just . . ." Her voice strengthened and she rose from her seat. "I have to go. Emergency call."

The server sighed knowingly through his trunk. "I am sorry for you. You must have to deal with a very great many of those in these uncomfortable times."

She did not succeed in mustering a reply.

Somehow, she donned her rain cape and found her way back to the Administration Center, thankful that the eating establishment lay within walking distance and she did not have to use a skimmer or slider. Pedestrians who knew her called out greetings and were taken by surprise when she did not respond. It occurred to her that she was in a mild state of shock.

She wrenched herself out of it. She was too busy to be in shock. If she wanted to spend time in shock, she would have to set aside an appropriate length of time on her appointment calendar.

She was dimly aware that Pandusky spoke to her as she entered and strode past him. Possibly one or two other staff members did so as well. She wasn't sure. She could hear nothing except her own searing, agitated thoughts.

Throwing herself into her welcoming chair, she ignored the insistent flashes of light from her desk. Whatever it was could wait. Everything could wait.

Kamis's testimony was damning—but it was not conclusive. The maintenance worker had said as much himself. She needed more proof. She needed hard evidence to go with the little man's eyewitness account. Bergovoy would be no help. What would, what could, constitute the proverbial smoking gun? Fully alert and active now, her mind ran through a long list of possibilities. Eventually, she addressed the waiting desk.

"Sanuel?"

"Administrator Matthias, is there something—"

"Not now, Sanuel," she interrupted brusquely. "Get in here. I've got a job for you."

Her assistant arrived within seconds. The look of concern on his face was not addressed. She had no time for it.

Without preamble or explanation, she said, "You know the bioprospector Sethwyn Case? He's been here to talk to me on several occasions."

Pandusky's expression remained perfectly neutral. "I remember him, yes."

"I'm not surprised. You remember everything, Sanuel." She did not give him time to respond to the mixed compliment. "I want to see his personal financial records for the past year, local time." She raised a hand to forestall the reaction she knew was coming. "I know it's illegal. I also know you have the skills and resources to do it. It's a matter of Authority security."

At that moment, her assistant looked more uncomfortable than she had ever seen him.

"I'll take full responsibility," she continued. "If there's any fall-out, I'll see to it that you are completely absolved of any liability."

Still, he hesitated. "A matter of Authority security, you said?"

She nodded. "Utmost importance. Questions of life and death."

Pandusky took a long, deep breath, didn't smile, and muttered, "Give me twenty minutes."

He was back in fifteen. Matter-of-factly, he dumped the hard copy on her desk. "Will there be anything else, Administrator?"

She was already poring over the report. It was not extensive. "Not for now, Sanuel. I'll let you know."

Nodding, he watched her read for a moment, then retreated gratefully from the room.

It did not take long to find what she was looking for. There were half a dozen suspicious transfers of credit. None was large enough to stand out, but they were all of approximately the same amount and in each instance the transfers into Case's account had taken place on consecutive days. One large payment broken up into several smaller ones to avoid drawing attention, she surmised. There was no proof that was the case, but it was not an unreasonable assumption. Particularly since every one of the suspect transfers was from a company called Poutukaa. She knew the name. It was part of her job to be at least cursorily familiar with such things.

Poutukaa was owned and operated by Sakuntala.

On the surface, there was nothing shady about the company. It dabbled in food processing and supply as well as the transshipment of goods among towns and villages. It might be involved in other enterprises as well; she couldn't remember. The key question was why and for what service was it paying Sethwyn Case substantial amounts of credit.

She ordered Poutukaa's confidential financial records accessed. With a look of reluctance and a sigh of distress, Pandusky went to work.

Geladu-tiv arrived in her office later that afternoon, escorted by two peaceforcers. She had the heavily armed soldiers remain, flanking the door to her outer office. The Sakuntala elder did not look happy. His tongue kept lolling out of one side of his mouth, and his tail would not be still. The strappings he wore were among the fanciest she had seen, an opulent mix of traditional weave, embossing, and engraving work that alternated with contemporary highlights.

She said as much. "Poutukaa must be doing well for its Hata to afford such costly raiment. I applaud your enterprise. You

are proof that the Deyzara are not the only ones who can succeed in doing commerce with the business entities of the Commonwealth."

Hauled off under armed guard to the office of the Authority
administrator, the last thing the senior Sakuntala had expected
was to be greeted with a compliment.

"Hauea, we do well enough." He was trying very hard not
to turn to look at the guards, who had their protective face
shields down and their weapons at the ready. "Administrator
Matthias, why have I been brought here? I a simple businessperson, just as you have declared."

"Businessperson I have no doubt. Simple—that is another
matter." She indicated a thick pile of hard copy on her desk. "I
have been reviewing your company records for the past year."

Geladu-tiv looked startled. "You not permitted to do such a
thing."

"On your way out you may request the proper form for filing an official complaint." She made a show of shuffling
through the hard copy. "There are a lot of payments here to
small groups and organizations that I am informed are active
participants in the current troubles."

As per prior instructions, one of the peaceforcers moved forward until he was standing close behind the Sakuntala senior.
Very close. Threat by implication would be difficult to prove.
Had a Church padre been present, he or she would have
protested vociferously. But no United Church presence hovered
over the little tableau that was being played out in her office.

Geladu-tiv struggled not to turn and meet the eyes of the
very tall peaceforcer. "Poutukaa is a respected clan-based
Sakuntala operation. It is no hotbed of radicals."

"I believe you." She indicated the hard copy. "However,
Poutukaa is guilty of providing financing and support to fac-
tions that are."

"To work profitably among Sakuntala is necessary to have
good relations with all clans and groups. Sometimes payments
necessary to buy not just goods but goodwill. That not a

crime." He hesitated, not entirely certain of the relevant bit of Commonwealth law. "Is it?"

"No, it's not." His relief was palpable. "Anyway, I'm not interested in your company's political activities. That's your business."

Now the senior appeared genuinely bewildered. "Then why I here? What you want from me?"

She extracted one piece of hard copy from the pile and pushed it toward him. He glanced down at it without making a move to pick it up, as if it were a lurking bai-mou just waiting to leap at his throat.

"On the dates specified, you made a number of sizable payments to a human named Sethwyn Case."

One did not become the head of a successful company operated and owned by Sakuntala without possessing at least a degree of shrewdness. "I cannot verify that without first check with company fiduciary."

"For now, take my word for it."

Having yet to be openly accused of breaking a law, the Sakuntala entrepreneur was starting to feel a little better about things. "Is also not illegal?"

"No." She stared hard at the senior. "All I want to know is, what were these payments made for? What services did the bioprospector Sethwyn Case render to the company Poutukaa to be worthy of all this credit? You didn't pay him in *mulat*."

Geladu-tiv let his tongue and tail tip fall to the floor, a dual sign of abject submission. "You must believe me, Administrator Matthias, when I tell you that I not know." Before she could object, he added helpfully, "If they are indeed accurately recorded and stated as you claim them to be, then all payments to which you refer would be ones made at behest of respected radical Hata-yuiqueru Aniolo-jat."

Sitting back in her chair, she nodded slowly. To the senior's discernible relief, the hulking peaceforcer who had been standing immediately behind him stepped back and resumed his original position next to the doorway.

"What business does Poutukaa have with an extremist like Aniolo-jat?"

"Trade," Geladu-tiv responded without hesitation. "Insurance."

"Weapons?" she retorted.

The senior looked alarmed. "No, no! Poutukaa would never be involved in the traffic of such things!"

Matthias was relentless. "Yet you make payments on behalf of a Hata-yuiqueru like Aniolo-jat."

"It is as I told you. Business is business. Among other things, heesa, credit buys goodwill."

She grunted, folding her hands in front of her. "In my language we would call it protection money, but so be it. You have no idea why Aniolo-jat wanted you to transfer large sums to the human Case?"

"No, Administrator. If you want to know, I think you must have to ask the Hata-yuiqueru yourself. We did what we did because we felt it good business." He swallowed. "Necessary business."

"You did it because you felt you had no choice. Did Aniolo-jat or some of his minions threaten you or your company?" The senior did not reply. "No matter. That's between his people and yours. You can go."

"Wistha?" Surprised by yet another unexpected turn in the interrogation, Geladu-tiv's ears flicked sharply in her direction.

"Heesa." She waved a hand indifferently. "Yes, go on; go. You are free to leave."

"I not—I am not under restraint?"

"You can stay if you want to," she told him crisply.

He left in such a hurry that he forgot to tongue her goodbye. It was just as well. She was in no mood to deal with a wet Sakuntala tongue wrapping around her face.

"You two. You can go outside, but stay in the building. I may need you later."

The two peaceforcers flashed simultaneous salutes. They had been sworn to secrecy concerning whatever took place in the

administrator's office. Now they departed, themselves unsure
of the significance of what they had just witnessed.

That was because they had been given access to only a few
pieces of the puzzle, she knew. The only one who held them all
was Lauren Matthias, chief administrator of the Commonwealth Authority on Fluva. And that was the trouble. She only
had pieces. Enough to visualize a finished picture. Not enough
to lay before a tribunal.

It would be nice to have a confession from the Hata-
yuiqueru. One more bit of the puzzle. Bringing in Aniolo-jat,
however, would not be quite as easy as sending peaceforcers to
the head offices of the company Poutukaa. Like his fellow extremists, the Sakuntala war chief was hiding somewhere deep in
the Viisiiviisii, directing the uprising. Utilizing the advanced
technical resources at her command, she had no doubt she
could locate him eventually. "Eventually," however, was an im-
precise length of time. She was far too angry to be patient.

What else could she do? She had learned something from
Pandusky's illegal but efficacious probe of various financial
records. She had learned something more from her tense inter-
view with the Sakuntala business-Hata Geladu-tiv. In gambler's
parlance, she was on a roll. What did one do when she was on a
roll? Leaning forward slightly, she addressed herself to the air.
The appropriate concealed pickup relayed her voice to the
outer office.

"Sanuel. If he can be found, bring in the independent bioprospector Sethwyn Case."

"Straightaway, Administrator." While Pandusky did not respond with enthusiasm, neither was he audibly upset. More
than anything, he was plainly relieved that he was not being
asked yet again to break into someone's restricted private financial records.

18

He did not look very happy. It was something of a shock. She was used to seeing him happy. Happy-go-lucky, at ease, grinning and laughing, ready to tease her with smile and laugh and eyes. Those eyes, she reflected. Those god-damned gorgeous, penetrating, seductive eyes. With an effort of will, she forced herself to meet them.

Shaking himself free of the two peaceforcers who had escorted him into her office, Case spared them a single lingering murderous glance before shifting his attention to the quiet, poised redheaded woman seated behind the desk. On previous occasions he had always tried to read her mind. He did not know how fortunate he was that he could not.

"I don't know what's going on, Lauren, but it isn't funny."

Her reply was one of studied calm. "You're right, Seth. It isn't funny." Looking past him, she dismissed the peaceforcers. They retired to the outer office, leaving her alone with the bioprospector.

As soon as the doorway sealed behind them, he turned back to her. His face was by turns flustered and furious. "Something's up, beautiful. Want to let me in on what it is?"

"Right away, Seth. And from here on in it might be best if you address me as Administrator." Her insides were churning again, but her voice was steady as strilk.

He drew back from her, straightening stiffly. "Oh. So it's like that, is it?"

She nodded slowly, painfully. "Yes, Seth. It's like that. I won't waste your valuable time." She continued to study his face, his eyes. "I know that you're the one responsible for sabotaging the instrumentation of the two missing skimmers: the one piloted by the bioprospector Shadrach Hasselemoga, also known as Hasa, and the rescue craft that was sent to find him."

Mouth open, lips more than slightly parted, he stared down at her in disbelief. Then his familiar grin returned, jaunty and disarming. But it did not return, she felt, quite quickly enough.

"You don't know anything of the sort," he retorted with becoming self-confidence, "because it isn't true."

"Sure it is," she replied with an assurance she was nowhere near feeling. "Hasselemoga is a competitor of yours. He took off to work the same territory where you were looking to make important discoveries. Probably boasted about where he was heading. Remember me asking you not long ago how your luck was going, and you telling me that you had some good prospects down south?"

"Means nothing." He shrugged it off. "The southern Viisii-viisii is an enormous place. In case you haven't noticed lately, there are only four cardinal bearings on the compass."

She pressed on, grimly self-possessed. "You were seen working around both of the missing craft. I have an eyewitness. You've received credit, a very large sum of credit, from an extremist Sakuntala Hata-yuiqueru, funneled through a legitimate Sakuntala company. The credit was disguised to conceal the magnitude of the overall amount, which makes the transfers even more suspicious."

"So what?" he challenged her. "Maybe my political leanings are morally hard for some people to understand, but they're not illegal. If I choose to support one Sakuntala political faction over another one, that's my decision."

She nodded appreciatively. "Thank you for telling me that. It explains why you told me you weren't worried about the Sakuntala giving you trouble during your explorations. 'They won't bother me,' you said. No wonder you were so sure of yourself. You had a deal with a prominent war chief and could operate freely under his protection, even in the deep south."

He sighed heavily. "Look, if you don't have anything else— *Administrator*—unlike some people, I have real work to do."

Unable to contain herself, she started to rise from her chair. "The Sakuntala radicals approached you with an offer to make the Deyzara look bad, thus helping to mute human and therefore Commonwealth objections to the uprising against the Deyzara. Needing money in order to keep operating—and your financial records show that you were in serious fiscal straits before receiving the credit from Poutukaa—you offered to sabotage Hasselemoga's skimmer and spread the rumor that the Deyzara were somehow responsible. This opportunity dovetailed neatly with your desire to get rid of a dangerously efficient competitor nobody liked anyway. Then you had to do the same to the rescue skimmer to make sure no one would find your handiwork and possibly trace it back to you." When he didn't respond, she pushed on.

"You're finished, Seth. Your dire financial situation, your direct connection to the Sakuntala radicals, your need to eliminate Hasselemoga, plus the eyewitness who saw you monkeying with not one but both missing skimmers that I'm reliably told no Deyzara could have manipulated so subtly—it all fits together rather neatly, doesn't it? Not to mention your own words to me." She glanced in the direction of floating time. "I'm expecting the Sakuntala Hata-yuiqueru Aniolo-jat any minute. He'll confirm what I've just said. Not that I need his confirmation to have you indicted."

For the first time since he'd been brought into her office, Case looked unsettled instead of irate. "You can't bring Aniolo-jat here. You don't know where he is."

Her eyes snapped sharply back up to lock onto his. "Don't I? I had an interview a while ago with Geladu-tiv, the head of

the company Poutukaa. Your financial go-between. Think *he*
doesn't know where the Hata he regularly pays off is residing?"
She tried not to hold her breath, to remain calm, to give away
nothing. Which, she knew, was what she had.

From the moment she'd first met him, she'd thought of
Sethwyn Case as indestructible, unyielding. A fit individual to
challenge the lethal Viisiiviisii single-handedly. Tough, coura-
geous, charming, knowledgeable, able to look Death in the face
with one eye and stare it down even as he was enchanting
someone like herself with the other. As the silence continued,
she became convinced that there was no way this was going to
work, no chance that she would gain the final piece of the rank,
unfinished puzzle. He was going to turn and walk out of her
office and she was not going to be able to do a damn thing
about it.

As she was contemplating the maddening failure that lay
spread out before her in all its malign grandeur, he cracked.

Though still outwardly defiant, he seemed to shrink before
her. How she had ever thought this miserable narcissistic sorry
slab of ambulating testosterone worthy of contemplated infi-
delity she now could not understand. The press of too much
work was the only excuse she could come up with. She had
been blinded by perspiration as much as by flattery. Given time,
perhaps she could do better.

She consoled herself with the knowledge that she was not
the first woman in history who occupied a position of importance to have been so deceived.

"I need the name of the individual in Port Security you paid
off to help you circumvent interior surveillance."

Anesthetized by events, wholly preoccupied, he responded with a barely perceptible nod. That's when he pulled the
injector.

It was very small. Still, the peaceforcers who had brought
him in should have found the medical device. Maybe they had,
she thought, and Case had protested at having it confiscated.
Or perhaps they had been preoccupied in the search for more

overt weaponry. She would have to have a word with Security. Her serenity in the face of the device, loaded with chemicals of what potential deadliness she could not imagine, astonished her. It was possible she was too weary to be frightened.

She kept her hands in plain sight. A sharp word would raise a defensive screen between her desk and the rest of the office. Unfortunately, he was too close and inside the potential barrier. A different word would bring the waiting peaceforcers running from the outer office. That might, she reflected calmly, take too much time. She favored him with a mixture of sadness and pity.

"Are you going to shoot me with something, Seth? Here, in my office, in the heart of Administration? If you do, it had better be instantly lethal. Suppose you do? What happens afterward? You can't just walk out of here. I'd first have to tell the officers waiting in the outer room that it's okay for you to leave. Even if you could somehow con your way past them, then what? Where would you go? This is Fluva. You'd never be able to get off-world. Is that the existence you want to look forward to for the rest of your life, hiding out in the Viisiiviisii? Because you'd have to hide, you know. With the offer of a modest reward you'd have every Deyzara and Sakuntala on the planet looking for you."

The injector wavered along with the look on his face. Keeping the business end aimed in her direction, he worked his way around the desk until he was standing next to the window. The same window through which she had stared so long and so often ever since she had accepted her promotion to her present position. Beyond the protective exterior overhang, a light rain was visible.

Still keeping his attention focused on her, he reached back with his free hand and tried to open the window. He failed, because there was no lock and no handle. She shook her head slowly.

"Like so much else in this office, Seth, it only responds to my voice. Like the screen that's been up between you and me ever since you pulled that toy out of your pocket."

"You're lying." His eyes flicked from side to side, searching for suggestions of an ethereal shield.

She shrugged. "Then go ahead and try to shoot me. If you succeed, you're further damned. If you fail, I'll see you put up on charges of making the attempt. In addition to everything else."

He hesitated a moment longer. Then he put the nasty little power injector down on her desk and stepped back. A ghost of the familiar captivating smile she knew all too well played around the corners of his mouth.

"You're smarter than me, Lauren. You always were. I just thought that this one time I could stay a step ahead of you."

"You *were* a step ahead of me," she replied coldly. "It just took me a while to catch up."

Nodding, he looked momentarily hopeful. "I just want you to know that however things turn out, I always meant what I said about your attractiveness. That was no lie. I loved your personality as well as your—"

"Shut up, Seth."

The two peaceforcers took him away. He departed with a smile. Or maybe it was a smirk. She marveled that until now she had not been able to tell the difference. Fine details, she told herself as she stared at the resealed portal. Little things she ought to have noticed. So many little things . . .

She began to cry, long, heaving sobs that were punctuated by ferocious obscenities. Not only was she furious at the apprehended bioprospector, she was equally angry at herself. How could she have been so gullible? It had been so easy for him to fool, to flatter, and, ultimately, to betray. All the engaging conversation, the sweet words, the cunning kissing up—it hadn't been for her. Everything had been said and done to advance Case's own private agenda. He might have brought it off, too, if not for the suspicions of a low-level maintenance tech unwilling to see an innocent species unfairly vilified.

For most of a full hour she raged against Case and against herself, ignoring the brightly colored points of floating light that twinkled just above the surface of her restless desk. Then she went back to work.

As she was about to leave the building, Pandusky informed her that word had just come in from an extremely remote southern village of the arrival, tattered and tired but otherwise in good physical shape, of both the missing bioprospector Hasselemoga and the two members of the team that had been sent to rescue him.

"Wonderful news, isn't it, Administrator?" Her assistant was beaming. "After so many days missing in the Viisiiviisii, it's a miracle that they've turned up alive."

"Yes, wonderful." Her voice was a whisper.

Pandusky's brows drew toward each other. It looked as if—no. Surely Administrator Matthias had not been crying. It was the strain she was working under. That was it. Too much on her plate these past few days. And now this unpleasant business with the prospector Case. No wonder she looked so worn out.

"Should I authorize sending a third crew down to pick them up?" When she didn't reply, he repeated the query, adding, "Administrator?"

She blinked, looked over at him. "Yes, of course. Authorize it." She started past him.

"I'll take care of it, Administrator—Lauren. Don't worry. I'll remind whoever's picked to go down there to take extra precautions with both predeparture and in-flight procedures."

She glanced back. "Won't be necessary, Sanuel. There won't be any trouble—this time."

"As you say, Administrator." He dithered briefly. "If you don't mind my saying so, Lauren, you could do with a day off. A little rest would do you . . ."

His words trailed away. She was already out of hearing range.

By the time she got home she had convinced herself she was over it. She was wrong. Jack was waiting for her in the center room of their dwelling. Good Jack, kind Jack, faithful Jack. He had supper waiting for her. Again. That was all it took to start her weeping once more.

"Hey," he murmured in bewilderment as she slumped, sobbing, into his arms, "I'm not *that* bad a cook."

An alarmed Pandusky called the next morning when she failed to arrive at the office. His concern was understandable, given that Chief Administrator Matthias was noted for her reliability and punctuality.

"I'm fine." She smiled across at Jack, who was also more than a little late for work. Neither of them much cared. For the first time in weeks, they were enjoying instead of lamenting the steady patter of rain on the curved roof of their suspended home. "I'll be there in an hour. And, Sanuel?"

"Yes, Administrator?" the voice floating in the air above the bed responded.

"Have those two AAnn brought over from Medical. I'll need to talk to them first thing."

Closing the connection with a word, she turned back to her husband. As it turned out, it was a good deal more than an hour before she left for work.

The AAnn were not happy about being kept waiting. Not that it was very different waiting in the outer office of the chief administrator from waiting in the isolation ward where they had been held for the past several days. They were not very happy about a great many things.

Thessu let her know as much the minute she arrived, punctuating his declamation with more than a dozen first-degree gestures of indignation.

"Truly, Administrator, it iss unconsscionable to keep uss locked up like thiss!"

"You are not locked up." Smoothly she slid back behind her desk. Unlike yesterday, this afternoon the position felt comfortable as well as completely familiar. "You are undergoing observation for your own protection."

"Protection from what?" Jallrii was so upset, his switching tail threatened to demolish the chair that had been provided for him. "There iss nothing wrong with uss!"

"Patience," she urged them, utterly unruffled by their ire. "I've brought you here to apologize to you."

Their reaction showed that those were words they were not expecting. After an exchange of several sibilant hisses, Thessu turned slitted eyes on the seated human.

"We accept your apology."

She smiled. "Don't you want to hear what it's for?"

The senior AAnn officer signaled third-degree uncertainty. "Truly, it musst be for forcibly resstraining uss on the mosst feeble of excussess." He hesitated. "Iss it not?"

"No, indeed. If you remember our previous meeting, I suggested that you might be somehow responsible for the sabotaging of two skimmers that had been lost in the southern Viisiiviisii. I now know that not to be the case. You have been proven innocent of such charges." Rising, she performed a third-degree double gesture of apology coupled with a second-degree forward bow of abasement. It was far from perfect, but her guests were impressed that she made the effort.

Taken aback, Jallrii recovered quickly. The rapid curling motion of his right hand, coupled with that of his tail, constituted the AAnn equivalent of a corporal smirk. "It iss alwayss gratifying to catch a human in a misstake, though it iss rare to have one express contrition in sso classical a fasshion."

She resumed her seat. "Thank you. I pride myself on my studies. Please recall my earnest sympathy when you are returned to your isolation ward."

Thessu started. "Returned? But you have jusst ssaid that we are abssolved of ressponssibility for the dissappearance of the two craft in quesstion."

"Truly." She smiled across at them. "That has nothing to do with your ongoing medical condition."

"What 'ongoing medical condition'?" Being slightly more excitable than his colleague, Jallrii was beside himself. "*There iss no ongoing medical condition.* It wass a russe on your part to hold uss here while you invesstigated the dissappearance of your two craft."

"Did I give that impression?" She smiled anew. "I certainly never meant to do so. No, good *nye,* I was being truthful from the beginning when I said that you were being held for medical observation." A sigh of sadness escaped her. "I regret to say that the tests that were run on you these past couple of days have come back positive. As a consequence, I regret to inform you that you are both to be deported from Fluva."

Now it was Thessu's turn to hiss so violently that he threatened to blow his pointed tongue right out of his mouth. "What nonssensse iss thiss? We are the accredited repressentativess of His Imperial Majesstic Navvur W. Our mission on Fluva iss authorized by your own government. It cannot be 'deported.' "

"You are quite right, noble *nye.* The AAnn observation mission to Fluva cannot be expelled." She folded her hands in front of her. "Its staff, however, can. I am sure replacements for the both of you will be sent out from Blassussar as soon as word of your situation here makes its way back to the Imperial home world."

The hissing that followed this pronouncement sounded like two steam engines fighting over the same sack of coal. "Thiss iss nothing but a crude ploy to get rid of my colleague and I."

Not at all, she mused. It's a fairly elaborate ploy. She held up a thick folder full of hard copy. "This is the report from my medical staff. I'm afraid that their worst fears have been borne out."

"Worsst fearss?" Thessu eyed her doubtfully.

"It seems that you indeed are infected with the suspect virus. No, don't be alarmed. I've been assured that an antidote exists. Not on Fluva, unfortunately. All relevant medical information will be provided so that you can receive proper treatment once you are on board a properly equipped vessel."

Jallrii's anger had given way to sudden uncertainty. "But truly, there iss nothing wrong with uss. We feel mosst excellently well." He blinked nictitating inner eyelids at his colleague. "At leasst, I do."

"I know it must be difficult for you to accept. Surely you are aware that many diseases, especially newly discovered agents on a world as fecund as Fluva, do not always manifest themselves immediately. I'm told that the symptoms of the viral infection that is spreading within your bodies even as we speak is particularly minimalist."

Reflexively Jallrii looked down at himself. Thessu, however, was having none of it. "I sstill think thiss is a trick. If we were contaminated as sserioussly as you ssay, we sshould feel *ssomething,* if only mild disscomfort."

"And I would say, be glad that you do not." She leaned forward slightly. "Please understand my position here, honored *nye.* If you were to sicken and die on my watch, I would be held responsible. It would result in a permanent black mark on my record of service. I'm sure you appreciate that I cannot take such a risk." She snapped a command. The peaceforcers who had escorted the two AAnn officers to Administration reentered the room.

"These soldiers will accompany you back to Medical, where you will remain until the time comes to evacuate you from Fluva. It was a pleasure meeting you both, and I'm sure I will establish the same courteous relationship with whoever the Imperial government appoints as your successors." She raised a hand in a futile attempt to forestall additional objections. "No, don't thank me."

"Thank you? *Thank you.* Truly, outrage, truly, thiss!" Thessu's protests continued to resound until the door had resealed completely behind him.

Interspersed with the irate officer's bellowing avowals of indignation was the notably softer reservation expressed by his colleague. "Truly," the now thoroughly subdued Jallrii could be heard to hiss softly, "now that I think hard on the matter, I musst confess that thesse lasst few dayss I have not been feeling at all that well."

She stared thoughtfully at the now sealed doorway. Then she picked up the folder full of medical hard copy and set it off to one side. Pandusky could retrieve it later. She knew he would make proper use of the sensitive recyclable material. He would not even have to wipe it before use, since every treated sheet within was already perfectly blank. With the room once more devoid of visitors, she smiled to herself this time.

She was getting better at this business of bluffing.

There was nothing wrong with the two AAnn officers. If anything, they were even healthier than Thessu claimed. And just as she had acknowledged, they would indeed be replaced as rapidly as the relevant Imperial bureau could ship suitable substitutes off to Fluva.

But in the meantime, there would be no scheming AAnn stationed on the world of the Big Wet to stir up trouble between Deyzara and Sakuntala.

Now all she had to do was figure out a way to settle the current conflict between those two fractious resident species and life would return to its previous familiar damp routine. Nothing to it. If only, she ruminated tiredly, it would turn out to be as easy as convincing her newly pubescent daughter to drop the unsuitable and whimsically inappropriate forename Fitzwinkle.

Turning toward the window, she looked to the ubiquitous rain for inspiration. As it turned out, she found it not there but in the calculated schemings of someone whom she knew all too well.

It was more ironic than satisfying, though, to realize that she had Sethwyn Case to thank for the breakthrough.

19

Aniolo-jat had just finished caucusing with Yeruna-hua and the rest of the war council when the delegation led by Sesesthi-toa arrived. More than a little surprised to discover that the female Hata-yuiqueru had managed to find him, since he had been moving daily from place to place to avoid possible Deyzara reprisals, he nonetheless prepared to receive her and those traveling in her company with all the proper regard and deference that was due her standing. The unexpected visitation might even turn out to be a good thing, one he might well turn to his advantage. The S'Toa were an important clan, most of whom were presently neutral in the ongoing drive to force the Deyzara off Fluva. He would use the unexpected opportunity to try to sway her into committing the support of all those who remained uncommitted.

It was therefore with hope as well as respect that he welcomed her and her cohorts into his temporary headquarters. So optimistic was he about the forthcoming encounter that he went so far as to have his own guards forsake the entryway to the house of the village elder where he was presently residing. Following the conference of Hatas, his team of communications and strategy specialists would return to the house to resume transmitting orders and directives to the valiant fighters who were busily engaged in pushing the abhorred Deyzara out of their homes and businesses all across Fluva.

There were suspension chairs out back, overlooking a still-water pond in the midst of the varzea. That was where he waited to greet Sesesthi-toa and her entourage. Food and drink, the best that the village could provide, was hastily brought over. Thus prepared, he settled down to await the arrival of the delegation. He did not have long to wait, nor to wonder what had brought them so far so quickly.

Sesesthi-toa's tongue did not linger long on his own. After the most cursory of greetings, it retracted into her cheek pouch with an audible *snap*. It was not quite an insult, but neither did it indicate an extension of affection.

"Hauea, Aniolo-jat. The S'Toa and its friends," she indicated the important personages who accompanied her, "are here to claim our share."

"Certainly," he agreed. Instead of swinging her chair in friendly fashion, the Hata-yuiqueru held it motionless. That was not a good sign. His initial hopes for the visit were growing shadowed. What had begun with promise was rapidly becoming something else. What was worse, he had no idea what had gone wrong.

"Your share of what?"

Angry mutterings rose from those warriors and representatives who had accompanied her. An increasingly wary Aniolo-jat was honestly confused. "I listen to my brothers and sisters, and I hear discontent. What troubles the S'Toa and its friends?"

"You ask for our support," she told him, "and some of us give it freely. Where the A'Jah and the Y'Hua lead, I should like all of the S'Toa and others to follow. But that cannot happen until we certain we follow as equals, not as servants."

What was going on here? he found himself wondering uncomfortably. "Was it ever said or implied otherwise?"

"There are many ways of saying things," declared an elder in the entourage. "We want our share."

Again, the laying of a cryptic claim. "You have your percentage of what booty has been taken from the Deyzara."

"We not talking of share of that," growled Sesesthi-toa. "We demand our share of additional credit paid you by our scale-skinned friends." Further grumbling from the assembled rose in support of her request.

Aniolo-jat's ears all but folded in upon themselves in confusion. "What are you talk about? Is no 'additional credit' from the AAnn. All funds given to support our cause are openly admitted to and accounted for."

She glared at him, nearly rising from her unmoving chair. "What about last four payments of two hundred thousand Commonwealth credits each? Where is admitting and accounting for *that*?"

Could they all be out of their minds? "Are no such payments. Where did you hear such crazy tales? Have you been talking military tactics with forest spirits?"

"We have seen the accounting," declared another member of the war chief's troupe. "It was very clear. Four payments of two hundred thousand apiece, paid into two accounts controlled by the A'Jah and two by the Y'Hua. That is great deal of credit. It has not been used to support the action against Deyzara or for anything else. It just sit and wait." Hands rested on knees, claws fully extended. "As do we."

Without waiting for permission from Hata or elder, a noted fighter spoke up from the back of the crowd. "Do the A'Jah and the Y'Hua think to become wealthy on blood of the P'Kei? By my ancestors, I vow such a thing will not happen!" His disrespectful outburst was echoed by many of those bunched up behind Sesesthi-toa and the other ranking warriors.

Aniolo-jat worked fast to dampen the rising anger that threatened to shift from discussion to outright hostility.

"You say you have seen accounting for these vast sums of credit. Where did this accounting come from?"

The elder seated in the suspension chair next to Sesesthi-toa sported a streak of bright gray fur running the length of his body. "From special branch of the company Poutukaa. The payments to Y'Hua and A'Jah accounts were authorized by

Geladu-tiv himself. When I go to inquire about them, he not available, but I was shown the relevant record-makings by a Sakuntala fiduciary. They said that the money was paid for 'services rendered.' " His fur, a gunmetal blue as well as gray, bristled. "What services have Y'Hua and A'Jah rendered to the Commonwealth Administration that they have not seen fit to tell their friends among the S'Toa, the P'Kei, the D'Sie, and the M'Rou about? Services that are worth eight hundred thousand Commonwealth credits."

Quick as was Aniolo-jat's mind, he was hard pressed to keep up with the avalanching chain of complaints. Eight hundred thousand credits? Paid into A'Jah and Y'Hua accounts? He decided to respond with the first thing that came to mind. That his reply was completely honest only served to exacerbate the already tense situation.

"I know nothing about any such funds."

Ears flicking forward, the elder murmured to the unblinking Sesesthi-toa, "I told you he would say that."

Heat rising in his own ears, Aniolo-jat barked back, "I know nothing about any such funds because there can't be any such. If our AAnn friends were going to transfer such an amount to us, the first thing they would have done was inform me about it."

"Maybe they did." Though an attractive female, Sesesthi-toa looked anything but mating material at the moment.

Primordial instincts threatened to overwhelm progressive thought as Aniolo-jat almost reached for the traditional long knife slung at his waist strappings. "Are you calling me a liar, Hata-yuiqueru?"

"The money exists. We want our share." She was not in the least intimidated by his attitude, his glare, his weapon, or the fact that she was a guest in his house.

With an effort, he forced himself to stay calm. Tranquillity provided room for thought, and thought led with blinding realization to a sudden revelation.

"This is a trick!"

Sesesthi-toa was not so easily dissuaded. "The money is real. How is that a trick?" A visitor could have smelled the tension accumulating behind her.

"To get us fighting among ourselves. It is trick of . . . of . . . the Deyzara! This is typical of them. If the clans fall to fighting each other again as we have always done, we will have no time for the Deyzara. They must realize this."

The elder with the business acumen responded, "No Deyzara could persuade, or pay, a true Sakuntala like Geladu-tiv to participate in such a scheme. You will have to do better than that, A'Jah thief."

Under ordinary circumstances, such an explicit insult would have called for immediate retribution. But the present circumstances, Aniolo-jat knew, were anything but ordinary. He saw years of careful planning, of organizing and preparation, coming apart like a soumeth flimsy. And the worst of it was, he didn't know how to put a stop to it because he did not know who or what was behind it.

Rising from his chair, he moved to pick up a communicator. He was immediately surrounded by his aroused guests.

"Calling for help?" Sesesthi-toa challenged him. At least, he reflected, she had not yet drawn a weapon of her own.

"Calling the AAnn Thessu. He will put this right. If you not believe me, will you believe him?"

The war chief glanced at her senior adviser, then over at several of her kinfolk and allies from the three other clans represented in her group. Finally she thrust both ears forward. "Call the hard-skinned ones."

He tried. Several times. But their AAnn allies seemed to have evaporated. Even the carrier wave was gone. It was as if the two toothy officers had vanished from Fluva itself.

Slowly, he set the expensive imported communicator aside— but not before furtively fingering one touch-spot on its surface. "They do not answer."

Sesesthi-toa's head bobbed knowingly. "For some reason, I not surprised."

He started backing away. As he did so, a host of armed clansfolk appeared in the doorway in response to the hasty emergency call he had placed via the communicator. Sesesthi-toa eyed the watchful arrivals impassively.

"So. This is how war chief of the A'Jah shares the spoils of battle with his allies."

"There are no spoils of which you speak, I am tell you! There is no eight hundred thousand Commonwealth credits. This is a deception to bring good friends to blows. Look at yourselves: it working!"

Sesesthi-toa hesitated. One did not become war chief of a clan as prominent as the S'Toa by being a fool. But behind her, knives were already being drawn, and she felt emotional as well as spiritual pressure against her back. Purely as a precaution, she started to draw her own weapon.

Aniolo-jat was among the most composed of all Sakuntala. But he was not made of stone. Indeed, he did not even know what stone was, having never seen such a thing. As the six fingers of Sesesthi-toa's left hand reached for the long knife at her waist, he brought his own weapon around in a horizontal slash. His intent was only to make her keep her distance. Unfortunately, she was pushed forward from behind and his blade sliced into her arm. Blood spurted.

Pandemonium filled the house as visitors and occupants clashed in violent but archetypal Sakuntala combat. By the time it ended with the arrival of Yeruna-hua and reinforcements, both Sesesthi-toa and Aniolo-jat were dead, along with an inexcusable number of warriors representing six different clans. Despite Yeruna-hua's attempts to keep the incident quiet, word inevitably escaped. Across the settled Viisiiviisii, clan promptly set upon clan in time-honored Sakuntala tradition. With the indigenous thus engaged, apprehensive but hopeful Deyzara began to return to their abandoned dwellings and ransacked places of business.

Aniolo-jat, Yeruna-hua, and their clannish co-conspirators never did figure out what had hit them.

• • •

Lauren Matthias was greatly pleased by the most recent news. With the Sakuntala once more fighting among themselves, the extremists' uprising against the Deyzara was dying of internal conflict and uncertainty. As soon as the combatants exhausted themselves battling one another, the more moderate elements among their kind, as exemplified by the Hata Naneci-tok, would step in to reassert control over the immature and hotheaded. These efforts would be discreetly supported (so as not to suggest favoritism among the clans) by the Commonwealth Authority, with favors and with credit.

Amazing what could be accomplished through the judicious distribution of a little money, she mused.

As for the refugee situation that had threatened to overwhelm the Authority itself, it was gradually being brought under control as more and more Deyzara were repatriated to their homes and businesses. Those Sakuntala who had not engaged in the uprising grudgingly consented to their return. Stores and shops reopened in town after town. Commerce resumed. Promises were made—and, more important, kept. Programs designed to foster mutual understanding and improve communication between the resident sentient species of Fluva were funded and activated. Though it was far from back to normal, life in parts of the inhabited Viisiiviisii once again began to approach the tolerable.

But there was still fighting going on, she knew. Still too much hatred and envy. Somehow, that would have to be dealt with.

She did not expect Jack to show up and practically drag her away from work.

"Where are we going?" He had hardly given her time to don her rain cape. A heavy downpour was in progress and some of the tepid water leaked through a small gap in the hydrophobic charge to run down her back. She struggled to seal the opening. "What's the hurry?"

"You'll see soon, love." He led her toward the Administration complex's small skimmer hangar.

"It must be something special, for you to haul me out of the office like this." She studied his face. "I haven't seen you this excited since Andrea agreed to stop visiting the forest with that intern from Hydrographics."

"It's special squared." Once inside the hangar, she was able to properly fasten her rain gear. "I had a visitor this morning. He showed me something. I could just tell you about it, but I think you should see it for yourself."

"Well, what is it?" Despite the press of her own work, she knew how important it was to show an interest in her mate's vocation.

When he turned back to her, his eyes were alive with the childlike delight all scientists express at times of great discovery. "A mushroom."

She started to say something, closed her mouth. There were no mushrooms on Fluva. A mushroom was a terrestrial growth. But there were innumerable analogs among the flourishing fungi of the endless forest. "Mushroom" was Jack's way of preparing her to see something familiar.

It better contain a genetic chain for curing something significant, she decided firmly. Or taste like Kansastan veal. She didn't like having her time wasted, even by her husband.

A driver was waiting for them in the open skimmer. As she climbed in, she noted with some discomfort that his greeting grin was directed not at her face but at a less public portion of her anatomy. This despite her official standing and the presence of her husband.

Settling excitedly into one of the three empty seats, Jack introduced the driver. "Lauren, meet Hasa. Hasa, this is my wife—the chief administrator."

Their pilot had the canopy sealing and the skimmer ready to go even before she was properly seated. "Pleasure, Administrator. What the hell took you so long to send someone out after me? And as long as you were at it, couldn't you have sent a couple of competent human techs instead of a stinking two-trunks and a moronic long-monkey?" Raising the skimmer, he scraped not one but two other parked craft as he recklessly gunned the compact vehicle out of the hangar and toward the forest, sending several pedestrians and the angry pilot of a delivery vehicle scattering for cover.

And that was her introduction to the exceedingly clever and much reviled Shadrach Hasselemoga.

After more than an hour in the skimmer with him, she, too, would not have been especially disappointed to see him vanish permanently into the depths of the unforgiving Viisiiviisii. But when they finally set down in a pile of fallen, decaying trees and Jack began to explain what their guide had located, she forgot all about his rude stares and loutish behavior.

Like magic, the black tendrils responded smoothly to her hand movements. Around them, the varzea sang and hooted and cackled. Hasa spoke while keeping watch, side arm at the ready.

"I came out searching as soon as I got cleaned up and had a decent meal. Took a few days, but it was a lot easier since I knew exactly what I was looking for. Found this occurrence a couple of days ago. Flew back into town, called for a meeting with a suitable specialist in the science division, ended up talking to Jack, here." He spit at something slender, bright, and chartreuse that scrambled to scurry away from his spit. "Didn't know he was married to the chief administrator. Makes things easier." He indicated the bobbing, weaving rhizomorphs. "Ask it which way to town."

"Ask it?" Kneeling beside the hypnotic ebon filaments, she looked questioningly at Jack. "Even if it could understand me, it has no ears."

Her husband was grinning like a little boy who'd just had his allowance doubled. "Turns out there are cilia on specialized rhizomorphs that can sense and interpret vibrations in the air.

Not all that different, really, from the way the tympanum in your ears handles sound waves."

As might be expected, she still found it all hard to believe. "Okay, I'll accept that. But sensing vibrations is one thing. Understanding them, deciphering them, is something else."

Moving close to her, Hasa reached down to caress the dozens of erect rhizomorphs. They lay down against his open palm like cats' paws. Observing the interaction, it was difficult to deny that some kind of connection was being made.

"I've been trying to train this one. Get it to connect words, sounds, with actions. It's very slow. For something so vast, it's not very smart. On the other hand," he said as he drew his hand back, "it's hard to say what kind of smarts the pannula does have. I'm not the guy to find that out." He nodded at Jack. "That's a job for your partner and his fellow dirt-rooters. Me, I just find stuff. Like my women, all my evaluations are quickies." He moved a little too close. "Go on, Administrator. Put your lips right up next to the filaments and ask it, 'Which way to town?' "

She hesitated. Given their present proximity, deliberately moving away from Hasa would only alert Jack to her disquiet. So, doing her best to ignore the husky, shameless presence beside her, she did as she was told, leaning forward until her mouth was almost touching several of the coiled black strands.

"Which . . . way . . . to . . . town?" As she mouthed each word slowly and deliberately, she saw what appeared to be very fine hairs lining several tendrils quiver as if in a gentle breeze.

As soon as she finished and straightened, every one of the dozens of slender tendrils dropped flat against the wood they were slowly decomposing. Flat and pointed in the direction of the center of Taulau.

Hasa rose triumphantly from his crouch. "Don't know why the pannula never made direct contact with the Sakuntala. Maybe their smell, maybe something else. Sakuntala don't know, either. Same goes for the Deyzara. Another mystery for the mycologists to resolve." He gazed paternally down at the tendrils, which had begun to rise skyward again.

"I'm gonna call it *Xenoarmillaria fluva hasselemoga*." He eyed her husband. "Jack says the naming of it is mine by right. Ain't that right, Jack?"

"*Xenoarmillaria fluva* would be taxonomically easier," the scientist replied.

"Nope. *Xenoarmillaria fluva hasselemoga* it is. Unless you or one of your squinty-eyes is gonna argue about it."

"No." Jack sighed good-naturedly "As you are the discoverer, it's yours to name."

Lauren had turned to inspect the handsome reddish-purple basidiocarps emerging from a nearby fallen trunk. "What about input from your companions on your difficult journey to the village where you were finally picked up?"

Hasa made a face. "They didn't see anything. I found it. Me. They didn't believe me about it even after I explained everything to them. I'm the sole discoverer, and I expect to be treated as such."

"I'm sure you will be." Commonwealth citizen or not, she decided, she positively did not like this man. Skilled and qualified he might be, but he was also vulgar, shallow, boastful, conceited, and self-centered. Furthermore, she did not like the way he looked at her at all. It was certainly not with the respect due the Commonwealth's ranking representative on Fluva.

"I want a parade," he declared brashly. "I want an official proclamation acknowledging my accomplishment. It's not every day a new intelligent species is discovered."

She eyed him dryly. The more she learned about the pannula's discoverer, the less enthused she was able to be about the undeniably astonishing discovery itself. "Anything else you want?"

He leered at her so blatantly she would have slapped him except for the distance between them. Jack never noticed the voiceless exchange. He was too busy examining exposed mycelium.

There was not much she could do by way of reprisal. Jack and a totally enthralled team from his department validated the obnoxious bioprospector's claims. The two members of the first rescue party, the Sakuntala Jemunu-jah and the Deyzara Masurathoo, did not dispute Hasa's claim of sole finding. As much as she disliked having to do so, she was forced to affix her official endorsement to the affidavit of discovery that was forwarded a week later to Commonwealth Science Headquarters on Earth and Hivehom.

Compensation for having to tender congratulations to a repellent specimen like Hasa came in the form of an unexpected and unusually expeditious reply from Earth to her most recent communiqué. She read through the lengthy space-minus response several times. Only when she was sure it meant everything it said and that she fully understood all the implications did she decide to call the summit.

20

~~~~~~~~~~~~~~~~~~~~~~~~~~~~~~

It was as big a room as could be safely, easily, and reasonably erected on Fluva. Considering that the entire structure was suspended by strilk cables from a combination of pylons and trees, it was relatively spacious. The astonishingly lightweight dome itself was made from an aerogel alloy. Not as strong as plexalloy, but it didn't have to be. The crystal-clear structure had been blown into place, not poured or welded.

Beneath the arching transparency were curving walls of similar material, stained to translucence to block out views of the town and varzea outside. The sturdy interior walls had been covered with patterned tri-reliefs of scenes from the Viisiiviisii and of Deyzara and Sakuntala village life.

Filling the wall at the far end of the circular edifice was a grand semidrift map of the Commonwealth, framed with quotations from the United Church and symbols of both secular and spiritual power. The overall effect on someone entering from the outside was inspiring without being oppressive. It ought to be: the entire layout had been vetted by the appropriate branches of the Commonwealth Department for Contact with New Sentient Species, Class V sector. Every visual effect was intentional and nothing had been left to chance—or improvisation.

Matthias liked the building. She would have preferred to have had her offices in the large, airy space. But the dome had been designed to accommodate and impress large groups, not to facilitate the often dull, boring work of daily administration. It was entirely functional, but not for bureaucrats.

The dais behind which she stood was equipped with instrumentation that would allow her to amplify her voice, have it instantly and simultaneously translated into as many as a hundred different languages, defend her position from attack by explosive and energy weapons, project elaborate tridee diagrams and constructs into the air between her and the audience, and, if necessary, supply a quick meal. It faced dozens of seats. Some balanced on three legs in the style favored by the Deyzara. Others were suspended in the fashion of the Sakuntala. Not from the dome, which could not handle such weight, but from graceful arcs of supportive composite. No column of rain fell through the center of the building in the manner of traditional Sakuntala meetinghouses. Humans desired to avoid the relentless, unending downpours of Fluva, not invite it inside their buildings. That much leeway in construction had been granted to her predecessors.

The steady patter of rain was a distant susurration high overhead. Unlike individual rain gear, the roof of the gathering chamber was not static-charged to repel moisture. Raindrops ran in all directions from its apex, forming an attractive pattern overhead that gently dispersed the light falling within. The combination of smoothly dispersed liquid and distant beating had a soothing effect, which was exactly what its designers had intended.

Certainly none of the venerable personages who were slowly filling the available seats were exhibiting overt hostility to one another, although plenty of that lay seething beneath their diplomatic exteriors. She perceived it in the agitated way the Deyzara shifted their trunks, in the swift, short flicking of Sakuntala tails and ears. For now, it was enough that no one took a swing at another or openly flaunted weaponry.

While she had not personally made the acquaintance of everyone present, there were enough familiar faces to make her feel comfortable. On the indigenous side, Naneci-tok was present together with a small retinue representing the burgeoning Sakuntala merchant class. Jemunu-jah sat on her immediate left, in the place of honored influence. The administrator also recognized Cecolou, head of the powerful and influential C'Tiu clan, and a few others.

Representing the Deyzara, Masurathoo sat in front in the middle of a row of respected members of the mercantile and social communities. Her attention tended to focus on the assembling Sakuntala. Not because she favored them, but because the body wrappings worn by the Deyzara were blinding in their richness and the sheer brilliance of their color schemes. The attractive strappings and mottled fur of the Sakuntala were subdued by comparison.

She was not present to judge appearances, however. When everyone had been seated, she moved one finger over a concealed portion of the dais. Instantly a slowly rotating three-dimensional map of the Commonwealth materialized above the heads of the assembled locals. It had the desired effect of stopping conversation.

"Like it or not, this is what you are a part of. What you make of your part in it is up to you." She zoomed in on Fluva, a cloud-swathed world circling a hot yellow sun. "It may not seem like much in the scheme of things, but this is your home. It's a nice place, though more to your liking than to my kind. It belongs to you." She paused for emphasis. "*All* of you."

A few subdued mutterings rose from the back rows of the assembled Sakuntala. They were matched by contentious hoots from within the crowd of seated Deyzara.

"I am pleased to announce," she declared, utilizing her prerogative as chief administrator to amplify her voice sufficient to drown out the incipient pugnacity on both sides, "that pursuant to my recent exchange of communications with Commonwealth center of operations, Fluva has now been upgraded from qualified to full Class Five status." Expectant, curious stares greeted her declaration. "It means that Fluva will receive

proportionately more attention from the relevant Commonwealth departments." The silence was sustained. "Also, more
aid, in the form of both material and credit."

That finally prompted the appropriate Sakuntala and Deyzara
equivalents of applause. She continued.

"As a corollary to this official change of status, my own
standing has similarly been upgraded." She shifted her stance
behind the dais. "I will now be able to do more on my own,
without having to wait for authorization from Earth or Hivehom. I can clear more exports, approve a greater volume of imports, sanction new aid for specific causes, and license more
businesses. Among other things. For the first time I can also,"
she added casually, "approve the use of force to settle local disputes."

That provoked sufficient howling and hooting to drown out
the sound of rain splattering on the top of the transparent
dome. The noise only began to die down when Cecolou-tiu
rose from her chair. Even the Deyzara quieted their hooting,
mindful of the revered Hata's status among her kind.

An aged but still steady six-fingered hand waved in the administrator's direction. "Humans may not interfere in affairs
between sentient native species. I know this thing to be true
because I have studied it." Ears, tail, and hand waved as one in
the direction of the seated Deyzara. "You may exercise your law
with the interlopers, but by your own regulations you cannot
do so among the Sakuntala." Despite her age, the elder succeeded in conveying an ample measure of confidence. Yelps and
yowls from her fellows showed how much her short speech was
appreciated.

Matthias was not taken aback by it because she had come
prepared for it.

"The esteemed Hata of the C'Tiu is right. No Commonwealth authority may intervene forcibly in sentient native affairs." She paused for effect. "Unless it is to defend the interests
of a second group of sentients who have no way of protecting
themselves."

A Hata-niu of the P'Lua clan slipped out of her seat to speak. "The Deyzara have many ways protect themselves. That they choose not use them does not mean they not exist." Muted Sakuntala laughter rose from her kinfolk, and a number of the seated Deyzara tensed visibly.

"I was not speaking of the Deyzara." Matthias waited for the noise to die down before resuming. "I was referring to the pannula."

That got their attention. As she knew it would.

One of the senior Hata-yuiquerus who had chosen not to fight with the extremists slipped out of his chair so forcefully that it swung wildly and banged into his neighbor. Indignation induced both Sakuntala to ignore the outrageous breach of etiquette. From behind the safety of the dais, Matthias watched and listened with interest. She was not sure she had ever seen a Sakuntala sputter before.

"The pannula is forest spirit, nothing more. It is not intelligent. What manner of trick is this?"

"It is no trick," she assured the speaker and the rest of her now completely attentive audience. "While the precise level of pannula sentience remains a matter for analysis, over the past several days Commonwealth researchers working in the Viisii-viisii have determined that a sufficient minimum level of awareness is present to qualify the species for such status. It therefore falls under Commonwealth regulations and policy governing the protection of particularly primitive intelligent species. The relevant Commonwealth law states that where multiple intelligences are perceived to be under threat, the most primal and helpless are to receive a proportionately greater degree of protection." She raised a hand to forestall the rising tide of protest—from both of the assembled groups.

"That means that I now have permission to send peaceforcers to intervene in any local dispute that I or my scientific people believe threatens the well-being of local pannula."

The Hata-yuiqueru's tone was acidic. "No Sakuntala is at war with the pannula." A few laughs greeted his response. They were less in number and intensity than previously and possessed of an underlying nervousness.

"Nor, I must say, is any Deyzara," added a well-known and floridly attired merchant from the other side of the dome.

"It is not a question of making war, but of danger and damage from wider conflicts spilling over to affect the pannula, who, after all, are unable to move out of the way of such clashes." She did not smile. "I assure you that the Commonwealth government takes such things very seriously."

"This a joke!" The speaker and several of the Sakuntala seated around him started to slip from their chairs, preparatory to walking out of the summit.

"If the Sakuntala or anyone else," she declared firmly, turning up the volume, "willfully disregard this judgment, they will have to deal with Commonwealth justice. Given the sensitivity of the matter, I am informed that more peaceforcers will soon be arriving to reinforce those already under my authority. As the safety and security of a newly eligible intelligent species is involved, they will be bringing with them heavy weapons of a type not yet seen on Fluva."

The dissenters paused. The warriors of the Sakuntala were bold, skillful, and brave, but they were not stupid. They knew what modern weapons could do. Those that had been obtained by the radicals for use against the Deyzara were impressive enough. They did not doubt that the Commonwealth to which they now belonged could fabricate devices even more lethal.

Cecolou-tiu spoke into the ensuing silence. "What you want of us?"

"Stop fighting each other. The extremists' move to drive the Deyzara off Fluva has devolved into internecine combat. That, too, must cease. You are going to have to learn how to live and work side by side without these intermittent explosions of senseless violence. The Deyzara are on Fluva to stay." Soft hoots of approval rose from the side of the chamber that was filled with their representatives.

"And regulations designed to protect the ingenuous Sakuntala

from mercantile predation by their more commercially sophisticated neighbors will be enforced by every means at my command." To this the Sakuntala responded with knowing, and
appreciative, yowls of awareness.

"Thanks to the official upgrading in status, Commonwealth
instruments and materials for improving the education and situation of all intelligences on Fluva will be increased." Leaning
forward against the dais, she tried to meet as many watching
eyes as possible. "My authority allows me to favor whichever
species proves to be the most cooperative and willing to embrace Commonwealth principles and values. If the Sakuntala
continue to wage war on their neighbors and themselves, it
could be the Deyzara. If certain Deyzara persist in using their
greater knowledge of Commonwealth ways to take advantage
of and impoverish their fellow citizens, it could be the Sakuntala." She paused meaningfully.

"If both the Deyzara and the Sakuntala continue as they
have before, then the Commonwealth Authority on Fluva will
have no choice but to favor the interests of the pannula to the
exclusion of all else."

A mixture of shock and disbelief ran through the entire assembly. No threats or words from a human speaker could instantly banish the fear the Deyzara felt for the Sakuntala or the
Sakuntala's dislike of the two-trunks. But they were forced to
put aside their mutual aversion and distrust of each other out of
fear of being one day dominated by . . . a fungus.

Naneci-tok quite liked what the humans often called mushrooms—to eat. The idea that she and her people might have
important decisions foisted on them by such growths, or by humans acting on behalf of such growths, no matter how "intelligent" the humans claimed the growths were, was considerably
less palatable.

"You all are going to have to learn how to live and work together," Matthias was saying. "That's what the Commonwealth
is all about: many different species living and working together

to grow knowledge, provide for a common defense, and offer the chance at a good life for everyone living within its stellar boundaries regardless of shape, size, color, belief, or what they respirate. The United Church embraces all sentiences. To my knowledge, it has never been able to count a fungoid intelligence among its flock. Possibly the pannula will be the first."

Moving with care, as befitted her advanced age, Cecolou-tiu walked slowly from her suspension chair to the other side of the room. There she embraced a surprised Masurathoo, wrapping her tongue several times around the Deyzara's head. To his credit, Masurathoo accepted the gesture without flinching (much).

"I declare to all who present within sound of my voice," the senior Hata announced, albeit with obvious reluctance, "that from this day forth the C'Tiu will work only for peace and accommodation between my people and the two-trunks."

As the demonstrative but wet tongue uncoiled from his head, Masurathoo fought through lingering Sakuntala saliva to respond. "I fear very much that I cannot speak for more than a few of the Deyzara, but I am sure that since it will greatly facilitate the conduct of proper commerce, my people will be of the same mind as the respected Hata Cecolou-tiu. Especially once the words of the most honorable and respected chief administrator have been dispersed to all and fully comprehended by them."

Matthias nodded approvingly. "Then I pronounce an ending to this gathering. May you all return to your homes and businesses, to your villages and clans, to explain the new way of things. Under these directives, Sakuntala and Deyzara will prosper. All of Fluva will prosper—and the pannula as well."

Afterward, many came forward to speak with her. Not to congratulate, since neither faction was especially happy with the prospects she had laid out for them, but to curry favor. She listened to them all, to every supplicant, and smiled and chatted politely while promising nothing. She'd meant what she had told them. Deyzara and Sakuntala would have to work things out between themselves, while all the while taking the interests of the pannula into careful account.

Privately, she was relieved at the way things had turned out. The discovery of the pannula had given her the excuse and the authorization to put an end to the interminable conflict that had existed between the planet's two dominant species ever since the first Deyzara worker had arrived on Fluva. Also, she looked forward with anticipation and fascination to the insights intensified contact with the Commonwealth's first known intelligent fungal life-form were likely to produce. It had all turned out rather well.

Except that none of the principals involved, not the Sakuntala or the Deyzara, or the reprehensible Case or the odious Shadrach Hasselemoga, had turned out to be very likable. In the elation of resolving the centuries-old conflict between Deyzara and Sakuntala, she had been forced to compromise a certain measure of personal compassion and kindness. The events of the previous weeks had left her a harder person. She had Case to thank for that. Dealing with him had stiffened her for the confrontation with the senior representatives of both Deyzara and Sakuntala.

Two figures who had been watching the summit from the rear of the chamber now came forward, making their way through the thinning crowd of flamboyantly clad Deyzara and dignified, solemn Sakuntala. Jack had brought Andrea with him. She was dressed sensibly for a change, the administrator noted. Among the Deyzara, Andrea could have been naked and painted bright yellow without standing out.

Then Lauren noticed the streak of color-shifting, luminescent composite hair that had been slack-weaved into Andrea's own natural tresses, and sighed. What would the girl be like at seventeen?

The teenager paused in front of her mother. Then she put both arms around her and hugged hard. "Mom, Dad and I listened to the whole thing, and I just want to tell you that I'm really, *really* impressed." Releasing the more than slightly stunned administrator, Andrea stepped back. Lauren Matthias saw that her incorrigible daughter had tears in her eyes. Standing close behind her, Jack Matthias was gazing down at his wife with a mixture of pride and affection.

"Oh, hell," she muttered, "this has taken much too long. I've got to get back to the office. There's so much to be done."

Stepping forward, her daughter took her by one arm and her husband by the other. "Sorry, Lauren," Jack told her firmly. "Like it or not, you're taking the rest of the day off."

For the first time in a long while, the chief of Commonwealth Authority on the full T Class V world known as Fluva found herself overruled.

Seated before the instrument panel of his salvaged and fully refurbished skimmer, Shadrach Hasselemoga contemplated the immensity of southern Viisiiviisii spread out before him. Hard rain ran in serpentine rivulets down the sides of the compact craft, kept clear of the front of the transparent canopy by a strong static charge. One readout was off by a tenth of a total, and he loudly cursed the unknown tech who had been charged with putting it back in proper working order.

Idiots! Morons! Fools and imbeciles, he was surrounded by nothing but. Add to that the need to have to deal with bloated, goggle-eyed two-trunks and smelly, oafish big-ears and it was a wonder he managed to keep a civil tongue in his head. He hated the cursed rain that hardly ever stopped; the turbid, mucky water that receded for only a few weeks out of the year; all the things that crawled and leapt and soared and hopped, that spit and bit and snapped and stung. It was a miserable, wretched dung ball of a world, and it was his misfortune to be stuck on it trying to eke out a living.

Despite his demand, there had been no parade in his honor. Grudgingly, he had been forced to admit that it would be hard to have one in the absence of dry ground. The official declaration had been nice, though, and the limp-lunged folks at the

science division had graciously shown him how he and his notable discovery had been entered into the official taxonomic
records of the greater Commonwealth. He had accepted the
honor and their associated accolades with his usual poor grace.
His only lingering regret was that they would not let him into
the local lockup and leave him alone for an hour with Sethwyn
Case.

Now Hasa hovered above the treetops just outside Taulau
Town, his craft on idle, contemplating the vast rain-swept
swath of the Viisiiviisii, the Fluvan varzea. In a few minutes, as
soon as the skimmer's internals had finished plotting out all the
details of his new zigzagging course, he would leave the town
and its brew of Deyzara, Sakuntala, and humans behind. It
couldn't come soon enough for him. Good riddance to them
all! Despite the ferocity of its flora and fauna, Fluva wouldn't
be such a bad place, he thought. If only you could get rid of all
the people.

A telltale winked to life in front of him and a small beep
sounded. He voiced a curt command, making it sound like a
curse. The skimmer, bless it, offered no objection. Its mechanical innards found him perfectly personable. Smoothly the re-
stored vehicle began to move forward, accelerating over the
treetops and away from civilization.

Discovering a new intelligent species was all very well and
good, he mused crossly, but there was never enough money in it.